BONE HEAD

Book 1

IMAGE COMICS, INC.

Robert Kirkman — Chief Operating Officer
Erik Larsen — Chief Financial Officer
Todd McFarlane — President
Marc Silvestri — Chief Executive Officer
Jim Valentino — Vice President
Eric Stephenson — Publisher / Chief Creative Officer
Corey Hart — Director of Sales
Jeff Boison — Director of Publishing Planning & Book Trade Sales
Chris Ross — Director of Digital Sales
Jeff Stang — Director of Specialty Sales
Kat Salazar — Director of PR & Marketing
Drew Gill — Art Director
Heather Doornink — Production Director
Nicole Lapalme — Controller
IMAGECOMICS.COM

For Top Cow Productions, Inc.
For Top Cow Productions, Inc.
Marc Silvestri - CEO
Matt Hawkins - President & COO
Elena Salcedo - Vice President of Operations
Henry Barajas - Director of Operations
Vincent Valentine - Production Manager
Dylan Gray - Marketing Director

To find the comic
shop nearest you, call:
1-888-COMICBOOK

Want more info? Check out:
www.topcow.com
for news & exclusive Top Cow merchandise!

COMIC SHOP LOCATOR SERVICE
888-COMICBOOK
888-266-4226

BONEHEAD, VOL. 1. First printing. OCTOBER 2018. Published by Image Comics, Inc. Office of publication: 2701 NW Vaughn St., Suite 780, Portland, OR 97210. Copyright © 2018 GLITCH.
All rights reserved. Contains material originally published in single magazine form as BONEHEAD #1-4. "BONEHEAD," its logos, and the likenesses of all characters herein are
trademarks of GLITCH, unless otherwise noted. "Image" and the Image Comics logos are registered trademarks of Image Comics, Inc. No part of this publication may be reproduced
or transmitted, in any form or by any means (except for short excerpts for journalistic or review purposes), without the express written permission of GLITCH, or Image Comics, Inc.
All names, characters, events, and locales in this publication are entirely fictional. Any resemblance to actual persons (living or dead), events, or places, without satirical intent, is
coincidental. Printed in the USA. For information regarding the CPSIA on this printed material call: 203-595-3636 and provide reference #RICH-811998. ISBN: 978-1-5343-0664-6

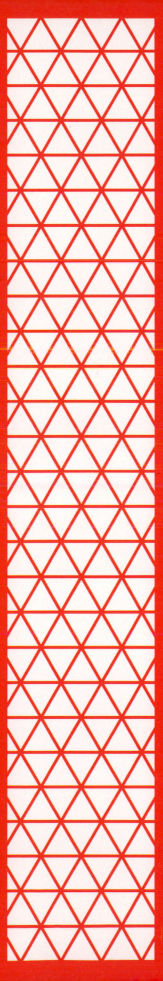

CREITS
—

created by
Machine56 / writer

Bryan Edward Hill / artist

Rhoald Marcellius /

colorist
Sakti Yuwono / cover artist

Rhoald Marcellius / letterer

Imam Eko & Jaka Ady /

graphics
Comolo / editor

Elena Salcedo / producer

Sunny Gho

(1P) Part No. MT-A0156 / D / **Test Subject no.56**

CHAPTER01

● ORIGINAL MITSURU.TECH SERIAL #
○ CLOSE QUARTER TYPE_

● SLAVE TYPE BONEHEAD01.
○ BODY STRUCTURE : N/A

● NODE TRACKING AFTER DELETION COURSE
○ EARTH: 7 MEGAPARSECS ACROSS_

▷ M56/001/A   ▷ Bonehead, RED, 16k-Zettabyte.   (1P) Part No. MT-A0156 / D / Test Subject no.56   ブラック・テス・ランナー   QC/P

Designed by Machine56, Assembled by Mitsuru.Tech
MK-I / Not suitable f

50601309

WELCOME!
DRONE XO102 IS READY TO DEPLOY.
XO102
ACTIVATING.
DRONE SYSTEM UPDATING (29 OF 77).
delivery to:
Taruna Rauf
2046 Feye st
cw. sector-02
DEPLOYING DRONES.
ACTIVATING DRONES.
DEPLOYING DRONES.
DRONE SYSTEM UPDATING.
DEPLOYING DRONES.
DEPLOYING DRONES.

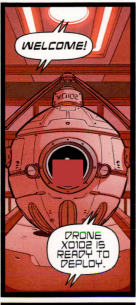

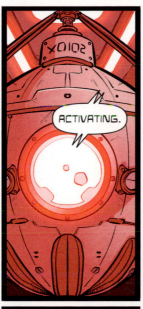

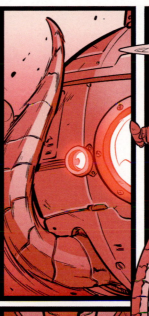

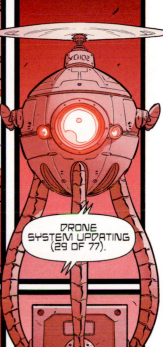

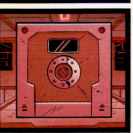

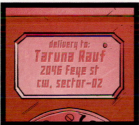

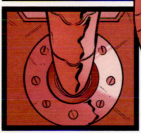

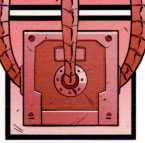

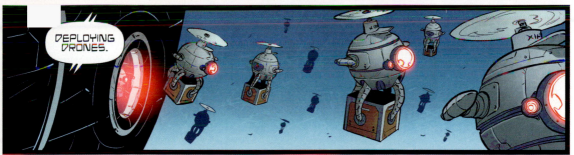

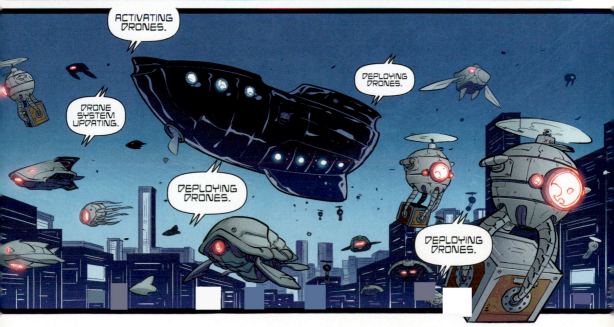

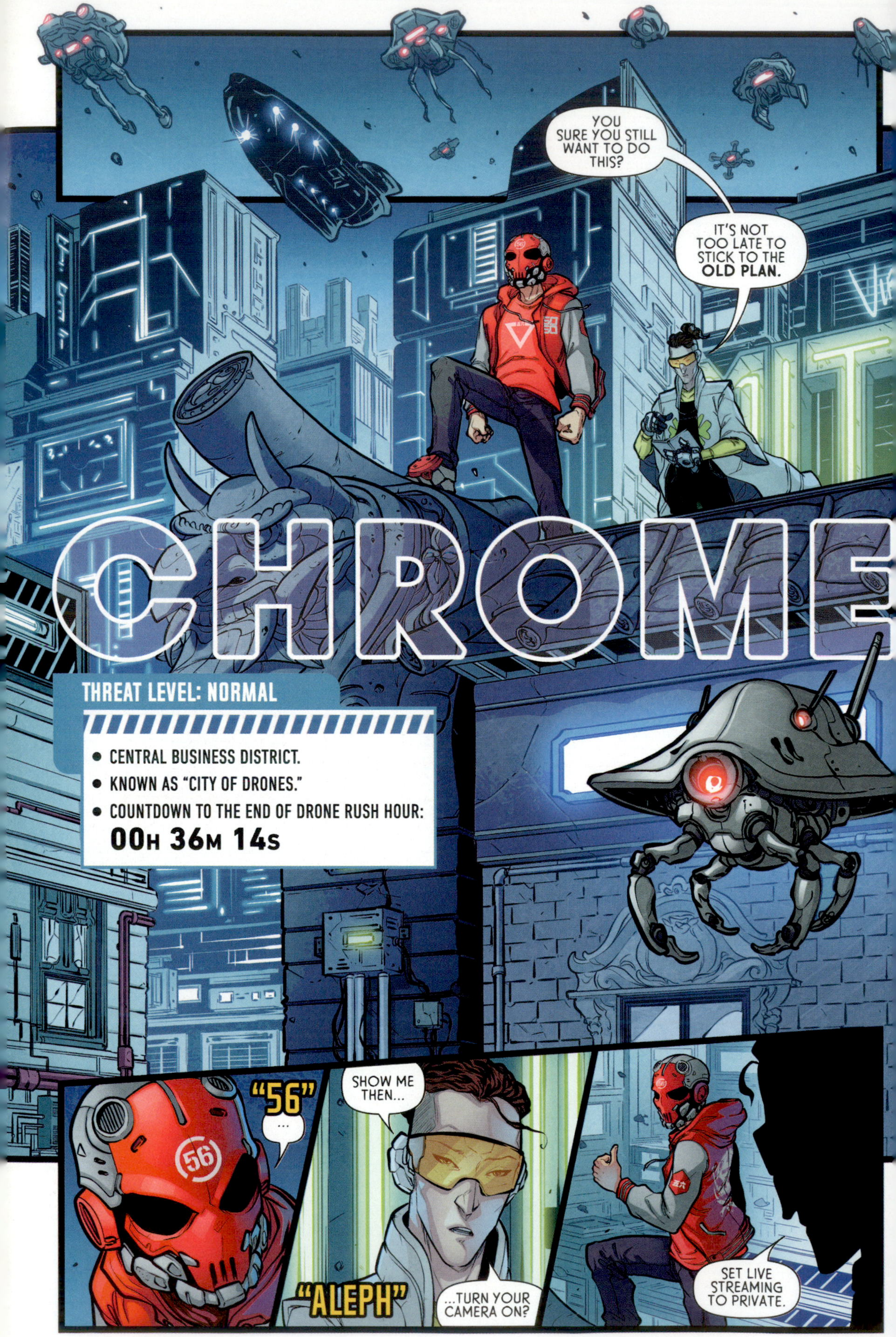
YOU SURE YOU STILL WANT TO DO THIS?
IT'S NOT TOO LATE TO STICK TO THE OLD PLAN.
CHROME
THREAT LEVEL: NORMAL
• CENTRAL BUSINESS DISTRICT.
• KNOWN AS "CITY OF DRONES."
• COUNTDOWN TO THE END OF DRONE RUSH HOUR:
00H 36M 14S
"56"
...
SHOW ME THEN...
"ALEPH"
...TURN YOUR CAMERA ON?
SET LIVE STREAMING TO PRIVATE.

"I LAUNCHED ONE OF MY DRONES ABOUT AN HOUR AGO.

A-L3PH

"THE *A-L3PH* IS OUT THERE RIGHT NOW, MINGLING WITH THE OTHER DRONES.

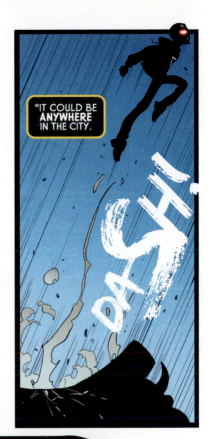

"IT COULD BE **ANYWHERE** IN THE CITY.

DASH!

"SEARCH FOR IT, FIND IT, GRAB IT, THEN **BRING IT** TO OUR MEETING PLACE.

"YOU CAN USE YOUR **BONEHEAD** TO TRACK ITS SIGNAL, BUT YOU'RE **NOT** GOING TO FIND IT...

"...NOT UNLESS YOU'RE IN CLOSE PROXIMITY TO A-L3PH.

"THE DRONES' RUSH HOUR WILL BE OVER IN EXACTLY THIRTEEN MINUTES...

"...SEE IF YOU CAN FIND MY A-L3PH IN TEN."

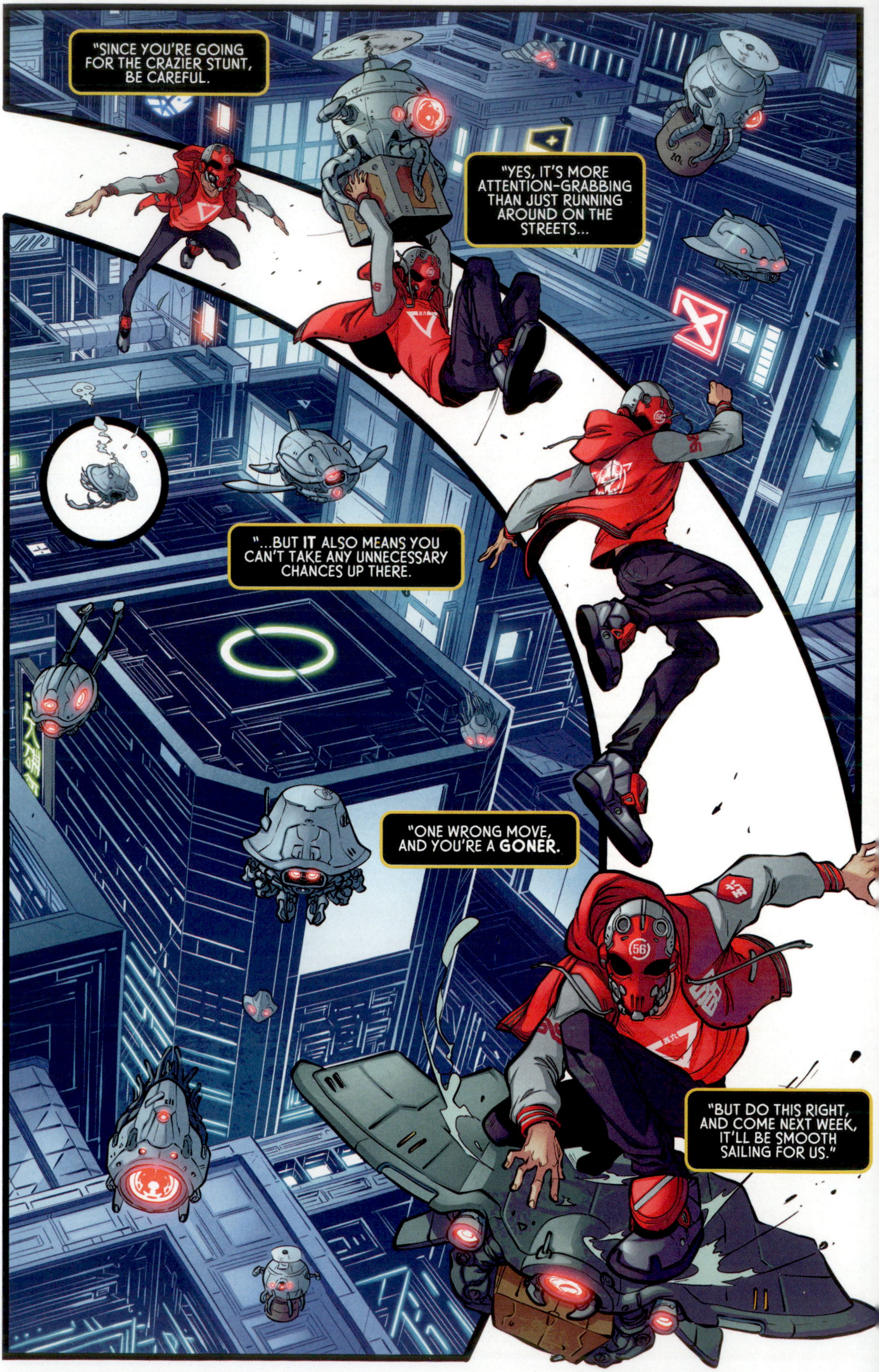
"SINCE YOU'RE GOING FOR THE CRAZIER STUNT, BE CAREFUL.
"YES, IT'S MORE ATTENTION-GRABBING THAN JUST RUNNING AROUND ON THE STREETS...
"...BUT IT ALSO MEANS YOU CAN'T TAKE ANY UNNECESSARY CHANCES UP THERE.
"ONE WRONG MOVE, AND YOU'RE A GONER.
"BUT DO THIS RIGHT, AND COME NEXT WEEK, IT'LL BE SMOOTH SAILING FOR US."

"OUR LITTLE PROJECT IS GOING TO BE BIG...

"...BONEHEADS BIG."

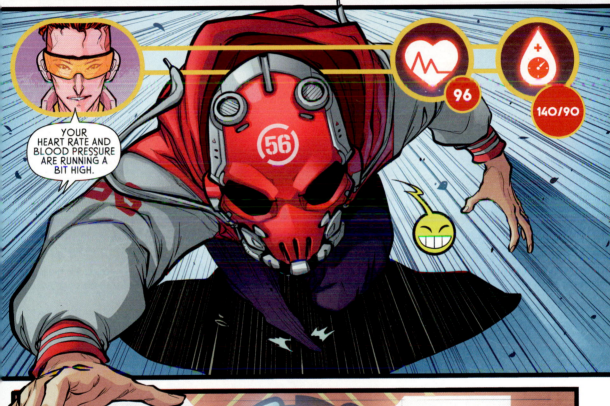

YOUR HEART RATE AND BLOOD PRESSURE ARE RUNNING A BIT HIGH.

96

140/90

I CAN FEEL THE ADRENALINE RUSH FROM OVER HERE.

YOU'VE NEVER FELT **THIS** FREE AND HAPPY BEFORE, HAVE YOU?

REPORT OF CODE 52-A ON SERGEY BRIN BOULEVARD.

CHARGING PERP FOR PUBLIC ENDANGERMENT.

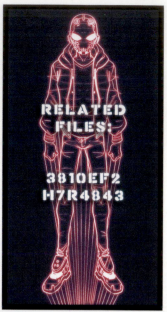

RELATED FILES:

3810EF2
H7R4843

UPDATING INFO: 52-A PERP IS A POSSIBLE MATCH FOR REPEATED OFFENSES.

UPDATE ON 52-A PERP. ACCESS TO V.R. HELMET **REJECTED.**

THE GLADIATORS' HEADQUARTERS

ADDING CHARGES ON 52-A PREP. CONFIRMED USE OF A **JAILBROKEN** V.R. HELMET.

REQUESTING PERMISSION TO SET A PATROL DRONE ON 52-A PERP.

PERMISSION GRANTED. RETASKING DRONE 79. PASSWORD: VESUVIO.

ALL GLADIATORS, THIS IS CENTRAL. BE ON THE LOOKOUT FOR ROGUE DELIVERY DRONES!

DISPATCH, THIS IS **GLADIATOR 32...**

...I HAVE **VISUALS** ON 52-A ON BANGALTER AND CHRISTO!

ONE MORE TIME?

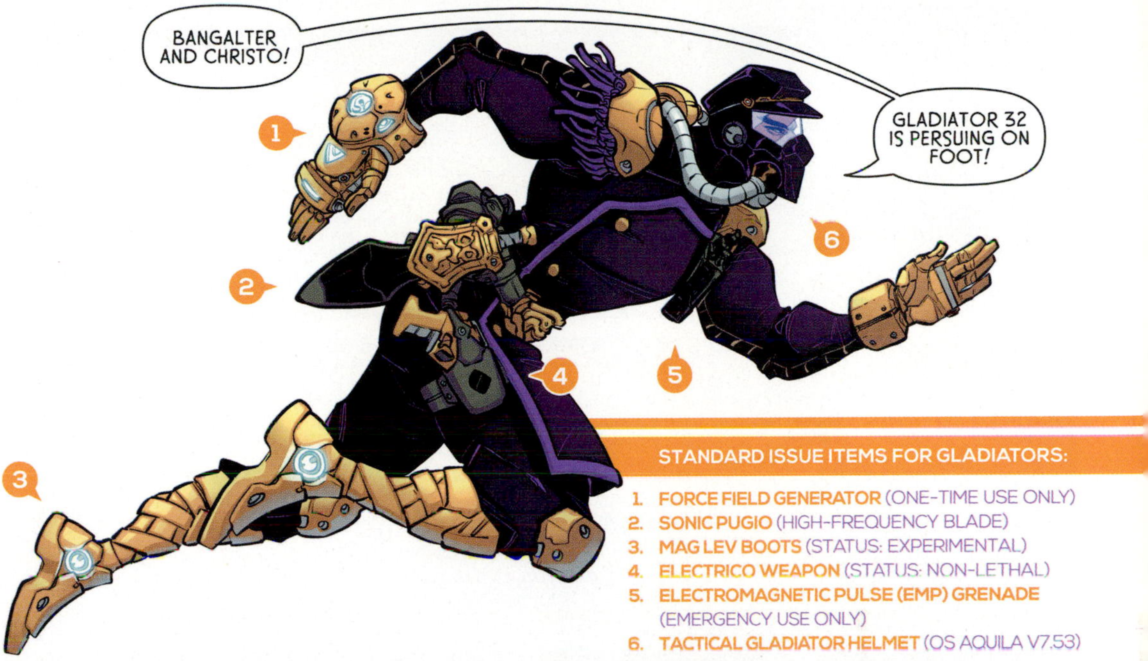
BANGALTER AND CHRISTO!
GLADIATOR 32 IS PERSUING ON FOOT!
1
2
3
4
5
6
STANDARD ISSUE ITEMS FOR GLADIATORS:
1. FORCE FIELD GENERATOR (ONE-TIME USE ONLY)
2. SONIC PUGIO (HIGH-FREQUENCY BLADE)
3. MAG LEV BOOTS (STATUS: EXPERIMENTAL)
4. ELECTRICO WEAPON (STATUS: NON-LETHAL)
5. ELECTROMAGNETIC PULSE (EMP) GRENADE (EMERGENCY USE ONLY)
6. TACTICAL GLADIATOR HELMET (OS AQUILA V7.53)

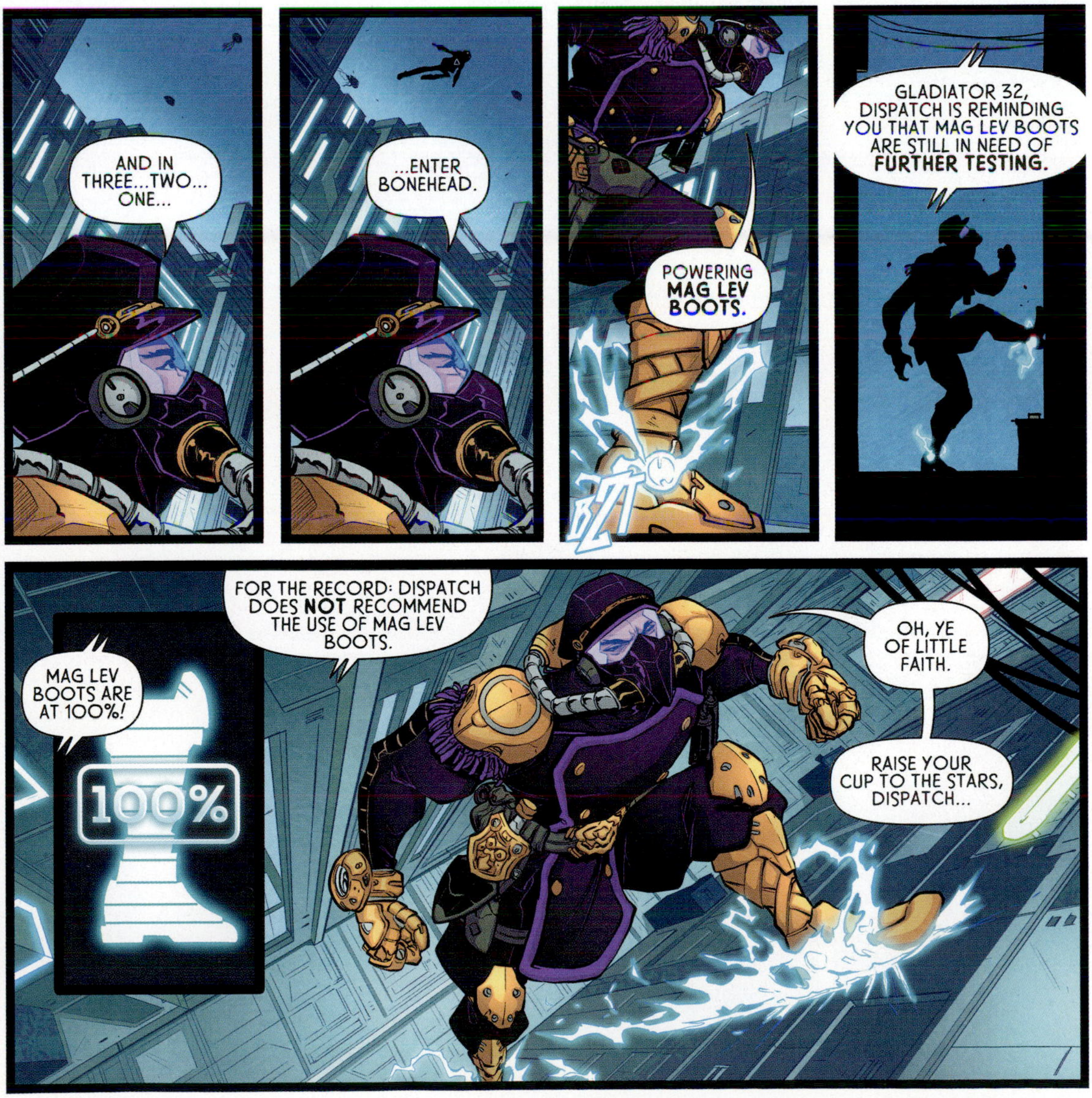
AND IN THREE...TWO... ONE...
...ENTER BONEHEAD.
POWERING MAG LEV BOOTS.
BZT
GLADIATOR 32, DISPATCH IS REMINDING YOU THAT MAG LEV BOOTS ARE STILL IN NEED OF FURTHER TESTING.
FOR THE RECORD: DISPATCH DOES NOT RECOMMEND THE USE OF MAG LEV BOOTS.
MAG LEV BOOTS ARE AT 100%!
100%
OH, YE OF LITTLE FAITH.
RAISE YOUR CUP TO THE STARS, DISPATCH...

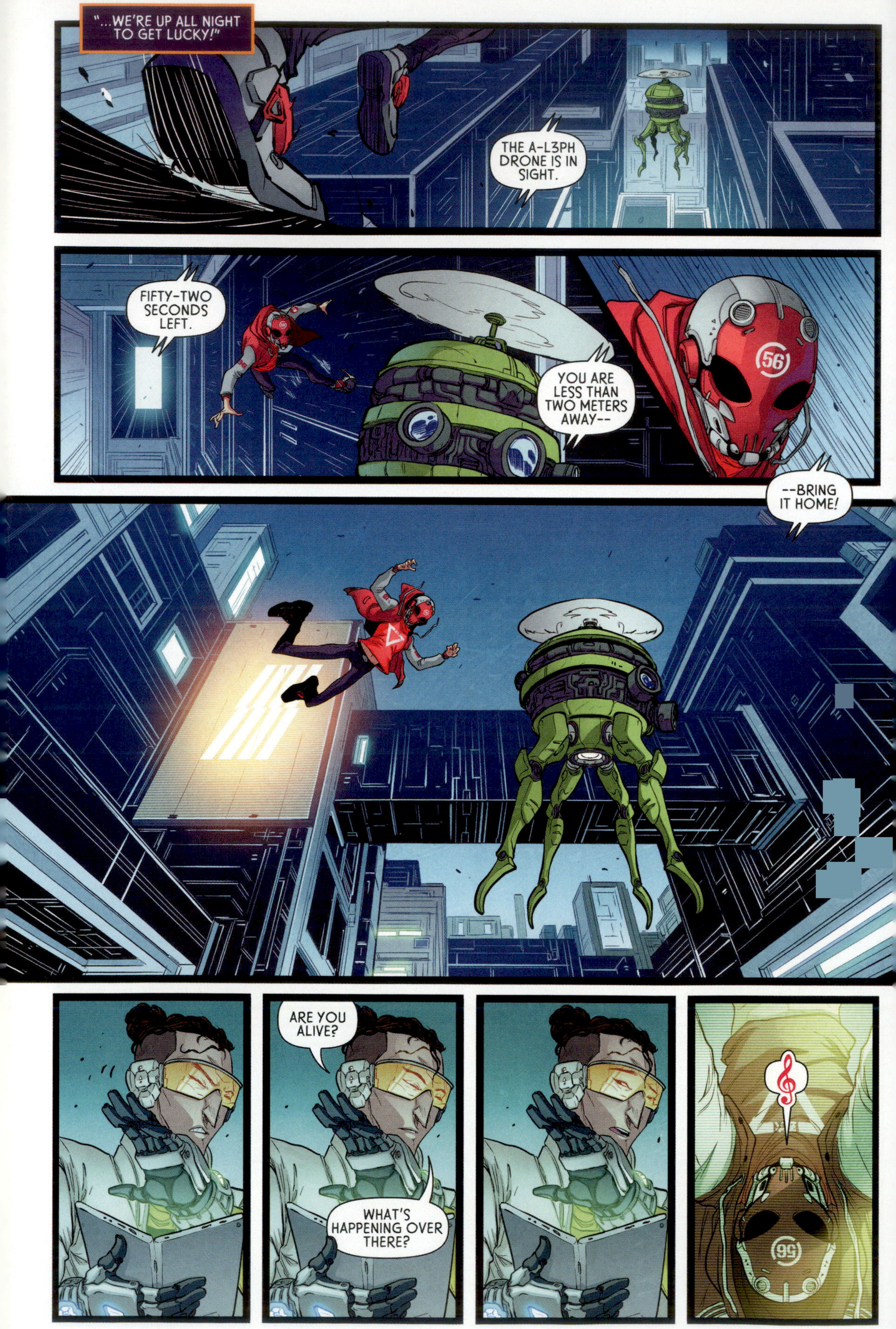
"...WE'RE UP ALL NIGHT TO GET LUCKY!"
THE A-L3PH DRONE IS IN SIGHT.
FIFTY-TWO SECONDS LEFT.
YOU ARE LESS THAN TWO METERS AWAY--
--BRING IT HOME!
ARE YOU ALIVE?
WHAT'S HAPPENING OVER THERE?

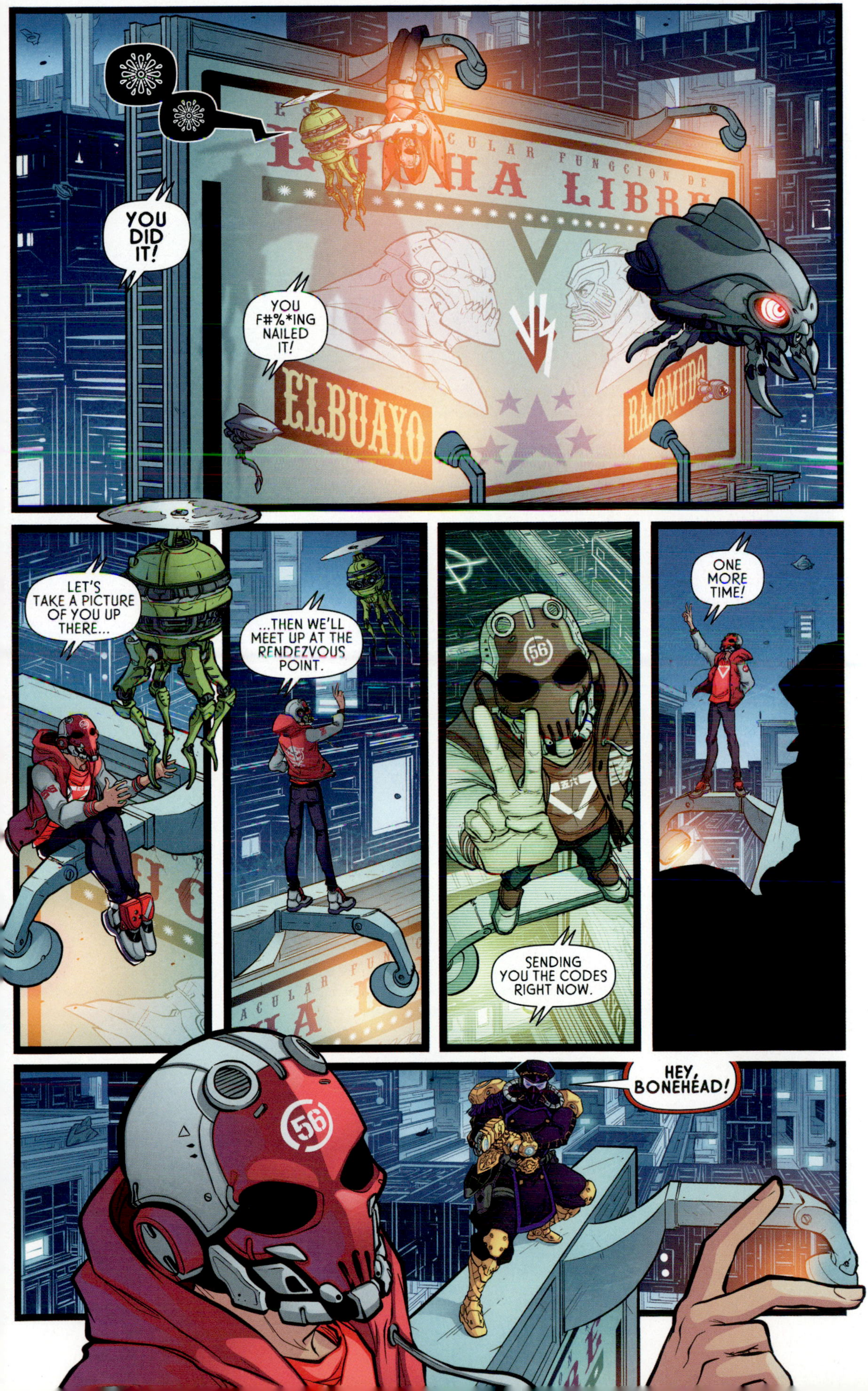
YOU DID IT!
YOU F#%*ING NAILED IT!
LUCHA LIBRE
ELBUAYO
VS
RAJOMUDO
LET'S TAKE A PICTURE OF YOU UP THERE...
...THEN WE'LL MEET UP AT THE RENDEZVOUS POINT.
SENDING YOU THE CODES RIGHT NOW.
ONE MORE TIME!
HEY, BONEHEAD!

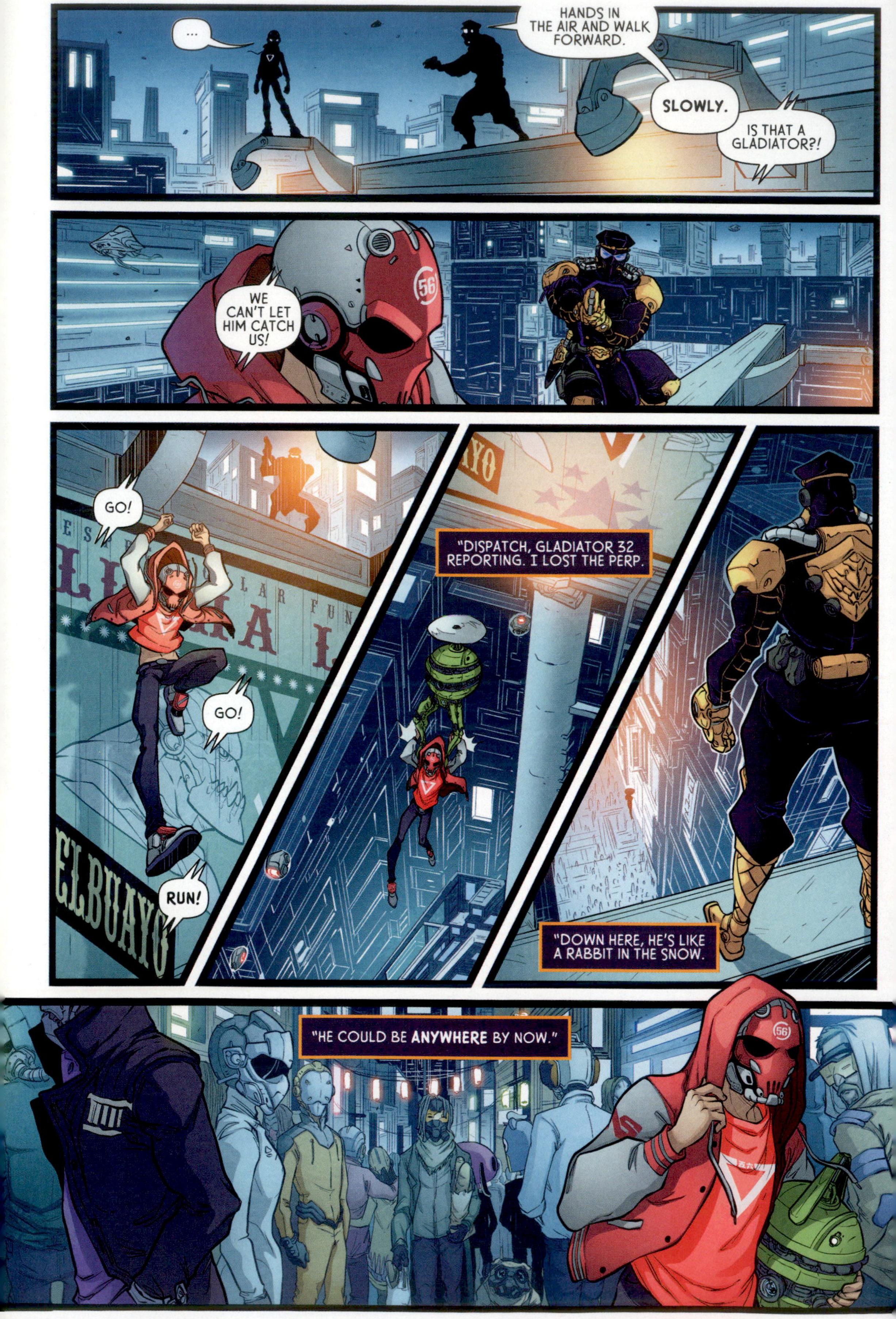
...
HANDS IN THE AIR AND WALK FORWARD.
SLOWLY.
IS THAT A GLADIATOR?!
WE CAN'T LET HIM CATCH US!
GO!
GO!
RUN!
ELBUAYO
"DISPATCH, GLADIATOR 32 REPORTING. I LOST THE PERP.
"DOWN HERE, HE'S LIKE A RABBIT IN THE SNOW.
"HE COULD BE **ANYWHERE** BY NOW."

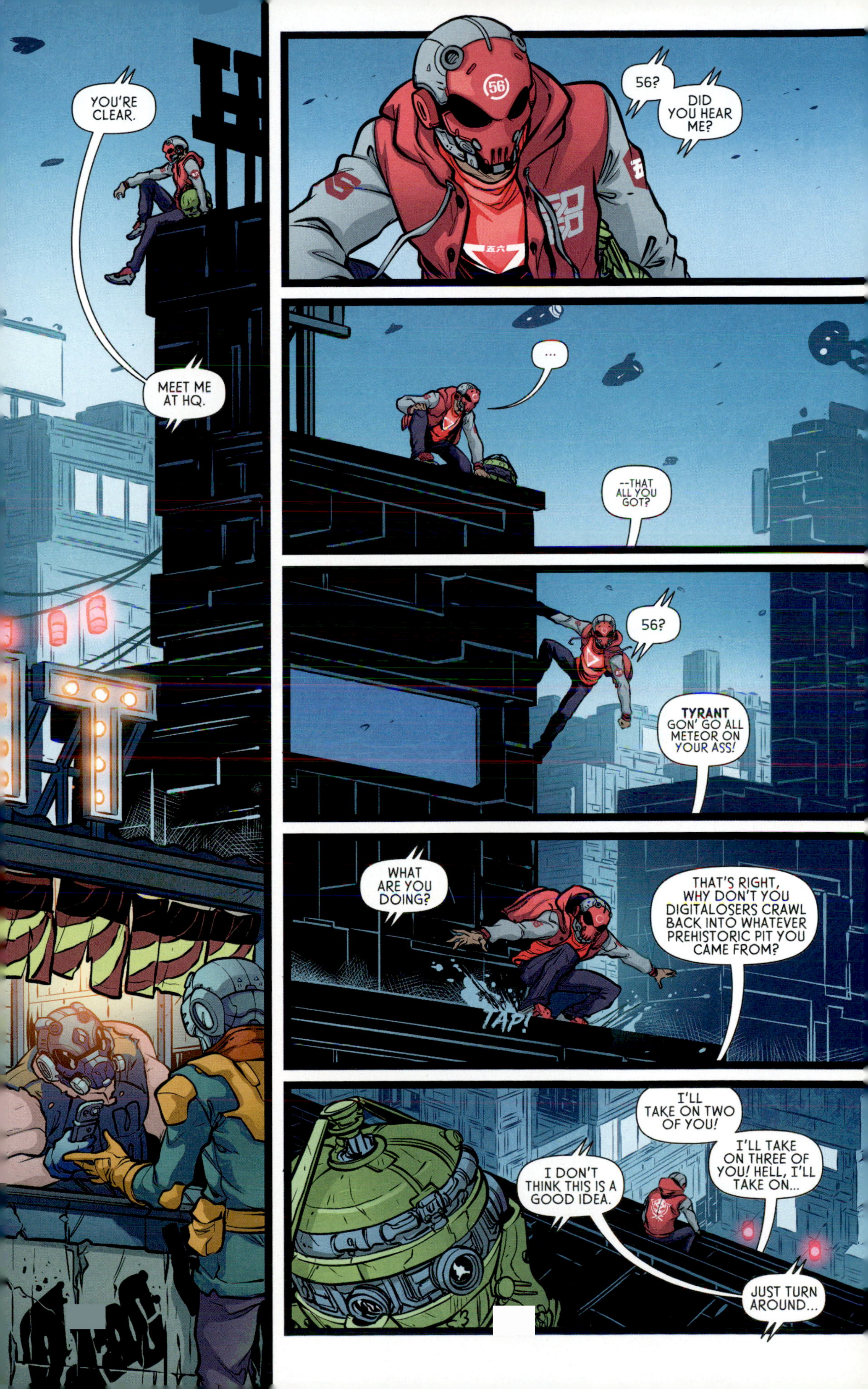
YOU'RE CLEAR.
MEET ME AT HQ.
56?
DID YOU HEAR ME?
...
--THAT ALL YOU GOT?
56?
TYRANT GON' GO ALL METEOR ON YOUR ASS!
WHAT ARE YOU DOING?
THAT'S RIGHT, WHY DON'T YOU DIGITALOSERS CRAWL BACK INTO WHATEVER PREHISTORIC PIT YOU CAME FROM?
TAP!
I'LL TAKE ON TWO OF YOU!
I'LL TAKE ON THREE OF YOU! HELL, I'LL TAKE ON...
I DON'T THINK THIS IS A GOOD IDEA.
JUST TURN AROUND...

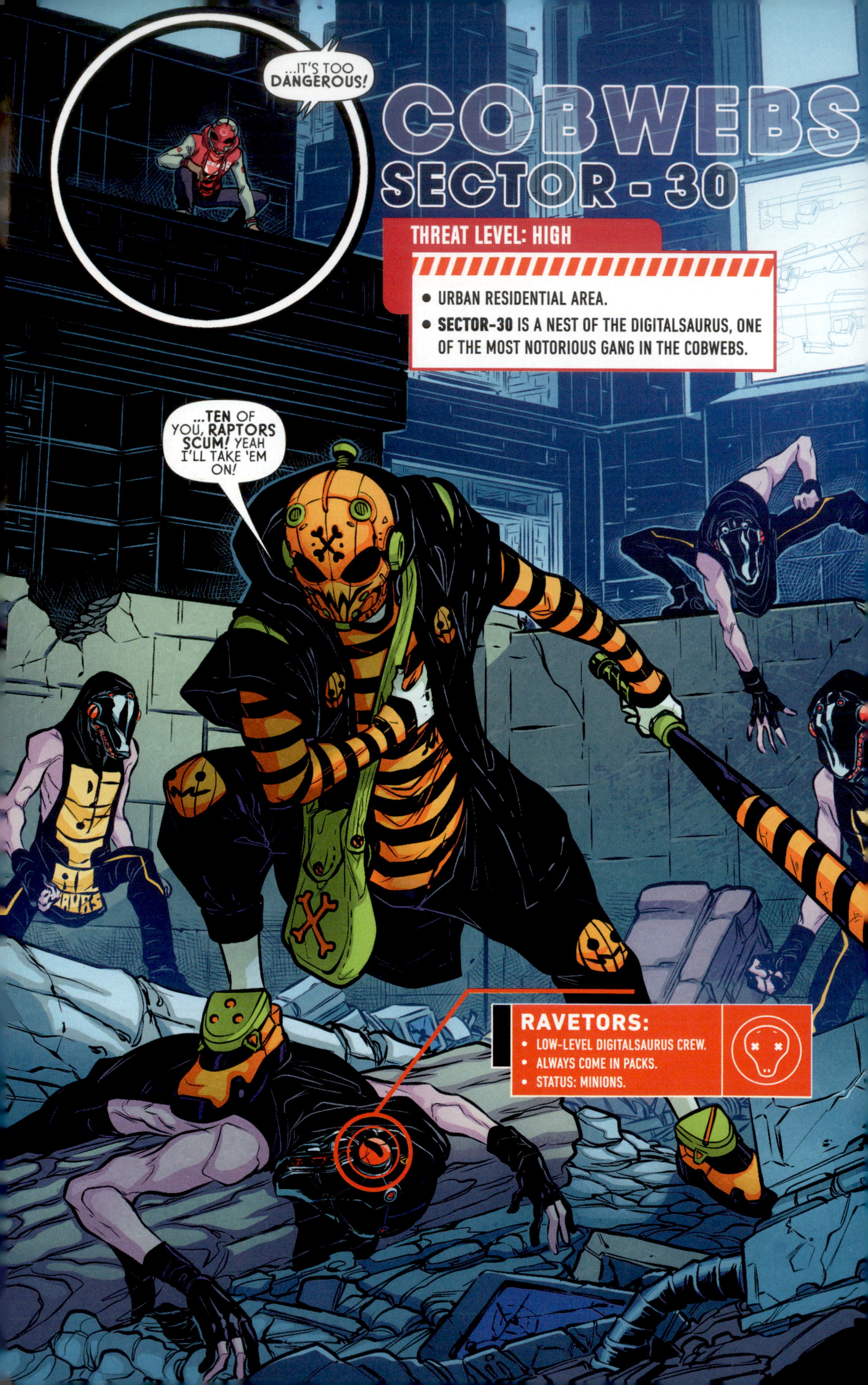

...IT'S TOO DANGEROUS!
COBWEBS
SECTOR - 30
THREAT LEVEL: HIGH
• URBAN RESIDENTIAL AREA.
• SECTOR-30 IS A NEST OF THE DIGITALSAURUS, ONE OF THE MOST NOTORIOUS GANG IN THE COBWEBS.
...TEN OF YOU, RAPTORS SCUM! YEAH I'LL TAKE 'EM ON!
RAVETORS:
• LOW-LEVEL DIGITALSAURUS CREW.
• ALWAYS COME IN PACKS.
• STATUS: MINIONS.

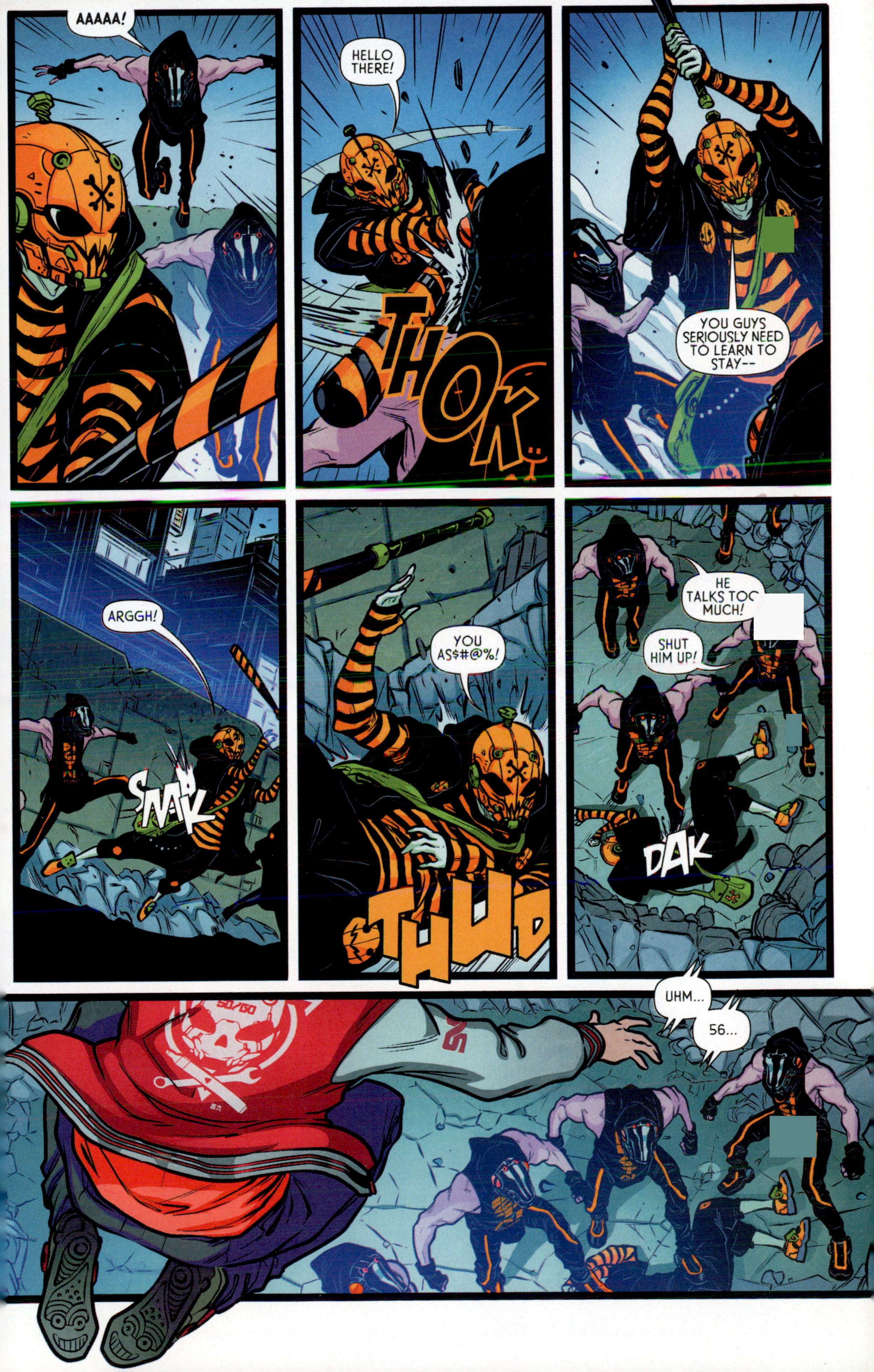
AAAAA!
HELLO THERE!
THOK
YOU GUYS SERIOUSLY NEED TO LEARN TO STAY--
ARGGH!
SNAK
YOU AS$#@%!
THUD
HE TALKS TOO MUCH!
SHUT HIM UP!
DAK
UHM...
56...

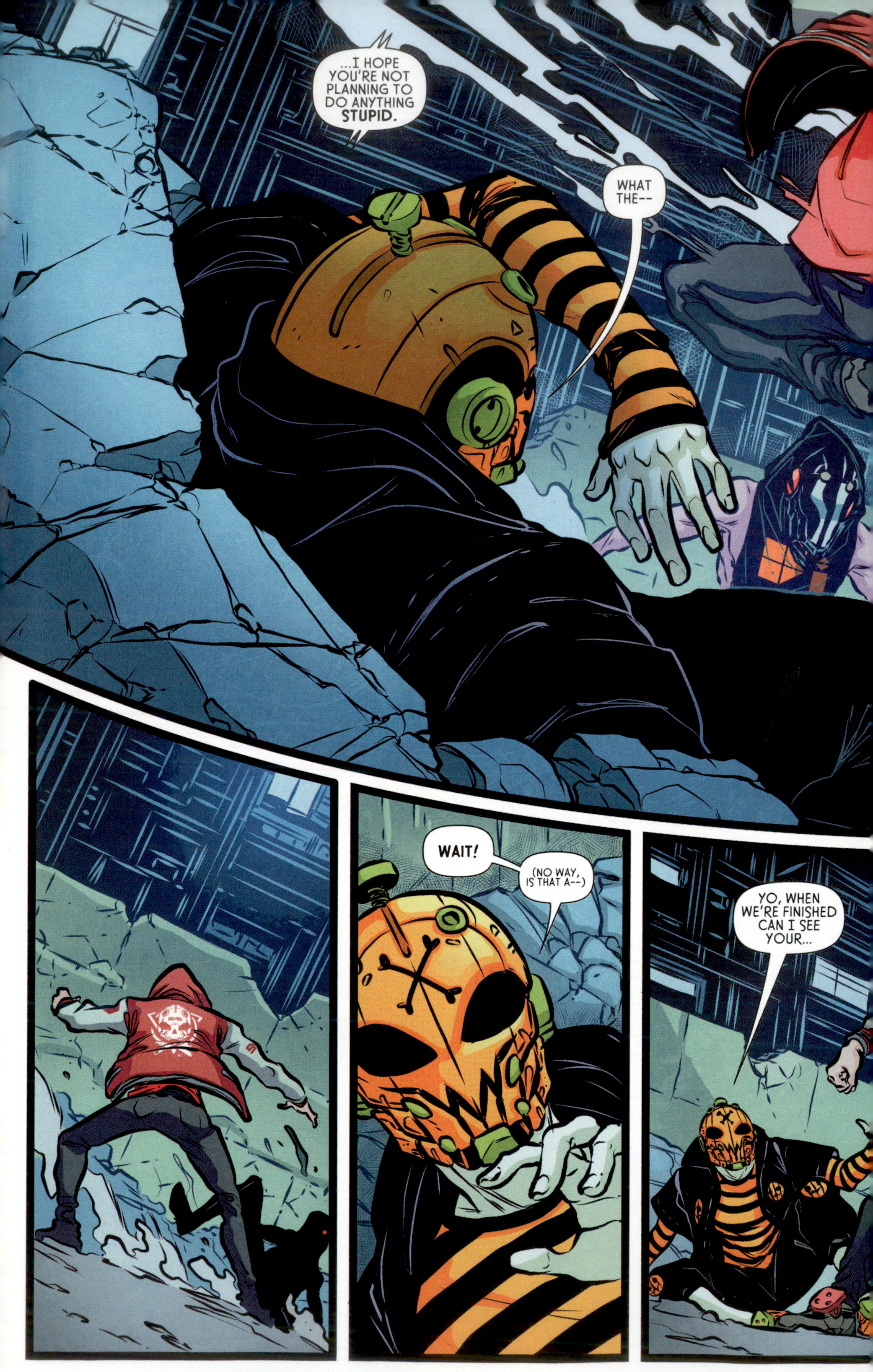
...I HOPE YOU'RE NOT PLANNING TO DO ANYTHING **STUPID.**
WHAT THE--
WAIT!
(NO WAY, IS THAT A--)
YO, WHEN WE'RE FINISHED CAN I SEE YOUR...

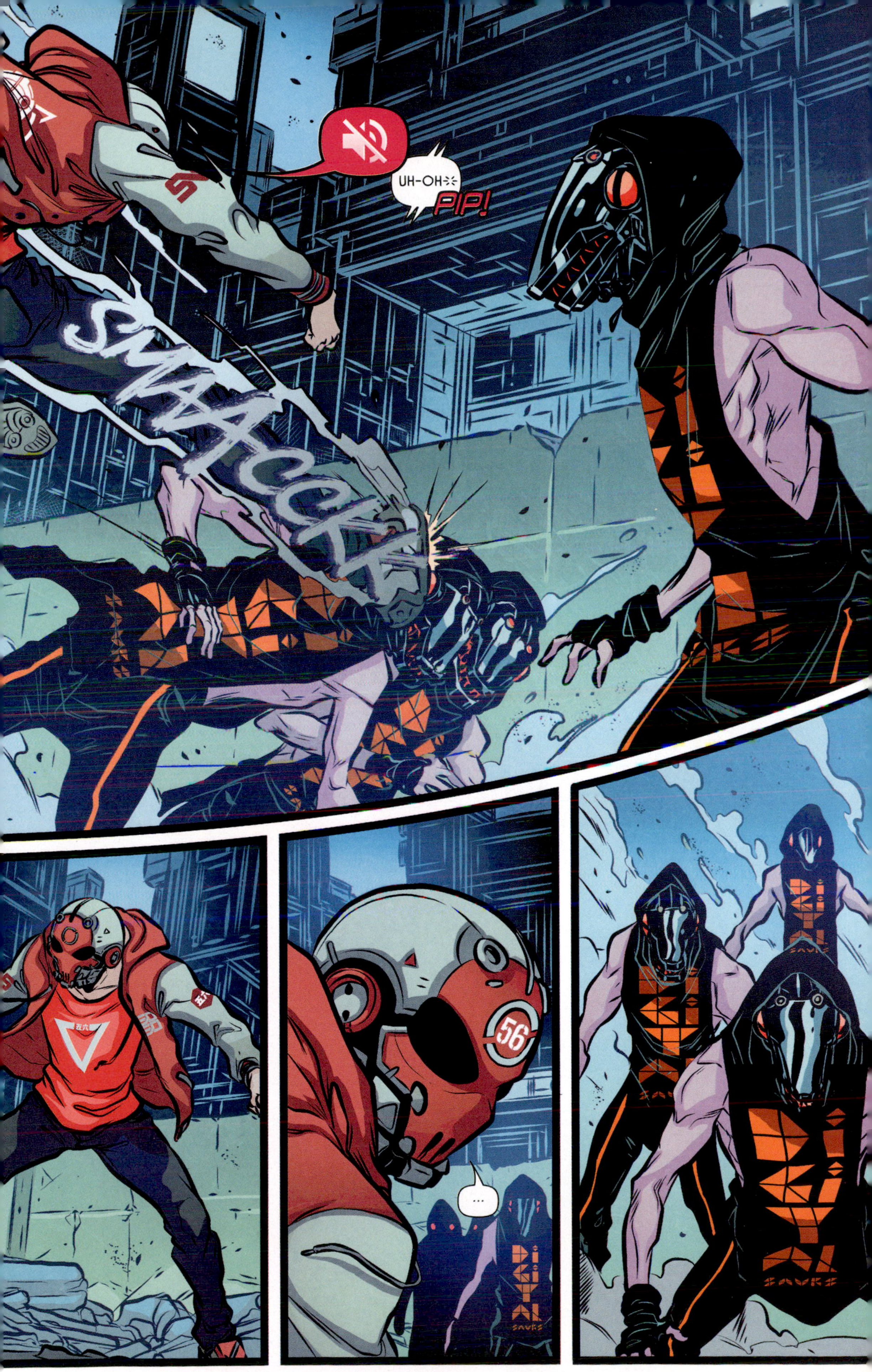

UH-OH
PIP!
SMACCK!
...

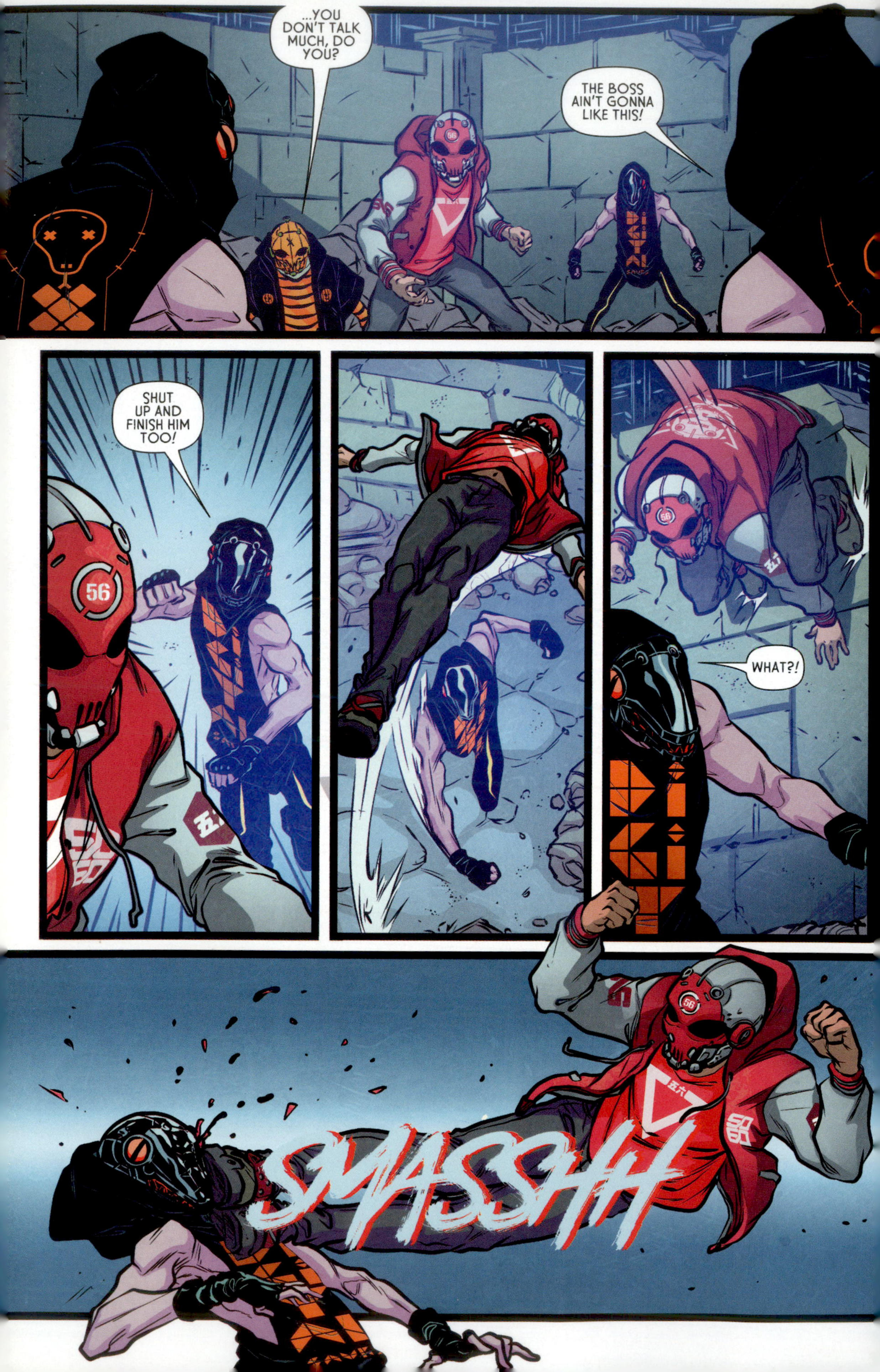
...YOU DON'T TALK MUCH, DO YOU?
THE BOSS AIN'T GONNA LIKE THIS!
SHUT UP AND FINISH HIM TOO!
WHAT?!
SMASSHH

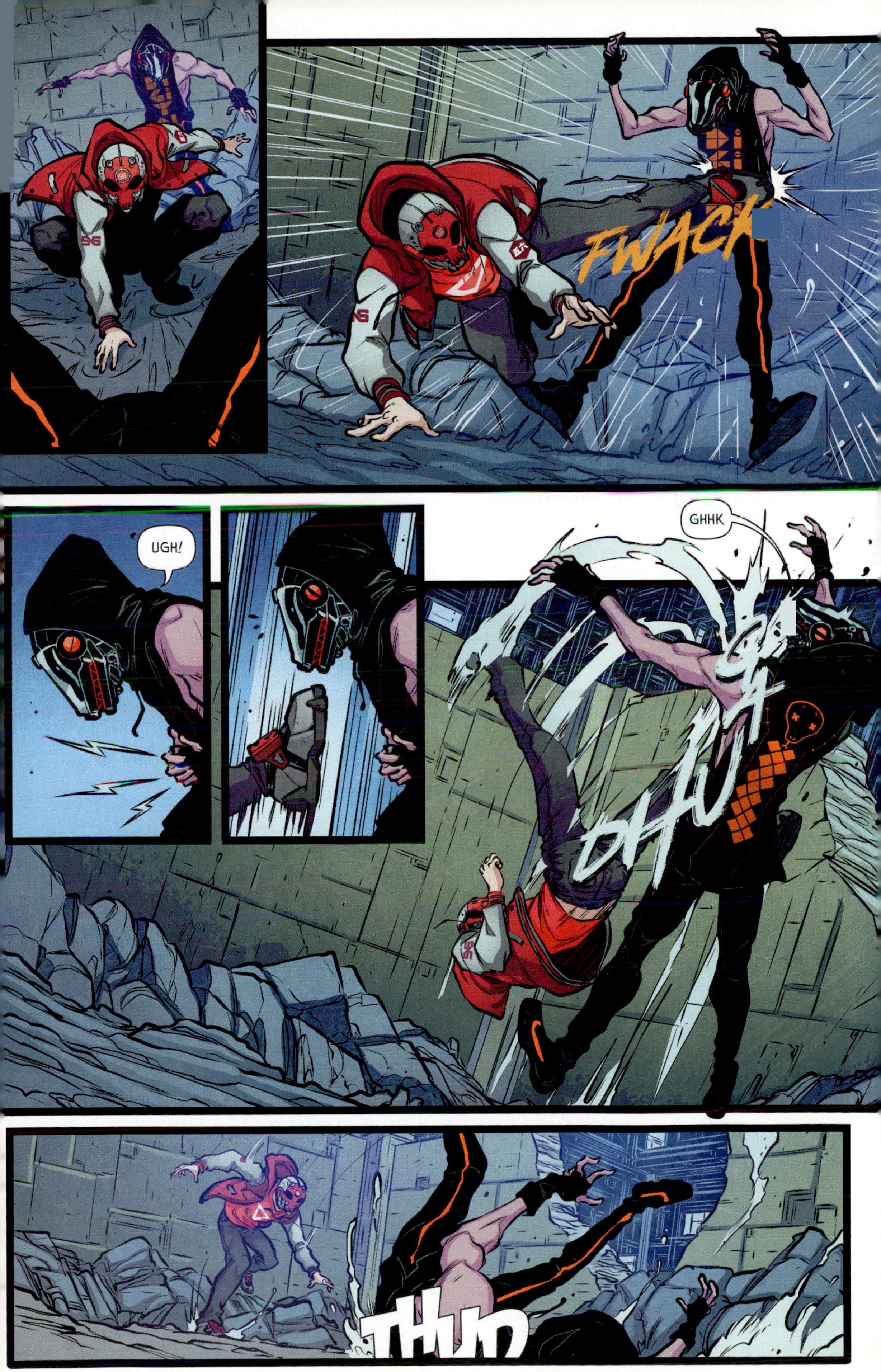
FWACK
UGH!
GHHK
THUD

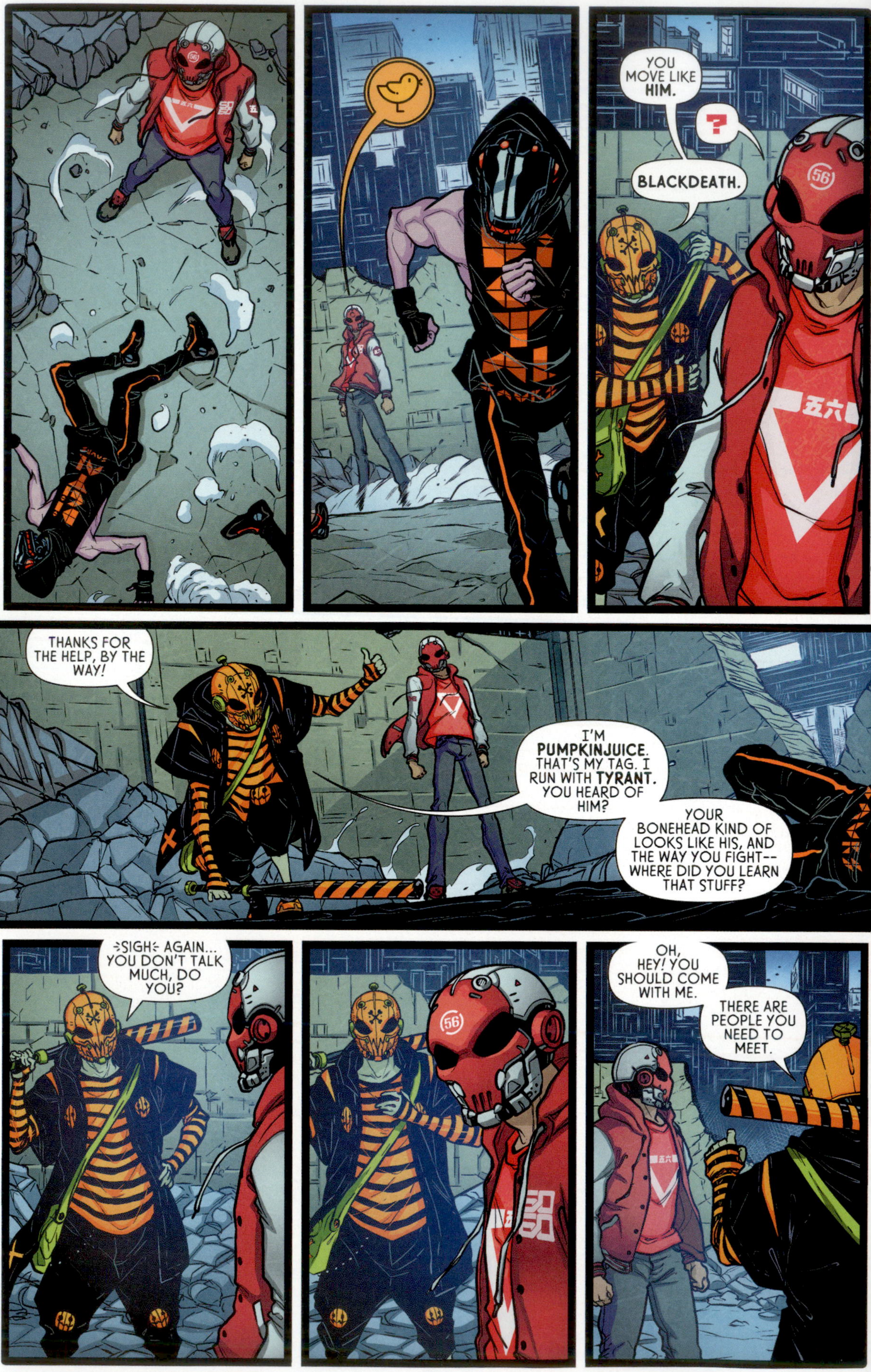
YOU MOVE LIKE HIM.
?
BLACKDEATH.
THANKS FOR THE HELP, BY THE WAY!
I'M PUMPKINJUICE. THAT'S MY TAG. I RUN WITH TYRANT. YOU HEARD OF HIM?
YOUR BONEHEAD KIND OF LOOKS LIKE HIS, AND THE WAY YOU FIGHT-- WHERE DID YOU LEARN THAT STUFF?
SIGH AGAIN... YOU DON'T TALK MUCH, DO YOU?
OH, HEY! YOU SHOULD COME WITH ME.
THERE ARE PEOPLE YOU NEED TO MEET.

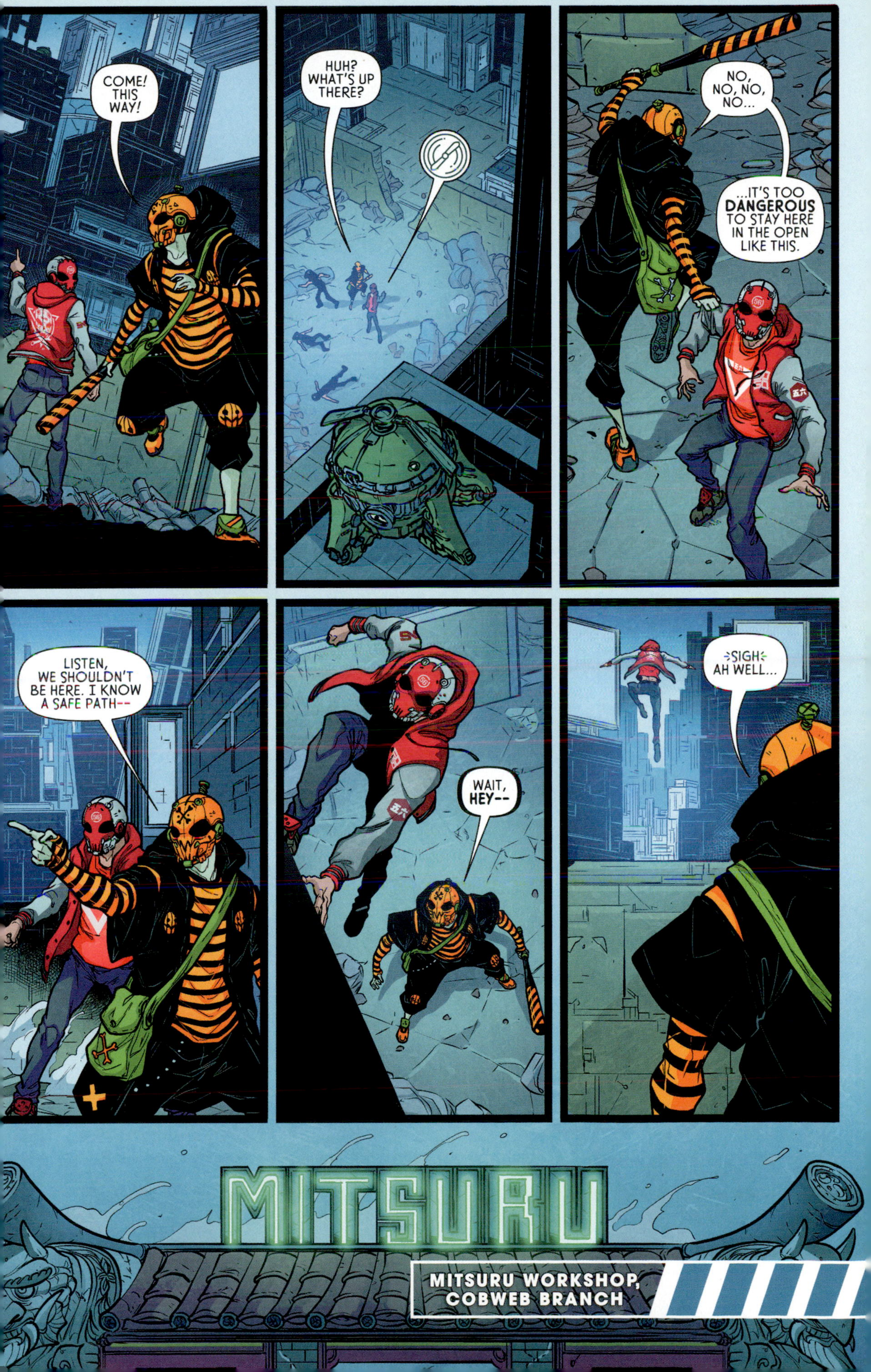
COME! THIS WAY!
HUH? WHAT'S UP THERE?
NO, NO, NO, NO...
...IT'S TOO DANGEROUS TO STAY HERE IN THE OPEN LIKE THIS.
LISTEN, WE SHOULDN'T BE HERE. I KNOW A SAFE PATH--
WAIT, HEY--
SIGH AH WELL...
MITSURU
MITSURU WORKSHOP, COBWEB BRANCH

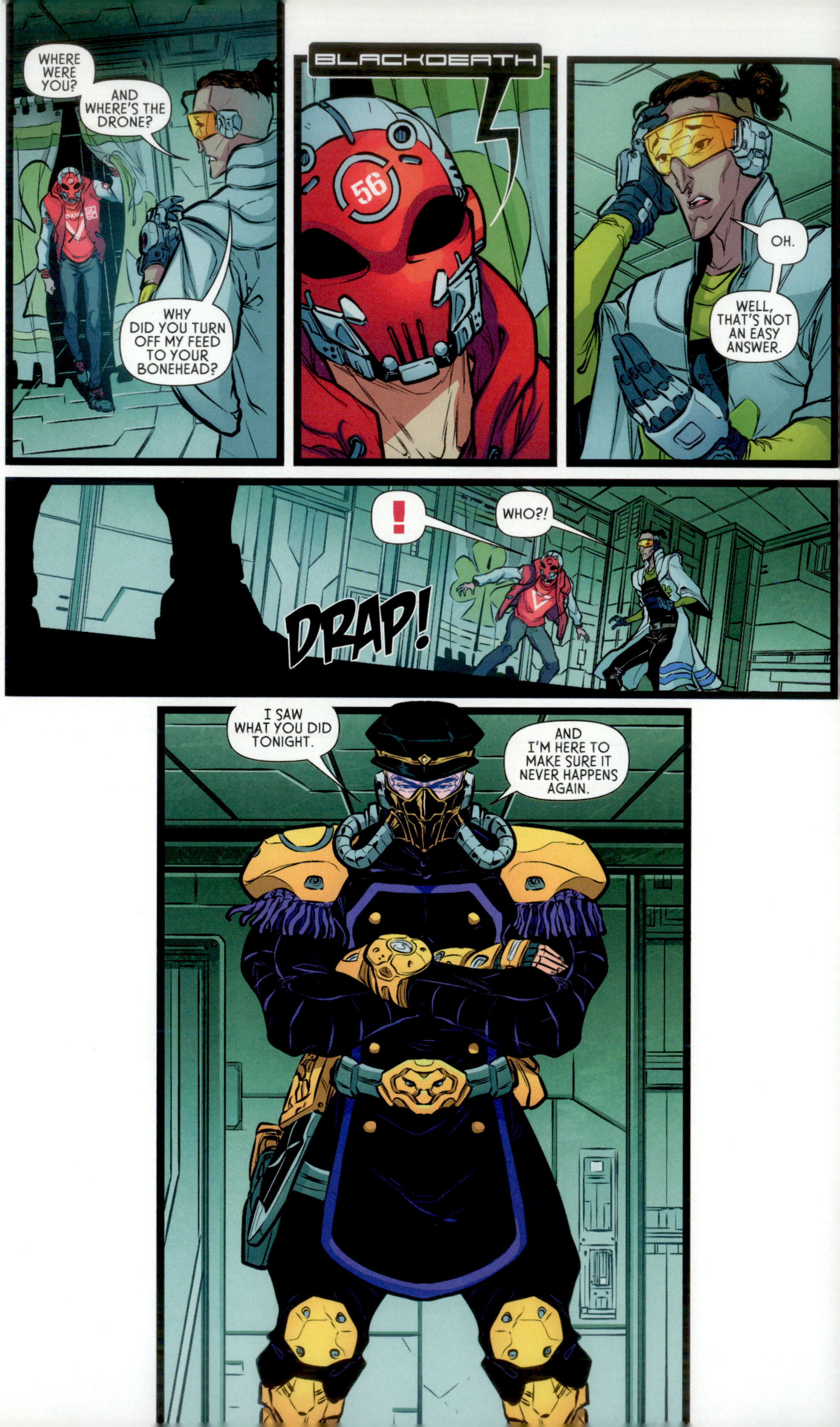

WHERE WERE YOU?
AND WHERE'S THE DRONE?
WHY DID YOU TURN OFF MY FEED TO YOUR BONEHEAD?
BLACKDEATH
OH.
WELL, THAT'S NOT AN EASY ANSWER.
DRAP!
!
WHO?!
I SAW WHAT YOU DID TONIGHT.
AND I'M HERE TO MAKE SURE IT NEVER HAPPENS AGAIN.

CHAPTER02

● ORIGINAL MITSURU.TECH SERIAL #   ● SLAVE TYPE BONEHEAD01.   ● NODE TRACKING AFTER DELETION COURS
○ CLOSE QUARTER TYPE_   ○ BODY STRUCTURE : N/A   ○ EARTH: 7 MEGAPARSECS ACROSS_

▶ **M56/001/A**   ▶ Bonehead, RED, 16k-Zettabyte.   (1P) Part No. MT-A0156 / D / Test Subject no.56   ブラック・デス・ランナー   QC/

Designed by Machine56, Assembled by Mitsuru.Tech
MK-I / Not suitable f

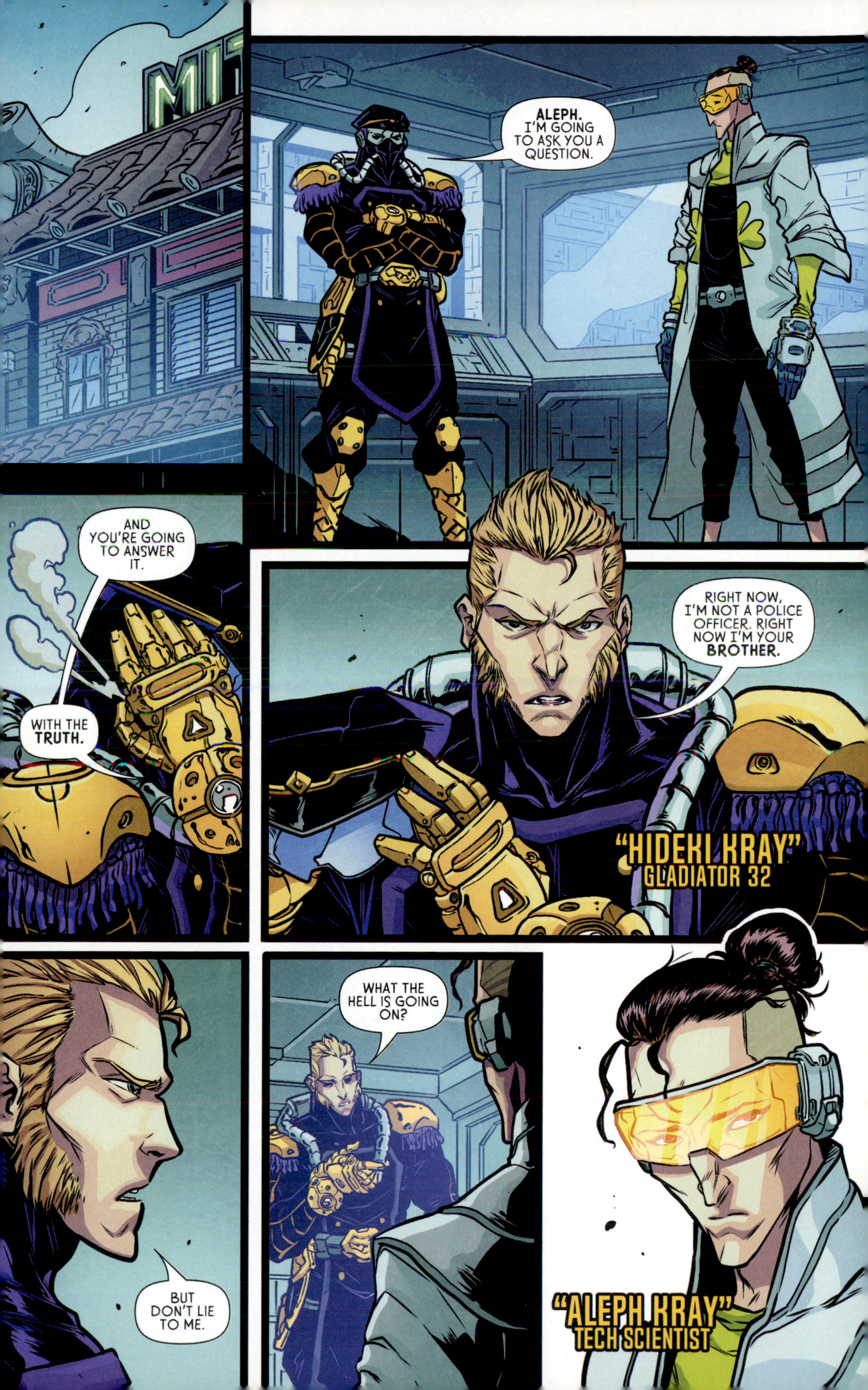
MIT
ALEPH. I'M GOING TO ASK YOU A QUESTION.
AND YOU'RE GOING TO ANSWER IT.
WITH THE TRUTH.
RIGHT NOW, I'M NOT A POLICE OFFICER. RIGHT NOW I'M YOUR BROTHER.
"HIDEKI KRAY" GLADIATOR 32
BUT DON'T LIE TO ME.
WHAT THE HELL IS GOING ON?
"ALEPH KRAY" TECH SCIENTIST

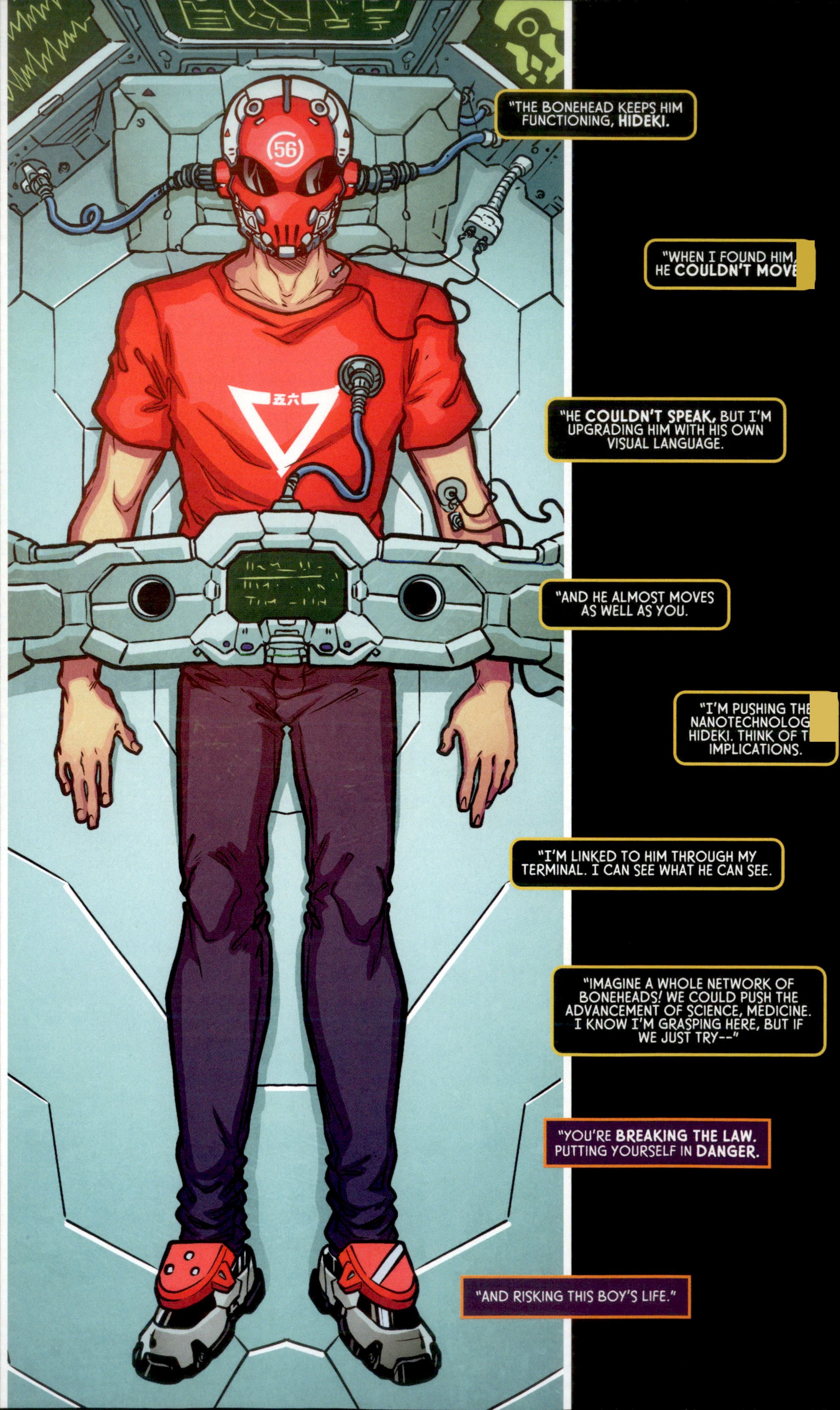
"THE BONEHEAD KEEPS HIM FUNCTIONING, HIDEKI.
56
"WHEN I FOUND HIM, HE COULDN'T MOVE
五六
"HE COULDN'T SPEAK, BUT I'M UPGRADING HIM WITH HIS OWN VISUAL LANGUAGE.
"AND HE ALMOST MOVES AS WELL AS YOU.
"I'M PUSHING THE NANOTECHNOLOG HIDEKI. THINK OF T IMPLICATIONS.
"I'M LINKED TO HIM THROUGH MY TERMINAL. I CAN SEE WHAT HE CAN SEE.
"IMAGINE A WHOLE NETWORK OF BONEHEADS! WE COULD PUSH THE ADVANCEMENT OF SCIENCE, MEDICINE. I KNOW I'M GRASPING HERE, BUT IF WE JUST TRY--"
"YOU'RE BREAKING THE LAW. PUTTING YOURSELF IN DANGER.
"AND RISKING THIS BOY'S LIFE."

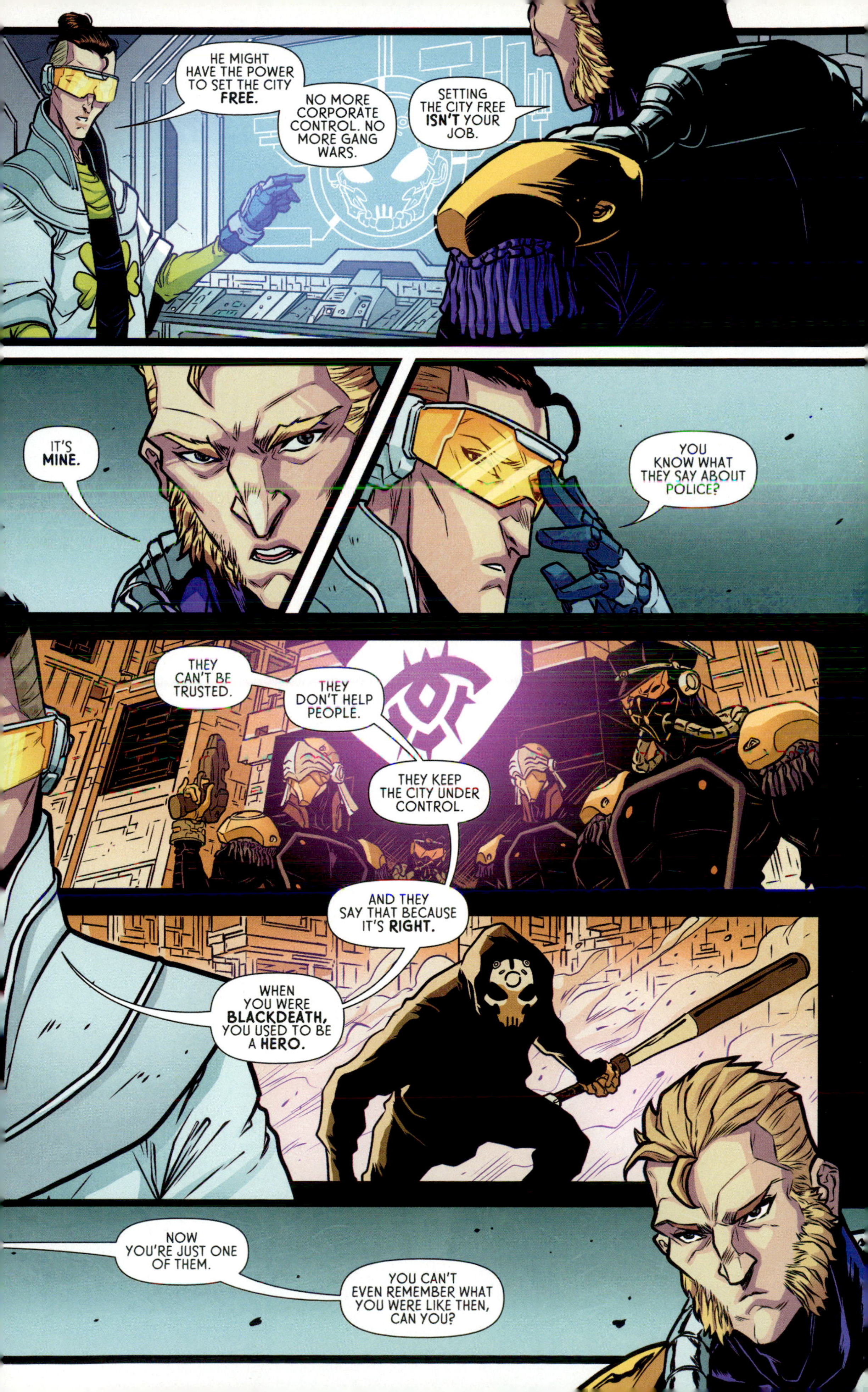
HE MIGHT HAVE THE POWER TO SET THE CITY **FREE.**
NO MORE CORPORATE CONTROL. NO MORE GANG WARS.
SETTING THE CITY FREE **ISN'T** YOUR JOB.
IT'S **MINE.**
YOU KNOW WHAT THEY SAY ABOUT POLICE?
THEY CAN'T BE TRUSTED.
THEY DON'T HELP PEOPLE.
THEY KEEP THE CITY UNDER CONTROL.
AND THEY SAY THAT BECAUSE IT'S **RIGHT.**
WHEN YOU WERE **BLACKDEATH,** YOU USED TO BE A **HERO.**
NOW YOU'RE JUST ONE OF THEM.
YOU CAN'T EVEN REMEMBER WHAT YOU WERE LIKE THEN, CAN YOU?

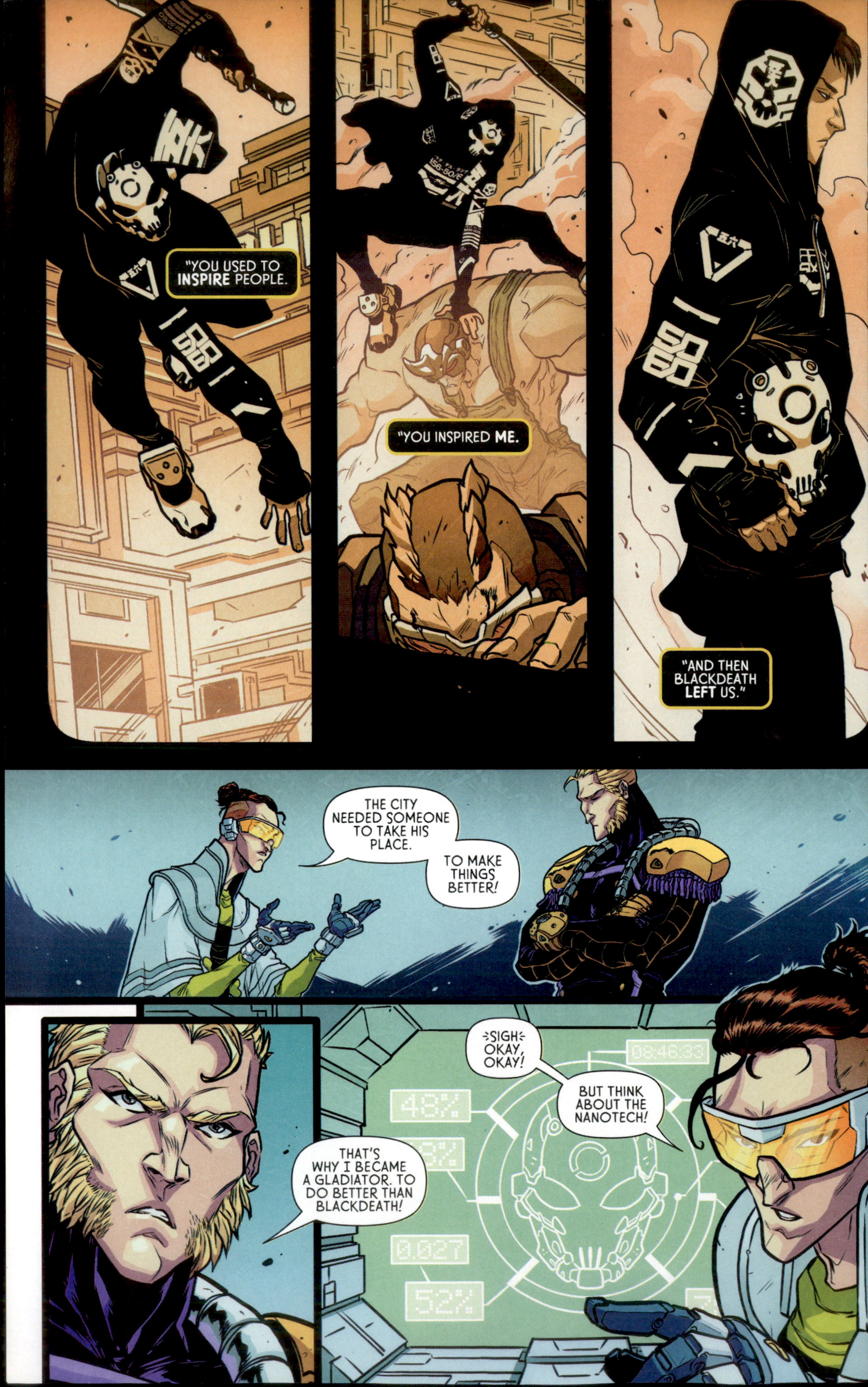
"YOU USED TO INSPIRE PEOPLE.
"YOU INSPIRED ME.
"AND THEN BLACKDEATH LEFT US."
THE CITY NEEDED SOMEONE TO TAKE HIS PLACE.
TO MAKE THINGS BETTER!
THAT'S WHY I BECAME A GLADIATOR. TO DO BETTER THAN BLACKDEATH!
SIGH OKAY, OKAY!
BUT THINK ABOUT THE NANOTECH!

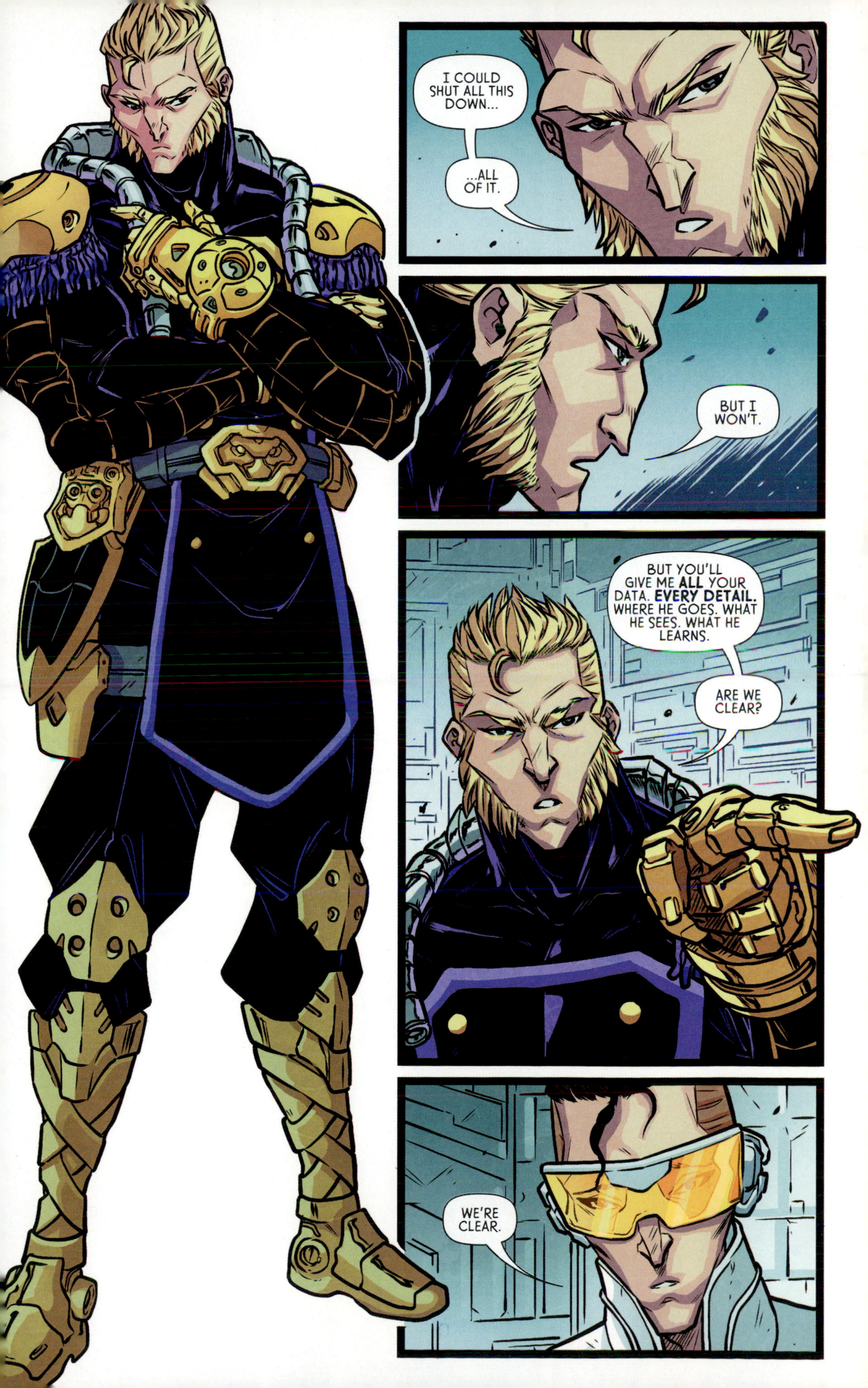
I COULD SHUT ALL THIS DOWN...
...ALL OF IT.
BUT I WON'T.
BUT YOU'LL GIVE ME **ALL** YOUR DATA. **EVERY DETAIL.** WHERE HE GOES. WHAT HE SEES. WHAT HE LEARNS.
ARE WE CLEAR?
WE'RE CLEAR.

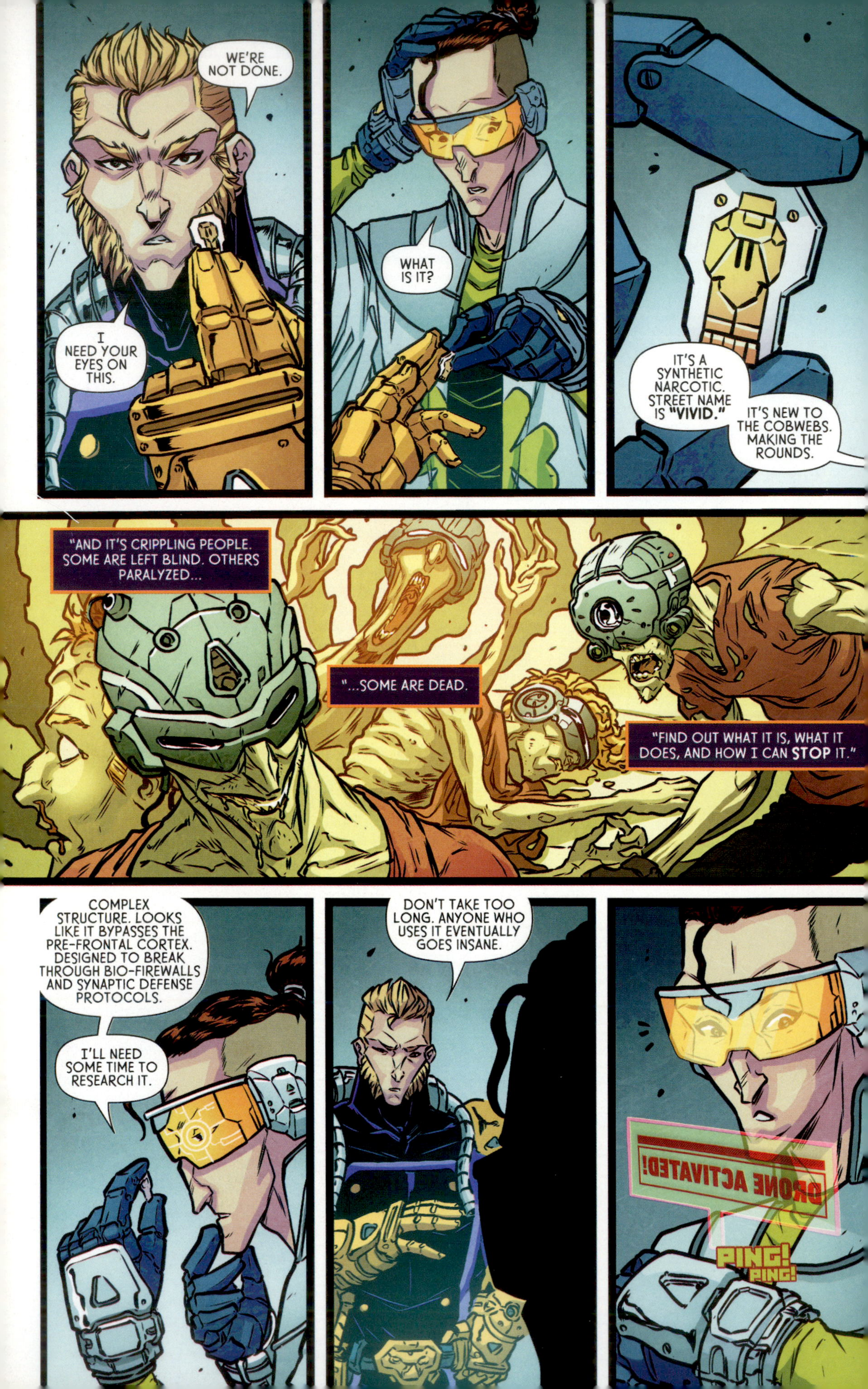
WE'RE NOT DONE.
I NEED YOUR EYES ON THIS.
WHAT IS IT?
IT'S A SYNTHETIC NARCOTIC. STREET NAME IS **"VIVID."**
IT'S NEW TO THE COBWEBS. MAKING THE ROUNDS.
"AND IT'S CRIPPLING PEOPLE. SOME ARE LEFT BLIND. OTHERS PARALYZED...
"...SOME ARE DEAD.
"FIND OUT WHAT IT IS, WHAT IT DOES, AND HOW I CAN **STOP** IT."
COMPLEX STRUCTURE. LOOKS LIKE IT BYPASSES THE PRE-FRONTAL CORTEX. DESIGNED TO BREAK THROUGH BIO-FIREWALLS AND SYNAPTIC DEFENSE PROTOCOLS.
I'LL NEED SOME TIME TO RESEARCH IT.
DON'T TAKE TOO LONG. ANYONE WHO USES IT EVENTUALLY GOES INSANE.
DRONE ACTIVATED!
PING! PING!

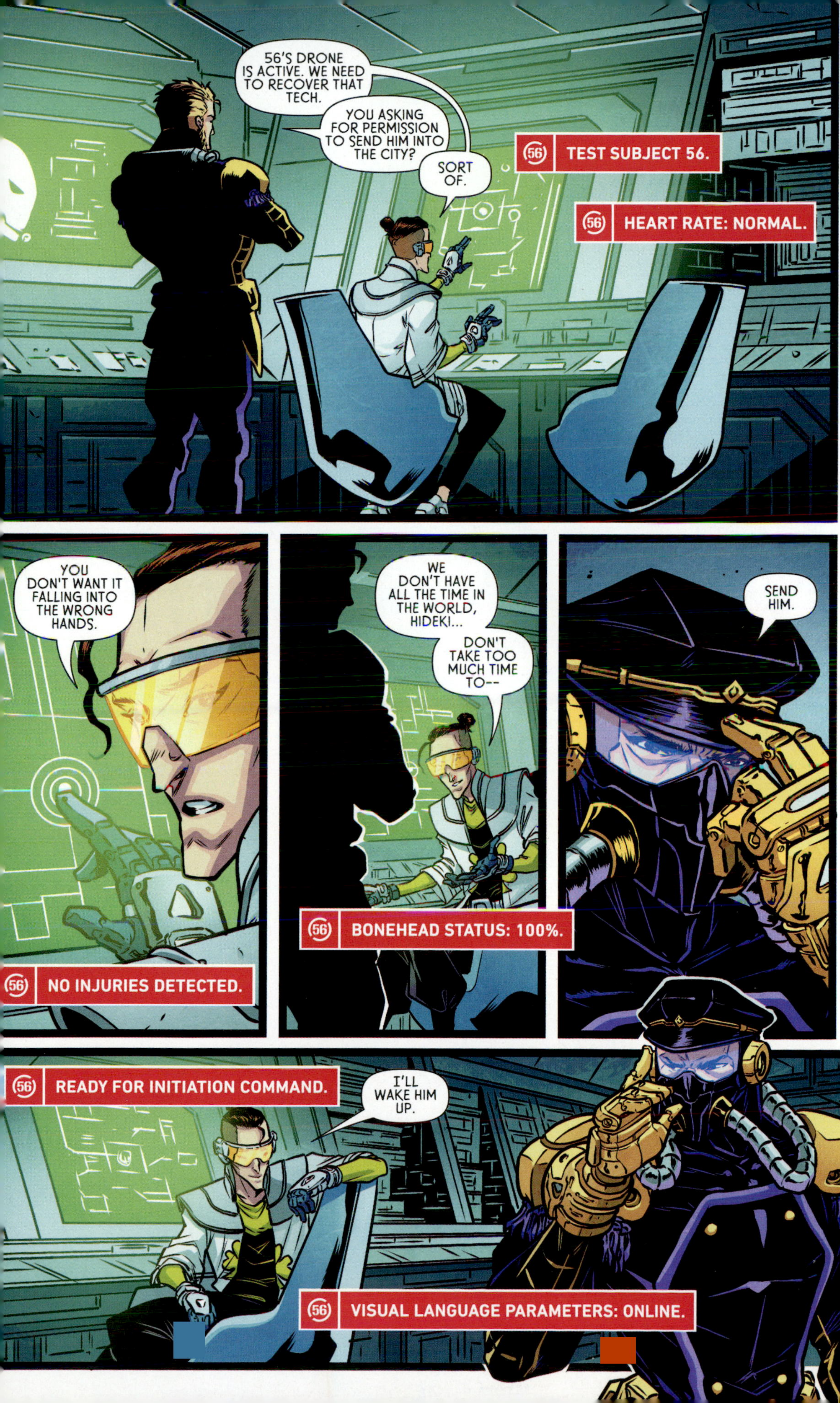
56'S DRONE IS ACTIVE. WE NEED TO RECOVER THAT TECH.
YOU ASKING FOR PERMISSION TO SEND HIM INTO THE CITY?
SORT OF.
56 TEST SUBJECT 56.
56 HEART RATE: NORMAL.
YOU DON'T WANT IT FALLING INTO THE WRONG HANDS.
56 NO INJURIES DETECTED.
WE DON'T HAVE ALL THE TIME IN THE WORLD, HIDEKI...
DON'T TAKE TOO MUCH TIME TO--
56 BONEHEAD STATUS: 100%.
SEND HIM.
56 READY FOR INITIATION COMMAND.
I'LL WAKE HIM UP.
56 VISUAL LANGUAGE PARAMETERS: ONLINE.

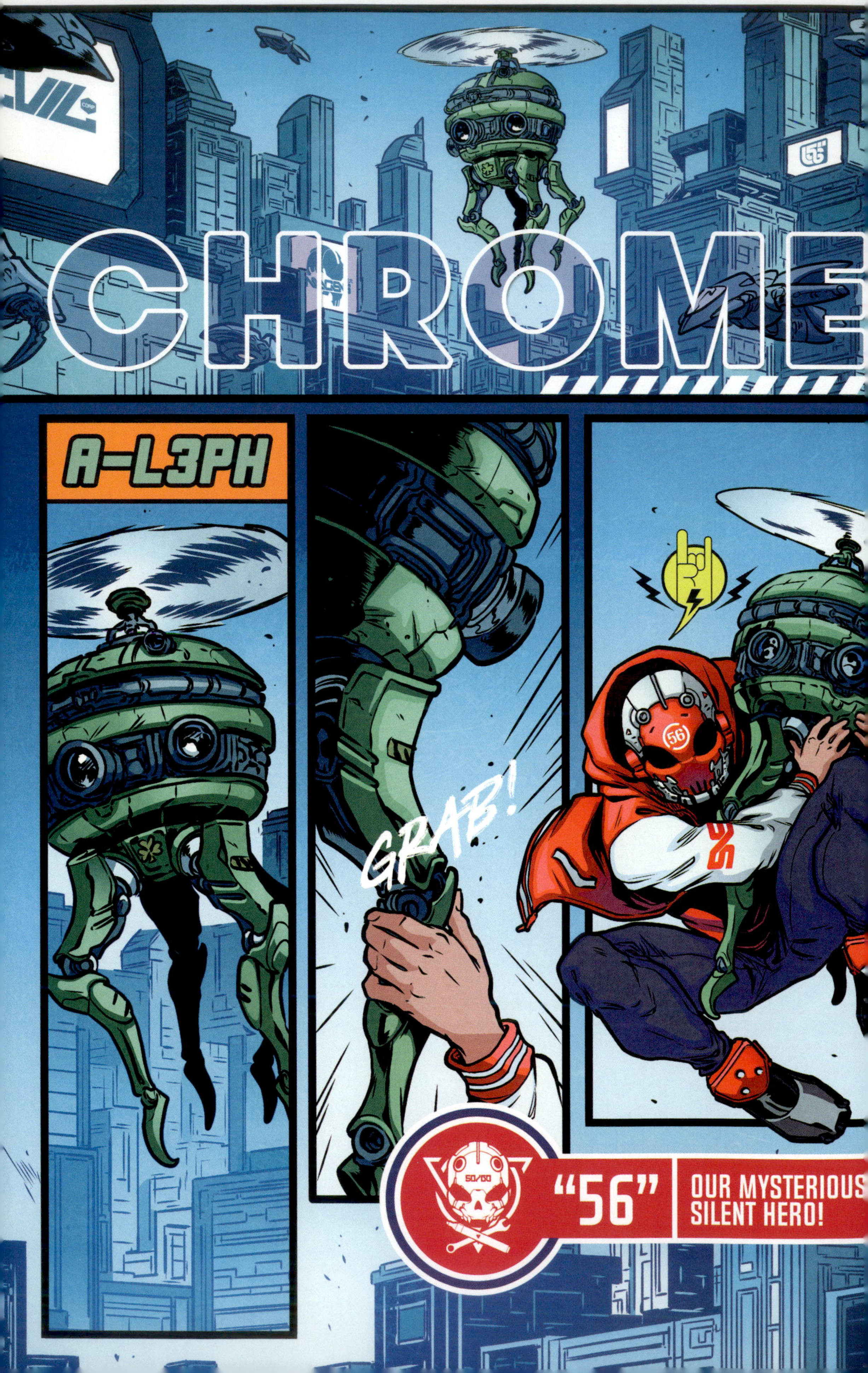

CHROME
A-L3PH
GRAB!
"56"
OUR MYSTERIOUS SILENT HERO!

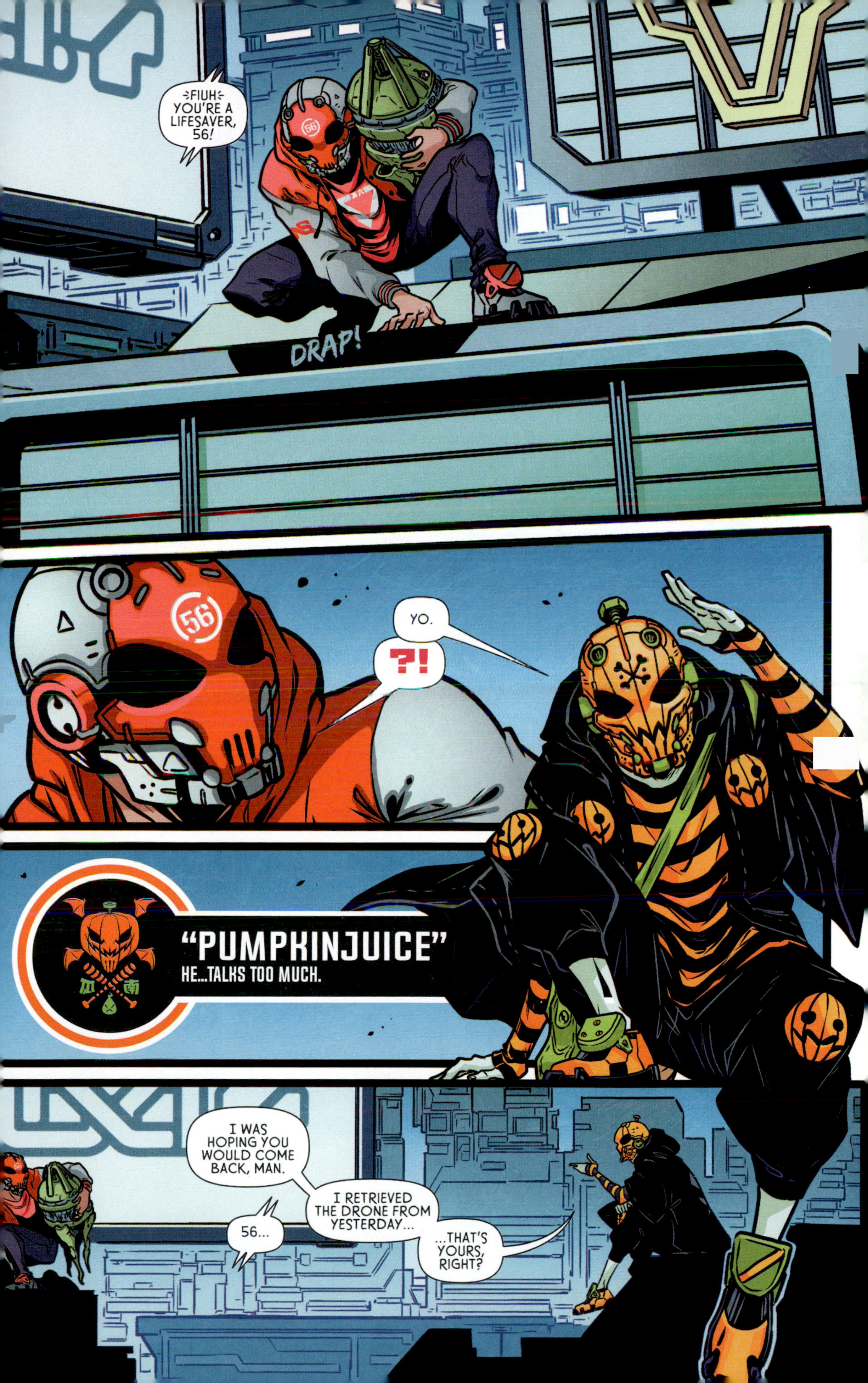

≈FIUH≈ YOU'RE A LIFESAVER, 56!
DRAP!
YO.
?!
"PUMPKINJUICE"
HE...TALKS TOO MUCH.
I WAS HOPING YOU WOULD COME BACK, MAN.
56...
I RETRIEVED THE DRONE FROM YESTERDAY...
...THAT'S YOURS, RIGHT?

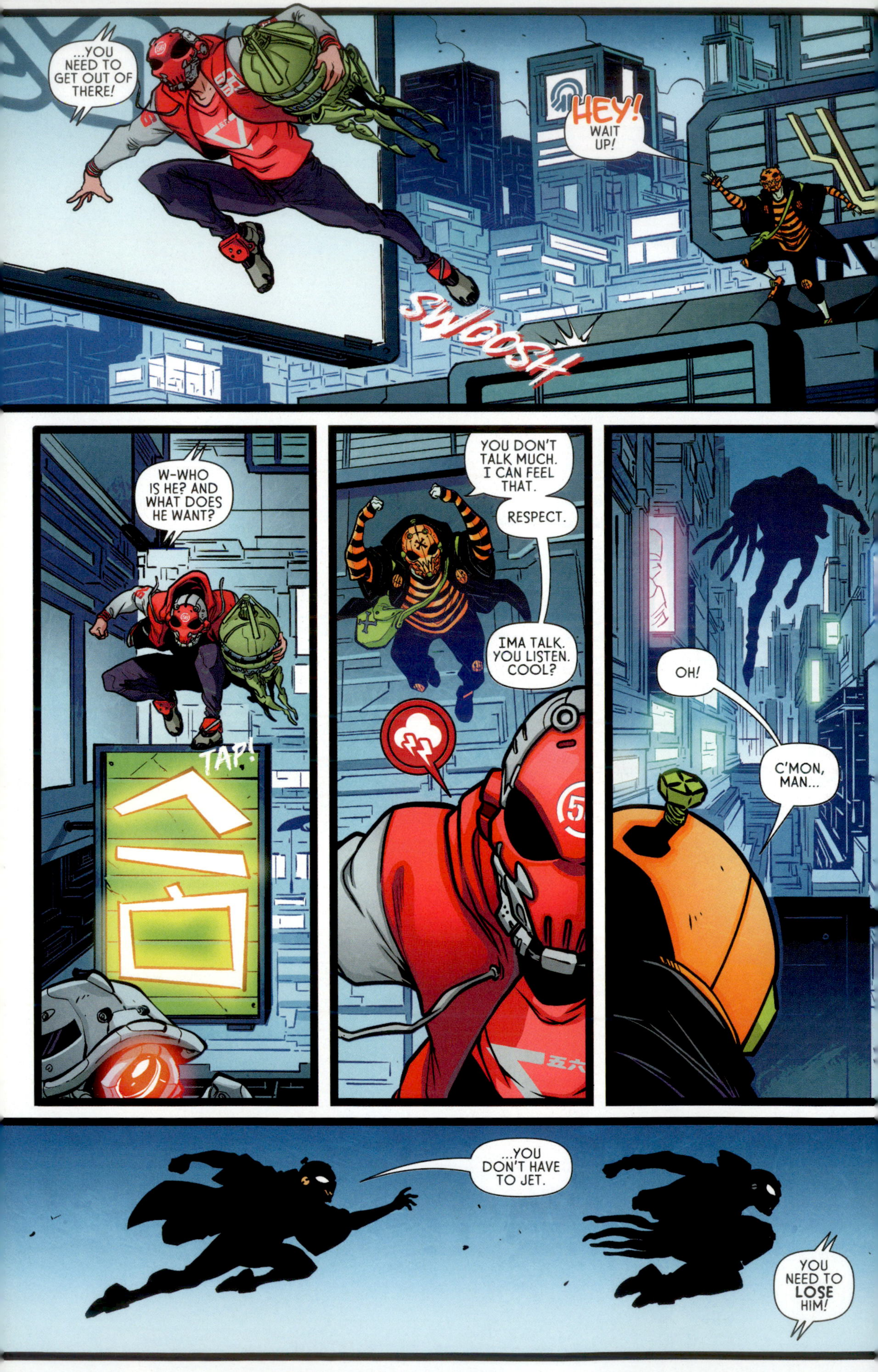
...YOU NEED TO GET OUT OF THERE!
HEY! WAIT UP!
SWOOSH
W-WHO IS HE? AND WHAT DOES HE WANT?
TAP!
YOU DON'T TALK MUCH. I CAN FEEL THAT.
RESPECT.
IMA TALK. YOU LISTEN. COOL?
OH!
C'MON, MAN...
...YOU DON'T HAVE TO JET.
YOU NEED TO LOSE HIM!

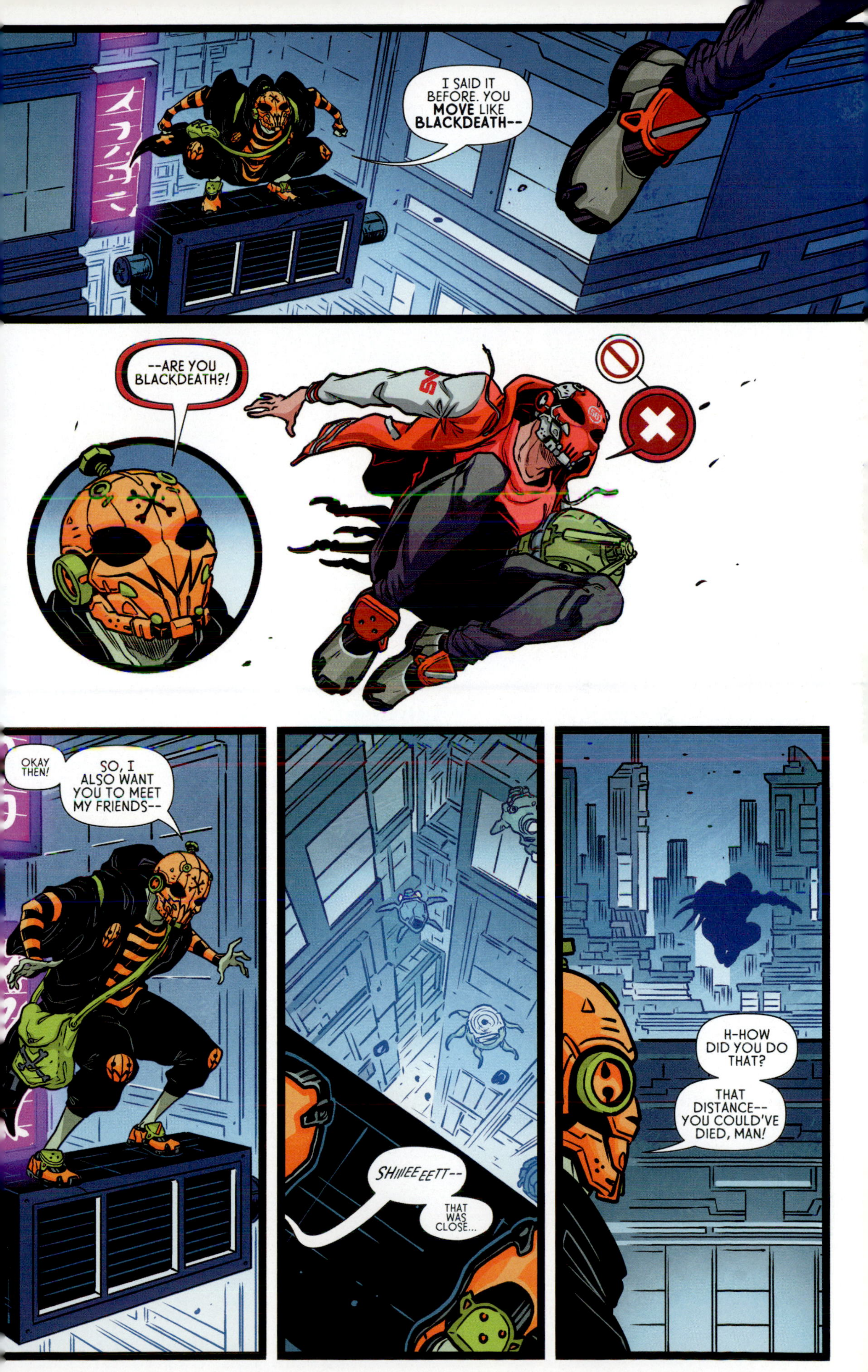
I SAID IT BEFORE. YOU MOVE LIKE BLACKDEATH--
--ARE YOU BLACKDEATH?!
OKAY THEN!
SO, I ALSO WANT YOU TO MEET MY FRIENDS--
SHIIIEE EETT--
THAT WAS CLOSE...
H-HOW DID YOU DO THAT?
THAT DISTANCE-- YOU COULD'VE DIED, MAN!

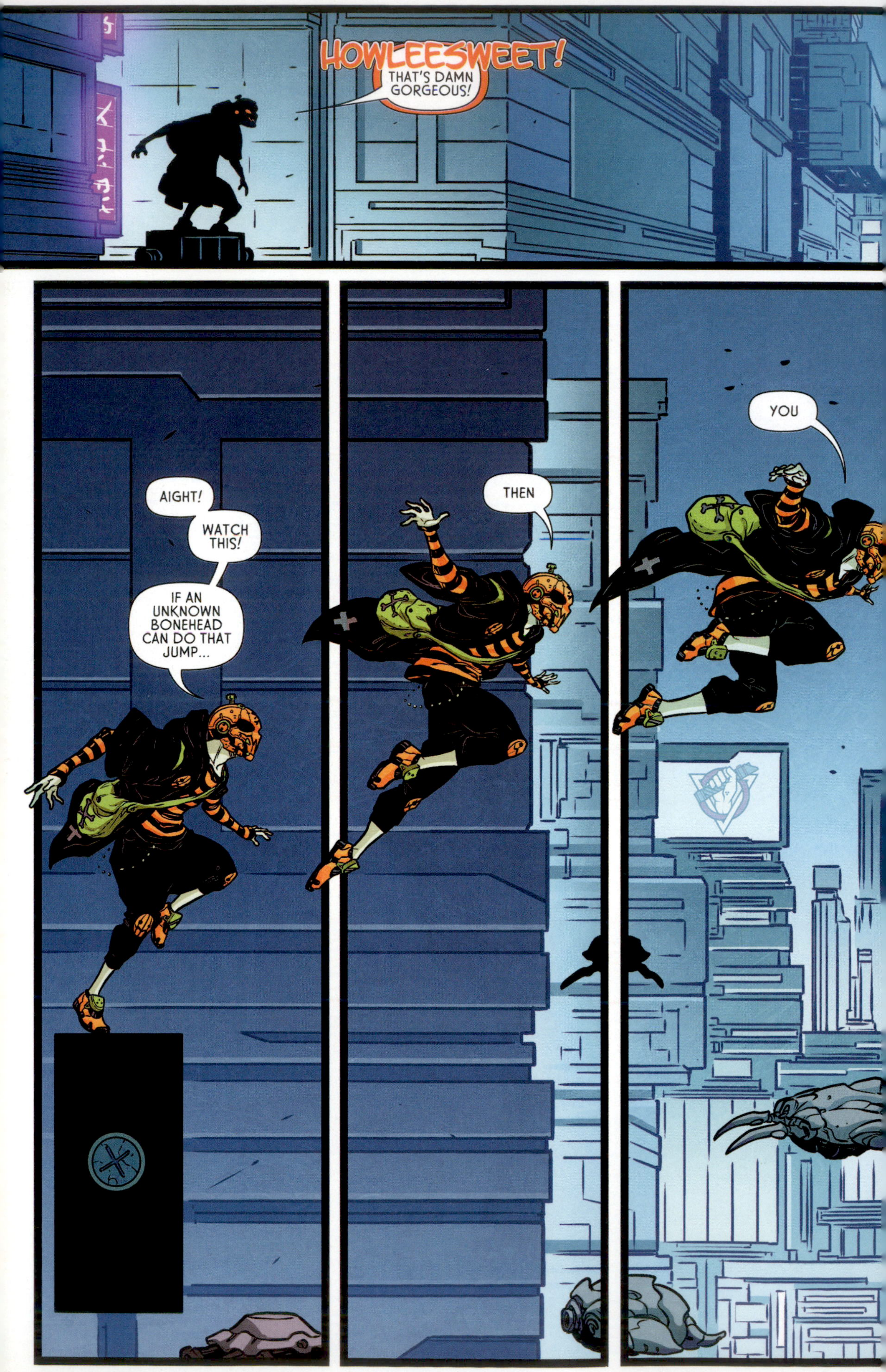

HOWLEESWEET!
THAT'S DAMN GORGEOUS!
AIGHT!
WATCH THIS!
IF AN UNKNOWN BONEHEAD CAN DO THAT JUMP...
THEN
YOU

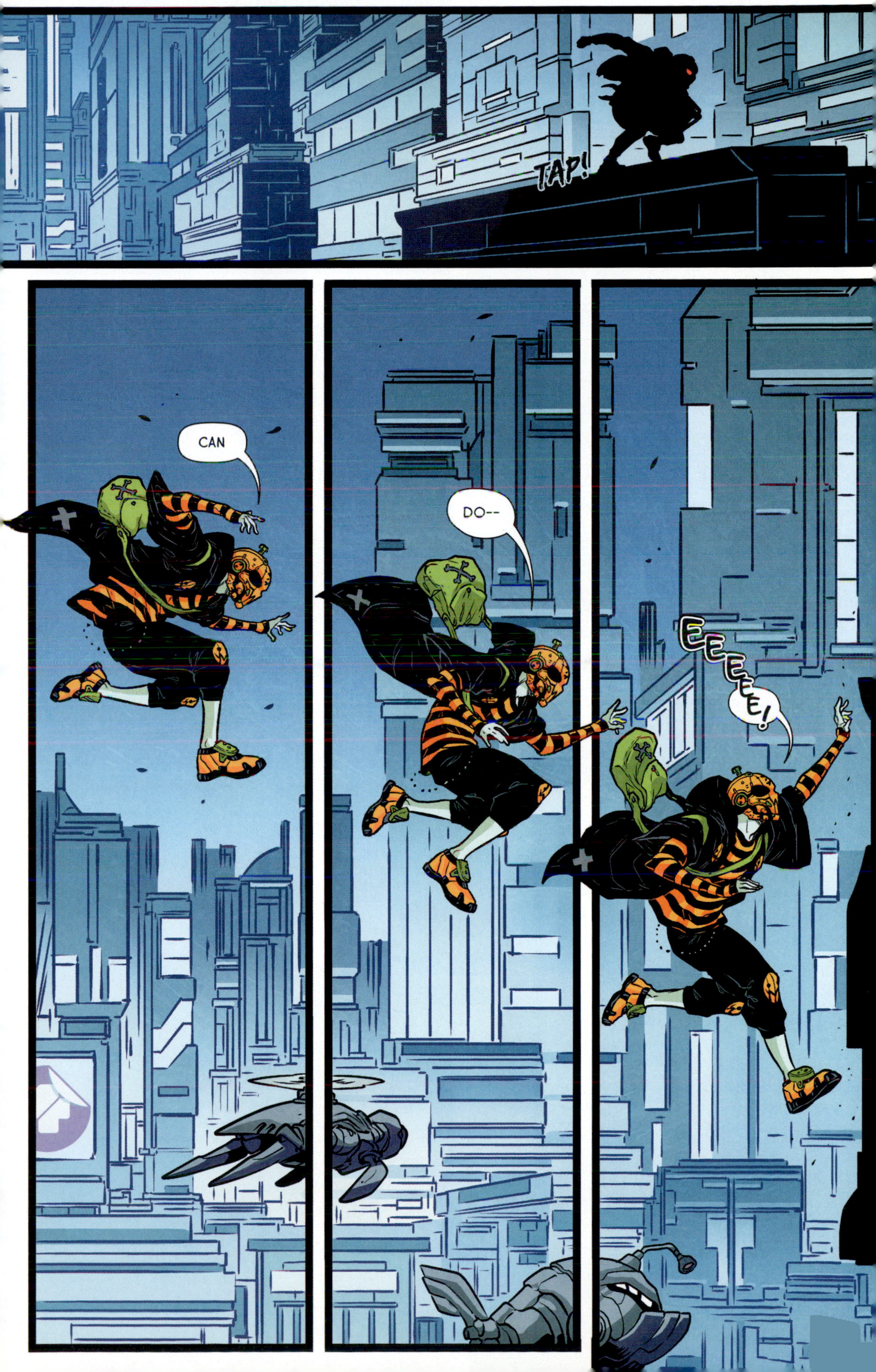
TAP!
CAN
DO--
EEEEEE!

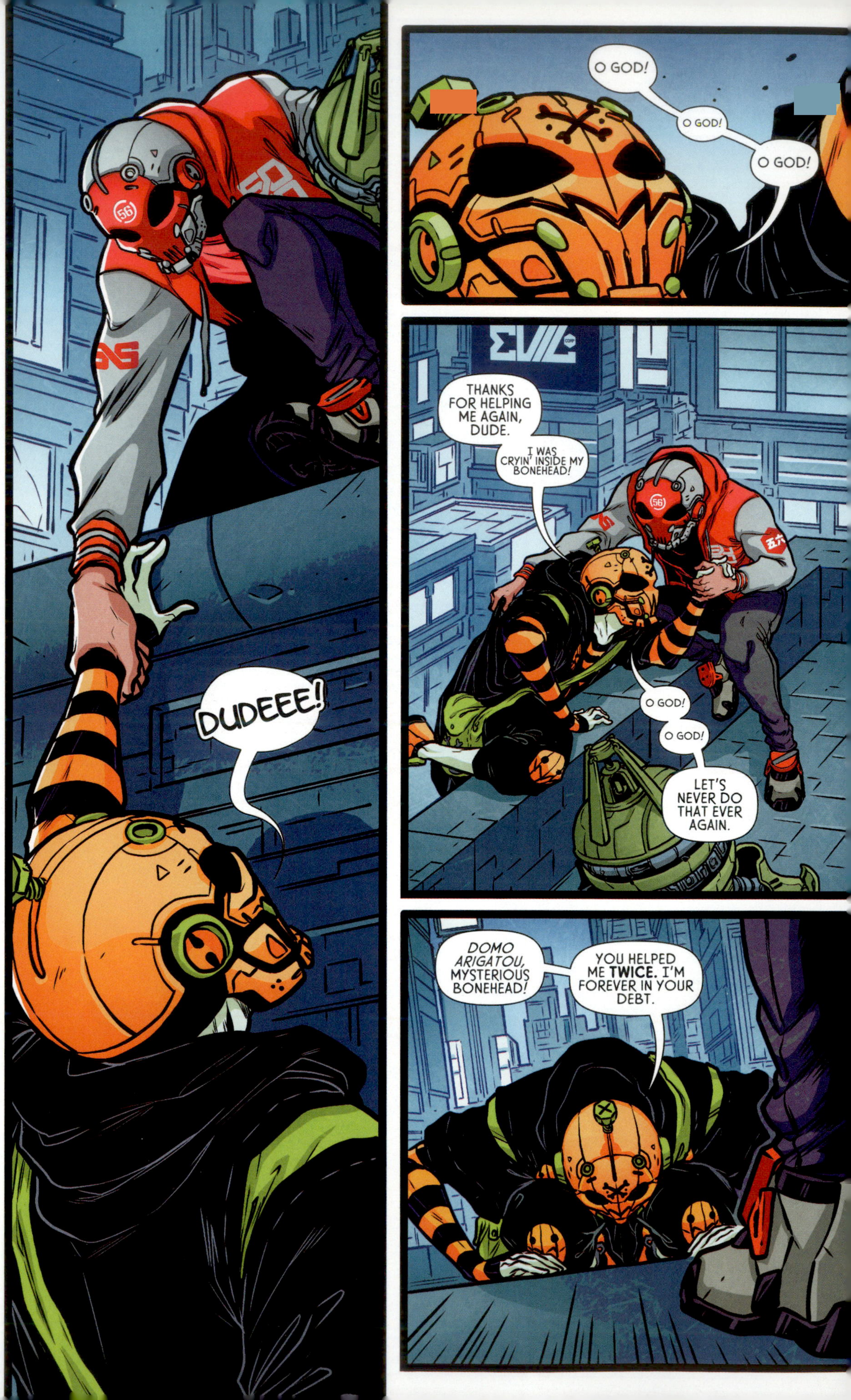
DUDEEE!
O GOD!
O GOD!
O GOD!
THANKS FOR HELPING ME AGAIN, DUDE.
I WAS CRYIN' INSIDE MY BONEHEAD!
O GOD!
O GOD!
LET'S NEVER DO THAT EVER AGAIN.
DOMO ARIGATOU, MYSTERIOUS BONEHEAD!
YOU HELPED ME **TWICE.** I'M FOREVER IN YOUR DEBT.

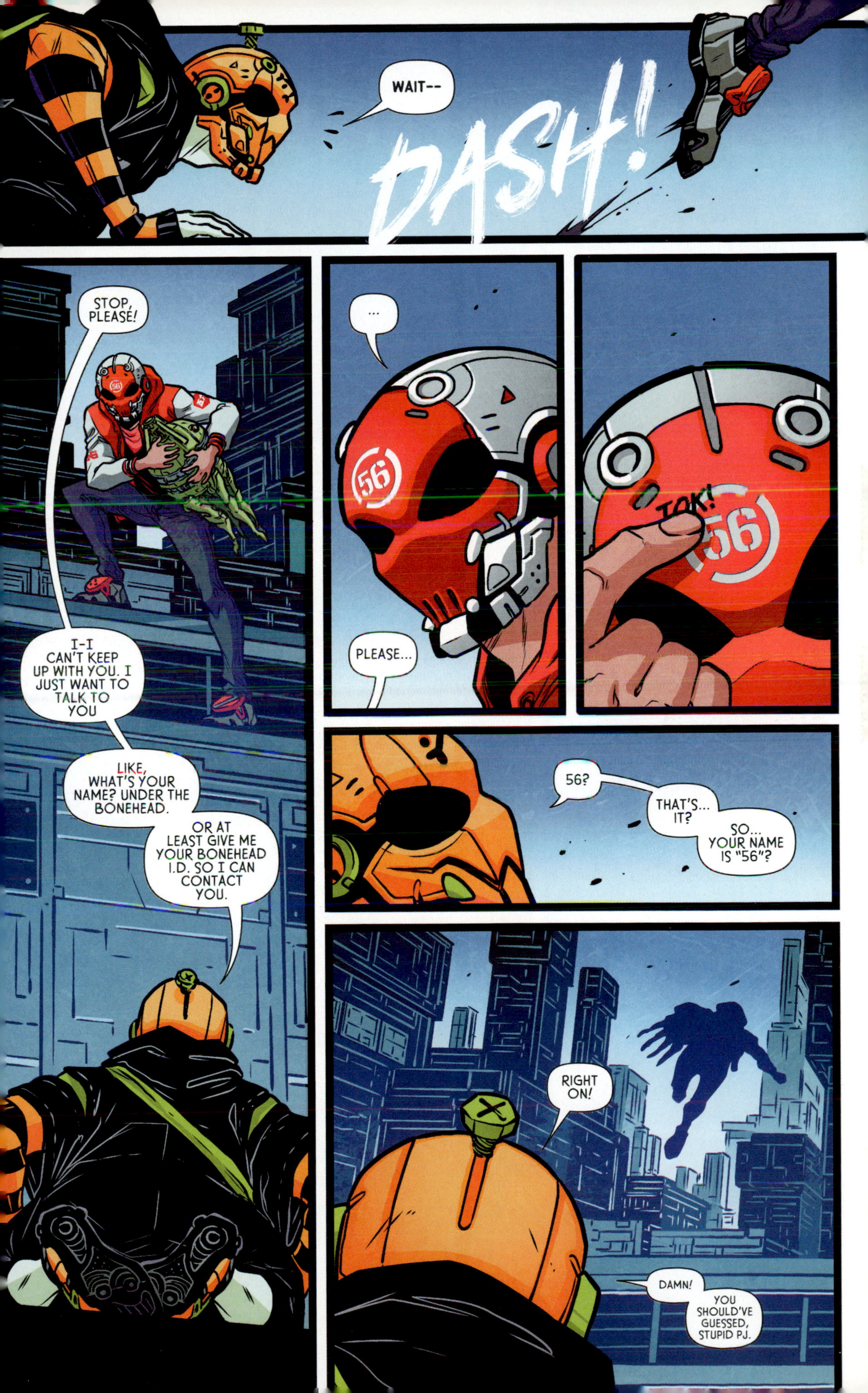
WAIT--
DASH!
STOP, PLEASE!
I-I CAN'T KEEP UP WITH YOU. I JUST WANT TO TALK TO YOU
LIKE, WHAT'S YOUR NAME? UNDER THE BONEHEAD.
OR AT LEAST GIVE ME YOUR BONEHEAD I.D. SO I CAN CONTACT YOU.
...
PLEASE...
TOK!
56?
THAT'S... IT?
SO... YOUR NAME IS "56"?
RIGHT ON!
DAMN!
YOU SHOULD'VE GUESSED, STUPID PJ.

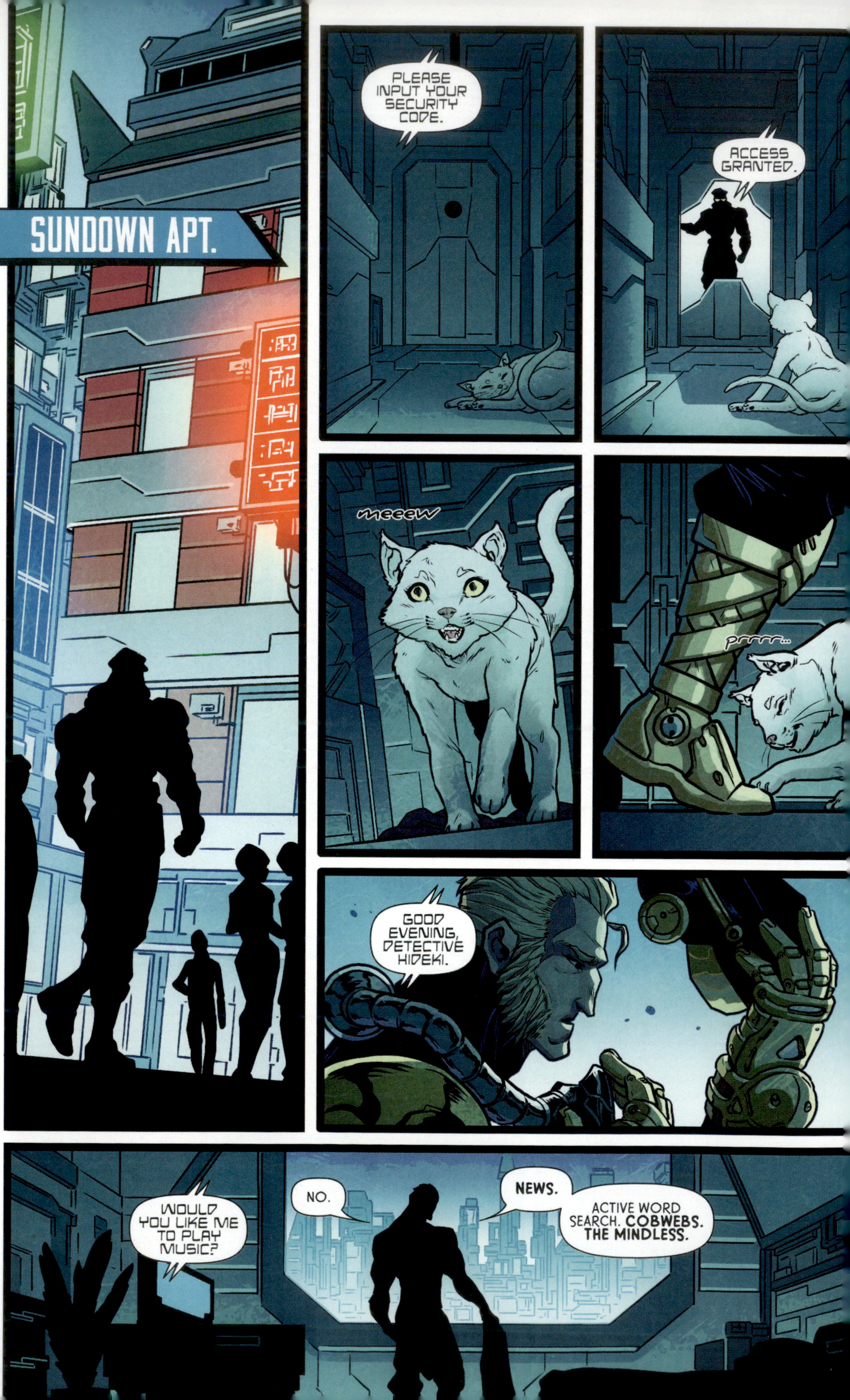

SUNDOWN APT.
PLEASE INPUT YOUR SECURITY CODE.
ACCESS GRANTED.
meeew
prrrr...
GOOD EVENING, DETECTIVE HIDEKI.
WOULD YOU LIKE ME TO PLAY MUSIC?
NO.
NEWS.
ACTIVE WORD SEARCH. COBWEBS. THE MINDLESS.

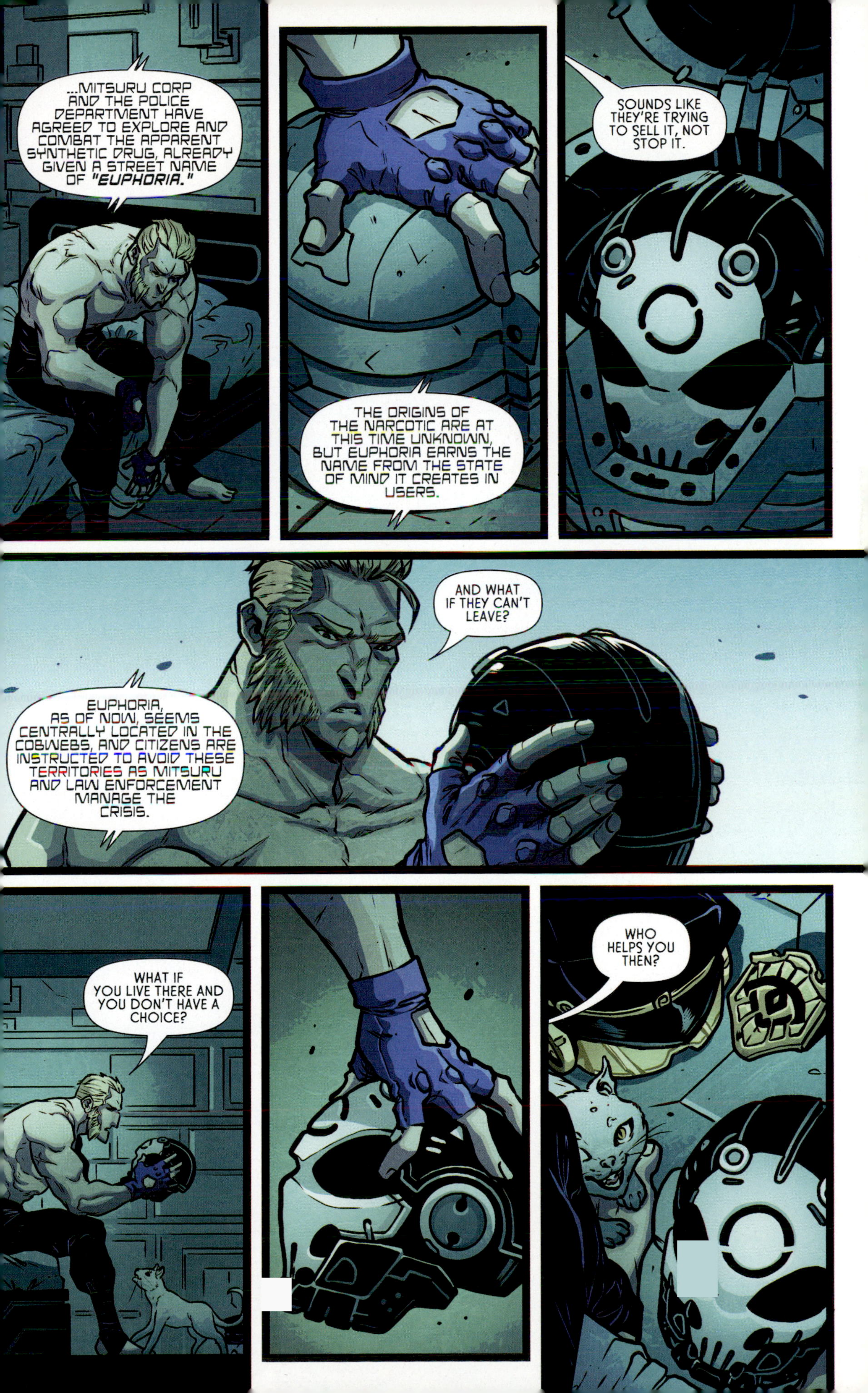
...MITSURU CORP AND THE POLICE DEPARTMENT HAVE AGREED TO EXPLORE AND COMBAT THE APPARENT SYNTHETIC DRUG, ALREADY GIVEN A STREET NAME OF "EUPHORIA."
THE ORIGINS OF THE NARCOTIC ARE AT THIS TIME UNKNOWN, BUT EUPHORIA EARNS THE NAME FROM THE STATE OF MIND IT CREATES IN USERS.
SOUNDS LIKE THEY'RE TRYING TO SELL IT, NOT STOP IT.
EUPHORIA, AS OF NOW, SEEMS CENTRALLY LOCATED IN THE COBWEBS, AND CITIZENS ARE INSTRUCTED TO AVOID THESE TERRITORIES AS MITSURU AND LAW ENFORCEMENT MANAGE THE CRISIS.
AND WHAT IF THEY CAN'T LEAVE?
WHAT IF YOU LIVE THERE AND YOU DON'T HAVE A CHOICE?
WHO HELPS YOU THEN?

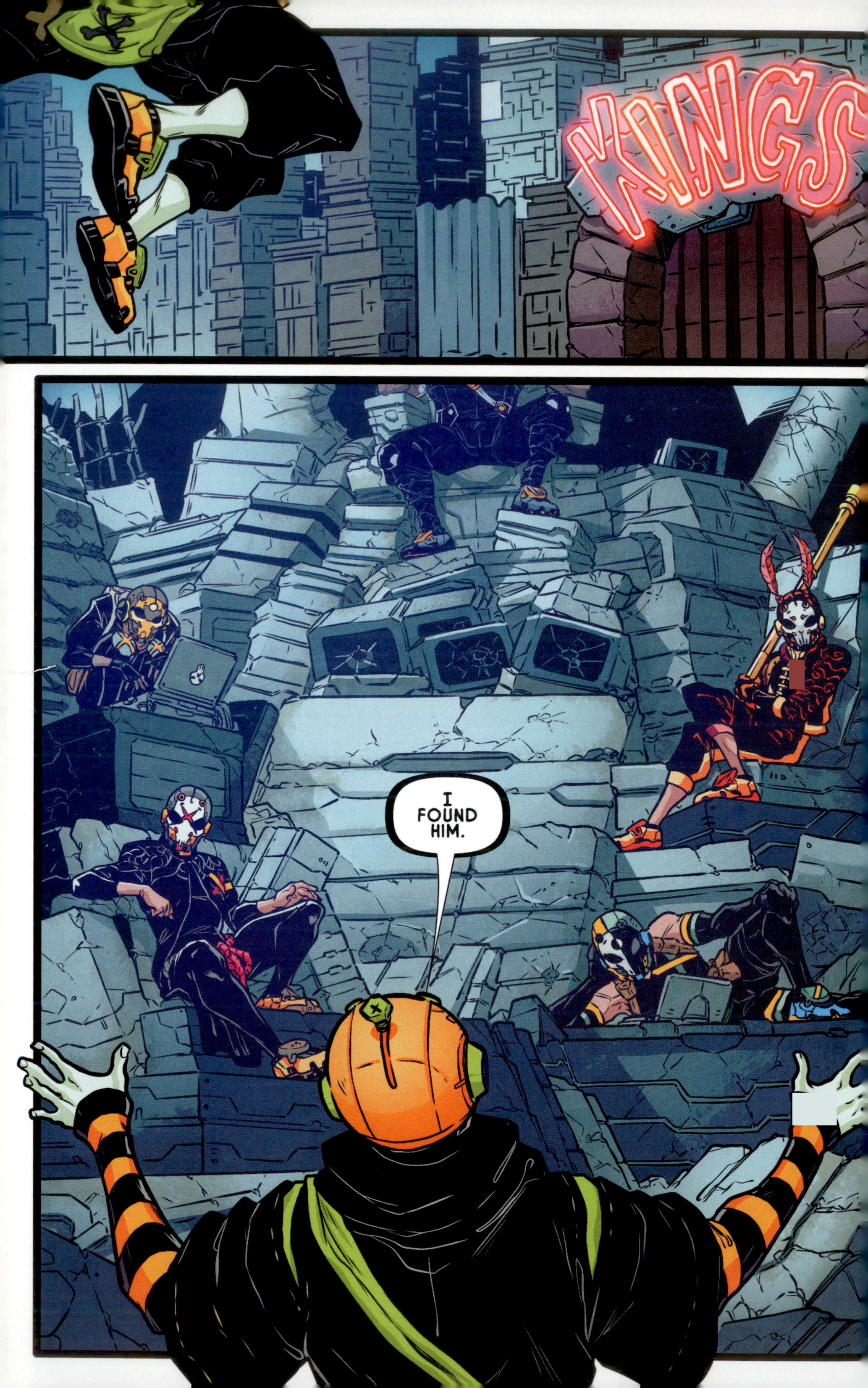
KINGS
I FOUND HIM.

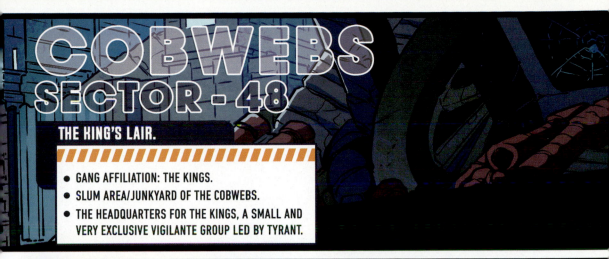

COBWEBS
SECTOR-48

THE KING'S LAIR.

- GANG AFFILIATION: THE KINGS.
- SLUM AREA/JUNKYARD OF THE COBWEBS.
- THE HEADQUARTERS FOR THE KINGS, A SMALL AND VERY EXCLUSIVE VIGILANTE GROUP LED BY TYRANT.

THE MYSTERIOUS BONEHEAD!

THE ONE WHO SAVED MY LIFE.

TWICE!

HIS TAG IS "56"!

HE MOVES JUST LIKE BLACKDEATH!

DOES HE?

WELL, THEN LET'S SEE--

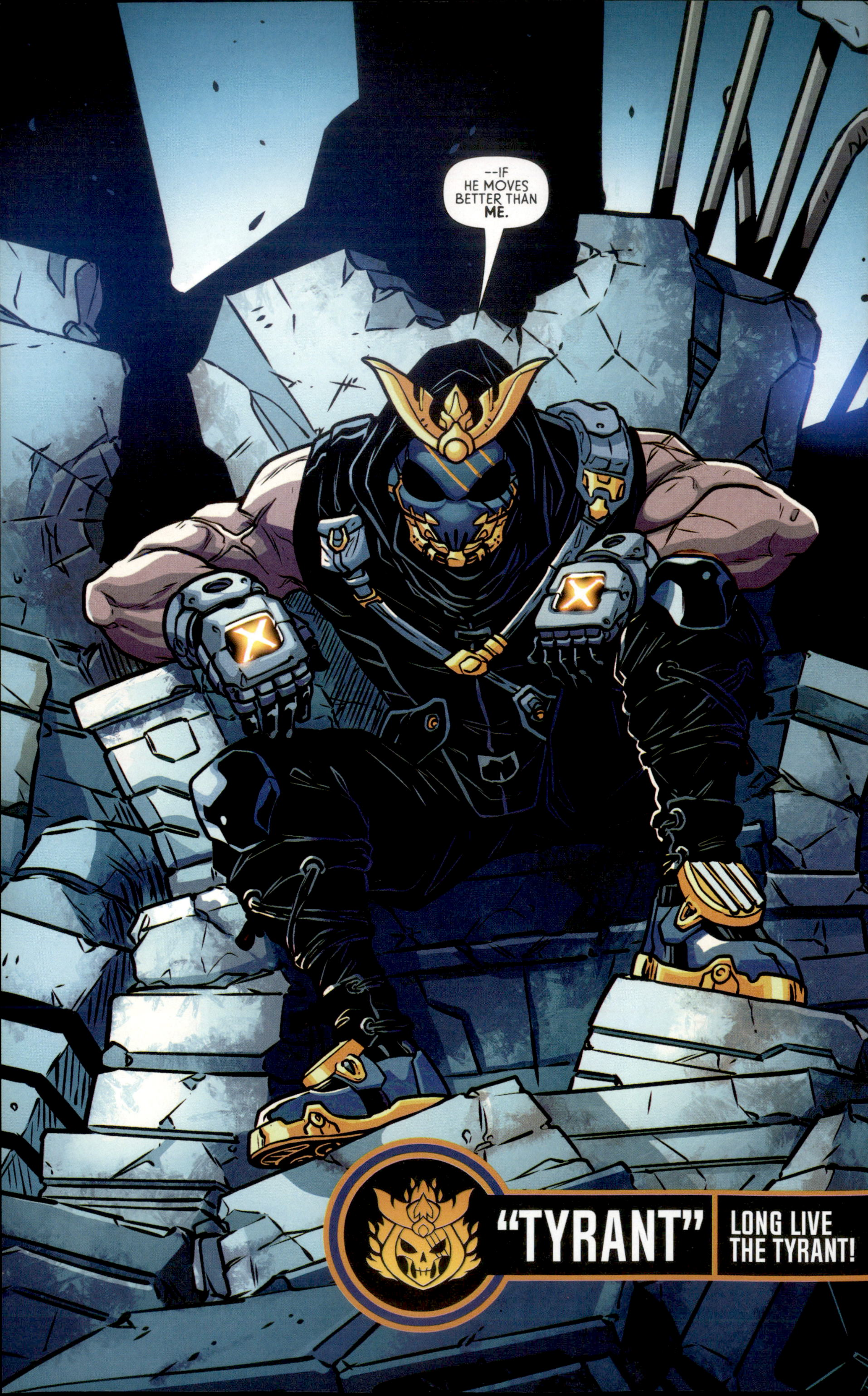
--IF HE MOVES BETTER THAN ME.
"TYRANT"
LONG LIVE THE TYRANT!

CHAPTER03

- ● ORIGINAL MITSURU.TECH SERIAL #
- ○ CLOSE QUARTER TYPE_
- ● SLAVE TYPE BONEHEAD01.
- ○ BODY STRUCTURE : N/A
- ● NODE TRACKING AFTER DELETION COURSE
- ○ EARTH: 7 MEGAPARSECS ACROSS_

▶ M56/001/A   ▶ Bonehead, RED, 16k-Zettabyte.
Designed by Machine56, Assembled by Mitsuru.Tech
MK-I / Not suitable f

(1P) Part No. MT-A0156 / D / Test Subject no.56

ブラック・デス・ランナー   QC/PA

50601309

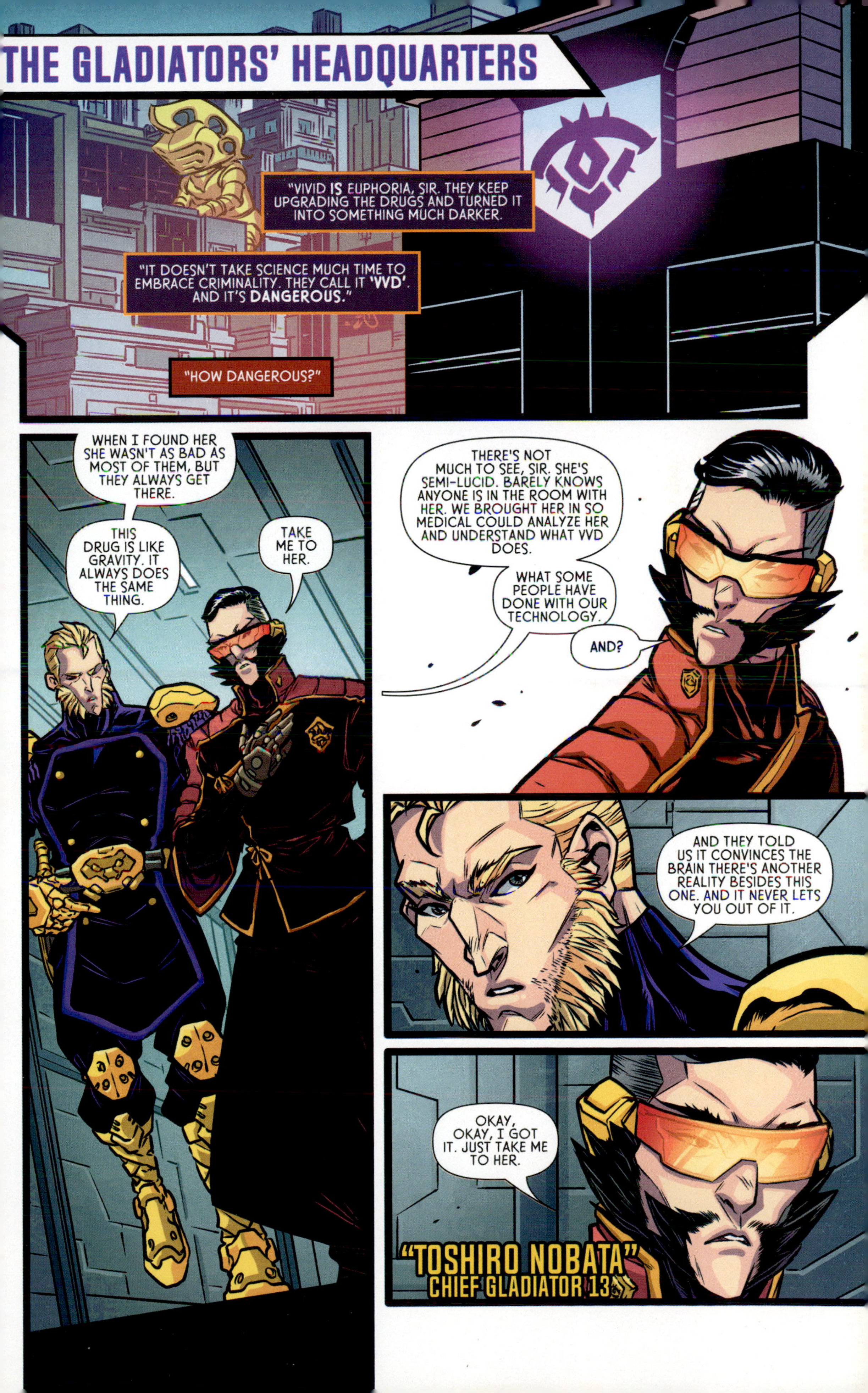
THE GLADIATORS' HEADQUARTERS
"VIVID IS EUPHORIA, SIR. THEY KEEP UPGRADING THE DRUGS AND TURNED IT INTO SOMETHING MUCH DARKER.
"IT DOESN'T TAKE SCIENCE MUCH TIME TO EMBRACE CRIMINALITY. THEY CALL IT 'VVD'. AND IT'S DANGEROUS."
"HOW DANGEROUS?"
WHEN I FOUND HER SHE WASN'T AS BAD AS MOST OF THEM, BUT THEY ALWAYS GET THERE.
THIS DRUG IS LIKE GRAVITY. IT ALWAYS DOES THE SAME THING.
TAKE ME TO HER.
THERE'S NOT MUCH TO SEE, SIR. SHE'S SEMI-LUCID. BARELY KNOWS ANYONE IS IN THE ROOM WITH HER. WE BROUGHT HER IN SO MEDICAL COULD ANALYZE HER AND UNDERSTAND WHAT VVD DOES.
WHAT SOME PEOPLE HAVE DONE WITH OUR TECHNOLOGY.
AND?
AND THEY TOLD US IT CONVINCES THE BRAIN THERE'S ANOTHER REALITY BESIDES THIS ONE. AND IT NEVER LETS YOU OUT OF IT.
OKAY, OKAY, I GOT IT. JUST TAKE ME TO HER.
"TOSHIRO NOBATA"
CHIEF GLADIATOR 13

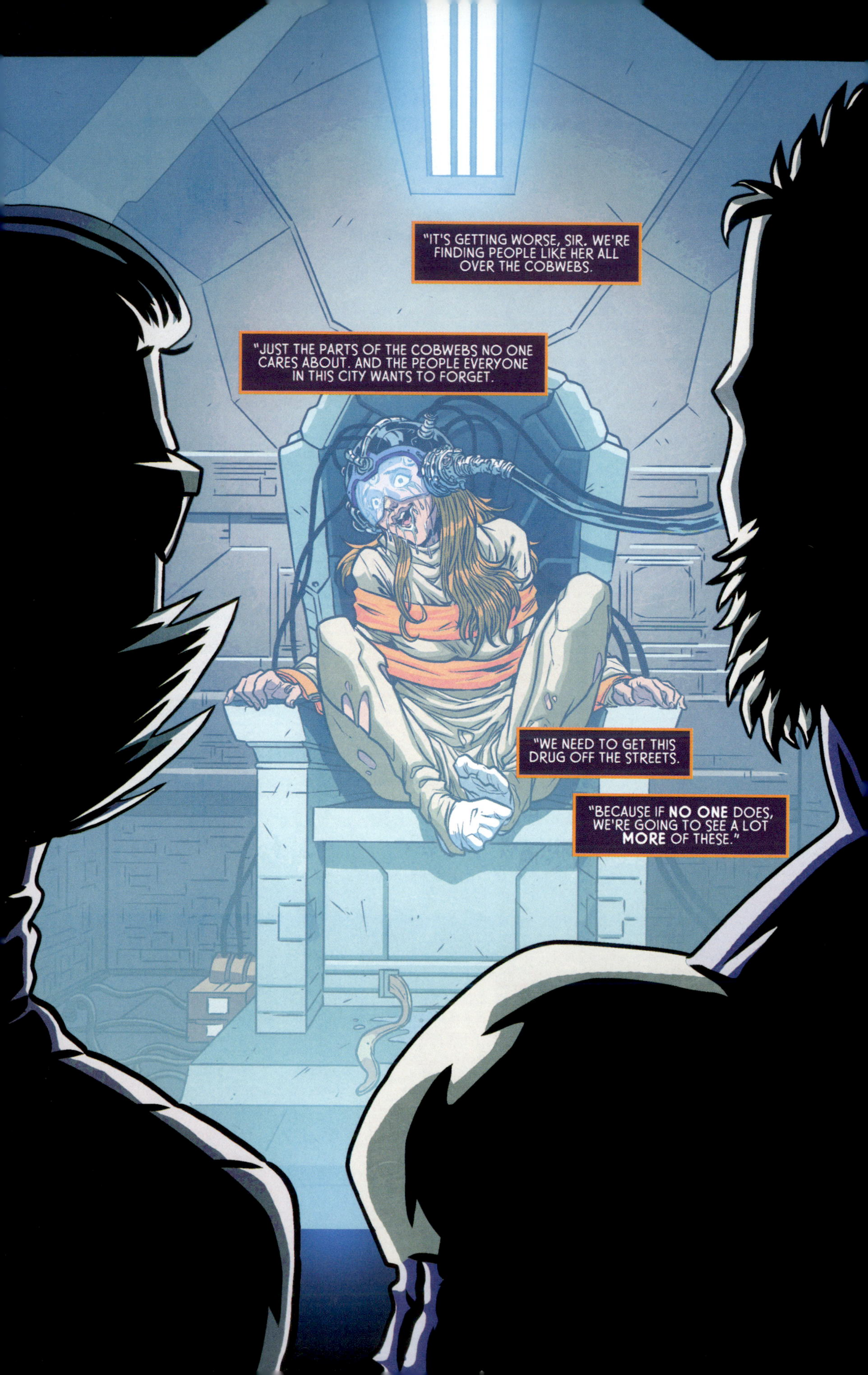
"IT'S GETTING WORSE, SIR. WE'RE FINDING PEOPLE LIKE HER ALL OVER THE COBWEBS.
"JUST THE PARTS OF THE COBWEBS NO ONE CARES ABOUT. AND THE PEOPLE EVERYONE IN THIS CITY WANTS TO FORGET.
"WE NEED TO GET THIS DRUG OFF THE STREETS.
"BECAUSE IF NO ONE DOES, WE'RE GOING TO SEE A LOT MORE OF THESE."

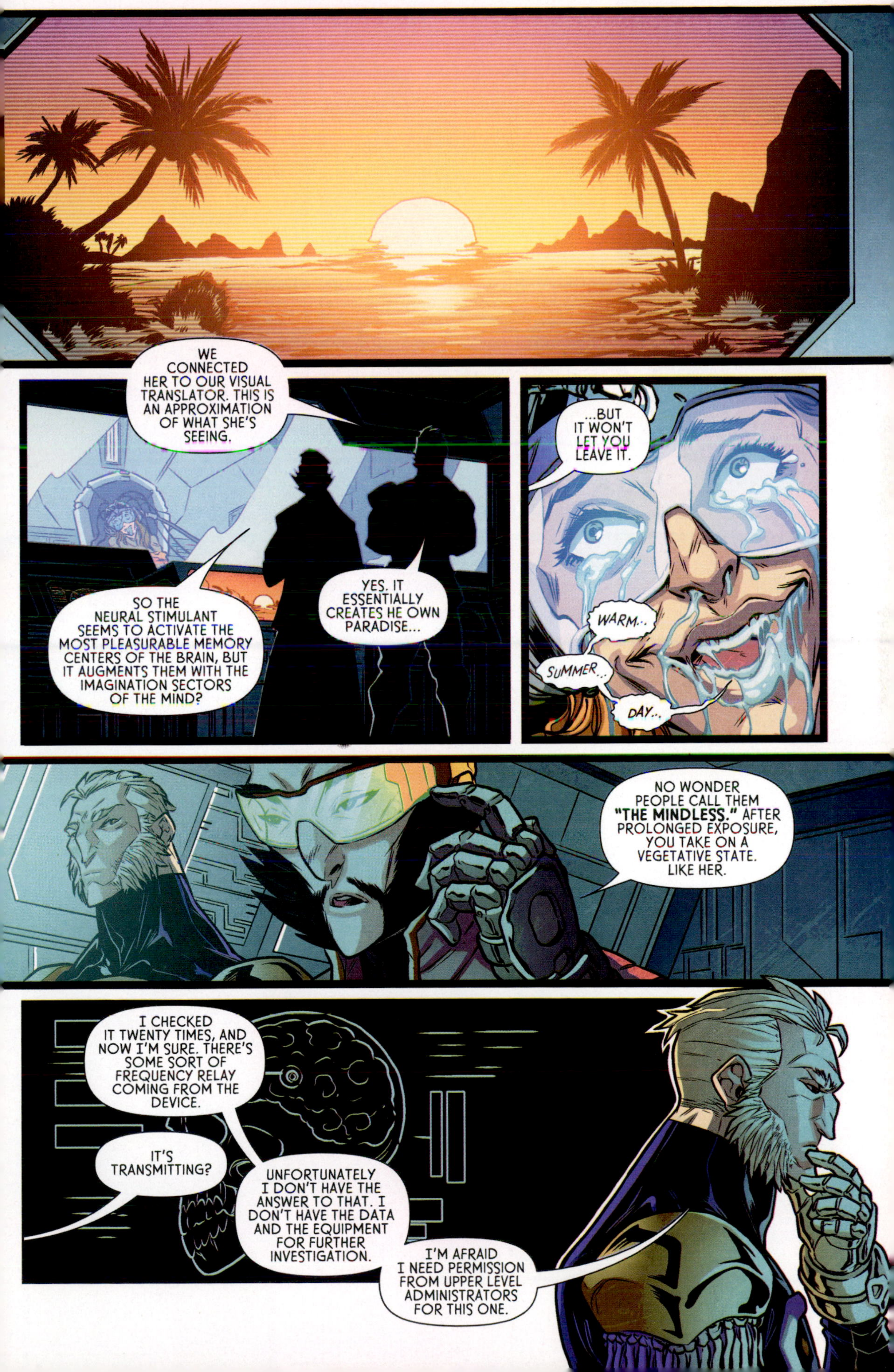
WE CONNECTED HER TO OUR VISUAL TRANSLATOR. THIS IS AN APPROXIMATION OF WHAT SHE'S SEEING.
SO THE NEURAL STIMULANT SEEMS TO ACTIVATE THE MOST PLEASURABLE MEMORY CENTERS OF THE BRAIN, BUT IT AUGMENTS THEM WITH THE IMAGINATION SECTORS OF THE MIND?
YES. IT ESSENTIALLY CREATES HE OWN PARADISE...
...BUT IT WON'T LET YOU LEAVE IT.
WARM...
SUMMER...
DAY...
NO WONDER PEOPLE CALL THEM **"THE MINDLESS."** AFTER PROLONGED EXPOSURE, YOU TAKE ON A VEGETATIVE STATE. LIKE HER.
I CHECKED IT TWENTY TIMES, AND NOW I'M SURE. THERE'S SOME SORT OF FREQUENCY RELAY COMING FROM THE DEVICE.
IT'S TRANSMITTING?
UNFORTUNATELY I DON'T HAVE THE ANSWER TO THAT. I DON'T HAVE THE DATA AND THE EQUIPMENT FOR FURTHER INVESTIGATION.
I'M AFRAID I NEED PERMISSION FROM UPPER LEVEL ADMINISTRATORS FOR THIS ONE.

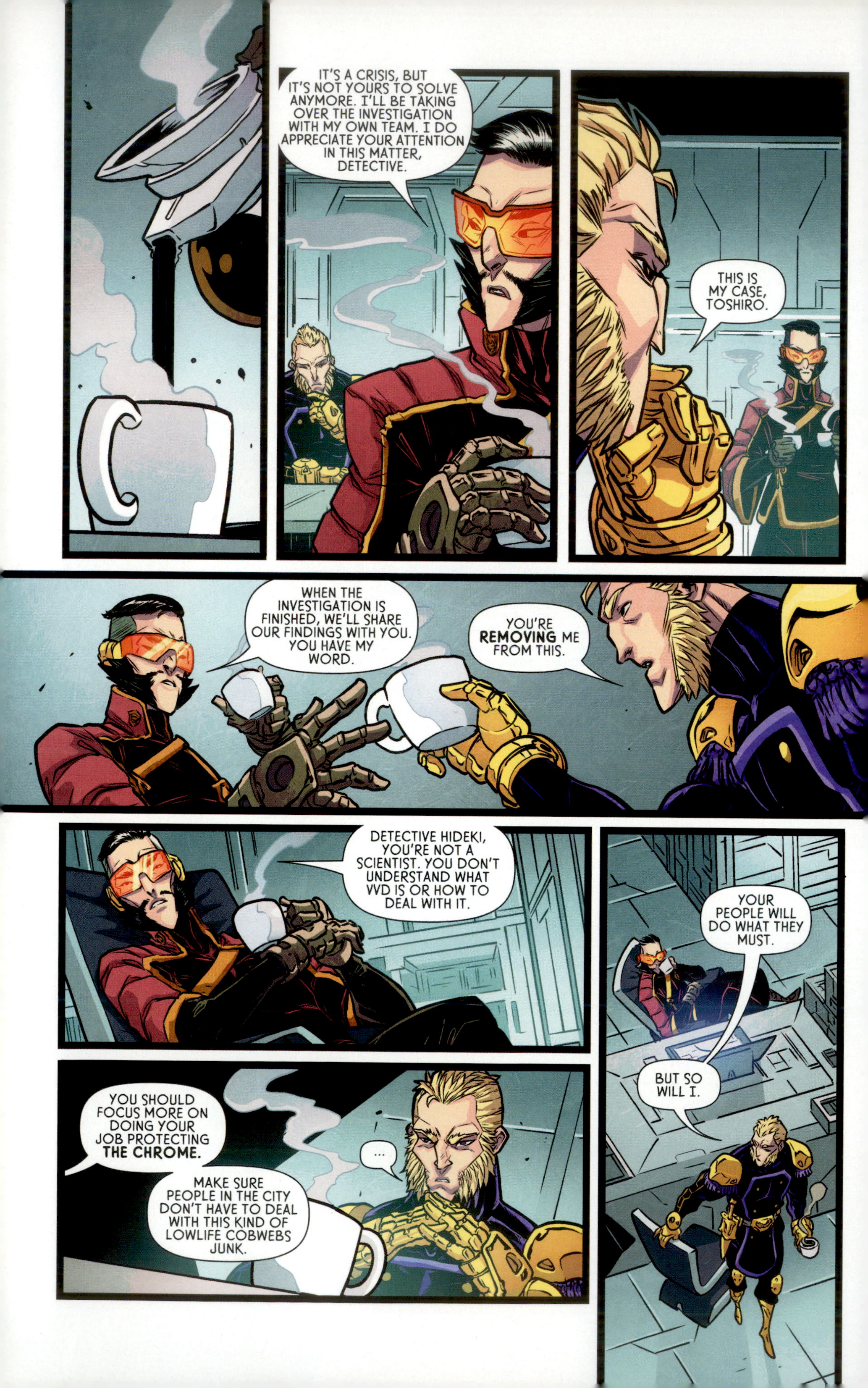
IT'S A CRISIS, BUT IT'S NOT YOURS TO SOLVE ANYMORE. I'LL BE TAKING OVER THE INVESTIGATION WITH MY OWN TEAM. I DO APPRECIATE YOUR ATTENTION IN THIS MATTER, DETECTIVE.
THIS IS MY CASE, TOSHIRO.
WHEN THE INVESTIGATION IS FINISHED, WE'LL SHARE OUR FINDINGS WITH YOU. YOU HAVE MY WORD.
YOU'RE **REMOVING** ME FROM THIS.
DETECTIVE HIDEKI, YOU'RE NOT A SCIENTIST. YOU DON'T UNDERSTAND WHAT VVD IS OR HOW TO DEAL WITH IT.
YOU SHOULD FOCUS MORE ON DOING YOUR JOB PROTECTING **THE CHROME.**
...
MAKE SURE PEOPLE IN THE CITY DON'T HAVE TO DEAL WITH THIS KIND OF LOWLIFE COBWEBS JUNK.
YOUR PEOPLE WILL DO WHAT THEY MUST.
BUT SO WILL I.

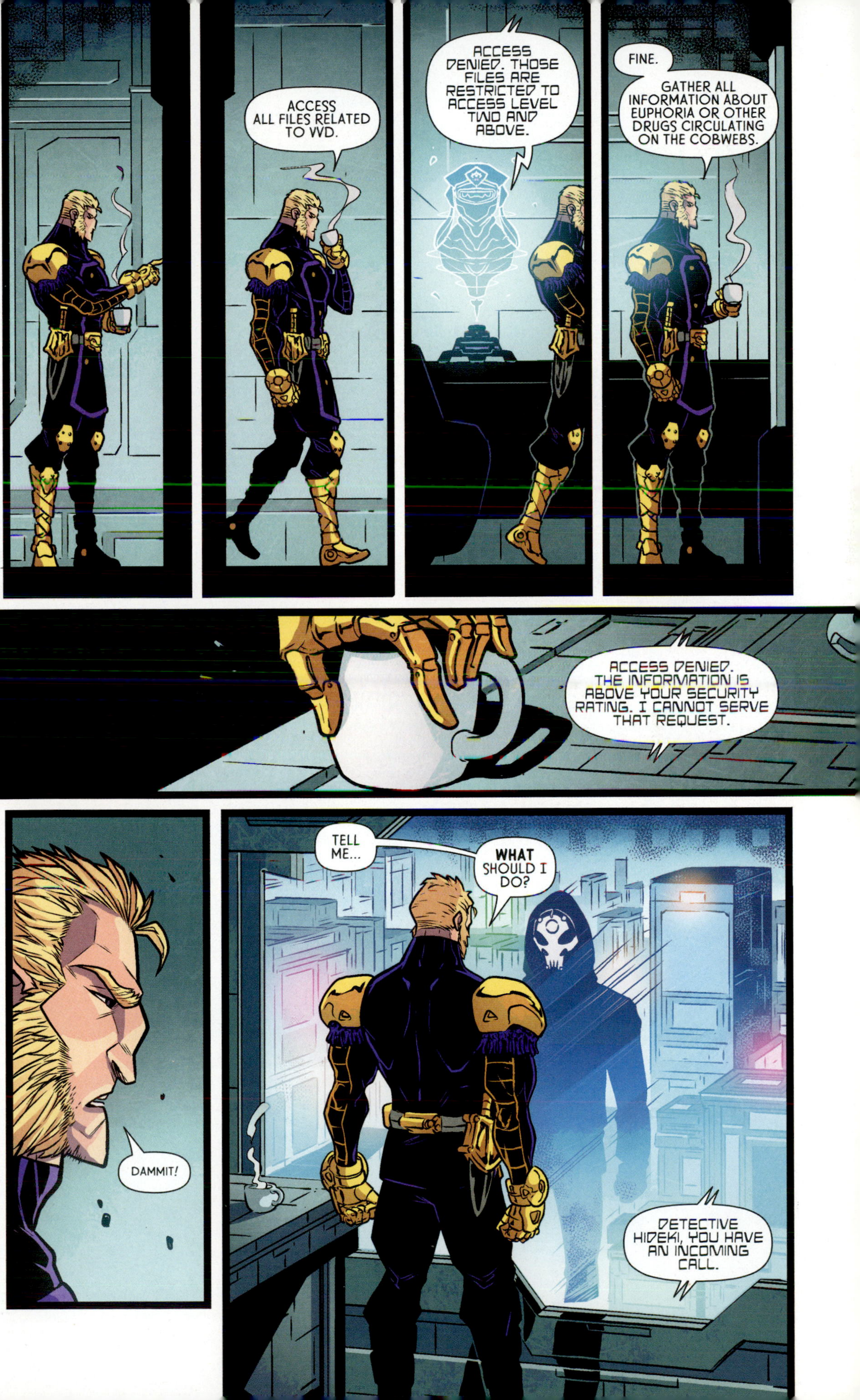
ACCESS ALL FILES RELATED TO WVD.
ACCESS DENIED. THOSE FILES ARE RESTRICTED TO ACCESS LEVEL TWO AND ABOVE.
FINE.
GATHER ALL INFORMATION ABOUT EUPHORIA OR OTHER DRUGS CIRCULATING ON THE COBWEBS.
ACCESS DENIED. THE INFORMATION IS ABOVE YOUR SECURITY RATING. I CANNOT SERVE THAT REQUEST.
DAMMIT!
TELL ME...
WHAT SHOULD I DO?
DETECTIVE HIDEKI, YOU HAVE AN INCOMING CALL.

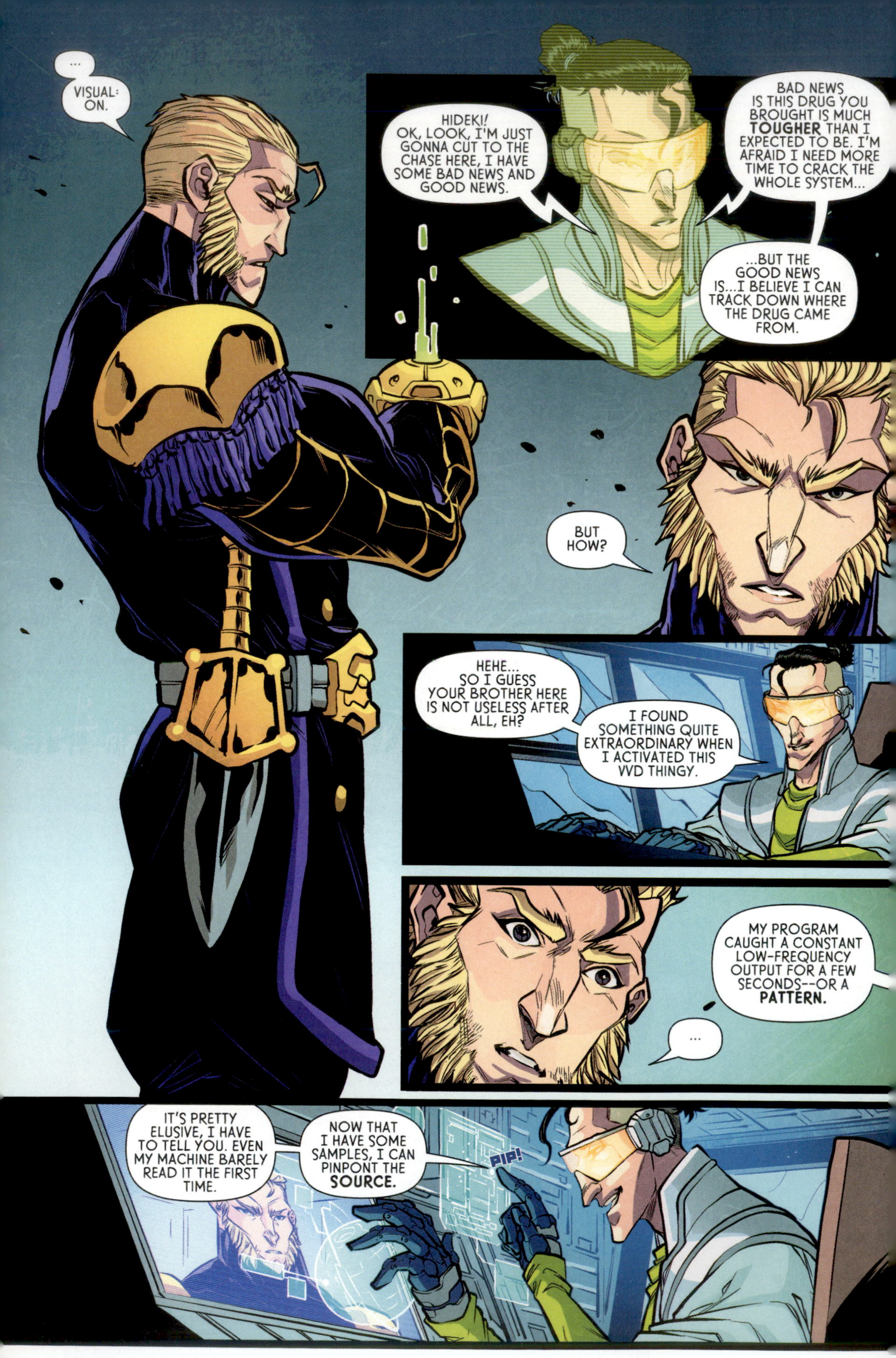
...
VISUAL: ON.
HIDEKI! OK, LOOK, I'M JUST GONNA CUT TO THE CHASE HERE, I HAVE SOME BAD NEWS AND GOOD NEWS.
BAD NEWS IS THIS DRUG YOU BROUGHT IS MUCH TOUGHER THAN I EXPECTED TO BE. I'M AFRAID I NEED MORE TIME TO CRACK THE WHOLE SYSTEM...
...BUT THE GOOD NEWS IS...I BELIEVE I CAN TRACK DOWN WHERE THE DRUG CAME FROM.
BUT HOW?
HEHE... SO I GUESS YOUR BROTHER HERE IS NOT USELESS AFTER ALL, EH?
I FOUND SOMETHING QUITE EXTRAORDINARY WHEN I ACTIVATED THIS VVD THINGY.
MY PROGRAM CAUGHT A CONSTANT LOW-FREQUENCY OUTPUT FOR A FEW SECONDS--OR A PATTERN.
...
IT'S PRETTY ELUSIVE, I HAVE TO TELL YOU. EVEN MY MACHINE BARELY READ IT THE FIRST TIME.
NOW THAT I HAVE SOME SAMPLES, I CAN PINPONT THE SOURCE.
PIP!

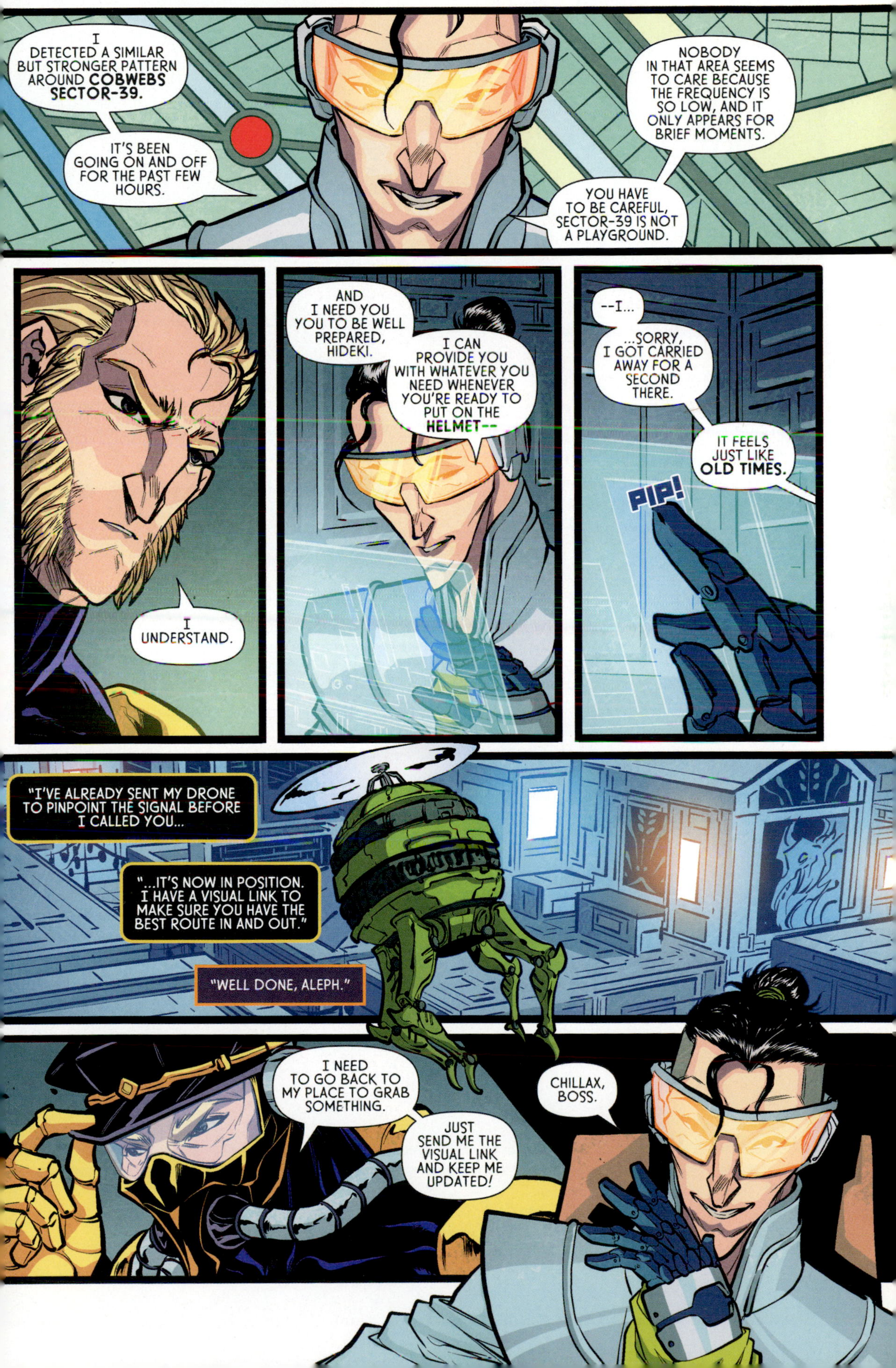
I DETECTED A SIMILAR BUT STRONGER PATTERN AROUND **COBWEBS SECTOR-39.**
IT'S BEEN GOING ON AND OFF FOR THE PAST FEW HOURS.
NOBODY IN THAT AREA SEEMS TO CARE BECAUSE THE FREQUENCY IS SO LOW, AND IT ONLY APPEARS FOR BRIEF MOMENTS.
YOU HAVE TO BE CAREFUL, SECTOR-39 IS NOT A PLAYGROUND.
I UNDERSTAND.
AND I NEED YOU YOU TO BE WELL PREPARED, HIDEKI.
I CAN PROVIDE YOU WITH WHATEVER YOU NEED WHENEVER YOU'RE READY TO PUT ON THE **HELMET--**
--I...
...SORRY, I GOT CARRIED AWAY FOR A SECOND THERE.
IT FEELS JUST LIKE **OLD TIMES.**
PIP!
"I'VE ALREADY SENT MY DRONE TO PINPOINT THE SIGNAL BEFORE I CALLED YOU...
"...IT'S NOW IN POSITION. I HAVE A VISUAL LINK TO MAKE SURE YOU HAVE THE BEST ROUTE IN AND OUT."
"WELL DONE, ALEPH."
I NEED TO GO BACK TO MY PLACE TO GRAB SOMETHING.
JUST SEND ME THE VISUAL LINK AND KEEP ME UPDATED!
CHILLAX, BOSS.

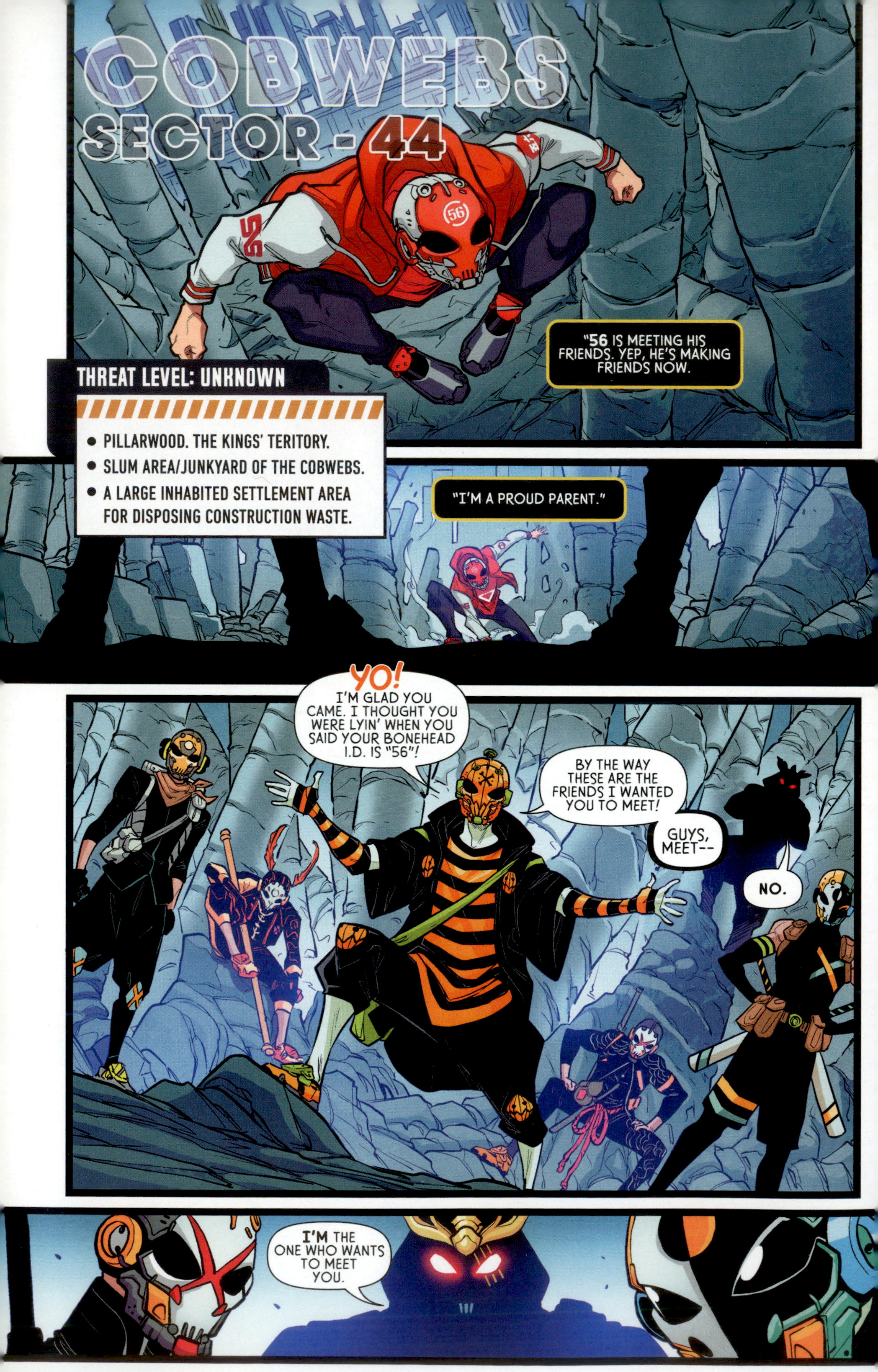
COBWEBS
SECTOR - 44
"56 IS MEETING HIS FRIENDS. YEP, HE'S MAKING FRIENDS NOW.
THREAT LEVEL: UNKNOWN
• PILLARWOOD. THE KINGS' TERITORY.
• SLUM AREA/JUNKYARD OF THE COBWEBS.
• A LARGE INHABITED SETTLEMENT AREA FOR DISPOSING CONSTRUCTION WASTE.
"I'M A PROUD PARENT."
YO! I'M GLAD YOU CAME. I THOUGHT YOU WERE LYIN' WHEN YOU SAID YOUR BONEHEAD I.D. IS "56"!
BY THE WAY THESE ARE THE FRIENDS I WANTED YOU TO MEET!
GUYS, MEET--
NO.
I'M THE ONE WHO WANTS TO MEET YOU.

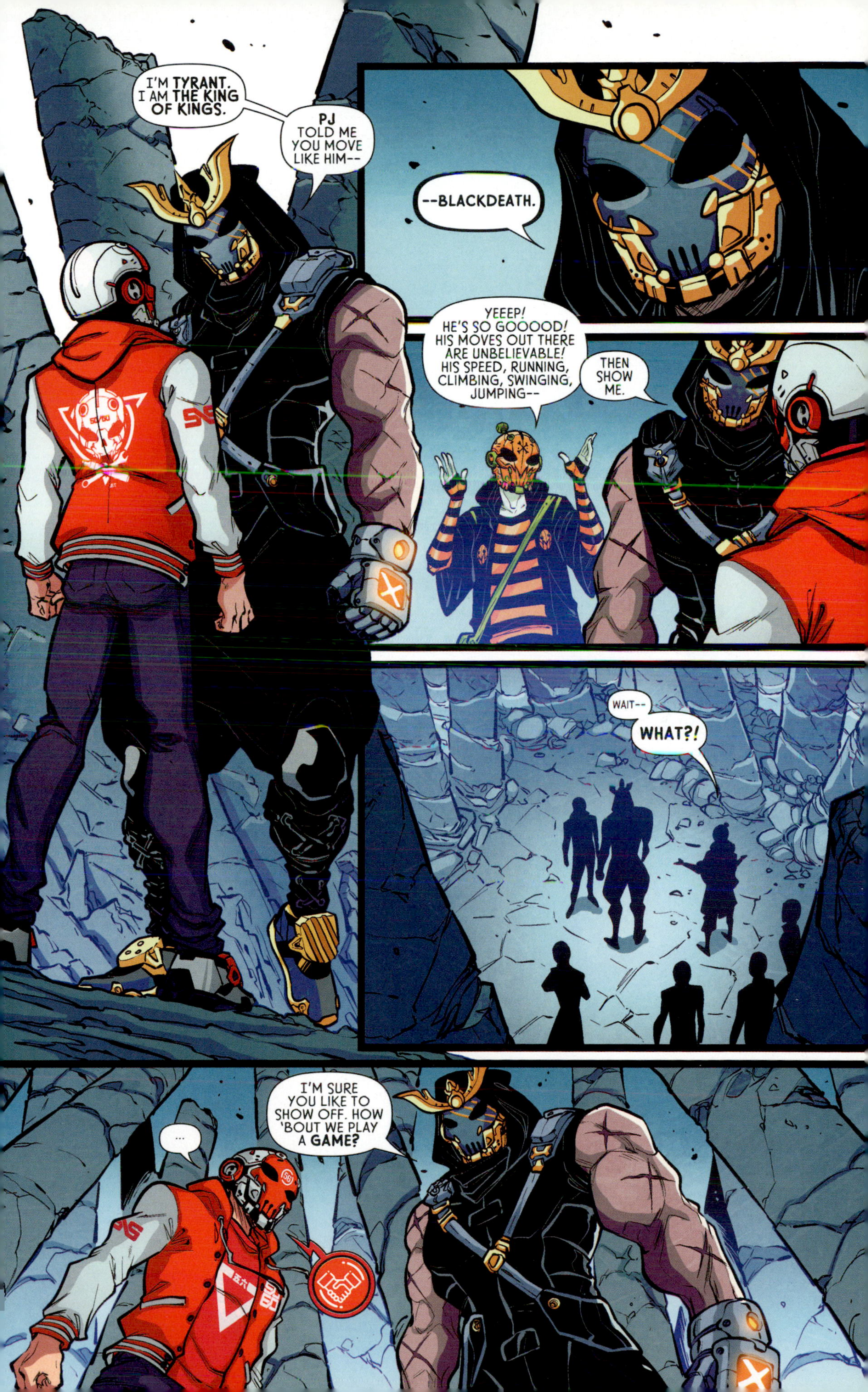
I'M TYRANT. I AM THE KING OF KINGS.
PJ TOLD ME YOU MOVE LIKE HIM--
--BLACKDEATH.
YEEEP! HE'S SO GOOOOD! HIS MOVES OUT THERE ARE UNBELIEVABLE! HIS SPEED, RUNNING, CLIMBING, SWINGING, JUMPING--
THEN SHOW ME.
WAIT--
WHAT?!
...
I'M SURE YOU LIKE TO SHOW OFF. HOW 'BOUT WE PLAY A GAME?

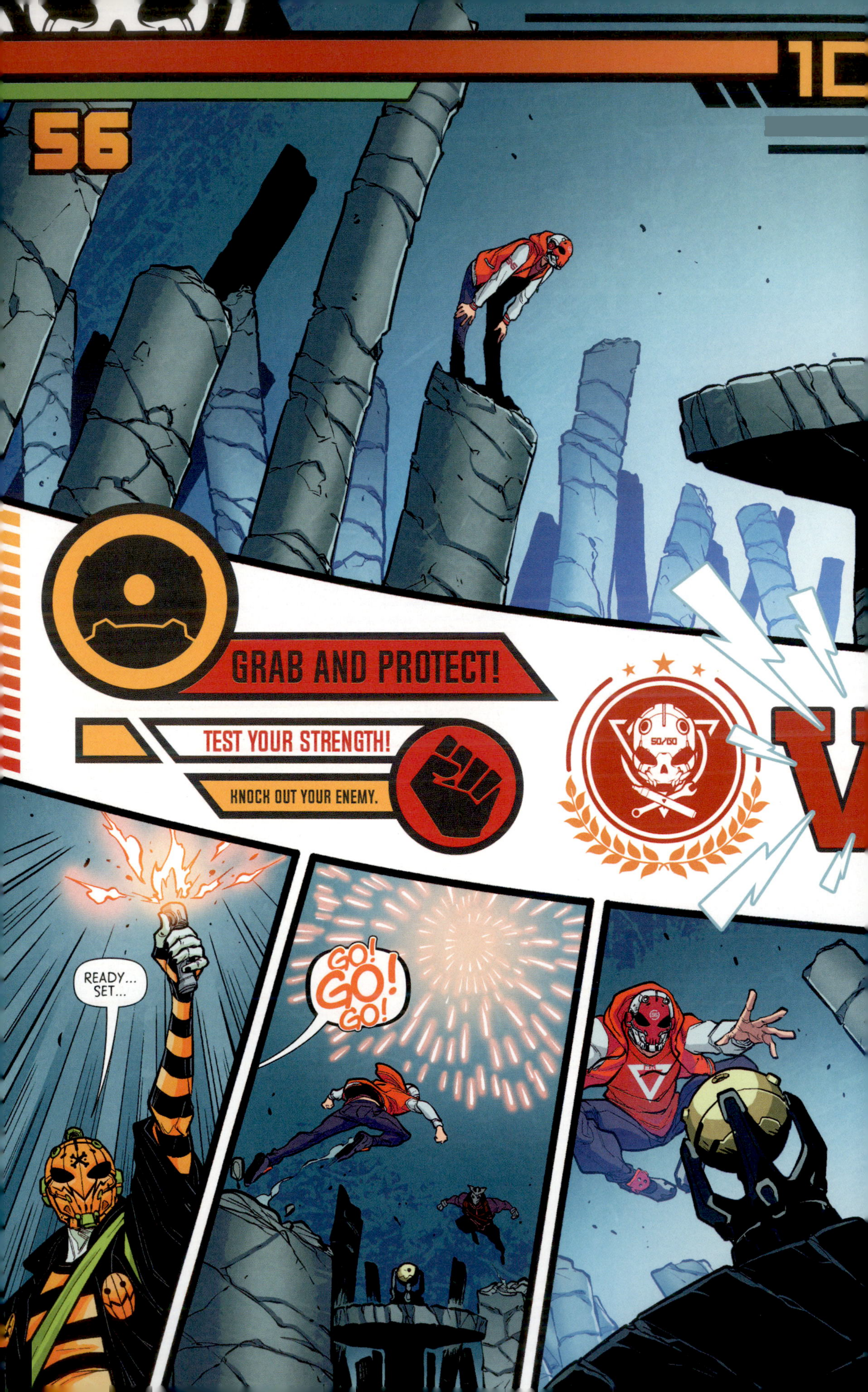
56
10
GRAB AND PROTECT!
TEST YOUR STRENGTH!
KNOCK OUT YOUR ENEMY.
50/50
READY... SET...
GO! GO! GO!

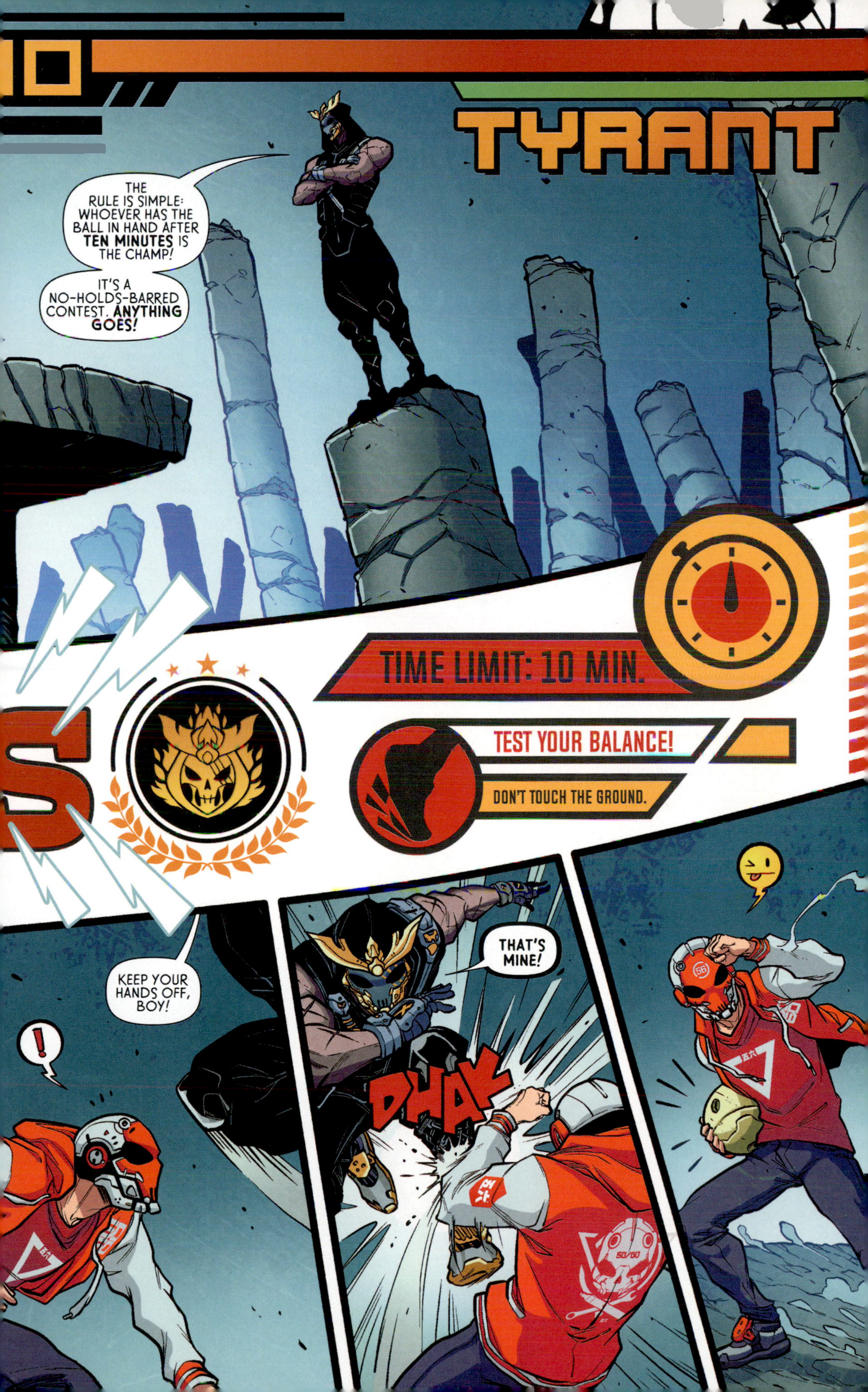
TYRANT
THE RULE IS SIMPLE: WHOEVER HAS THE BALL IN HAND AFTER TEN MINUTES IS THE CHAMP!
IT'S A NO-HOLDS-BARRED CONTEST. ANYTHING GOES!
TIME LIMIT: 10 MIN.
TEST YOUR BALANCE!
DON'T TOUCH THE GROUND.
KEEP YOUR HANDS OFF, BOY!
!
THAT'S MINE!
DHAK

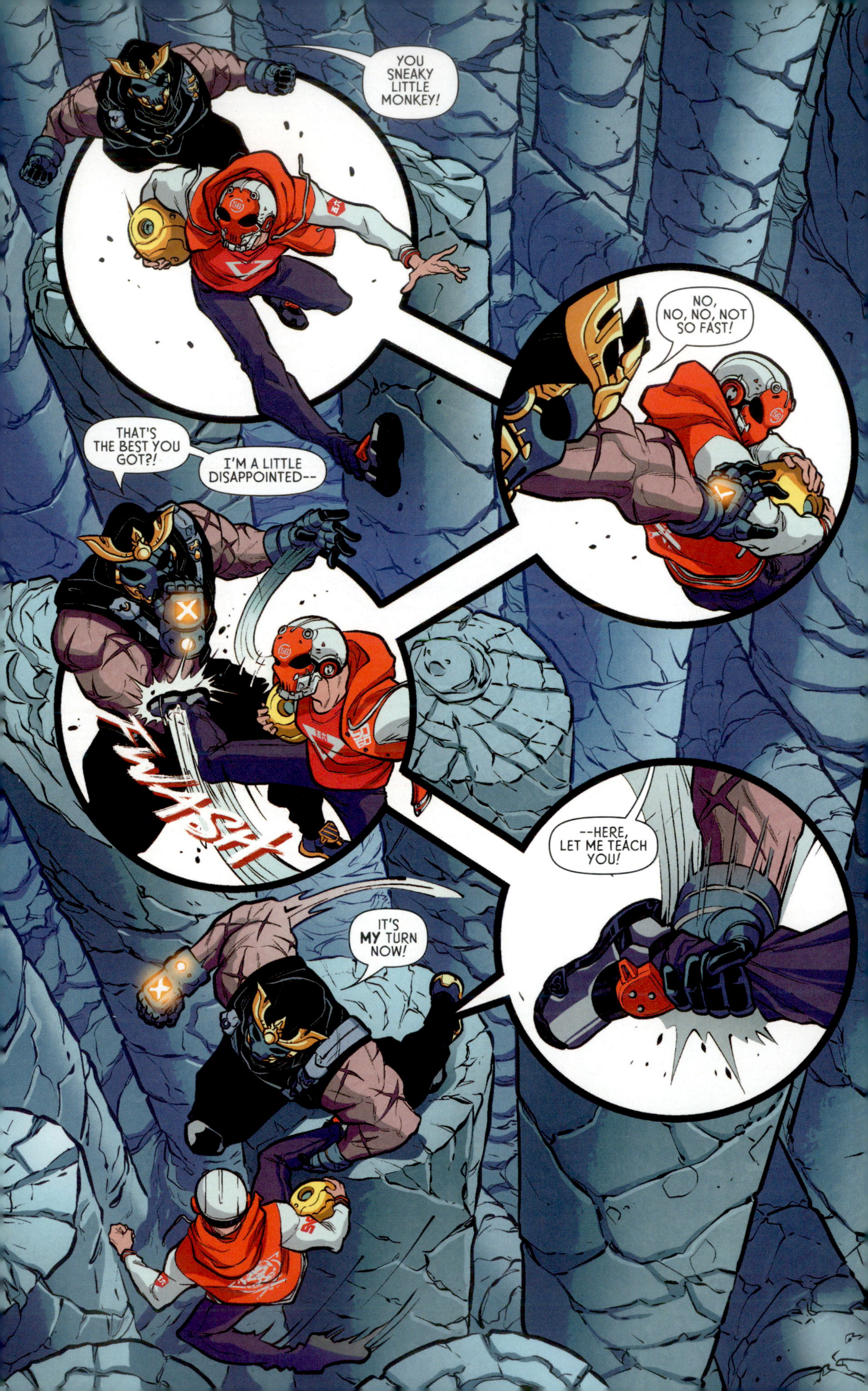
YOU SNEAKY LITTLE MONKEY!
NO, NO, NO, NOT SO FAST!
THAT'S THE BEST YOU GOT?!
I'M A LITTLE DISAPPOINTED--
FWASH
--HERE, LET ME TEACH YOU!
IT'S MY TURN NOW!

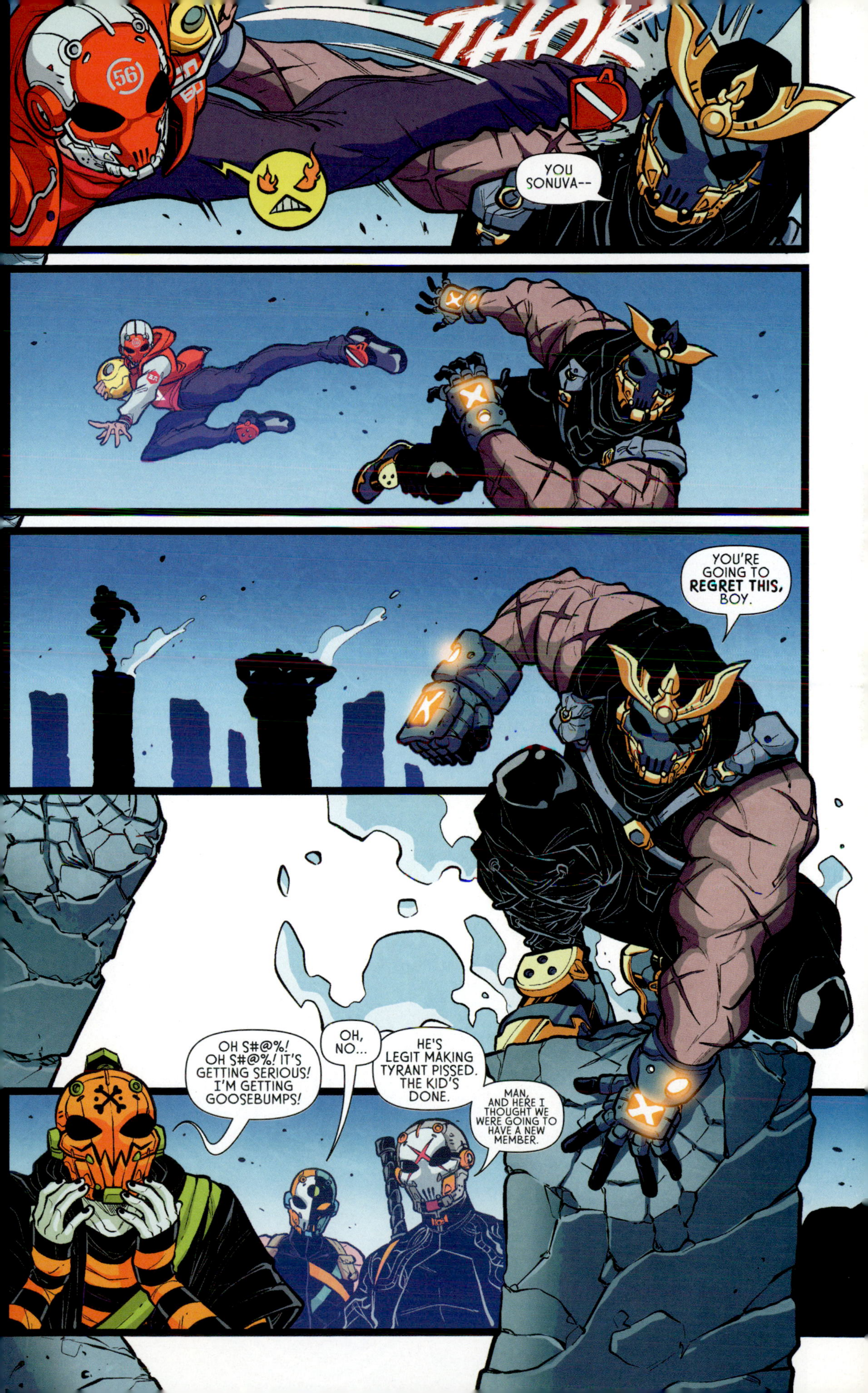
THOK
YOU SONUVA--
YOU'RE GOING TO REGRET THIS, BOY.
OH S#@%! OH S#@%! IT'S GETTING SERIOUS! I'M GETTING GOOSEBUMPS!
OH, NO...
HE'S LEGIT MAKING TYRANT PISSED. THE KID'S DONE.
MAN, AND HERE I THOUGHT WE WERE GOING TO HAVE A NEW MEMBER.

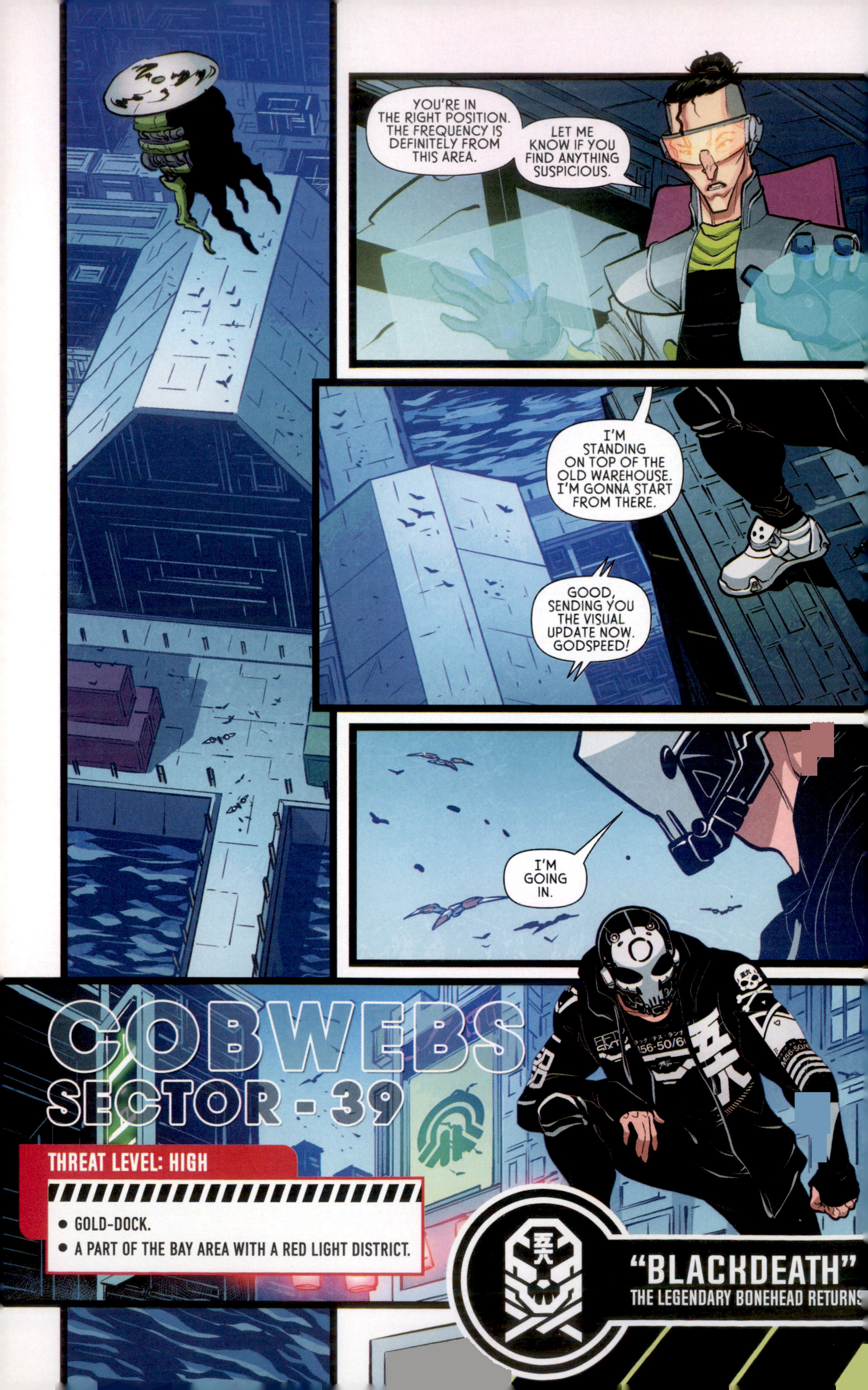
YOU'RE IN THE RIGHT POSITION. THE FREQUENCY IS DEFINITELY FROM THIS AREA.
LET ME KNOW IF YOU FIND ANYTHING SUSPICIOUS.
I'M STANDING ON TOP OF THE OLD WAREHOUSE. I'M GONNA START FROM THERE.
GOOD, SENDING YOU THE VISUAL UPDATE NOW. GODSPEED!
I'M GOING IN.
COBWEBS
SECTOR - 39
THREAT LEVEL: HIGH
• GOLD-DOCK.
• A PART OF THE BAY AREA WITH A RED LIGHT DISTRICT.
"BLACKDEATH"
THE LEGENDARY BONEHEAD RETURNS

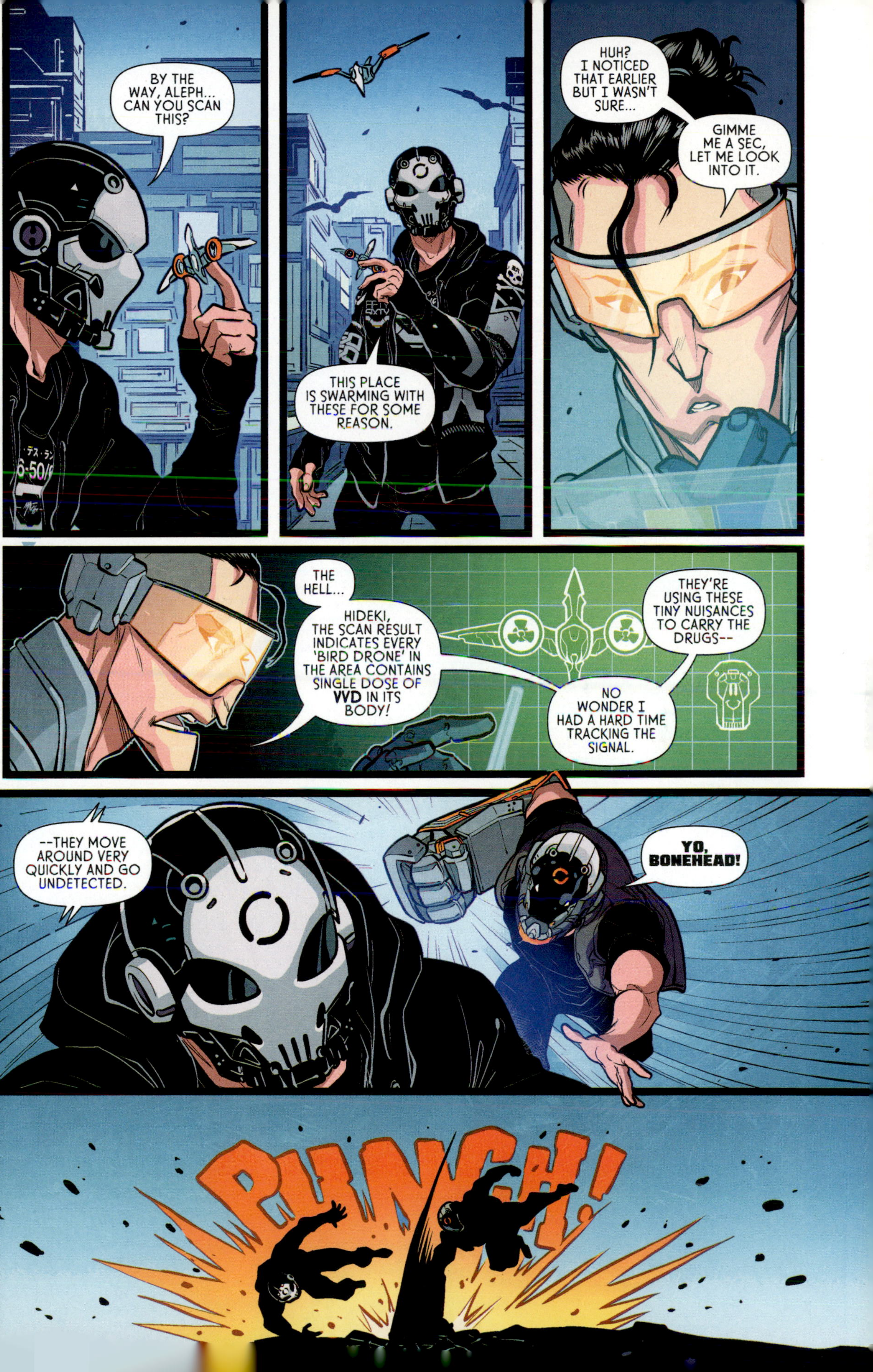

BY THE WAY, ALEPH... CAN YOU SCAN THIS?
THIS PLACE IS SWARMING WITH THESE FOR SOME REASON.
HUH? I NOTICED THAT EARLIER BUT I WASN'T SURE...
GIMME ME A SEC, LET ME LOOK INTO IT.
THE HELL...
HIDEKI, THE SCAN RESULT INDICATES EVERY 'BIRD DRONE' IN THE AREA CONTAINS SINGLE DOSE OF **VVD** IN ITS BODY!
NO WONDER I HAD A HARD TIME TRACKING THE SIGNAL.
THEY'RE USING THESE TINY NUISANCES TO CARRY THE DRUGS--
--THEY MOVE AROUND VERY QUICKLY AND GO UNDETECTED.
YO, BONEHEAD!
PUNCH!

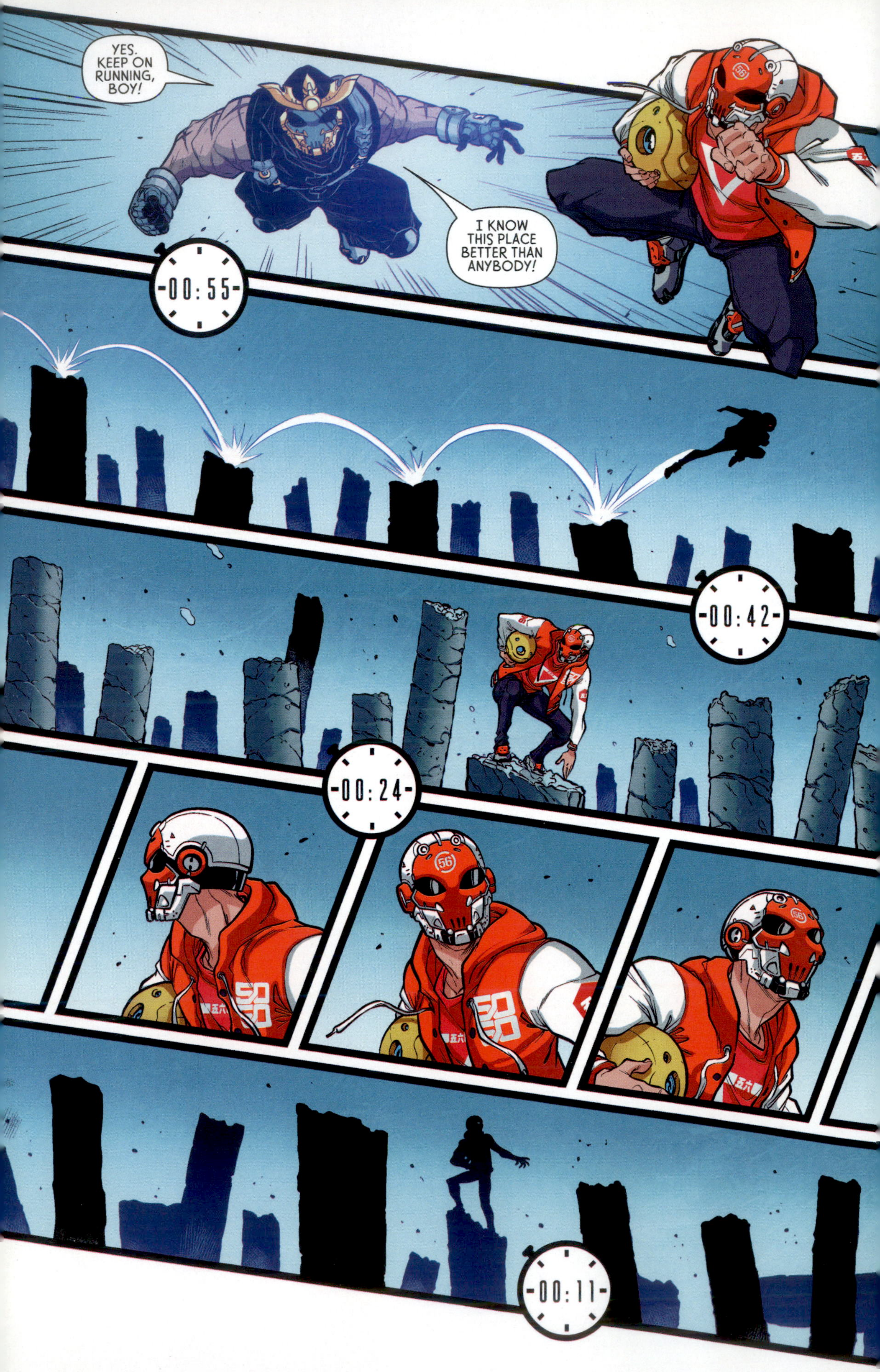
YES. KEEP ON RUNNING, BOY!
I KNOW THIS PLACE BETTER THAN ANYBODY!
00:55
00:42
00:24
00:11

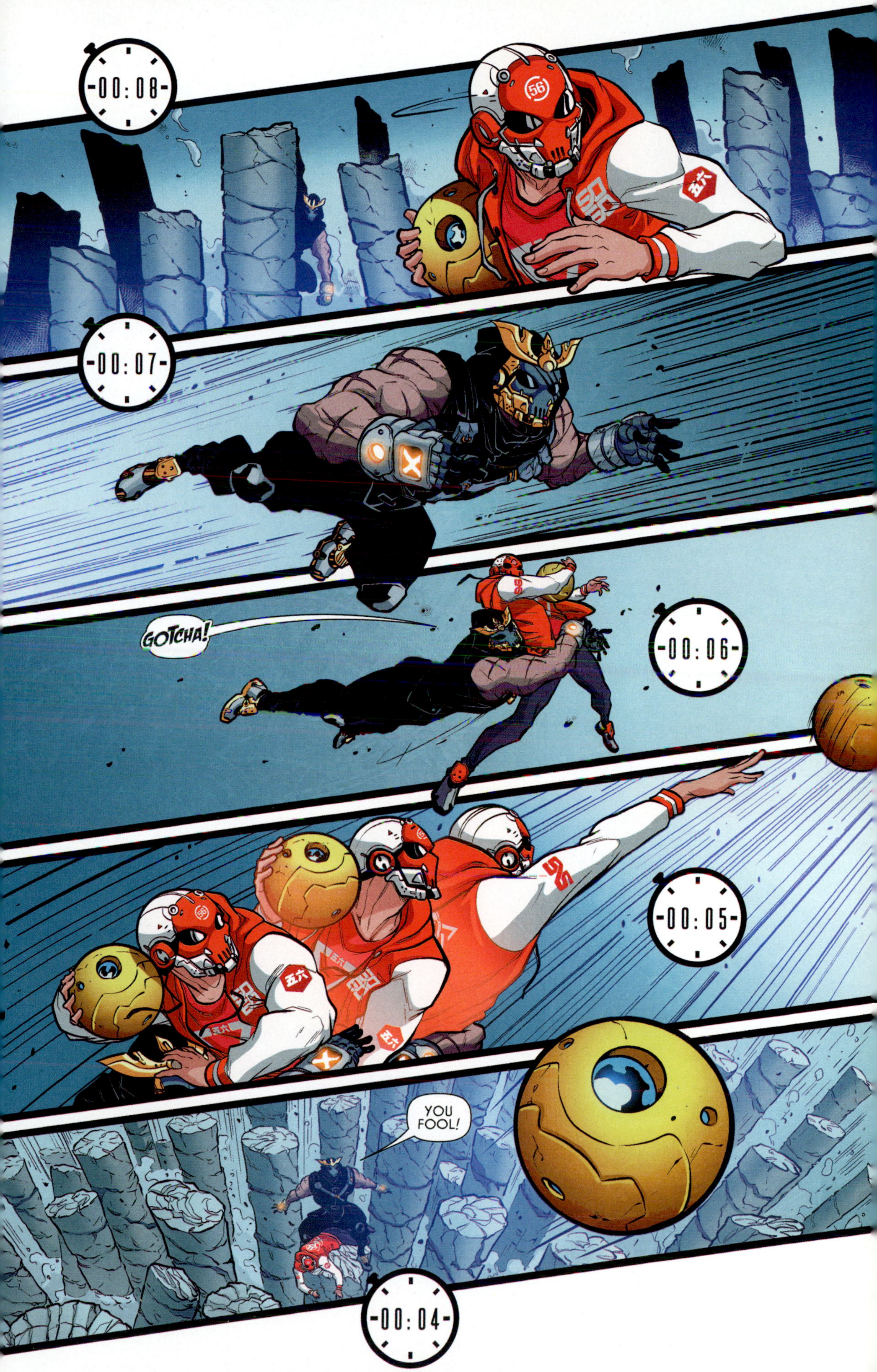
00:08
00:07
GOTCHA!
00:06
00:05
YOU FOOL!
00:04

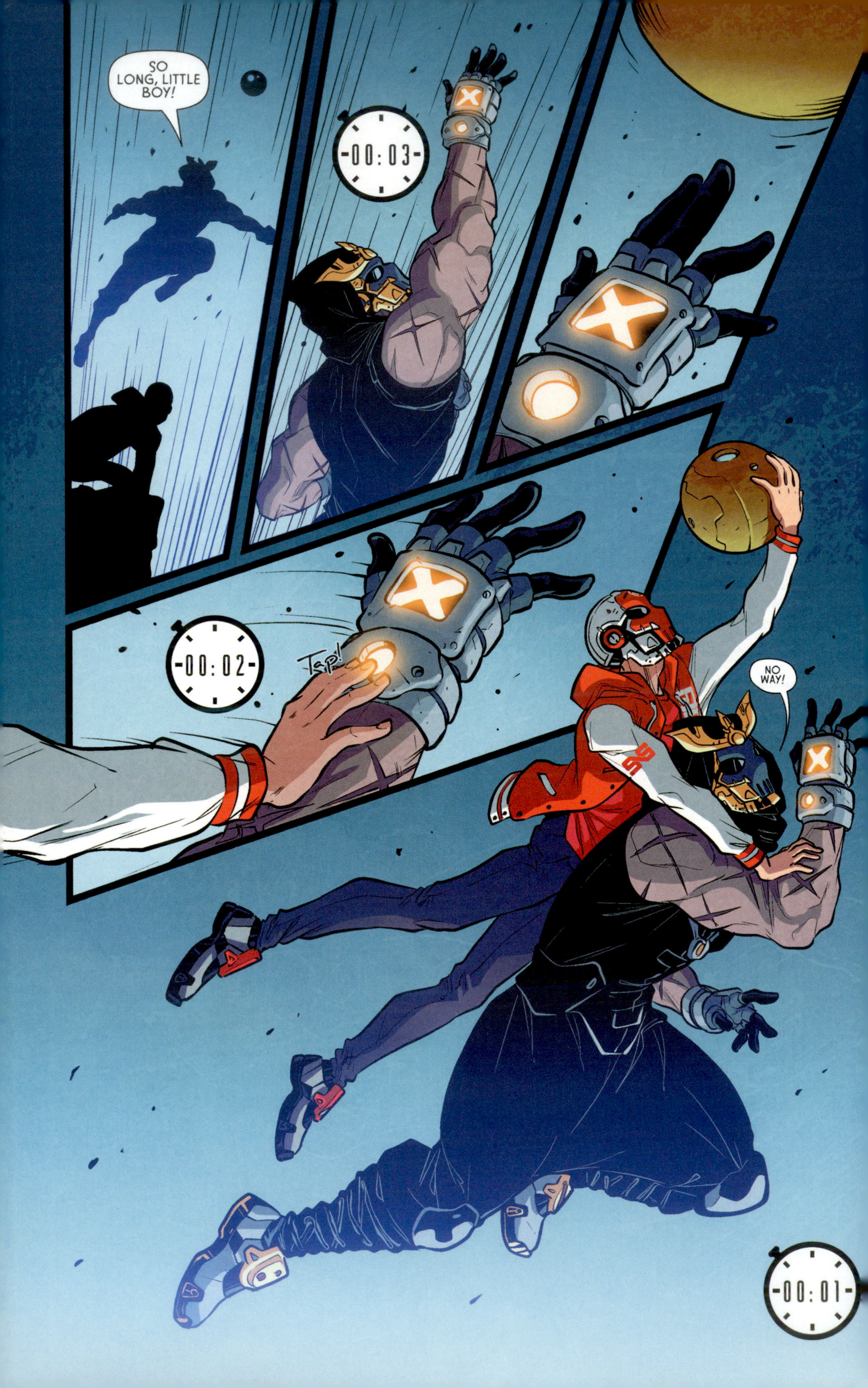
SO LONG, LITTLE BOY!
00:03
00:02
TAP!
NO WAY!
00:01

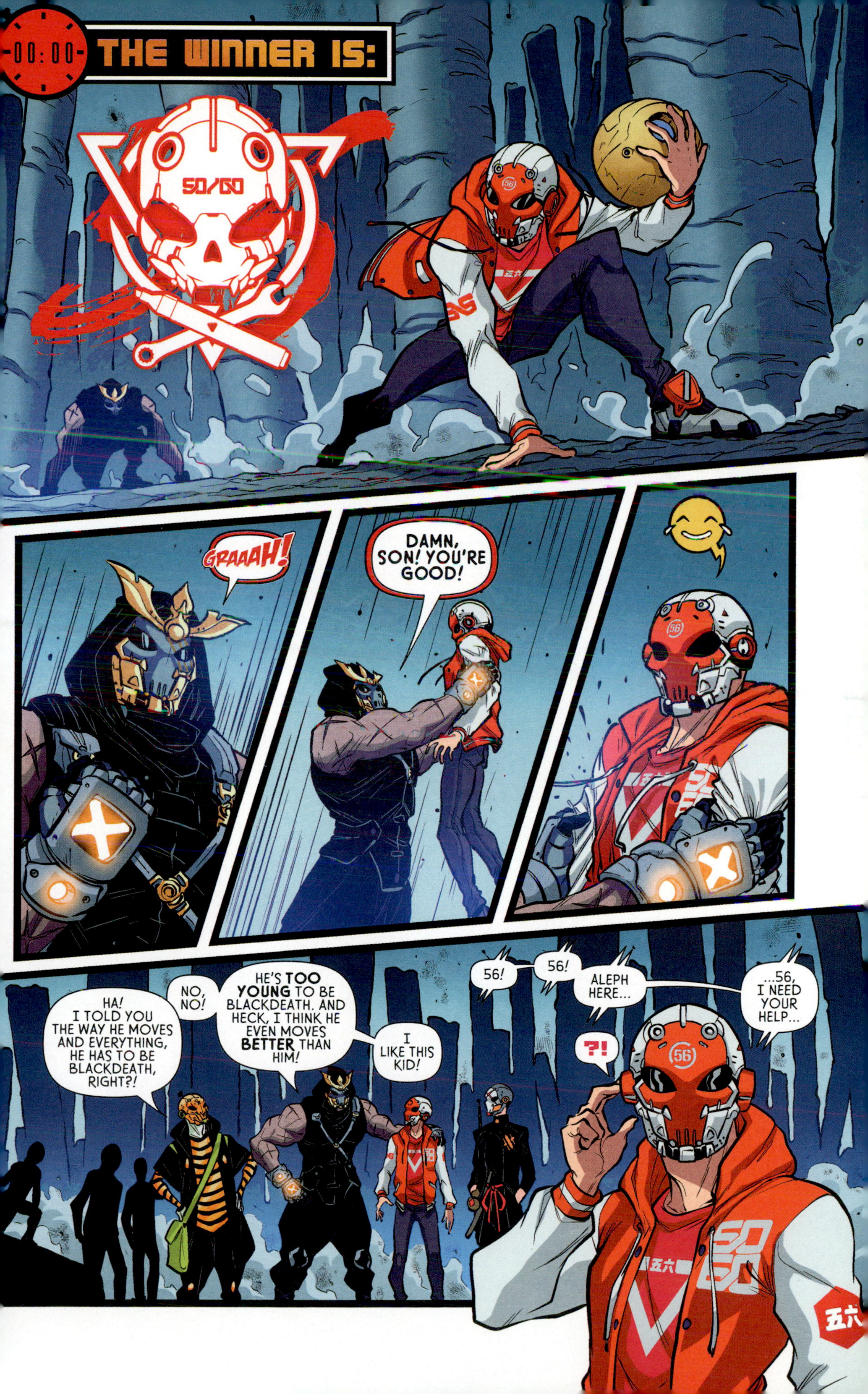
00:00
THE WINNER IS:
50/60
GRAAAH!
DAMN, SON! YOU'RE GOOD!
HA! I TOLD YOU THE WAY HE MOVES AND EVERYTHING, HE HAS TO BE BLACKDEATH, RIGHT?!
NO, NO!
HE'S TOO YOUNG TO BE BLACKDEATH. AND HECK, I THINK HE EVEN MOVES BETTER THAN HIM!
I LIKE THIS KID!
56!
56!
ALEPH HERE...
...56, I NEED YOUR HELP...
?!

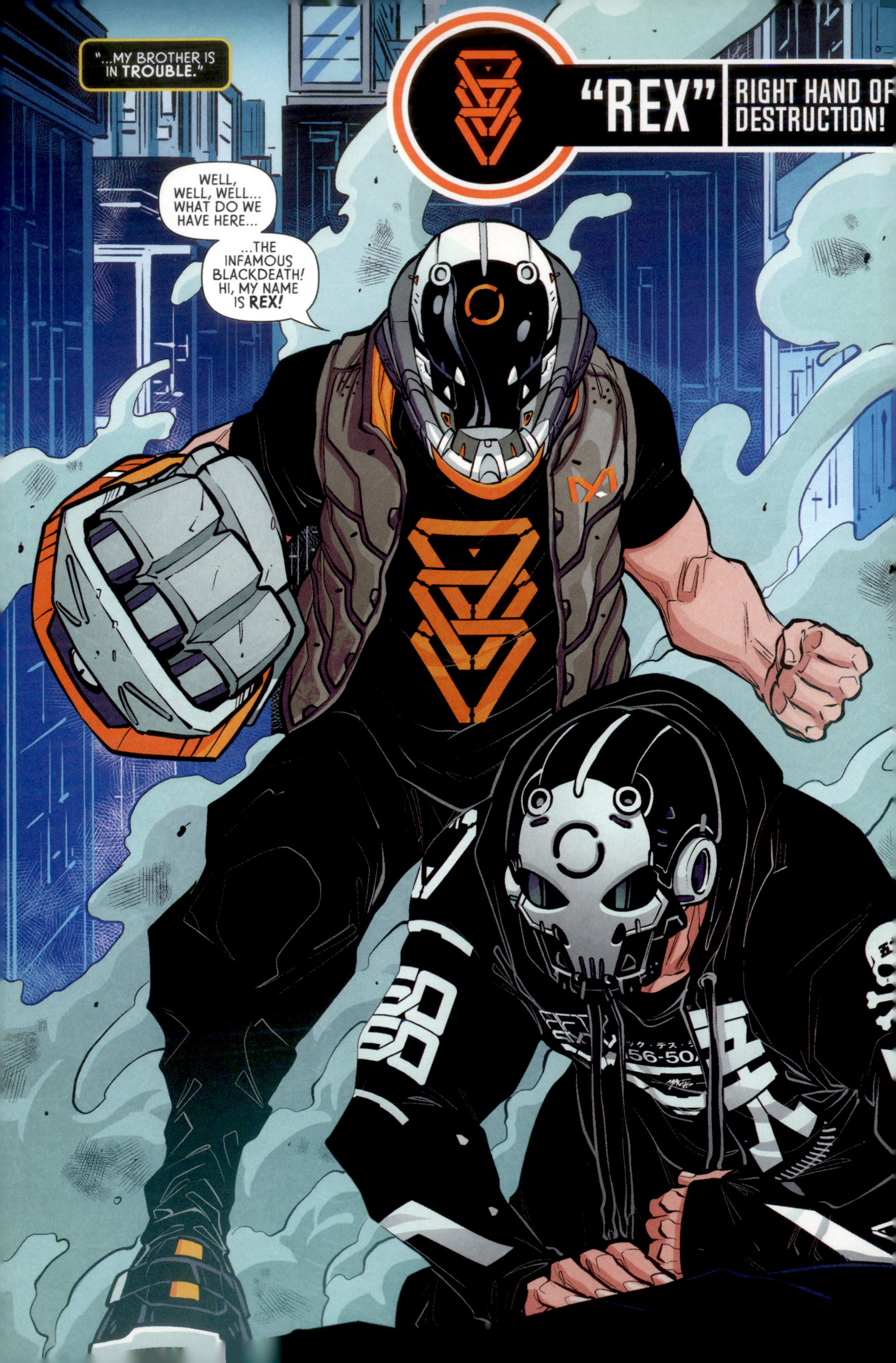
"...MY BROTHER IS IN TROUBLE."
"REX" RIGHT HAND OF DESTRUCTION!
WELL, WELL, WELL... WHAT DO WE HAVE HERE...
...THE INFAMOUS BLACKDEATH! HI, MY NAME IS REX!

CHAPTER04

● ORIGINAL MITSURU.TECH SERIAL #
○ CLOSE QUARTER TYPE_

● SLAVE TYPE BONEHEAD01.
○ BODY STRUCTURE : N/A

● NODE TRACKING AFTER DELETION COURSE
○ EARTH: 7 MEGAPARSECS ACROSS_

▶ M56/001/A   ▶ Bonehead, RED, 16k-Zettabyte.   (1P) Part No. MT-A0156 / D / Test Subject no.56   ブラック・デス・ランナー   QC/P

Designed by Machine56, Assembled by Mitsuru.Tech
MK-I / Not suitable f

5 0 6 0 1 3 0 9

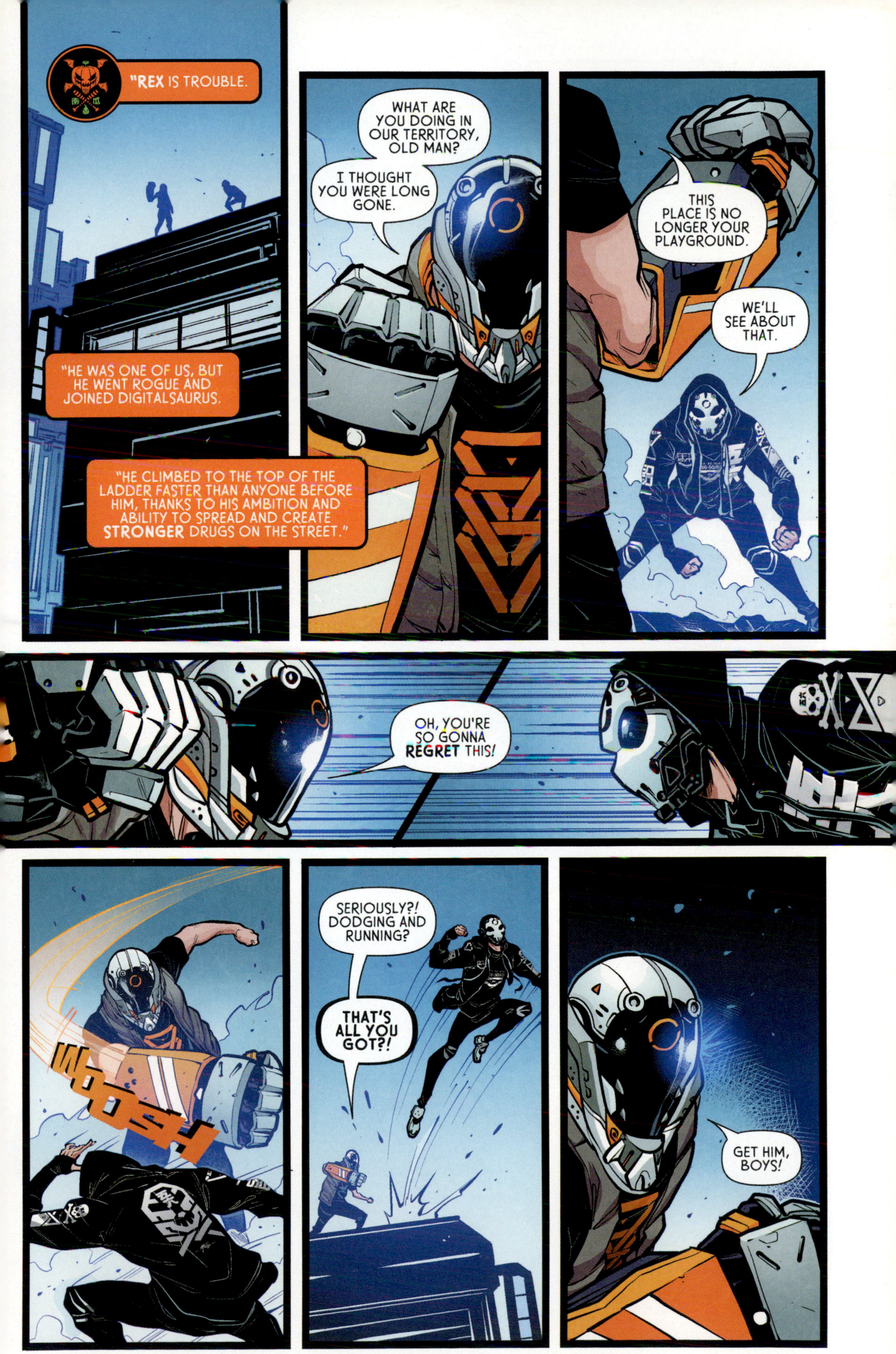
"REX IS TROUBLE.
"HE WAS ONE OF US, BUT HE WENT ROGUE AND JOINED DIGITALSAURUS.
"HE CLIMBED TO THE TOP OF THE LADDER FASTER THAN ANYONE BEFORE HIM, THANKS TO HIS AMBITION AND ABILITY TO SPREAD AND CREATE STRONGER DRUGS ON THE STREET."
WHAT ARE YOU DOING IN OUR TERRITORY, OLD MAN?
I THOUGHT YOU WERE LONG GONE.
THIS PLACE IS NO LONGER YOUR PLAYGROUND.
WE'LL SEE ABOUT THAT.
OH, YOU'RE SO GONNA REGRET THIS!
WOOSH
SERIOUSLY?! DODGING AND RUNNING?
THAT'S ALL YOU GOT?!
GET HIM, BOYS!

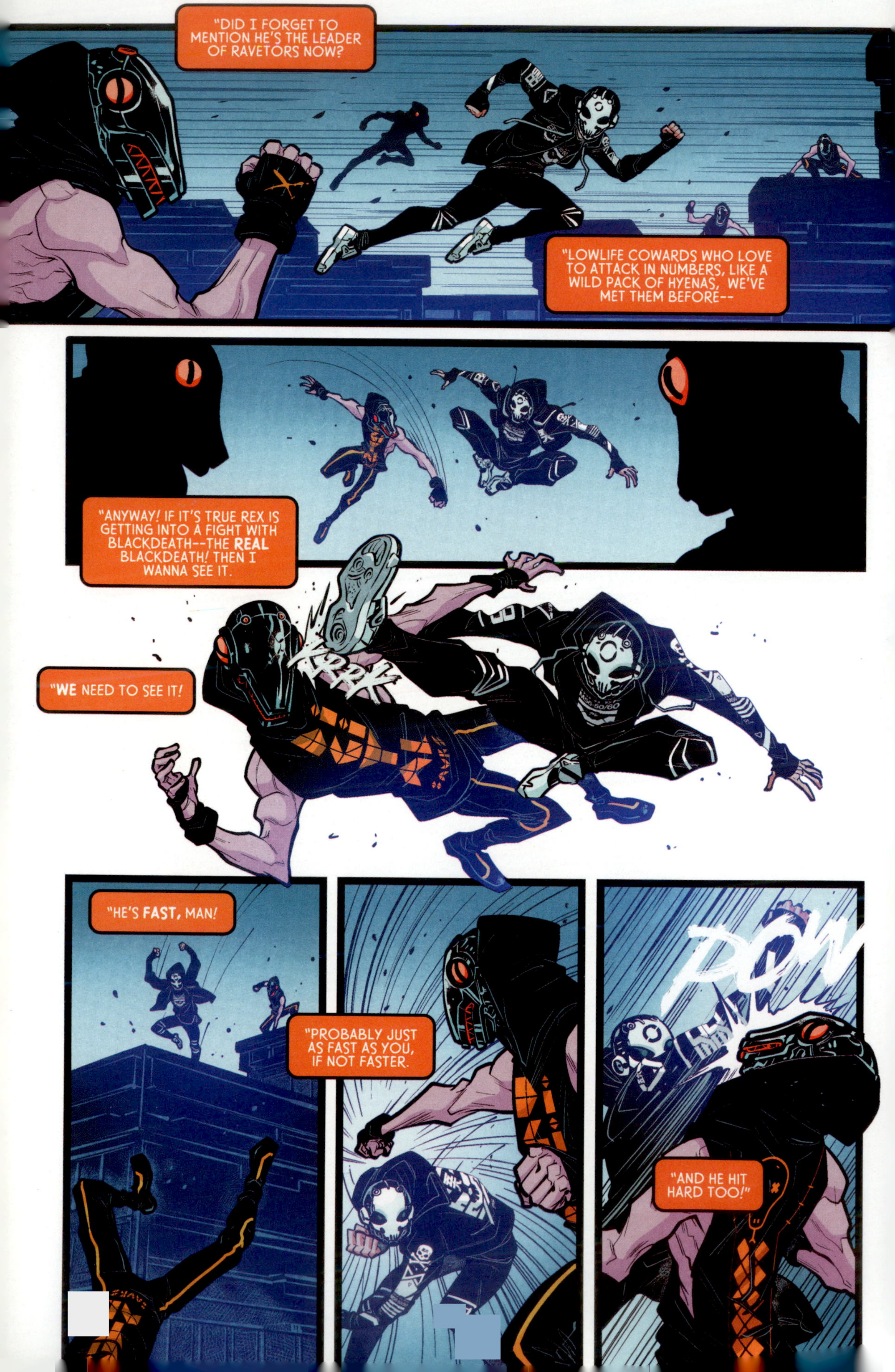
"DID I FORGET TO MENTION HE'S THE LEADER OF RAVETORS NOW?
"LOWLIFE COWARDS WHO LOVE TO ATTACK IN NUMBERS, LIKE A WILD PACK OF HYENAS, WE'VE MET THEM BEFORE--
"ANYWAY! IF IT'S TRUE REX IS GETTING INTO A FIGHT WITH BLACKDEATH--THE **REAL** BLACKDEATH! THEN I WANNA SEE IT.
"**WE** NEED TO SEE IT!
KRRK
"HE'S **FAST,** MAN!
"PROBABLY JUST AS FAST AS YOU, IF NOT FASTER.
POW
"AND HE HIT HARD TOO!"

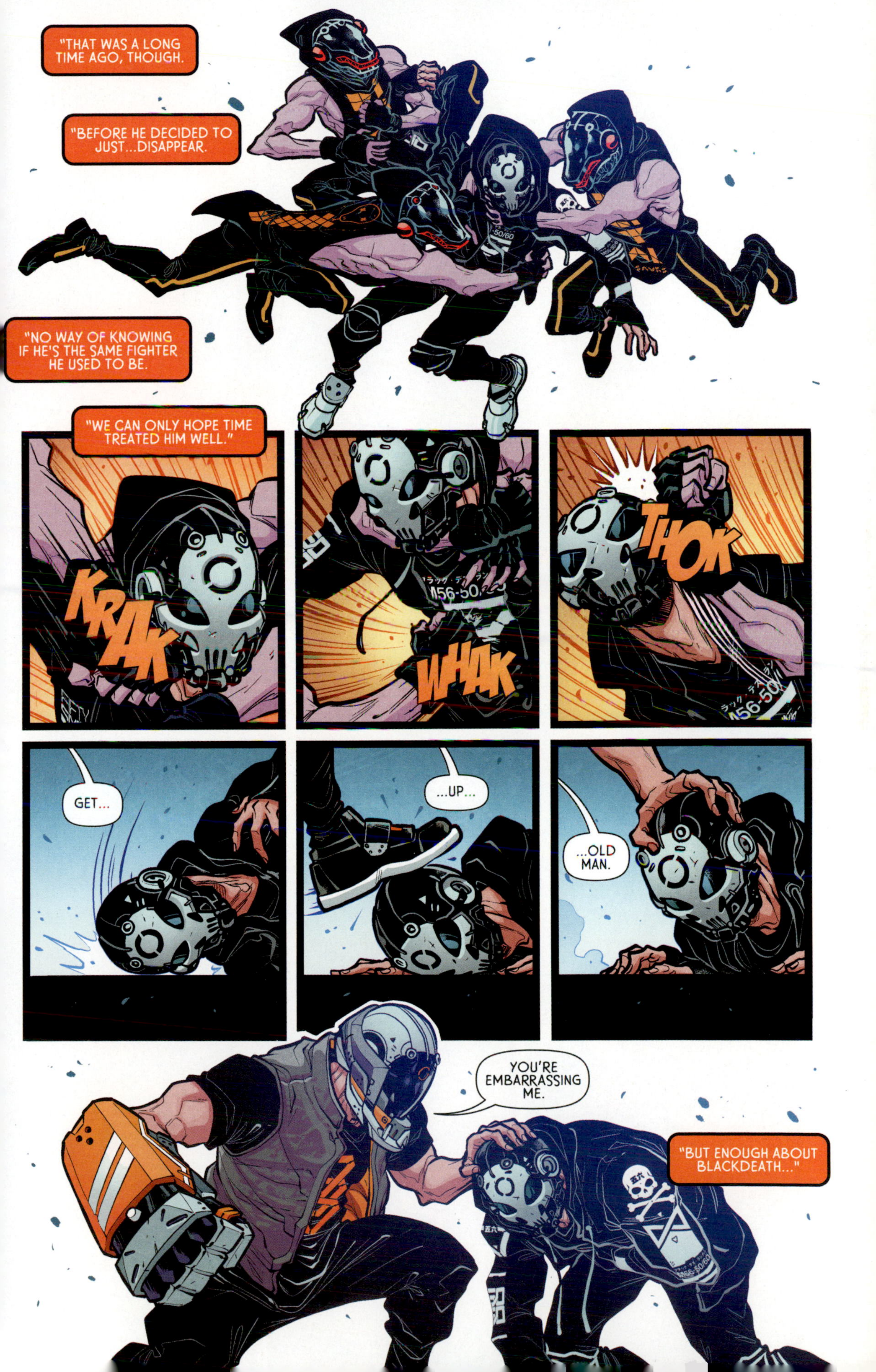
"THAT WAS A LONG TIME AGO, THOUGH.
"BEFORE HE DECIDED TO JUST...DISAPPEAR.
"NO WAY OF KNOWING IF HE'S THE SAME FIGHTER HE USED TO BE.
"WE CAN ONLY HOPE TIME TREATED HIM WELL."
KRAK
WHAK
THOK
GET...
...UP...
...OLD MAN.
YOU'RE EMBARRASSING ME.
"BUT ENOUGH ABOUT BLACKDEATH..."

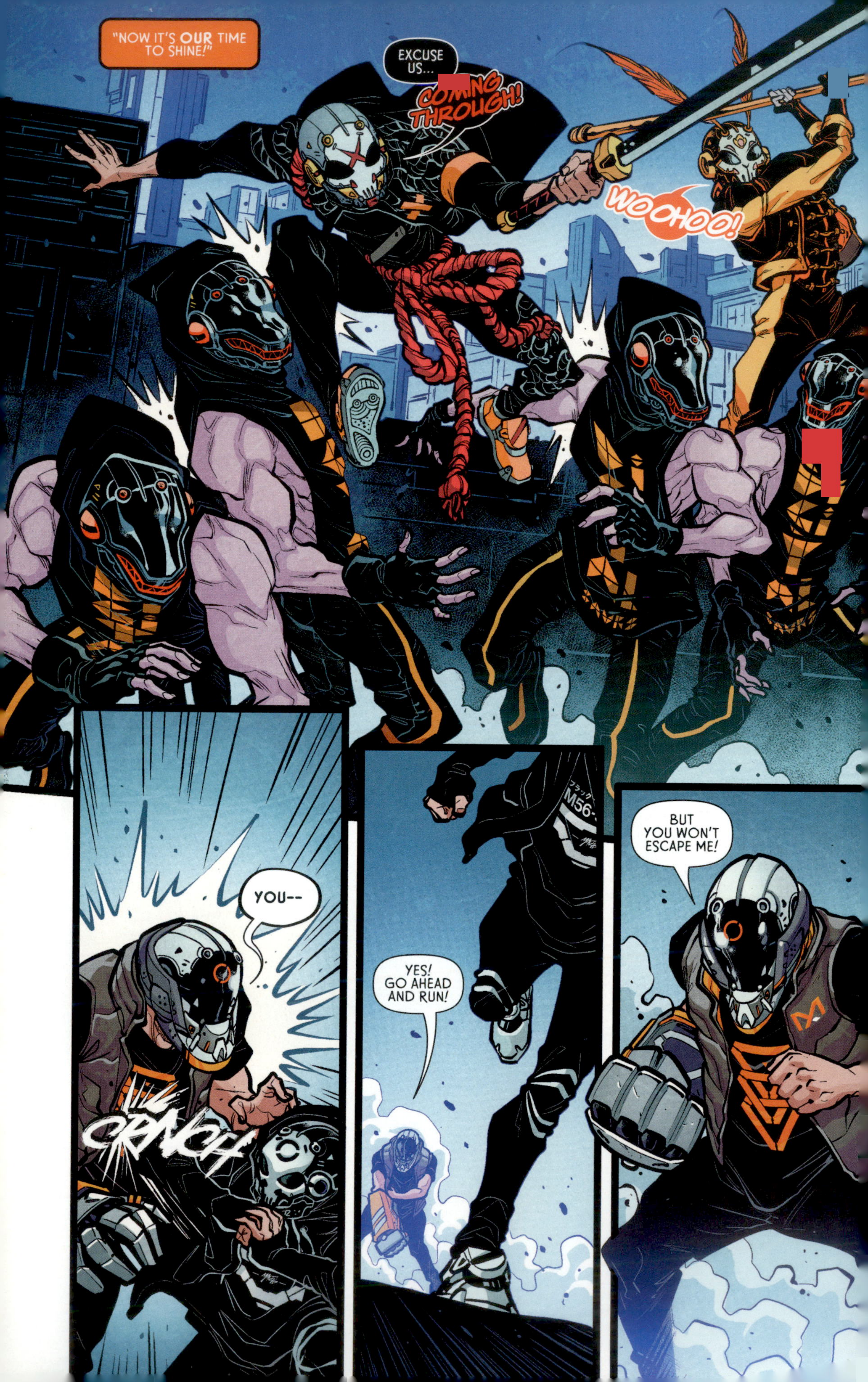
"NOW IT'S **OUR** TIME TO SHINE!"
EXCUSE US...
COMING THROUGH!
WOOHOO!
YOU--
CRNCH
YES! GO AHEAD AND RUN!
BUT YOU WON'T ESCAPE ME!

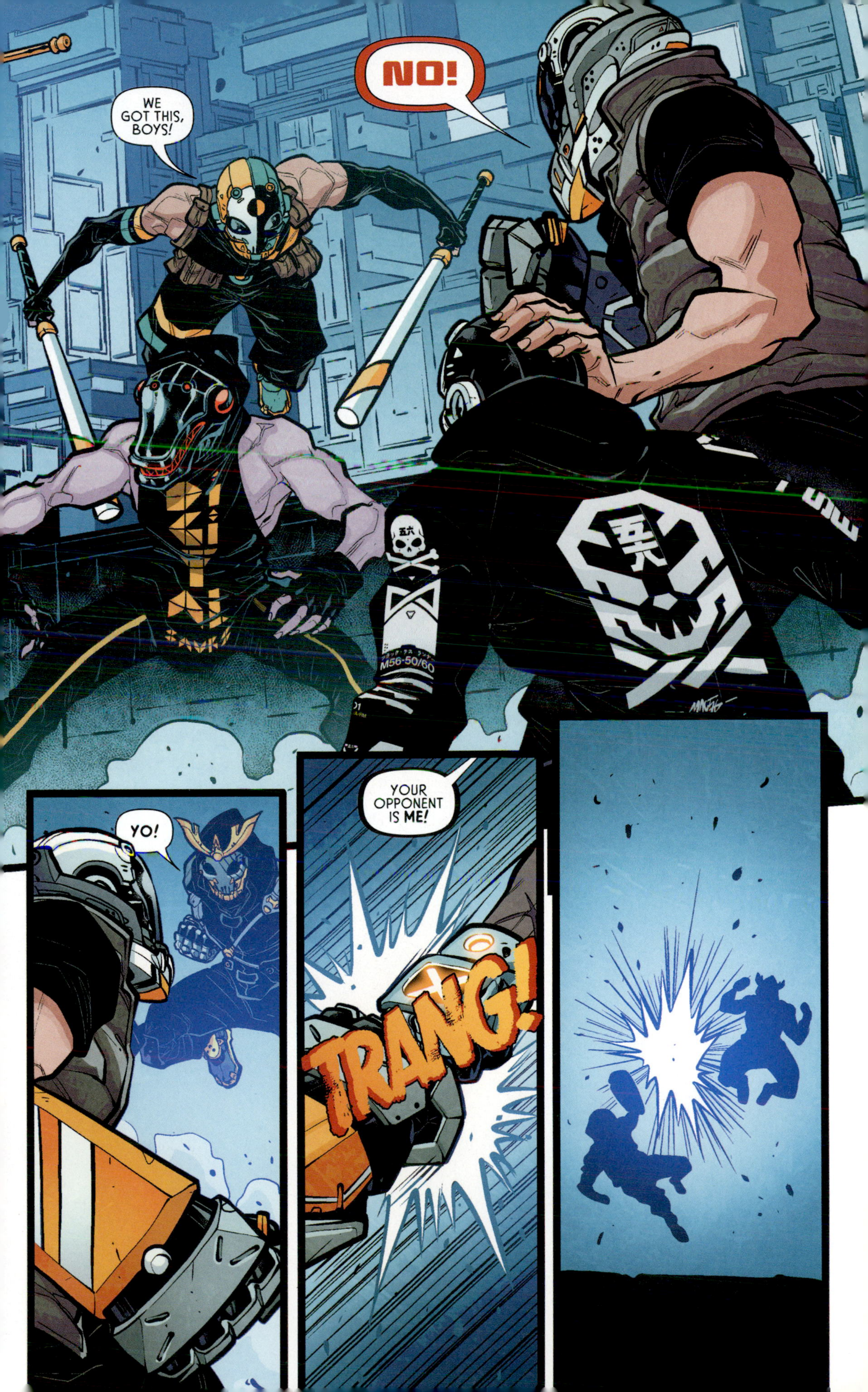
WE GOT THIS, BOYS!
NO!
YO!
YOUR OPPONENT IS ME!
TRANG!

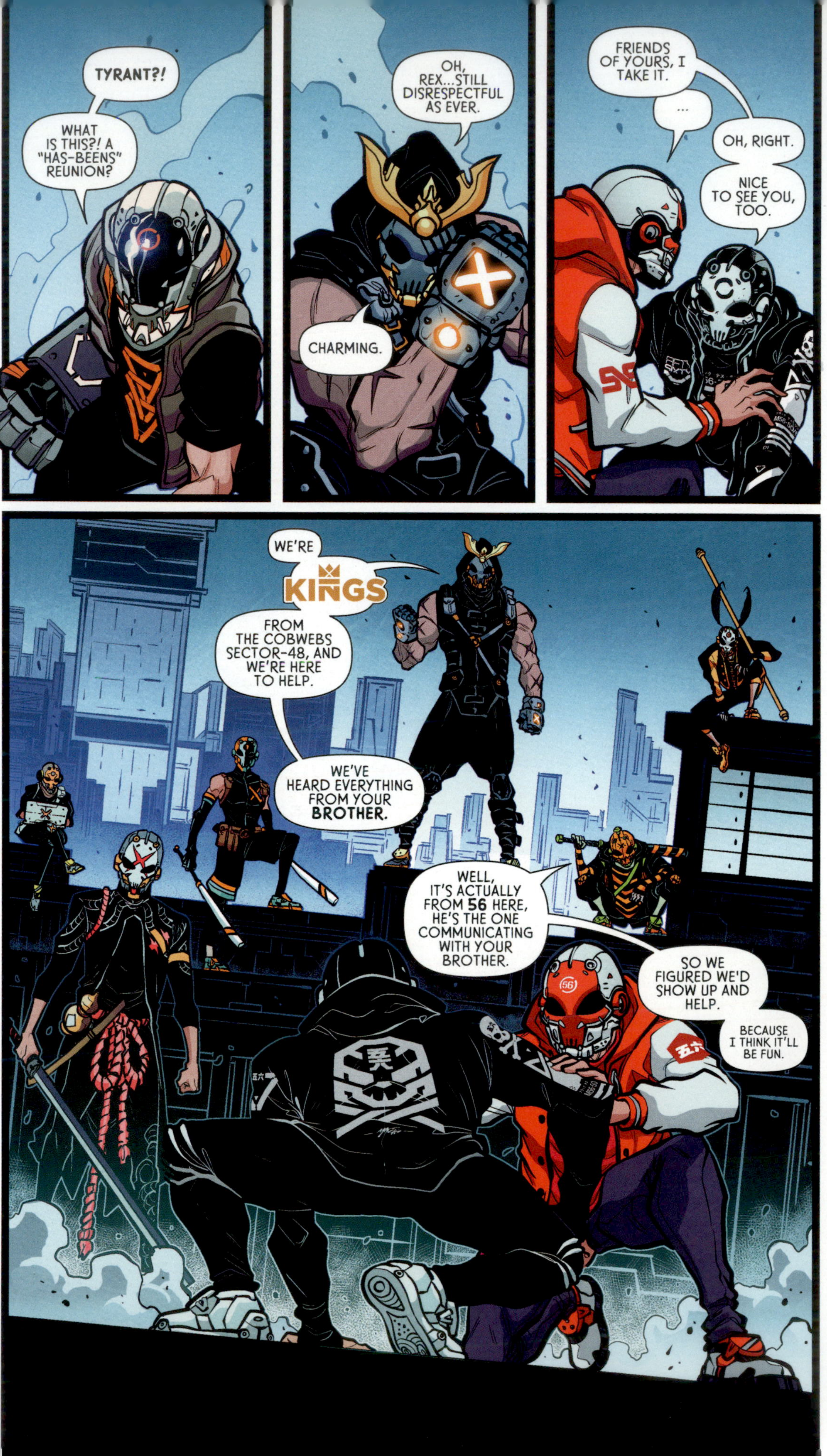
TYRANT?!
WHAT IS THIS?! A "HAS-BEENS" REUNION?
OH, REX...STILL DISRESPECTFUL AS EVER.
CHARMING.
FRIENDS OF YOURS, I TAKE IT.
...
OH, RIGHT.
NICE TO SEE YOU, TOO.
WE'RE KINGS FROM THE COBWEBS SECTOR-48, AND WE'RE HERE TO HELP.
WE'VE HEARD EVERYTHING FROM YOUR BROTHER.
WELL, IT'S ACTUALLY FROM 56 HERE, HE'S THE ONE COMMUNICATING WITH YOUR BROTHER.
SO WE FIGURED WE'D SHOW UP AND HELP.
BECAUSE I THINK IT'LL BE FUN.

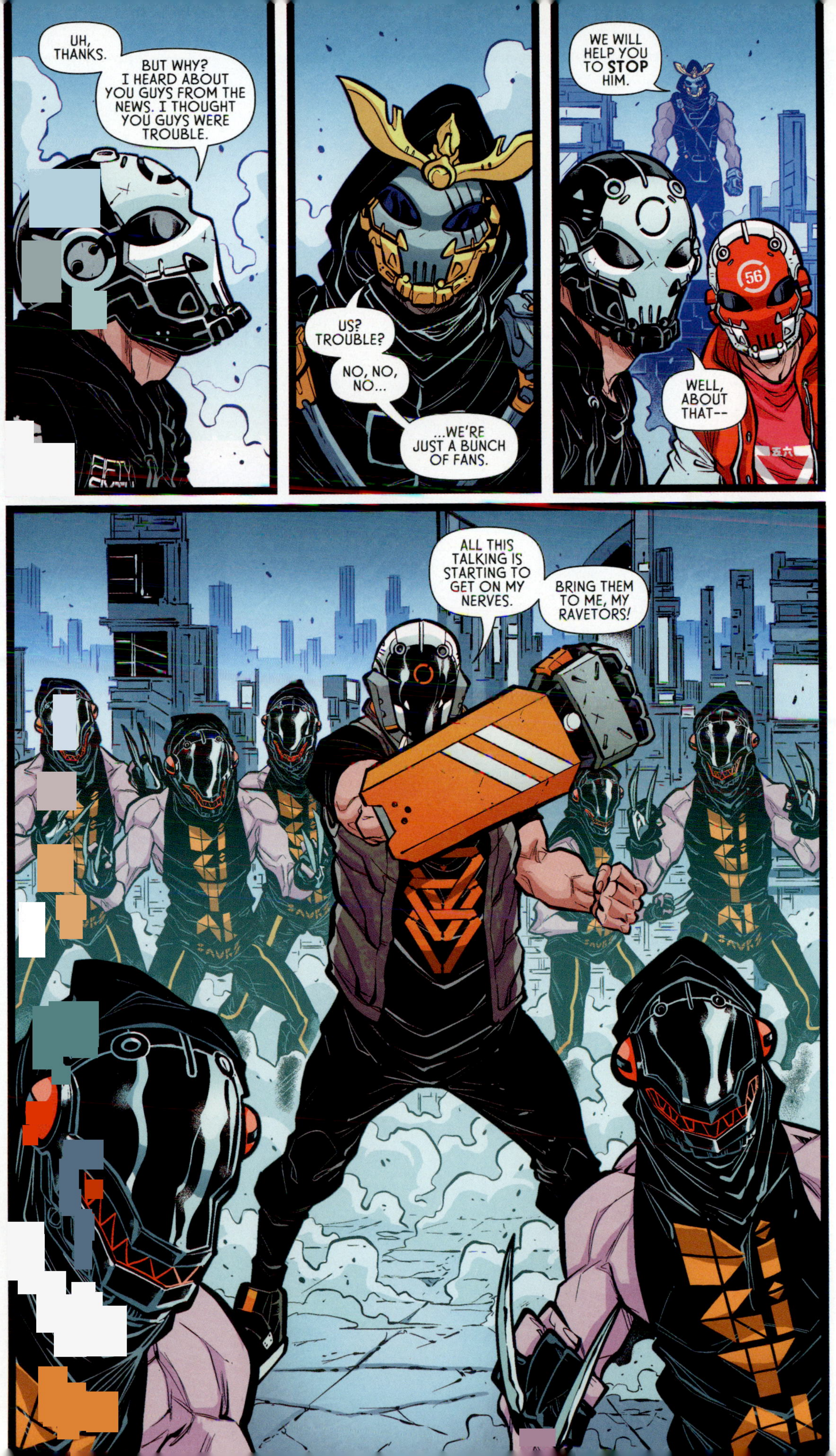
UH, THANKS.
BUT WHY? I HEARD ABOUT YOU GUYS FROM THE NEWS. I THOUGHT YOU GUYS WERE TROUBLE.
US? TROUBLE?
NO, NO, NO...
...WE'RE JUST A BUNCH OF FANS.
WE WILL HELP YOU TO **STOP** HIM.
WELL, ABOUT THAT--
ALL THIS TALKING IS STARTING TO GET ON MY NERVES.
BRING THEM TO ME, MY RAVETORS!

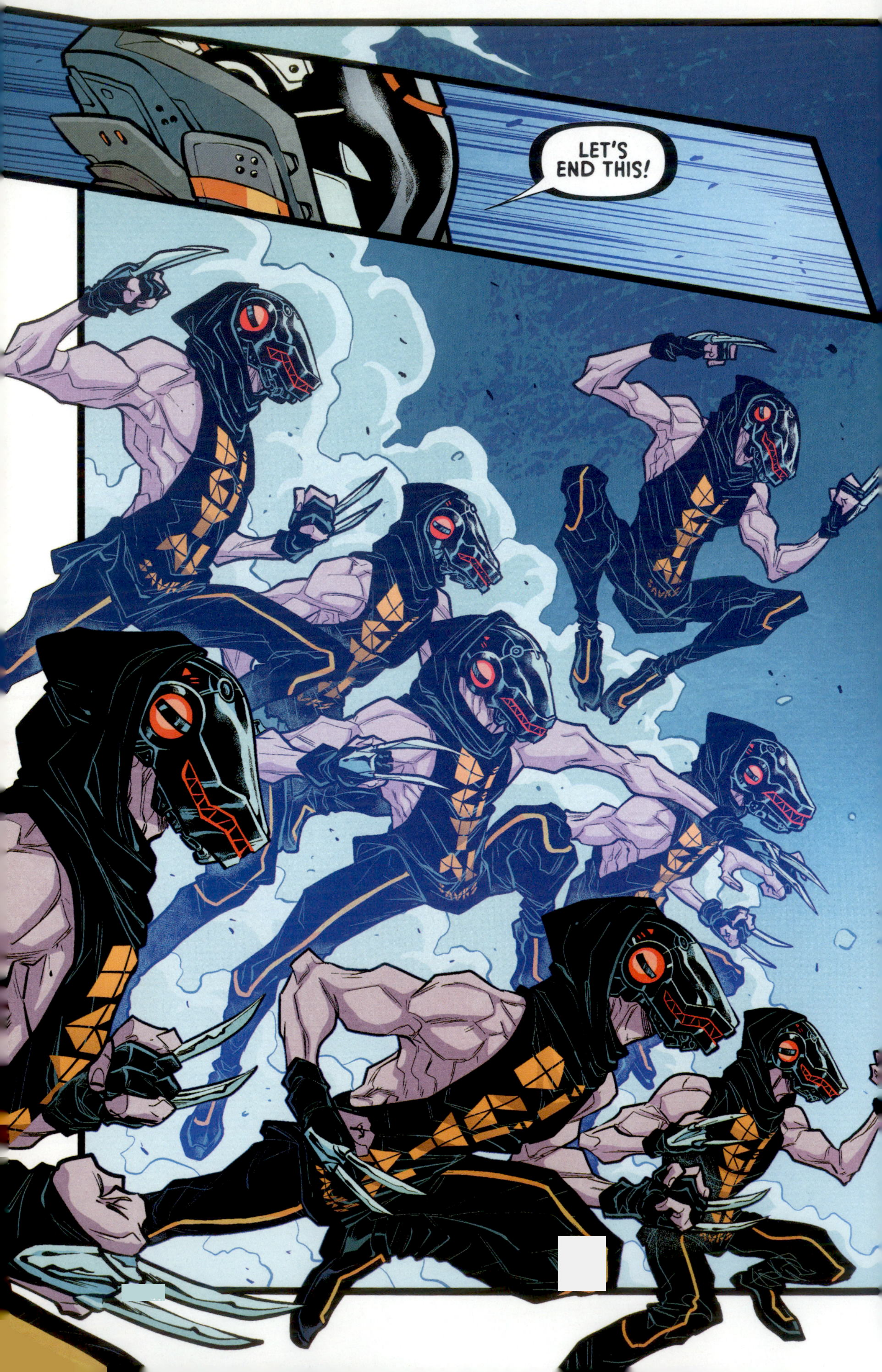
LET'S END THIS!

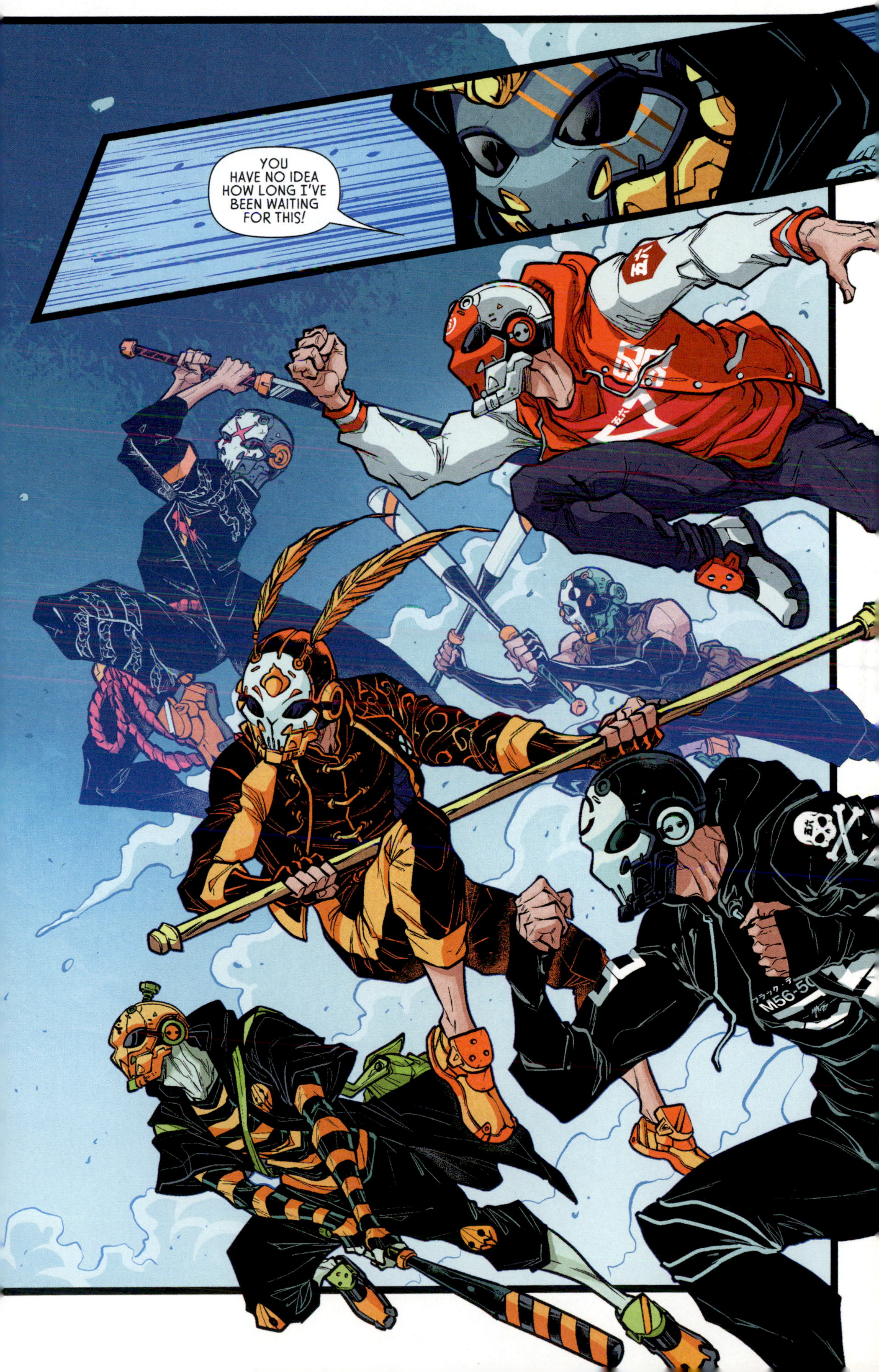
YOU HAVE NO IDEA HOW LONG I'VE BEEN WAITING FOR THIS!

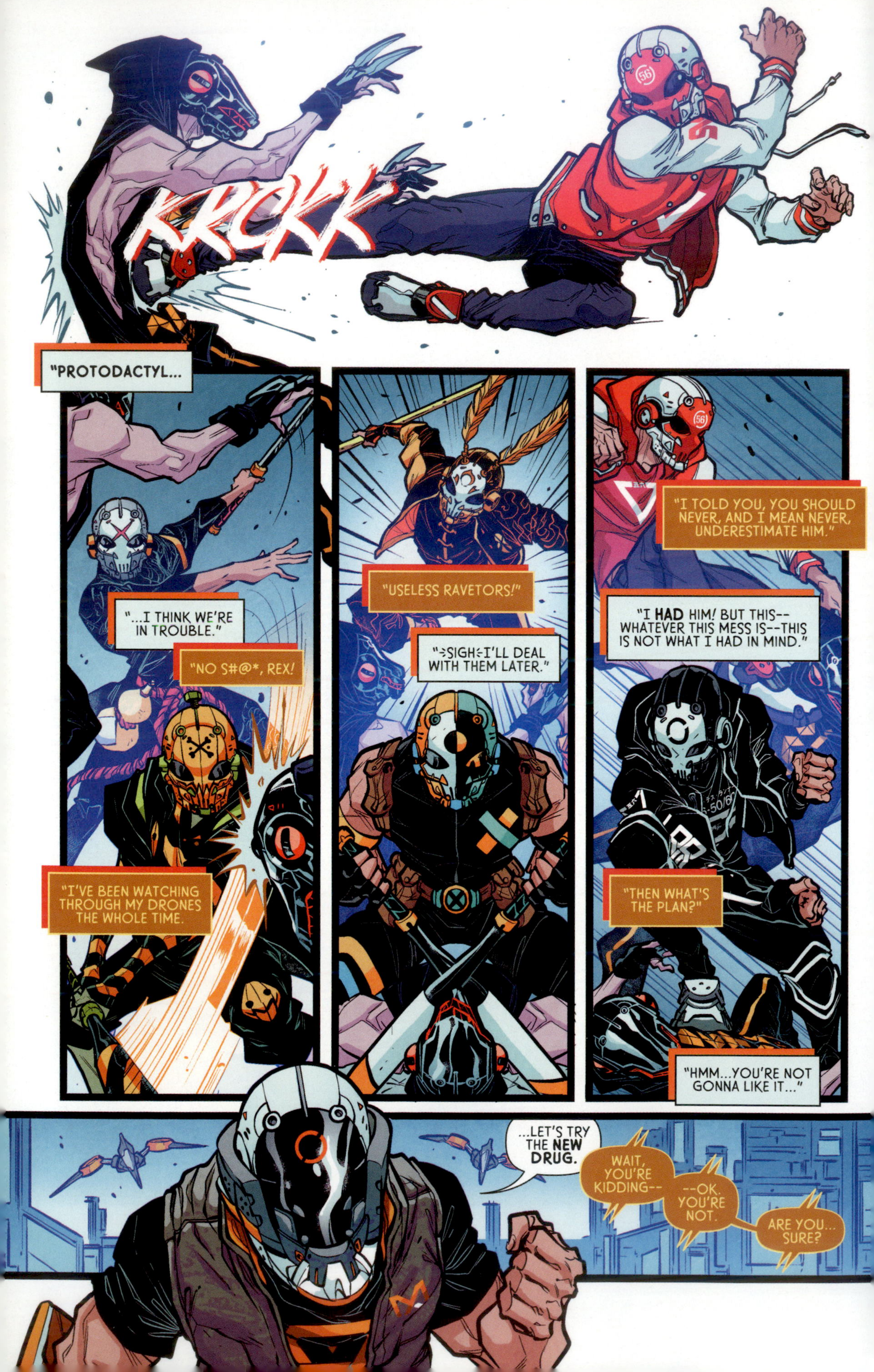
KRCKK
"PROTODACTYL...
"...I THINK WE'RE IN TROUBLE."
"NO S#@*, REX!
"I'VE BEEN WATCHING THROUGH MY DRONES THE WHOLE TIME.
"USELESS RAVETORS!"
"÷SIGH÷ I'LL DEAL WITH THEM LATER."
"I TOLD YOU, YOU SHOULD NEVER, AND I MEAN NEVER, UNDERESTIMATE HIM."
"I HAD HIM! BUT THIS--WHATEVER THIS MESS IS--THIS IS NOT WHAT I HAD IN MIND."
"THEN WHAT'S THE PLAN?"
"HMM...YOU'RE NOT GONNA LIKE IT..."
...LET'S TRY THE NEW DRUG.
WAIT, YOU'RE KIDDING--
--OK. YOU'RE NOT.
ARE YOU... SURE?

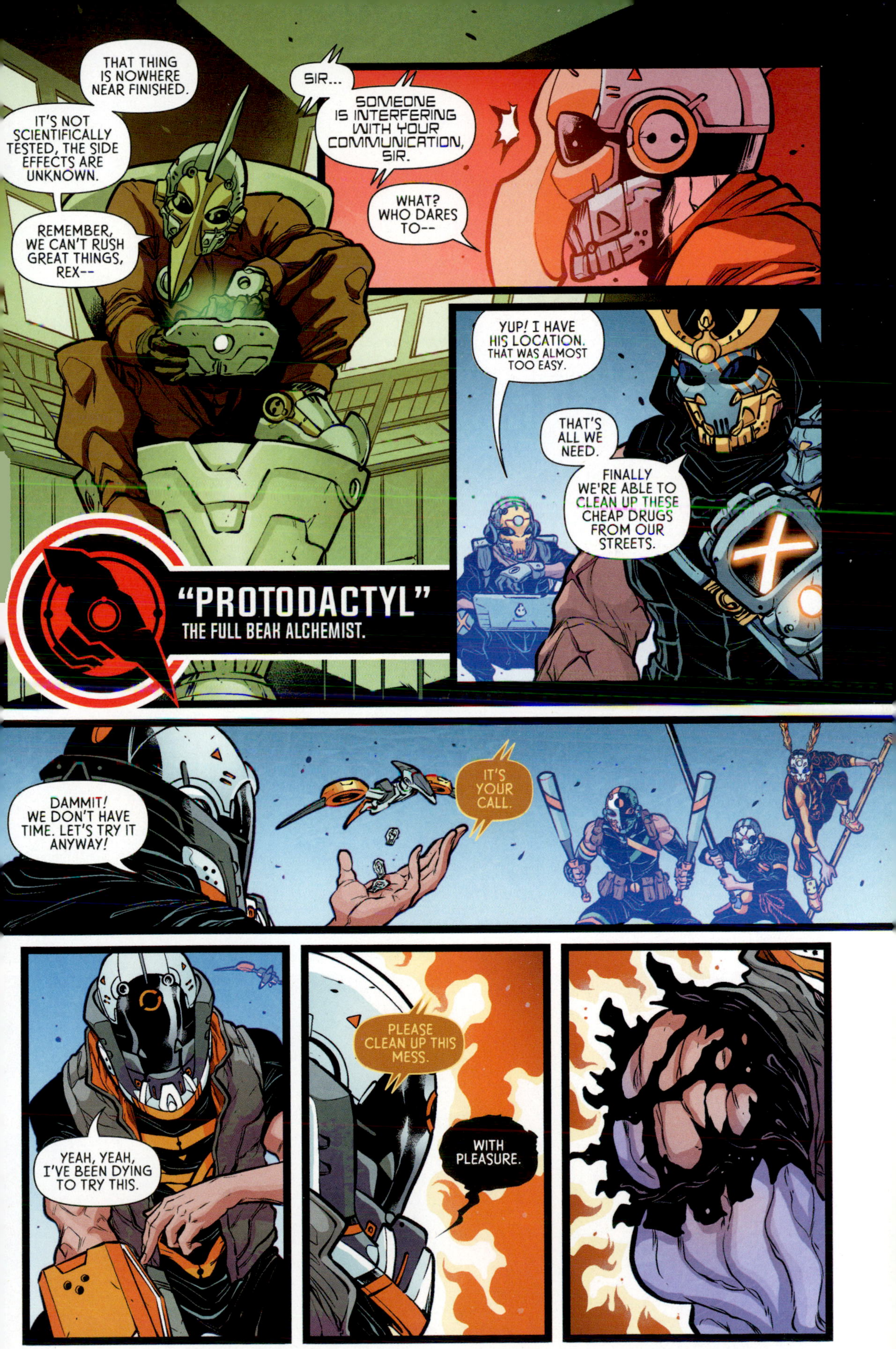

THAT THING IS NOWHERE NEAR FINISHED.
IT'S NOT SCIENTIFICALLY TESTED, THE SIDE EFFECTS ARE UNKNOWN.
REMEMBER, WE CAN'T RUSH GREAT THINGS, REX--
SIR...
SOMEONE IS INTERFERING WITH YOUR COMMUNICATION, SIR.
WHAT? WHO DARES TO--
YUP! I HAVE HIS LOCATION. THAT WAS ALMOST TOO EASY.
THAT'S ALL WE NEED.
FINALLY WE'RE ABLE TO CLEAN UP THESE CHEAP DRUGS FROM OUR STREETS.
"PROTODACTYL"
THE FULL BEAK ALCHEMIST.
DAMMIT! WE DON'T HAVE TIME. LET'S TRY IT ANYWAY!
IT'S YOUR CALL.
YEAH, YEAH, I'VE BEEN DYING TO TRY THIS.
PLEASE CLEAN UP THIS MESS.
WITH PLEASURE.

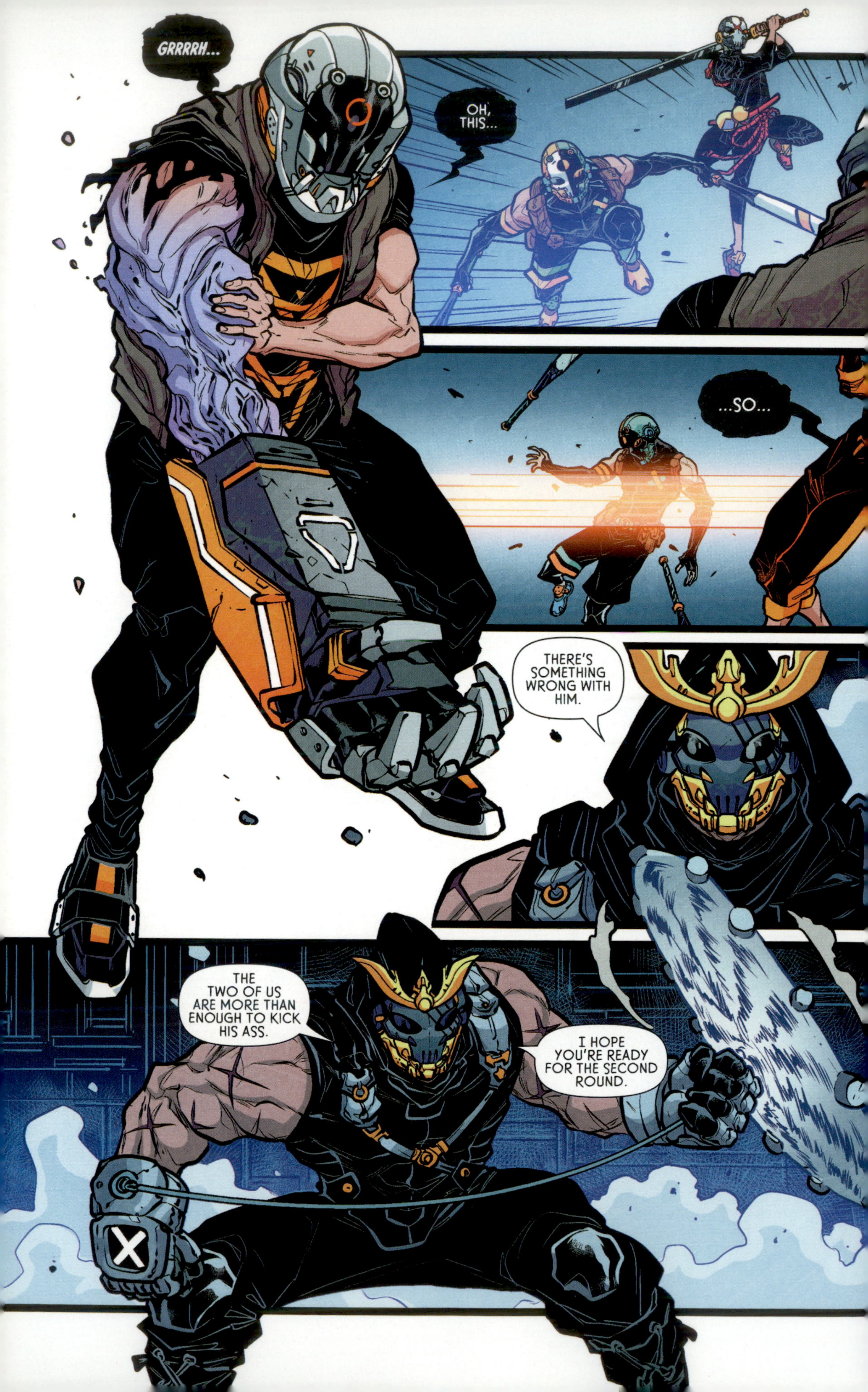
GRRRRH...
OH, THIS...
...SO...
THERE'S SOMETHING WRONG WITH HIM.
THE TWO OF US ARE MORE THAN ENOUGH TO KICK HIS ASS.
I HOPE YOU'RE READY FOR THE SECOND ROUND.

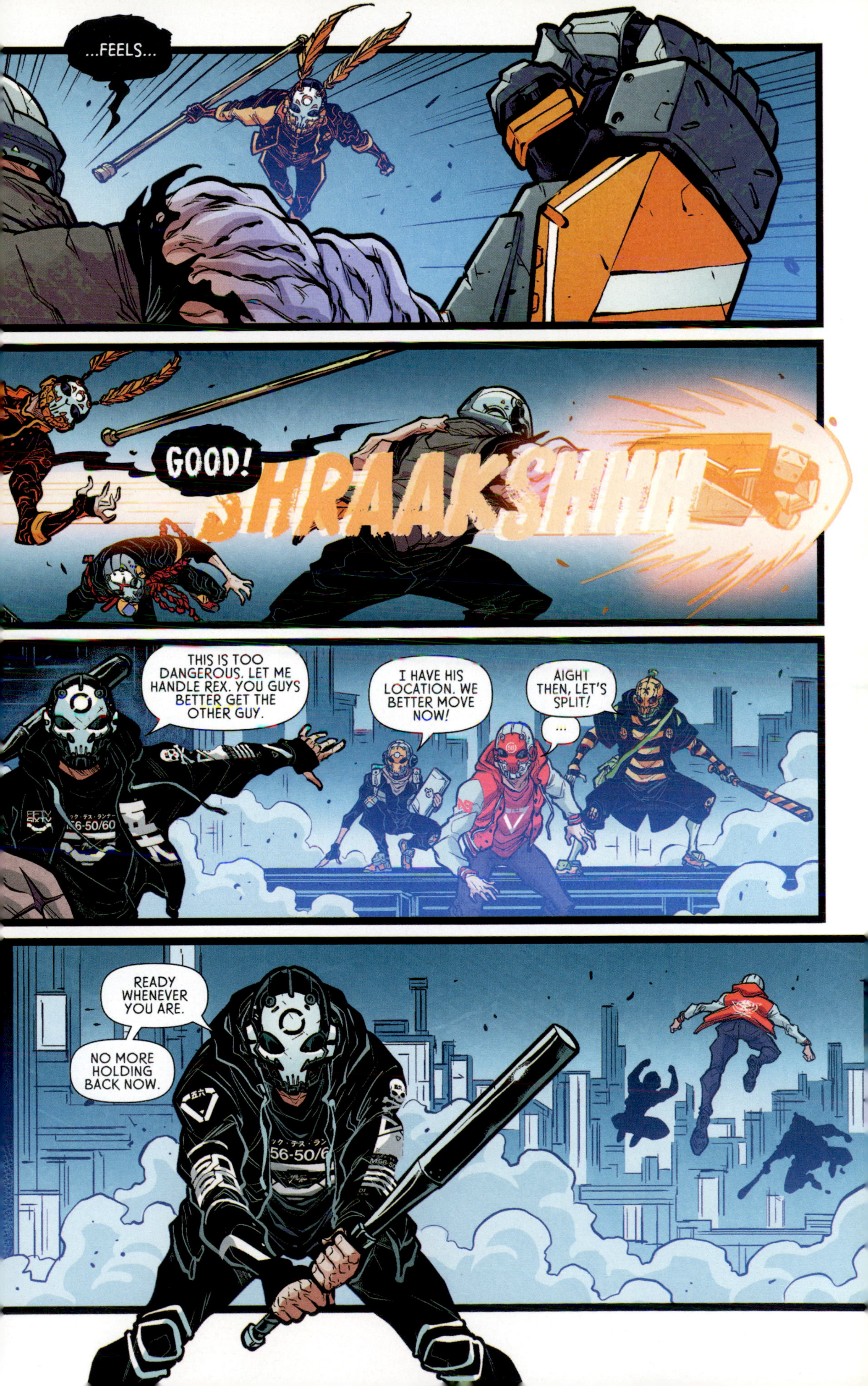
...FEELS...
GOOD!
SHRAAKSHHH
THIS IS TOO DANGEROUS. LET ME HANDLE REX. YOU GUYS BETTER GET THE OTHER GUY.
I HAVE HIS LOCATION. WE BETTER MOVE NOW!
AIGHT THEN, LET'S SPLIT!
...
READY WHENEVER YOU ARE.
NO MORE HOLDING BACK NOW.

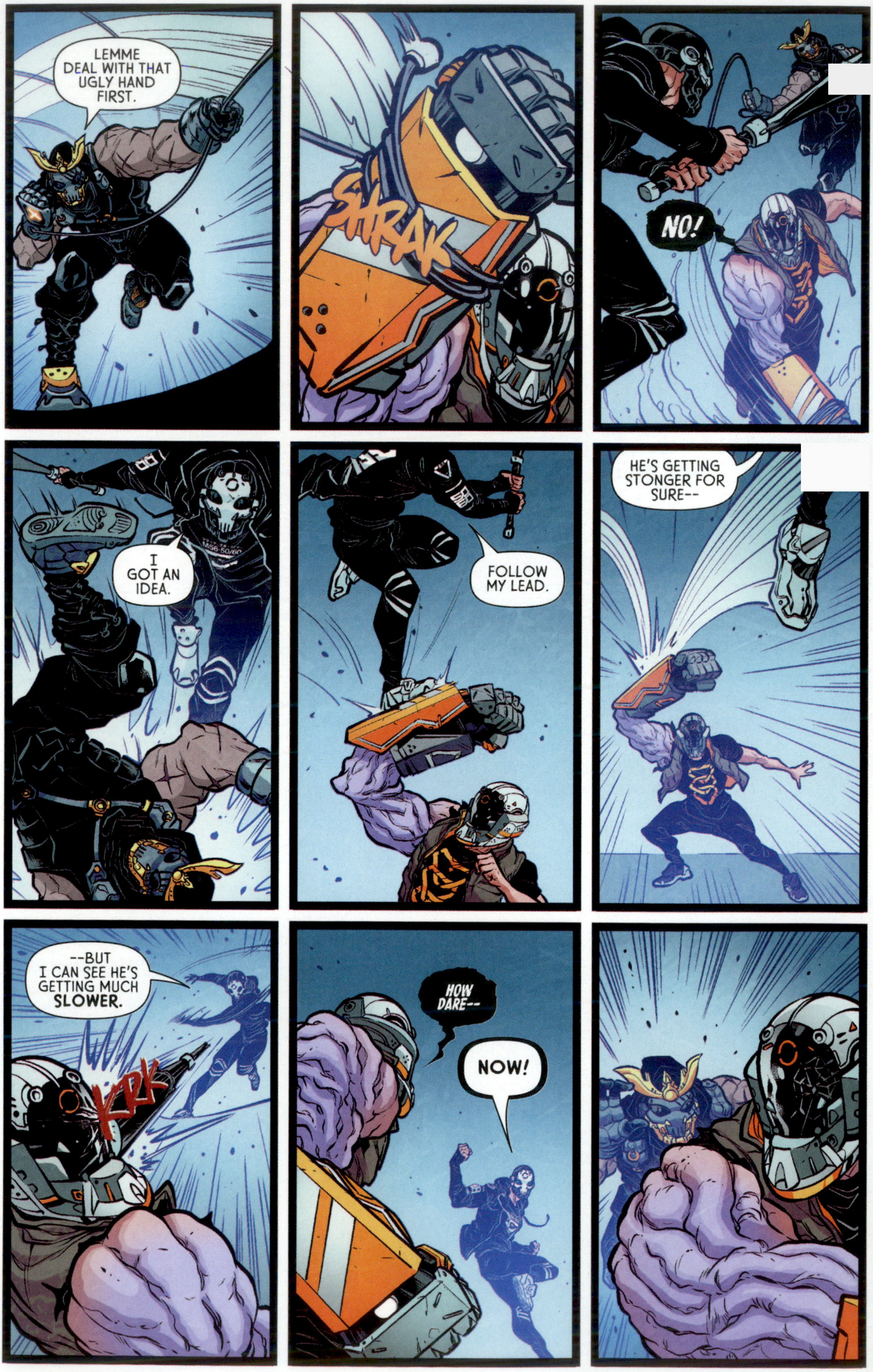
LEMME DEAL WITH THAT UGLY HAND FIRST.
SHRAK
NO!
I GOT AN IDEA.
FOLLOW MY LEAD.
HE'S GETTING STONGER FOR SURE--
--BUT I CAN SEE HE'S GETTING MUCH SLOWER.
KRK
HOW DARE--
NOW!

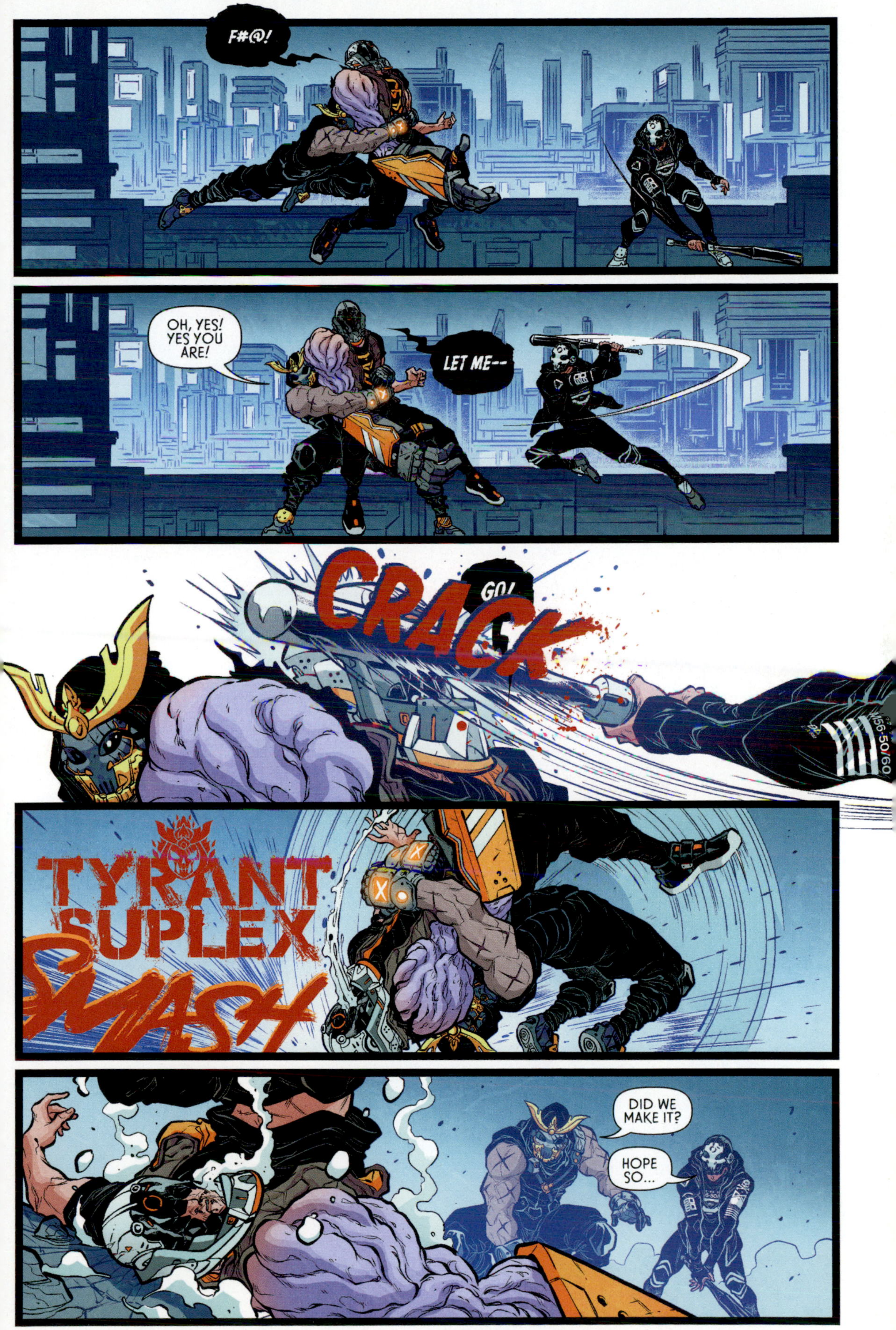
F#@!
OH, YES! YES YOU ARE!
LET ME--
CRACK
GO!
TYRANT SUPLEX
SMASH
DID WE MAKE IT?
HOPE SO...

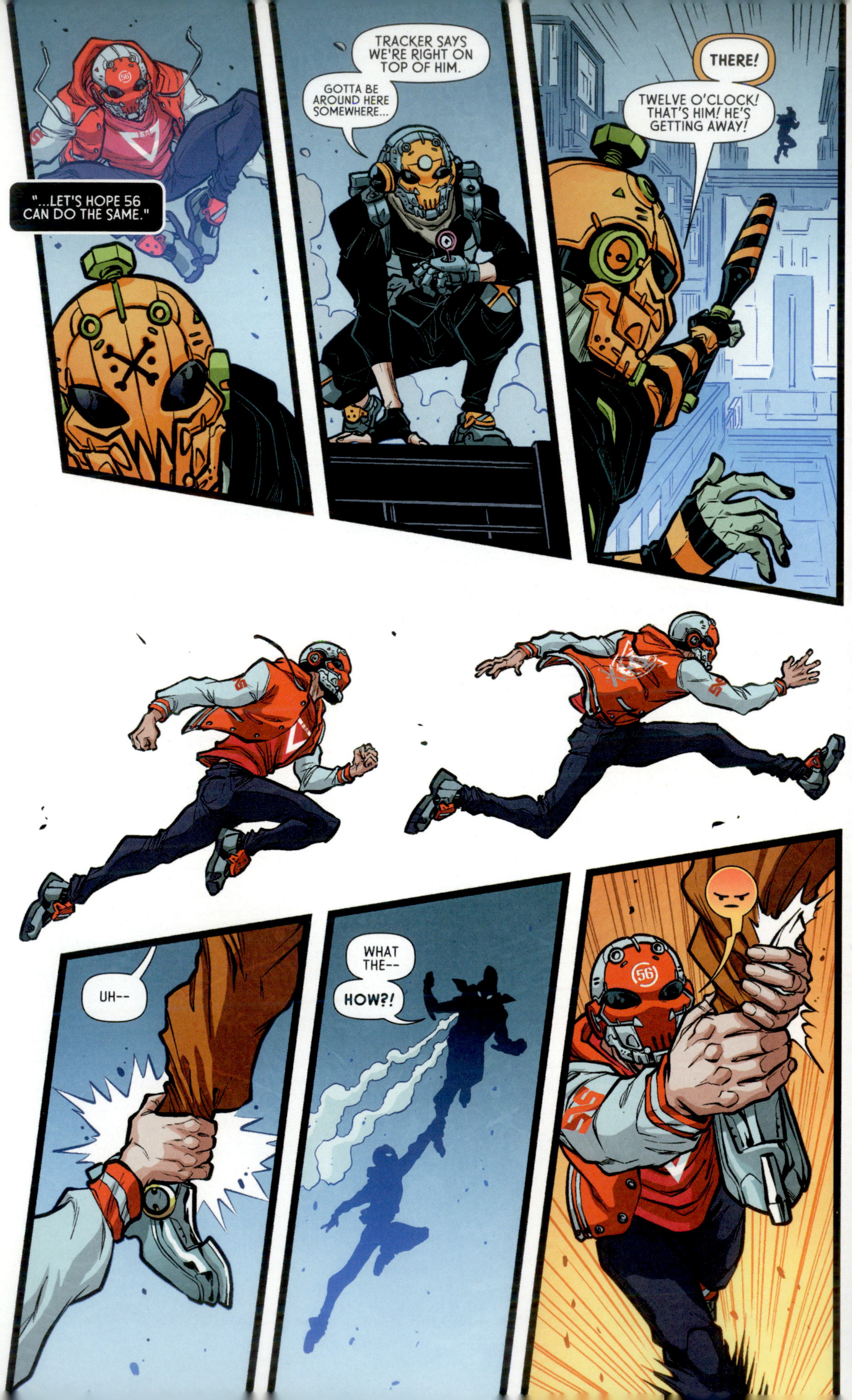
"...LET'S HOPE 56 CAN DO THE SAME."
TRACKER SAYS WE'RE RIGHT ON TOP OF HIM.
GOTTA BE AROUND HERE SOMEWHERE...
THERE!
TWELVE O'CLOCK! THAT'S HIM! HE'S GETTING AWAY!
UH--
WHAT THE--
HOW?!

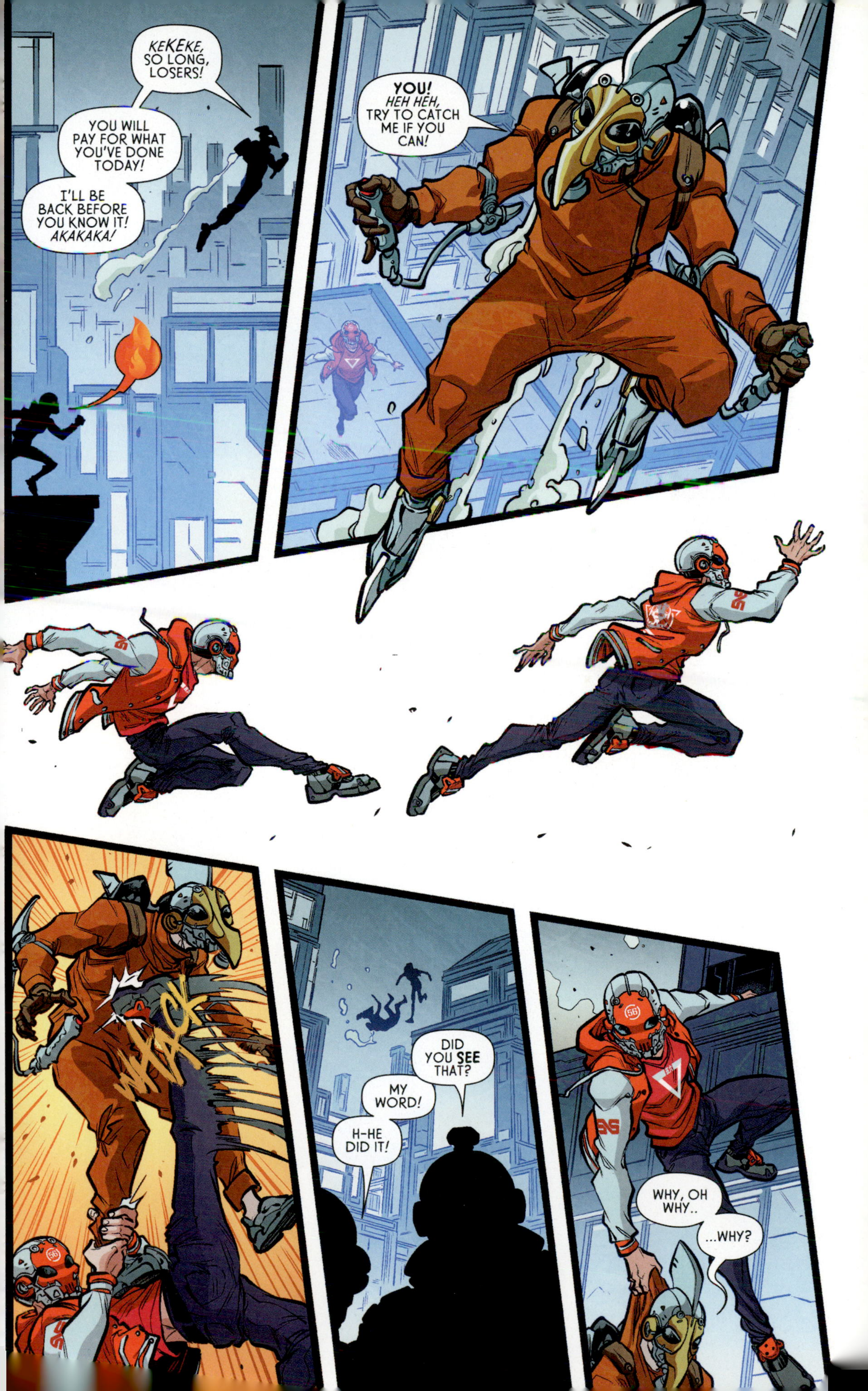
KEKEKE, SO LONG, LOSERS!
YOU WILL PAY FOR WHAT YOU'VE DONE TODAY!
I'LL BE BACK BEFORE YOU KNOW IT! AKAKAKA!
YOU! HEH HEH, TRY TO CATCH ME IF YOU CAN!
WHACK
DID YOU SEE THAT?
MY WORD!
H-HE DID IT!
WHY, OH WHY..
...WHY?

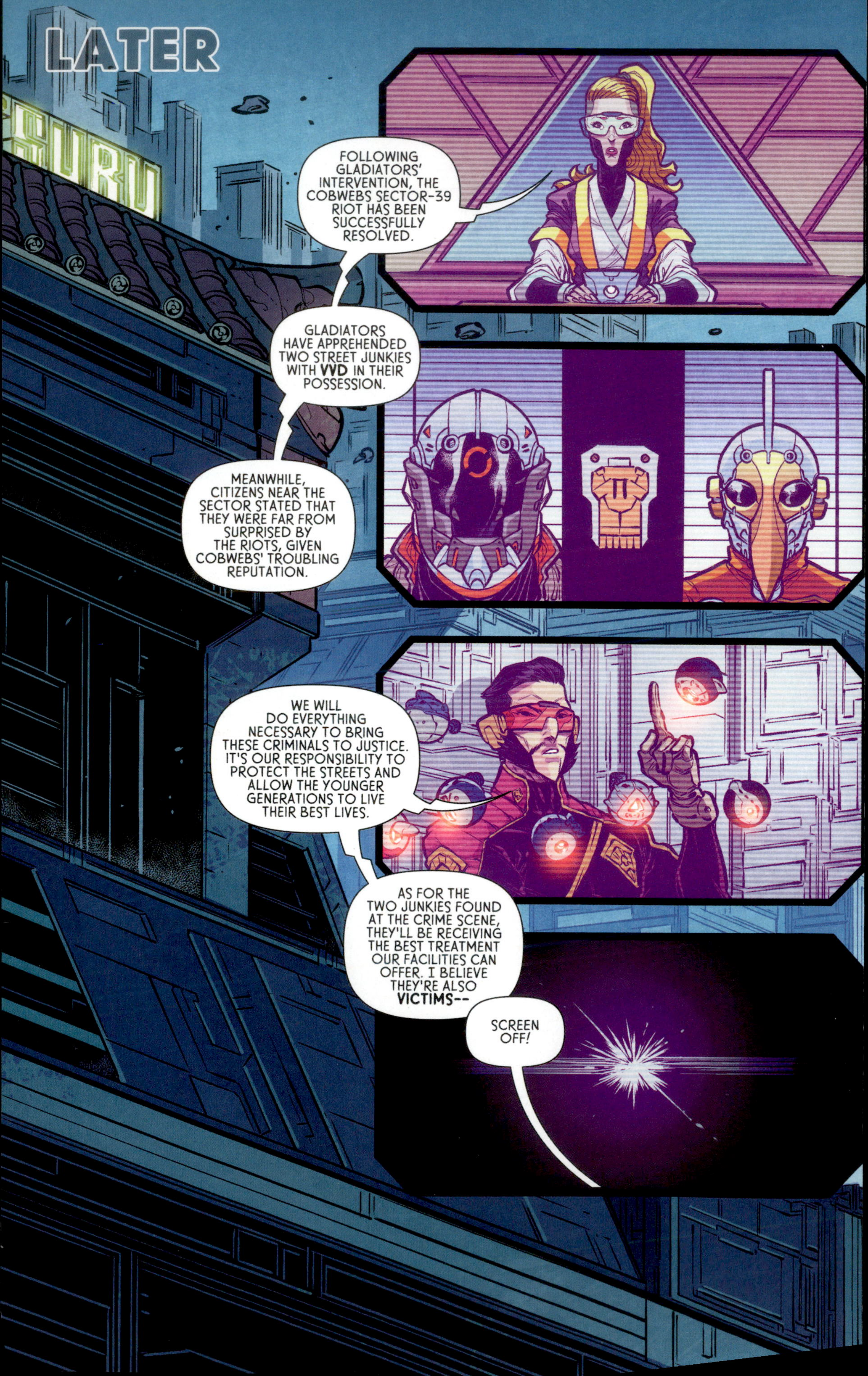
LATER
FOLLOWING GLADIATORS' INTERVENTION, THE COBWEBS SECTOR-39 RIOT HAS BEEN SUCCESSFULLY RESOLVED.
GLADIATORS HAVE APPREHENDED TWO STREET JUNKIES WITH **VVD** IN THEIR POSSESSION.
MEANWHILE, CITIZENS NEAR THE SECTOR STATED THAT THEY WERE FAR FROM SURPRISED BY THE RIOTS, GIVEN COBWEBS' TROUBLING REPUTATION.
WE WILL DO EVERYTHING NECESSARY TO BRING THESE CRIMINALS TO JUSTICE. IT'S OUR RESPONSIBILITY TO PROTECT THE STREETS AND ALLOW THE YOUNGER GENERATIONS TO LIVE THEIR BEST LIVES.
AS FOR THE TWO JUNKIES FOUND AT THE CRIME SCENE, THEY'LL BE RECEIVING THE BEST TREATMENT OUR FACILITIES CAN OFFER. I BELIEVE THEY'RE ALSO **VICTIMS--**
SCREEN OFF!

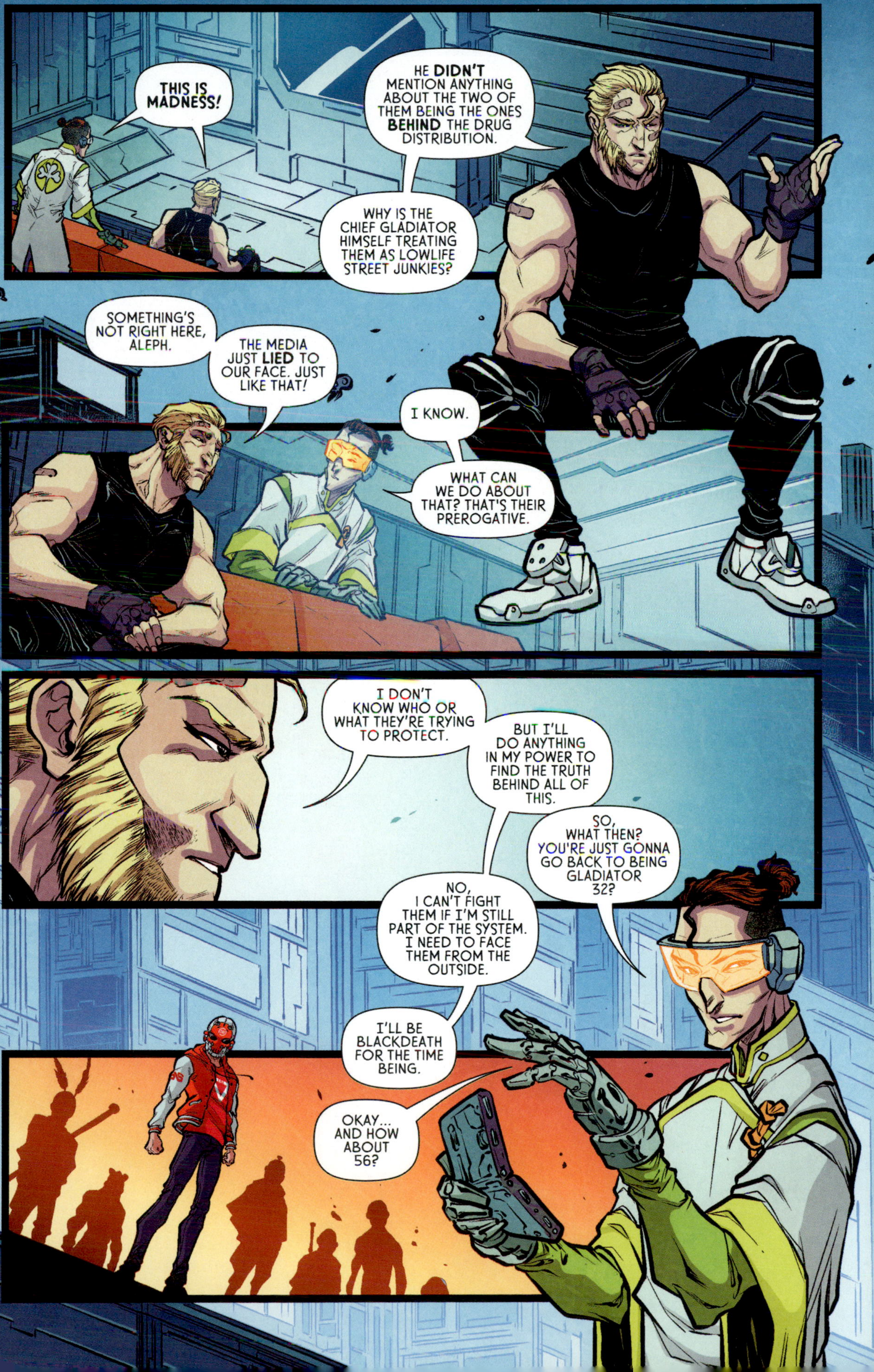
THIS IS MADNESS!
HE DIDN'T MENTION ANYTHING ABOUT THE TWO OF THEM BEING THE ONES BEHIND THE DRUG DISTRIBUTION.
WHY IS THE CHIEF GLADIATOR HIMSELF TREATING THEM AS LOWLIFE STREET JUNKIES?
SOMETHING'S NOT RIGHT HERE, ALEPH.
THE MEDIA JUST LIED TO OUR FACE. JUST LIKE THAT!
I KNOW.
WHAT CAN WE DO ABOUT THAT? THAT'S THEIR PREROGATIVE.
I DON'T KNOW WHO OR WHAT THEY'RE TRYING TO PROTECT.
BUT I'LL DO ANYTHING IN MY POWER TO FIND THE TRUTH BEHIND ALL OF THIS.
SO, WHAT THEN? YOU'RE JUST GONNA GO BACK TO BEING GLADIATOR 32?
NO, I CAN'T FIGHT THEM IF I'M STILL PART OF THE SYSTEM. I NEED TO FACE THEM FROM THE OUTSIDE.
I'LL BE BLACKDEATH FOR THE TIME BEING.
OKAY... AND HOW ABOUT 56?

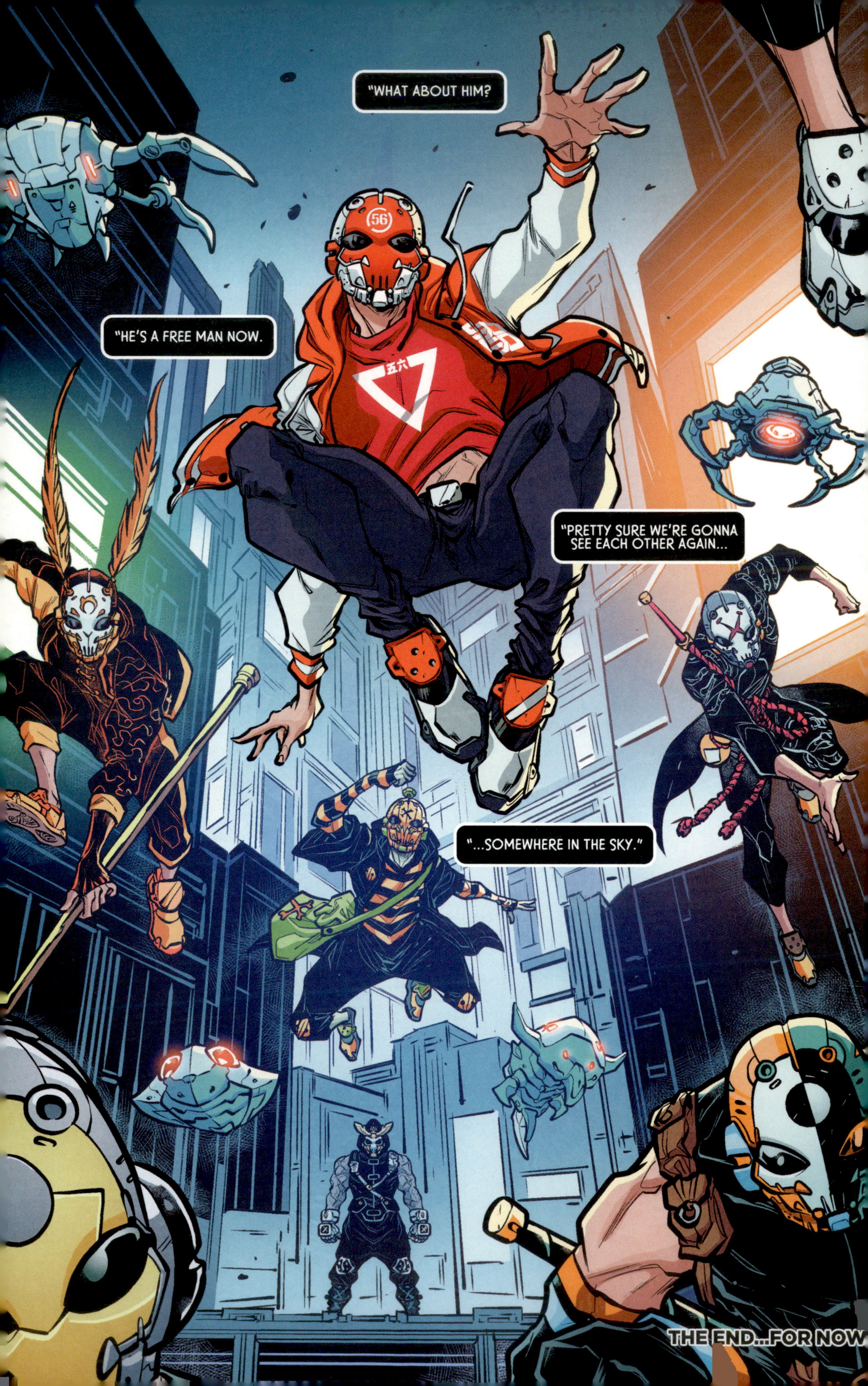
"WHAT ABOUT HIM?
"HE'S A FREE MAN NOW.
"PRETTY SURE WE'RE GONNA SEE EACH OTHER AGAIN...
"...SOMEWHERE IN THE SKY."
THE END...FOR NOW

COVER GALLERY

● ORIGINAL MITSURU.TECH SERIAL #
○ CLOSE QUARTER TYPE_

● SLAVE TYPE BONEHEAD01.
○ BODY STRUCTURE : N/A

● NODE TRACKING AFTER DELETION COURSE
○ EARTH: 7 MEGAPARSECS ACROSS_

ART BY: RHOALD MARCELLIUS

▶M56/001/A   ▶ Bonehead, RED, 16k-Zettabyte.
Designed by Machine56, Assembled by Mitsuru.Tech
MK-I / Not suitable f

(1P) Part No. MT-A0156 / D / Test Subject no.56

ブラック・デス・ランナー

QC/P

五六

5 0 6 0 1 3 0 9

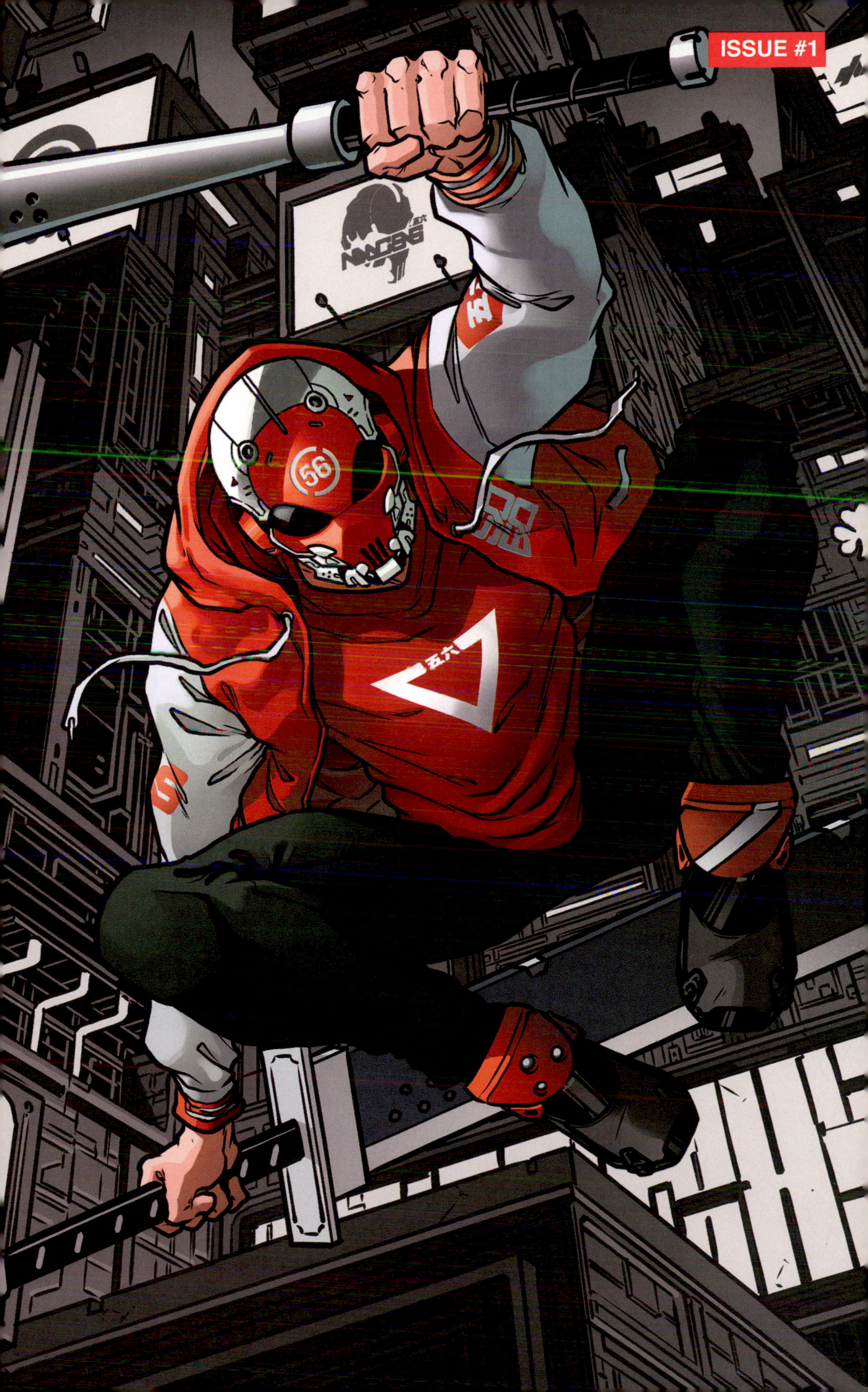
ISSUE #1
56

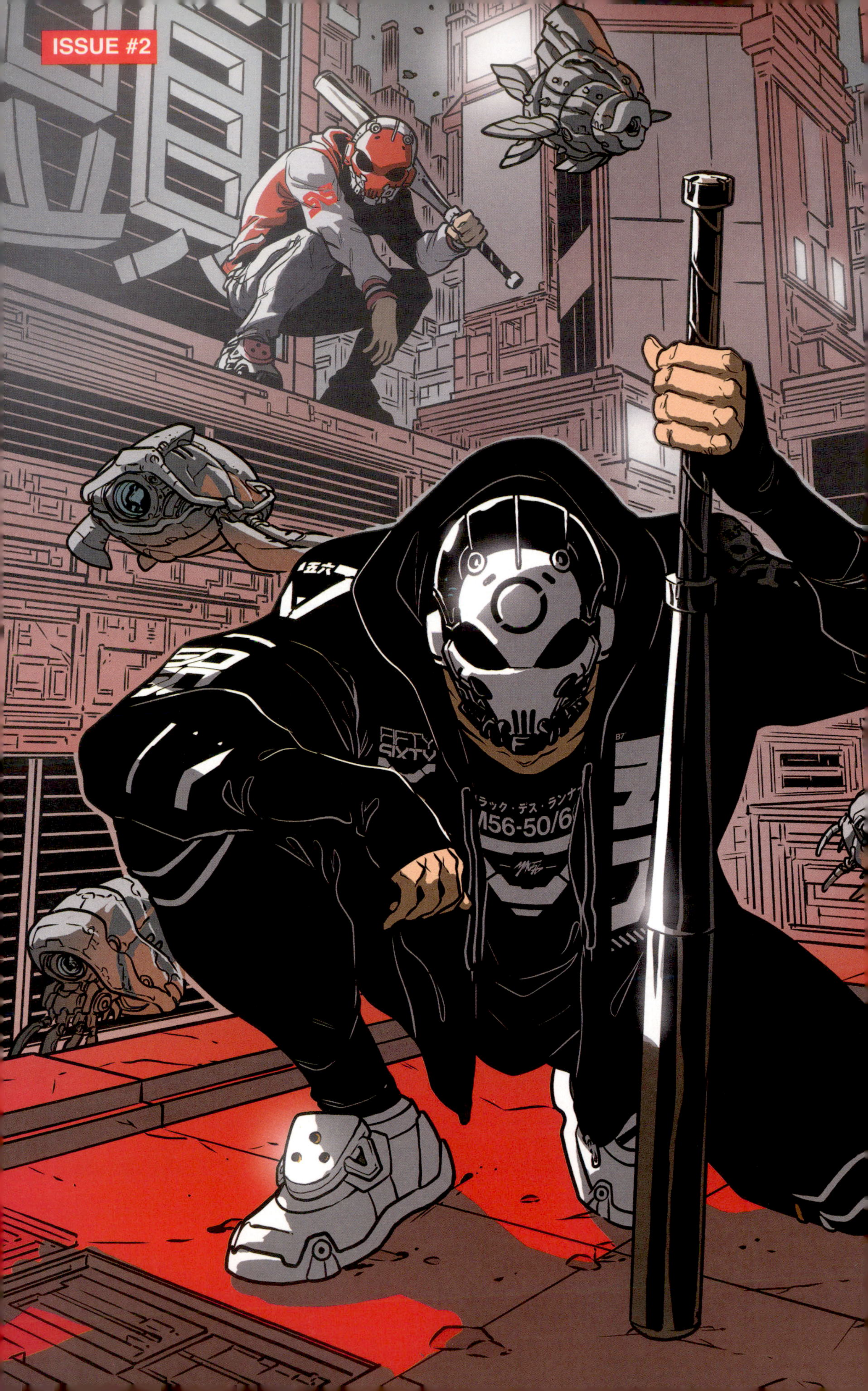
ISSUE #2

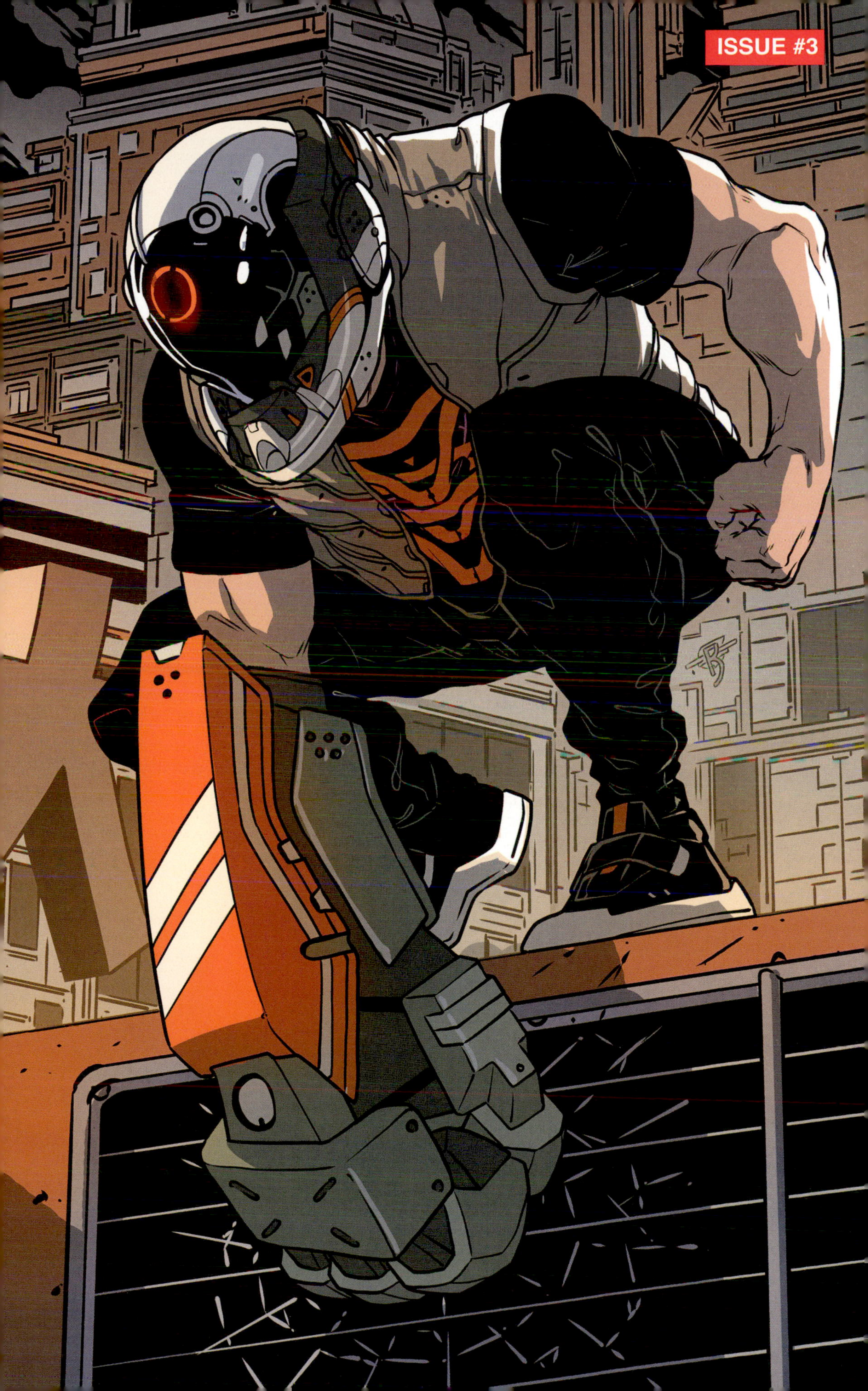
ISSUE #3

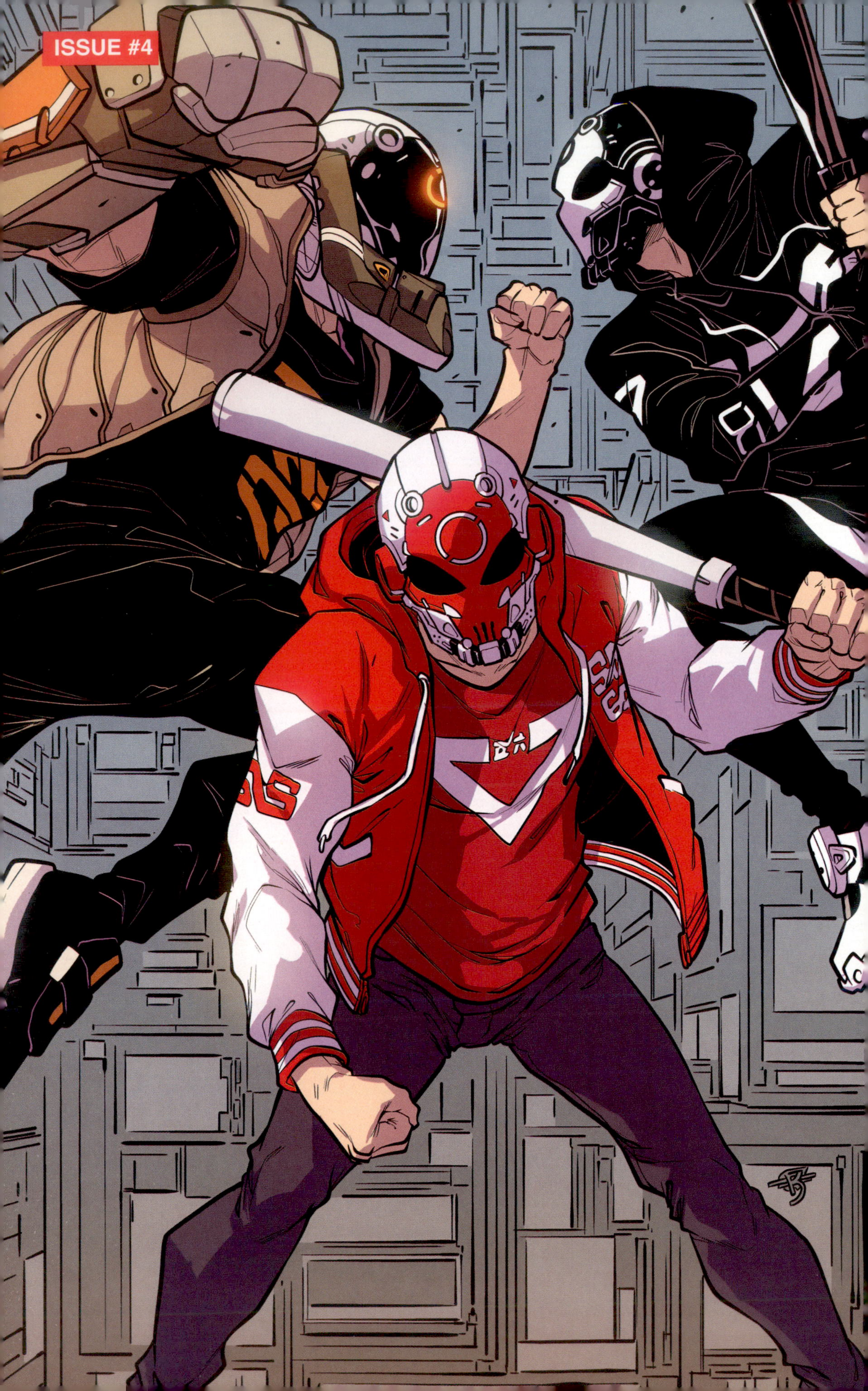
ISSUE #4

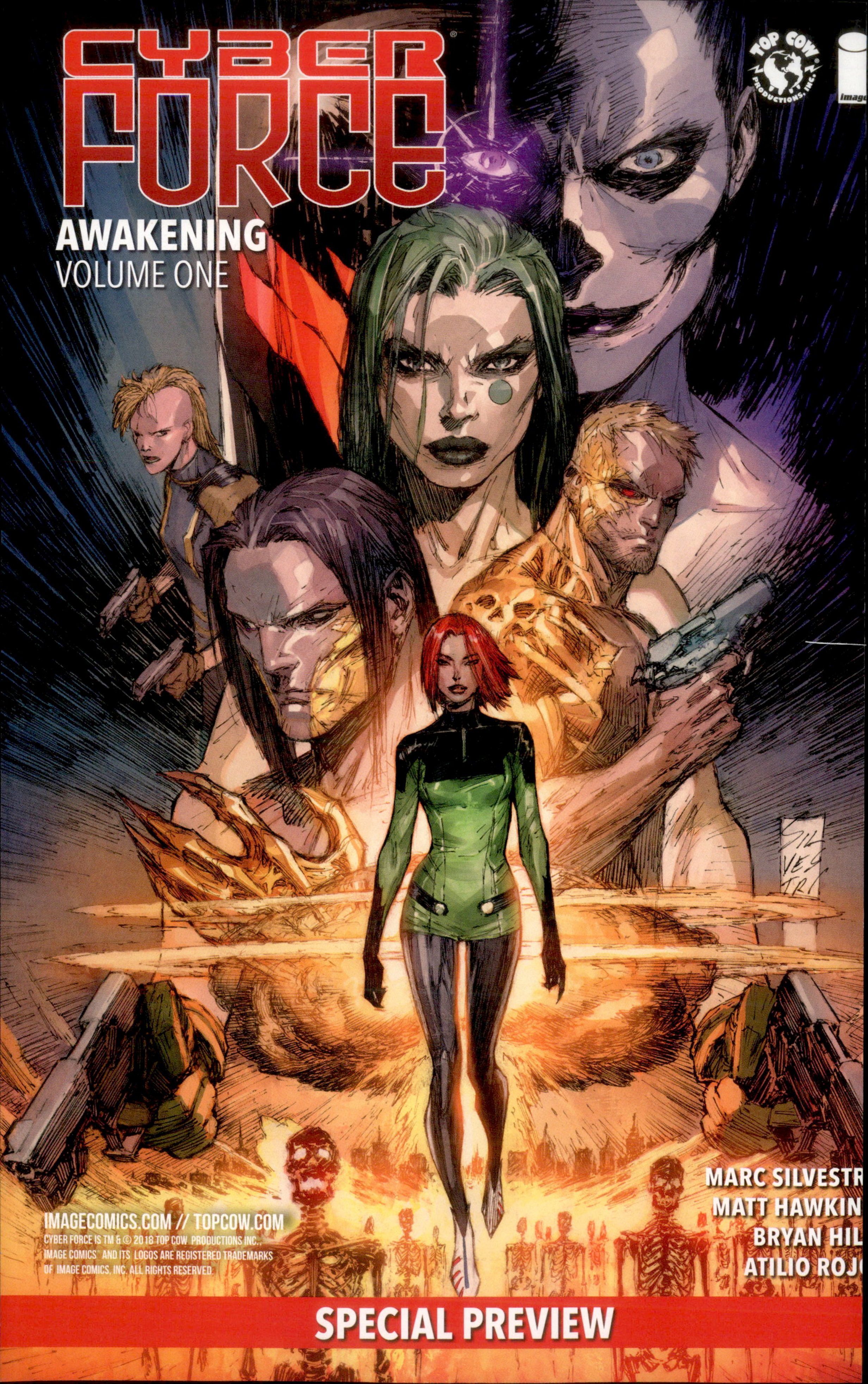
CYBER FORCE
AWAKENING
VOLUME ONE
MARC SILVESTR
MATT HAWKIN
BRYAN HIL
ATILIO ROJ
IMAGECOMICS.COM // TOPCOW.COM
CYBER FORCE IS TM & © 2018 TOP COW PRODUCTIONS INC., IMAGE COMICS® AND ITS LOGOS ARE REGISTERED TRADEMARKS OF IMAGE COMICS, INC. ALL RIGHTS RESERVED.
SPECIAL PREVIEW

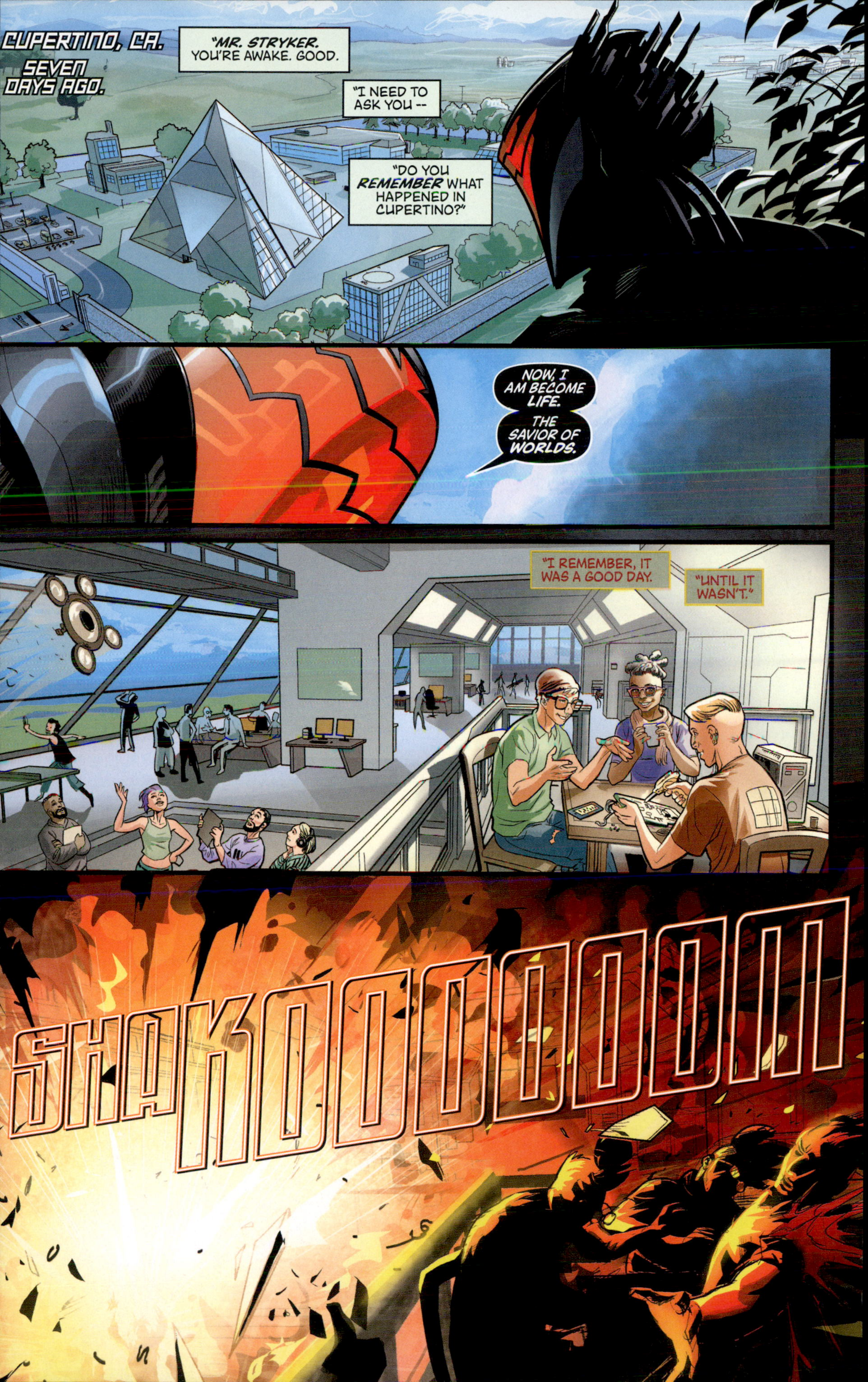
CUPERTINO, CA.
SEVEN DAYS AGO.
"MR. STRYKER. YOU'RE AWAKE. GOOD.
"I NEED TO ASK YOU --
"DO YOU REMEMBER WHAT HAPPENED IN CUPERTINO?"
NOW, I AM BECOME LIFE.
THE SAVIOR OF WORLDS.
"I REMEMBER, IT WAS A GOOD DAY.
"UNTIL IT WASN'T."
SHAKOOOOOOM

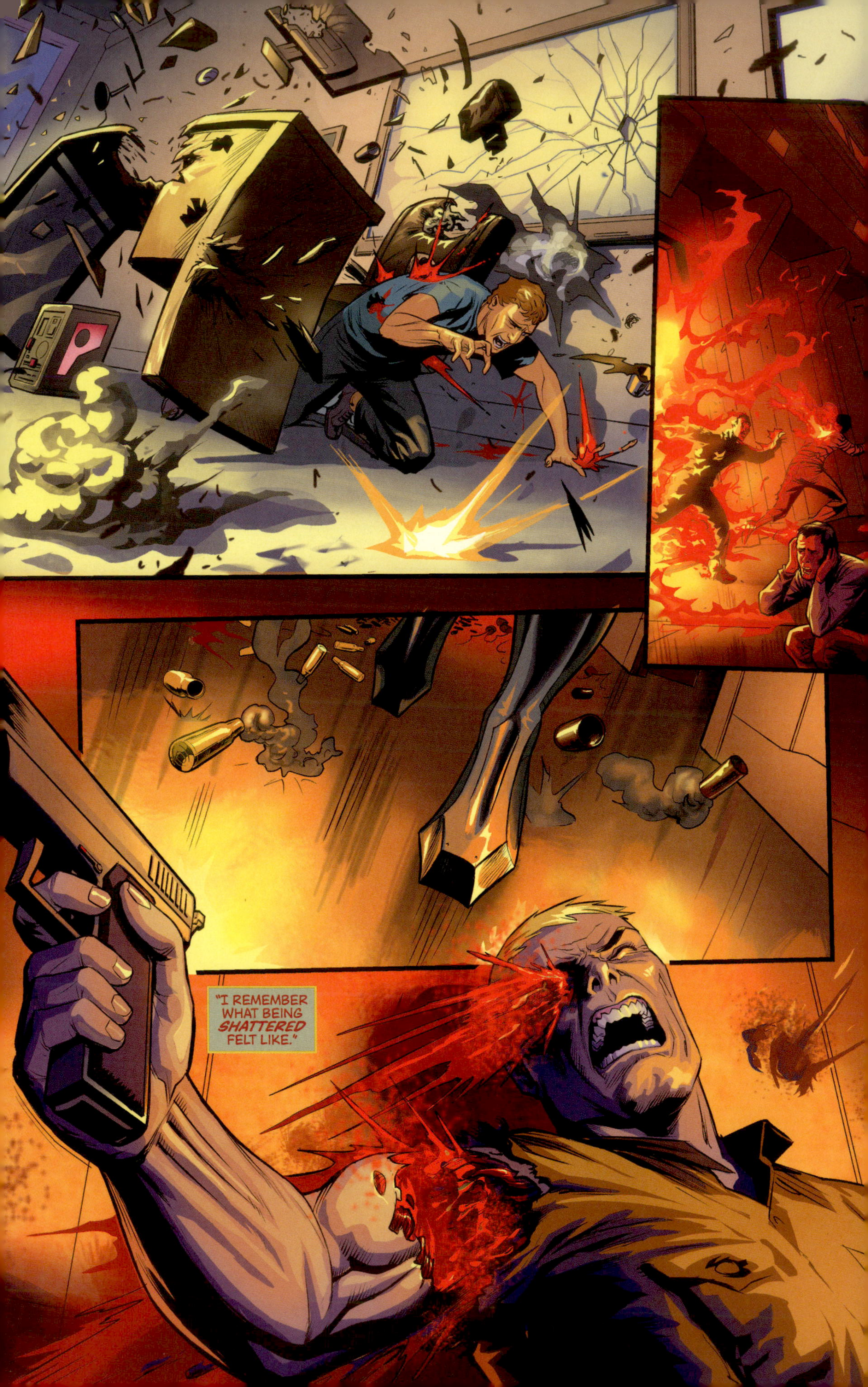
"I REMEMBER WHAT BEING SHATTERED FELT LIKE."

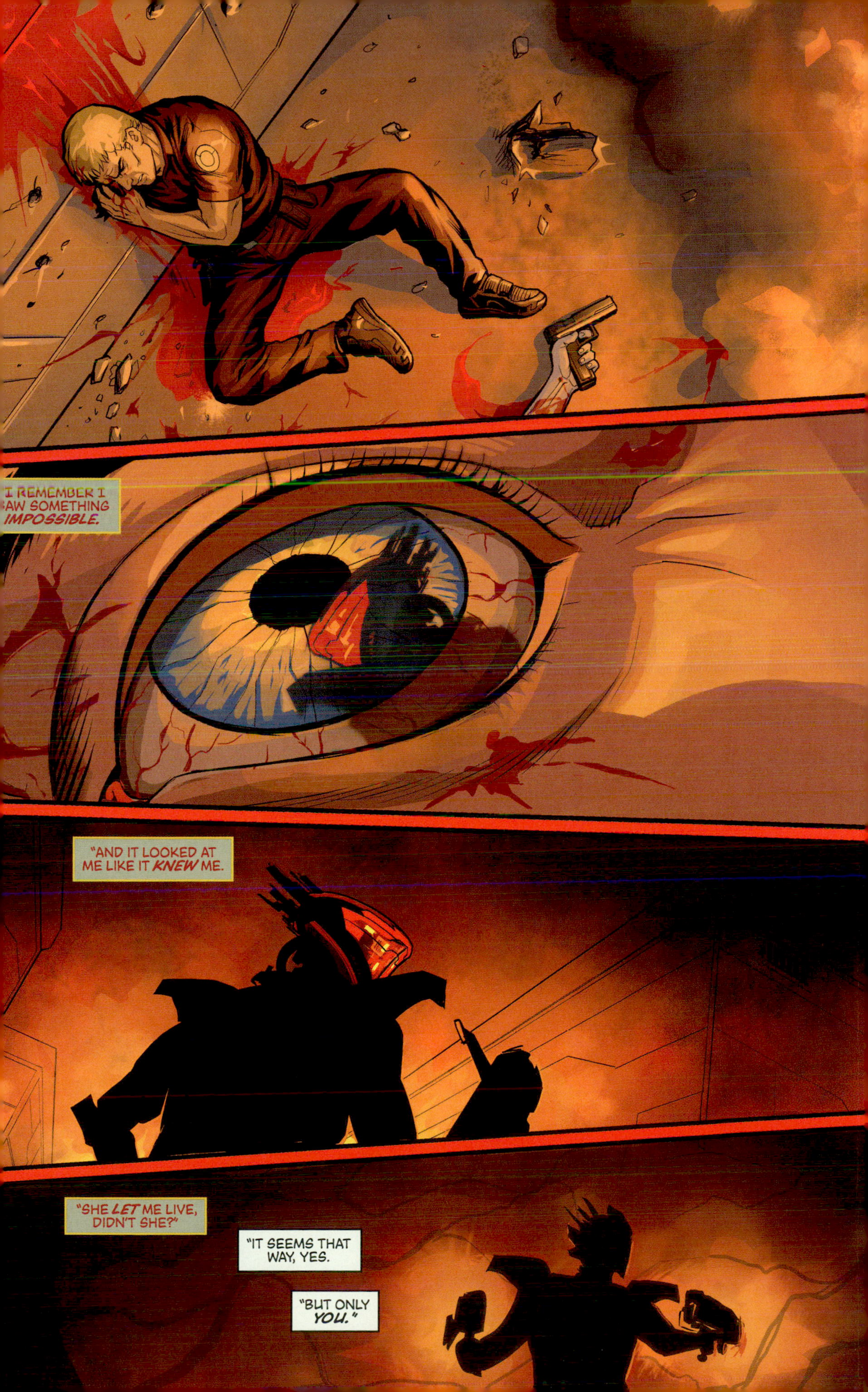
I REMEMBER I SAW SOMETHING IMPOSSIBLE.
"AND IT LOOKED AT ME LIKE IT KNEW ME.
"SHE LET ME LIVE, DIDN'T SHE?"
"IT SEEMS THAT WAY, YES.
"BUT ONLY YOU."

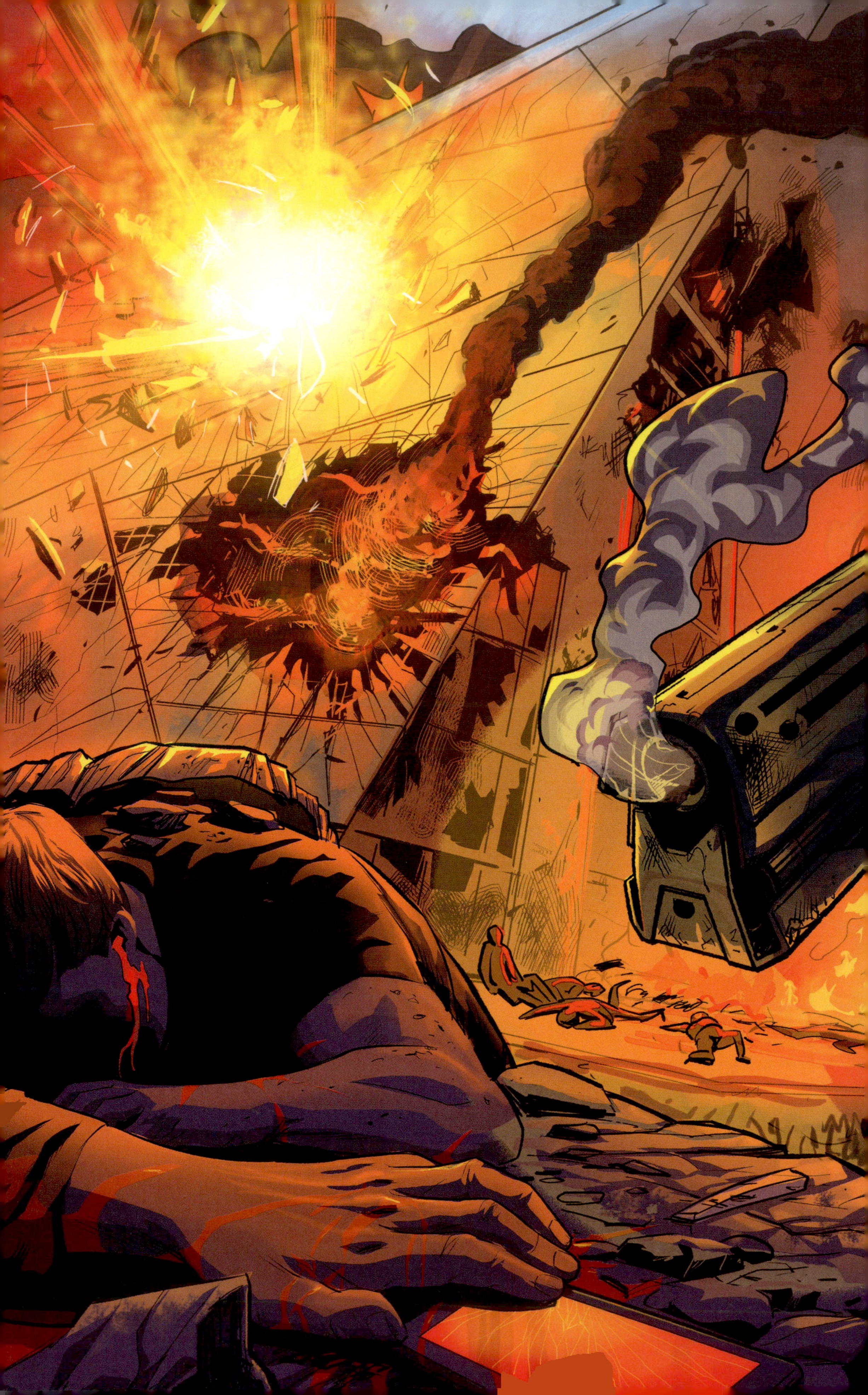

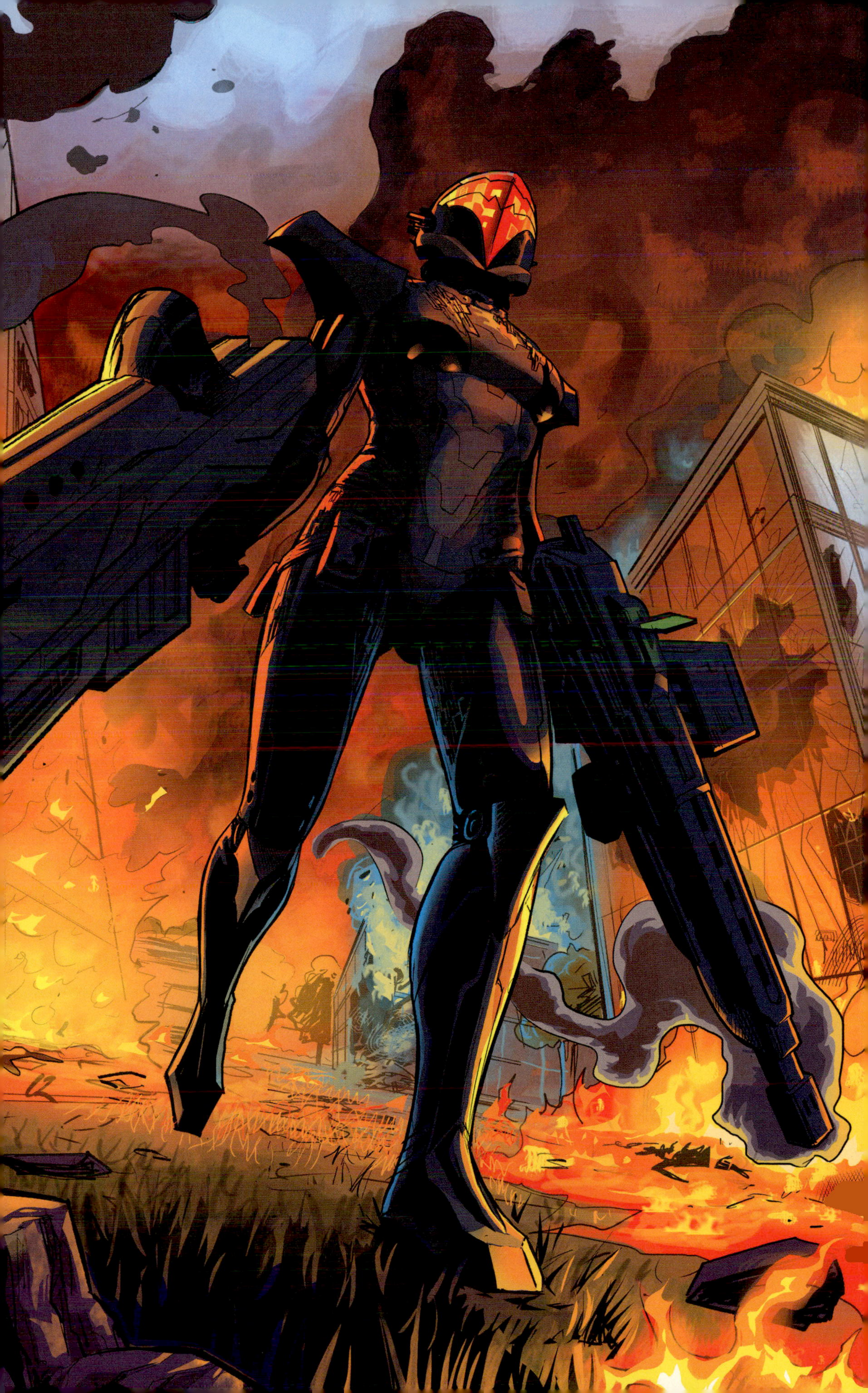

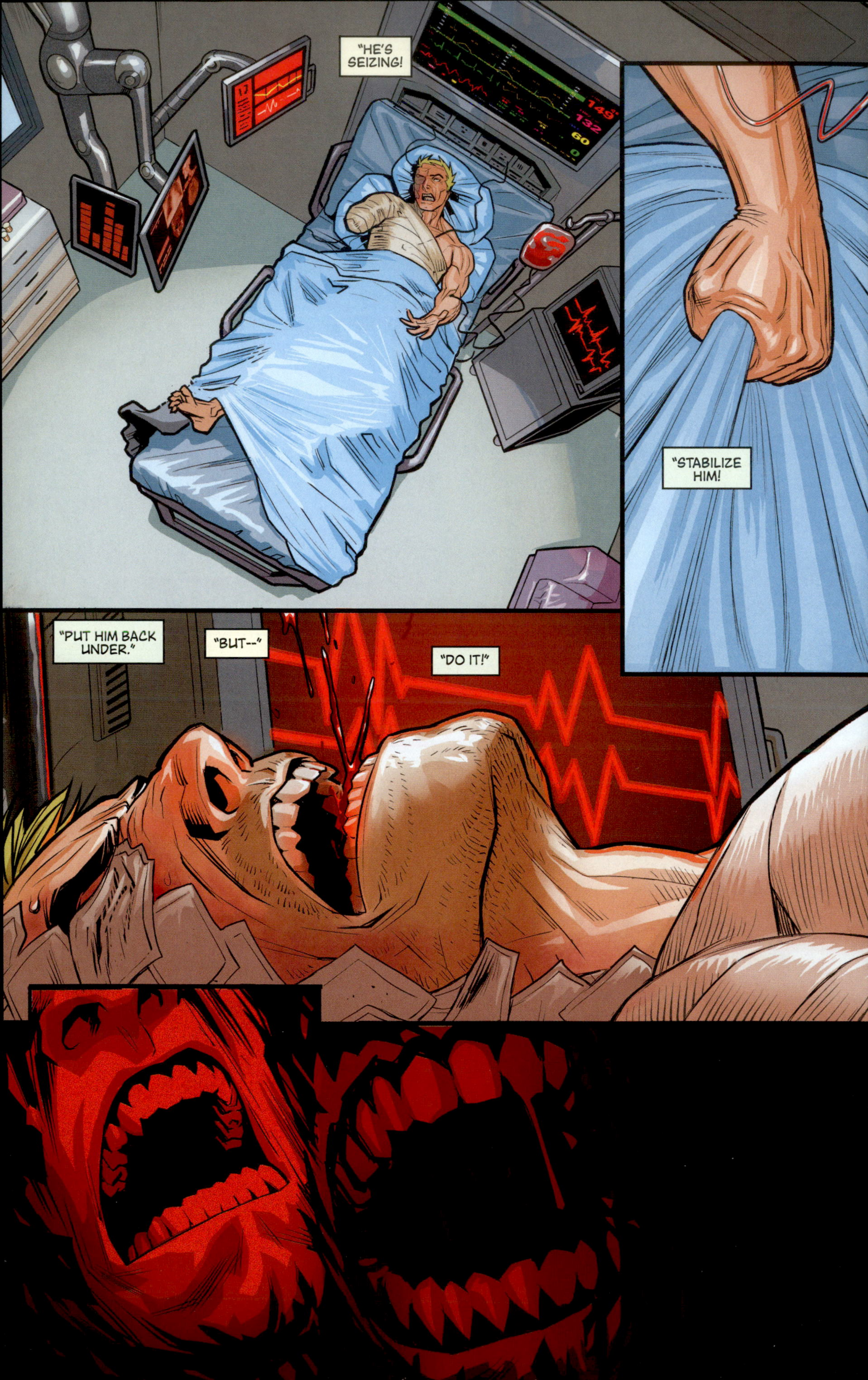
"HE'S SEIZING!
"STABILIZE HIM!
"PUT HIM BACK UNDER."
"BUT--"
"DO IT!"

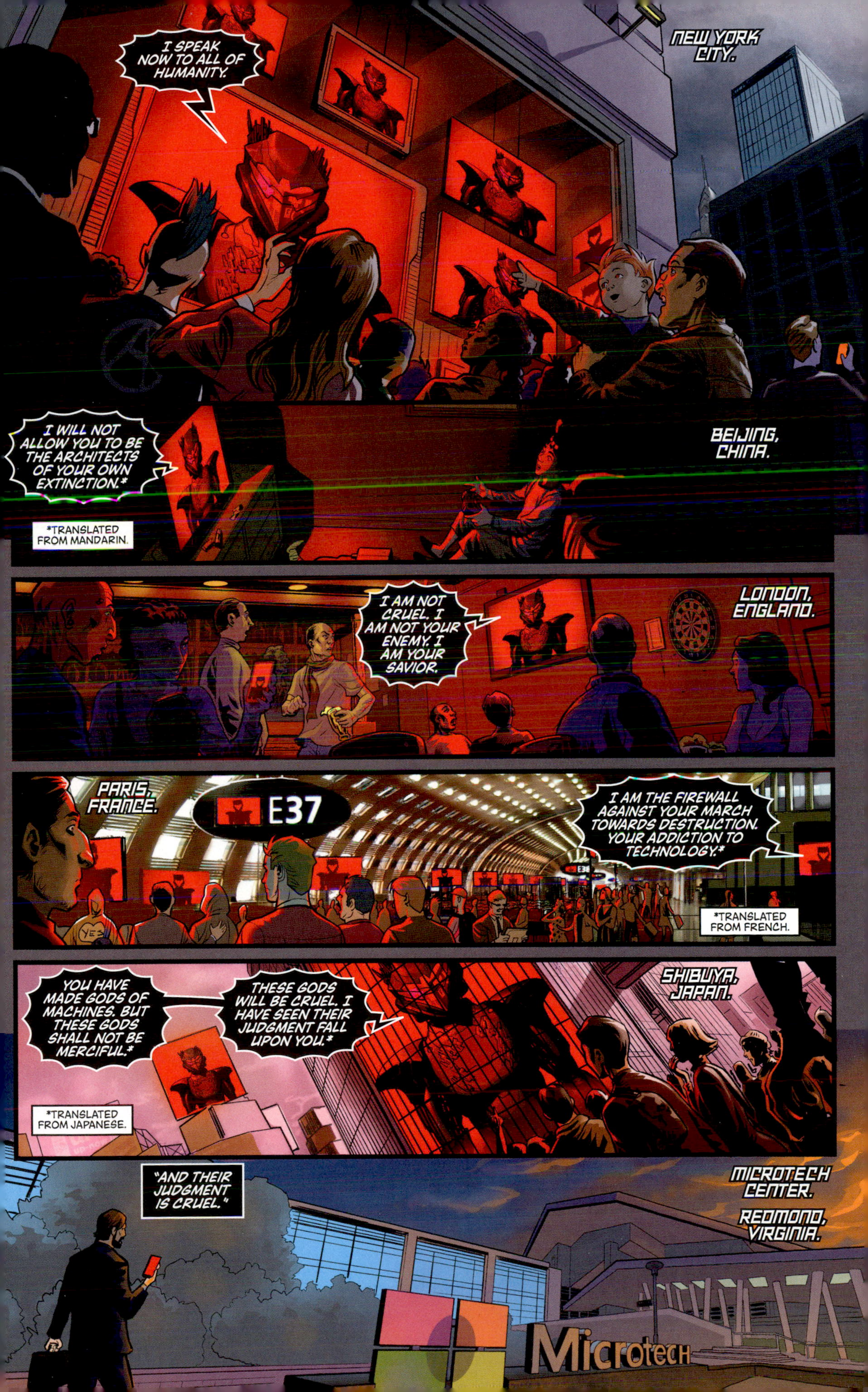
NEW YORK CITY.
I SPEAK NOW TO ALL OF HUMANITY.
BEIJING, CHINA.
I WILL NOT ALLOW YOU TO BE THE ARCHITECTS OF YOUR OWN EXTINCTION.*
*TRANSLATED FROM MANDARIN.
LONDON, ENGLAND.
I AM NOT CRUEL. I AM NOT YOUR ENEMY. I AM YOUR SAVIOR.
PARIS, FRANCE.
E37
I AM THE FIREWALL AGAINST YOUR MARCH TOWARDS DESTRUCTION. YOUR ADDICTION TO TECHNOLOGY.*
*TRANSLATED FROM FRENCH.
SHIBUYA, JAPAN.
YOU HAVE MADE GODS OF MACHINES. BUT THESE GODS SHALL NOT BE MERCIFUL.*
THESE GODS WILL BE CRUEL. I HAVE SEEN THEIR JUDGMENT FALL UPON YOU.*
*TRANSLATED FROM JAPANESE.
"AND THEIR JUDGMENT IS CRUEL."
MICROTECH CENTER.
REDMOND, VIRGINIA.
Microtech

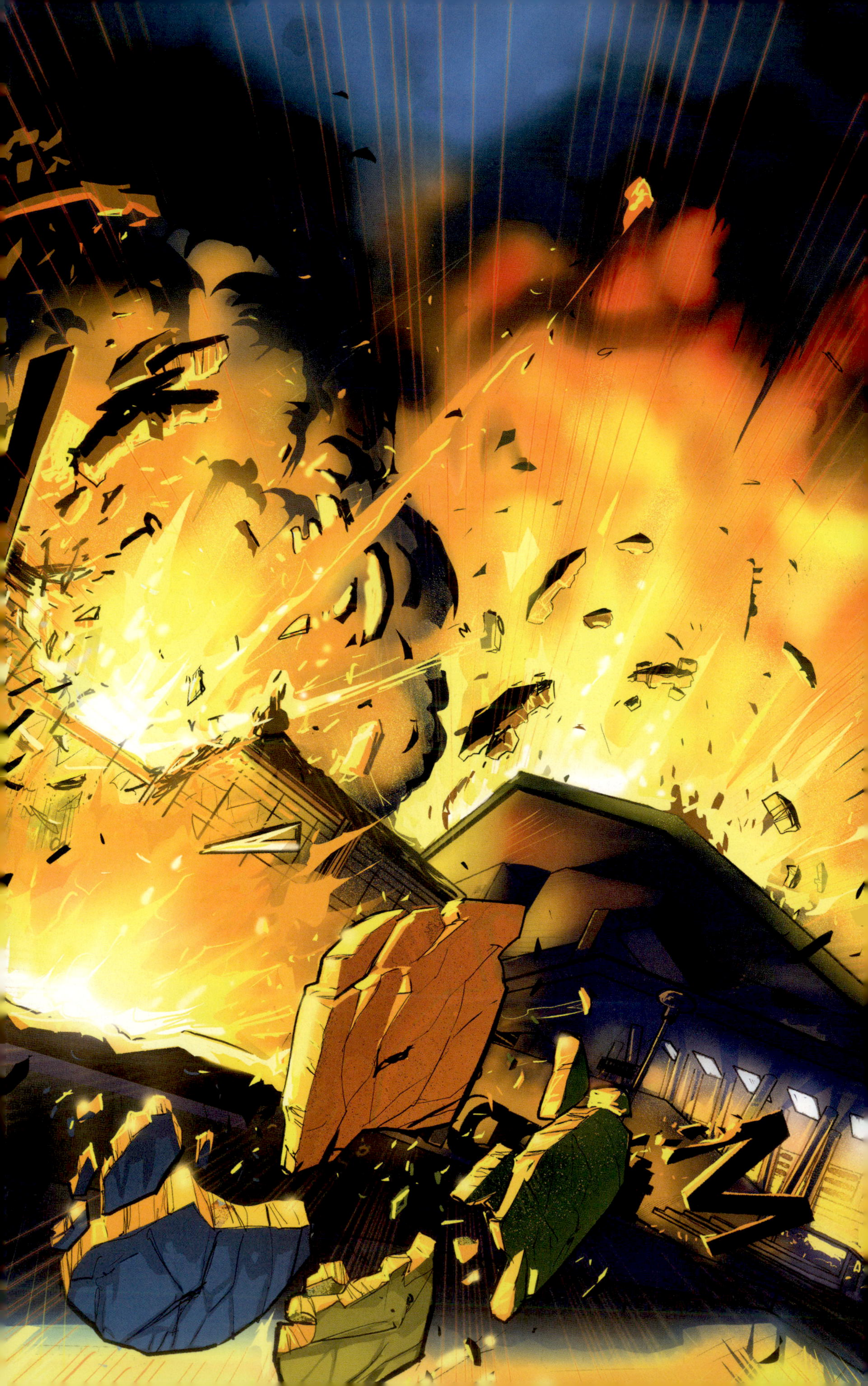

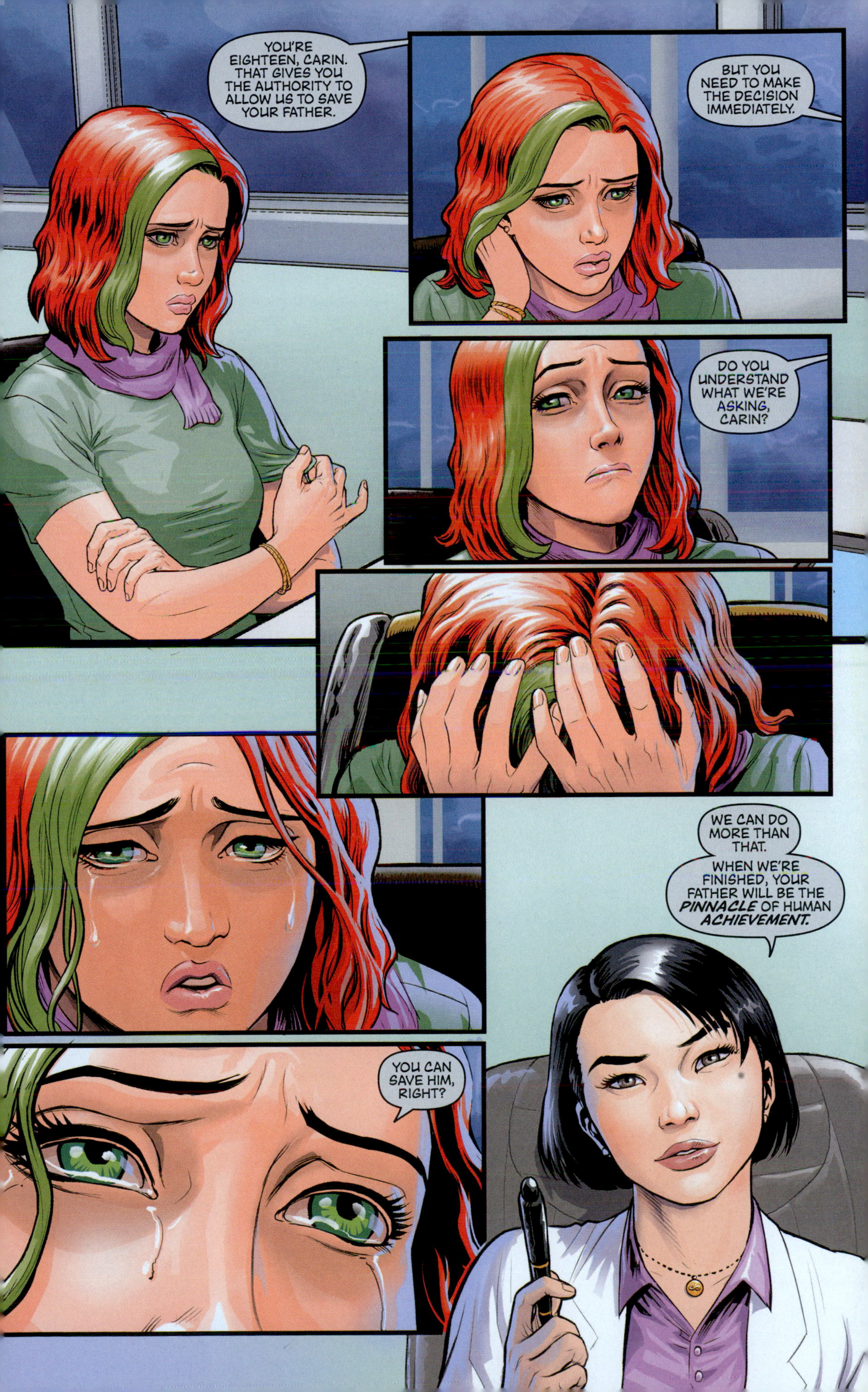
YOU'RE EIGHTEEN, CARIN. THAT GIVES YOU THE AUTHORITY TO ALLOW US TO SAVE YOUR FATHER.
BUT YOU NEED TO MAKE THE DECISION IMMEDIATELY.
DO YOU UNDERSTAND WHAT WE'RE ASKING, CARIN?
YOU CAN SAVE HIM, RIGHT?
WE CAN DO MORE THAN THAT.
WHEN WE'RE FINISHED, YOUR FATHER WILL BE THE PINNACLE OF HUMAN ACHIEVEMENT.

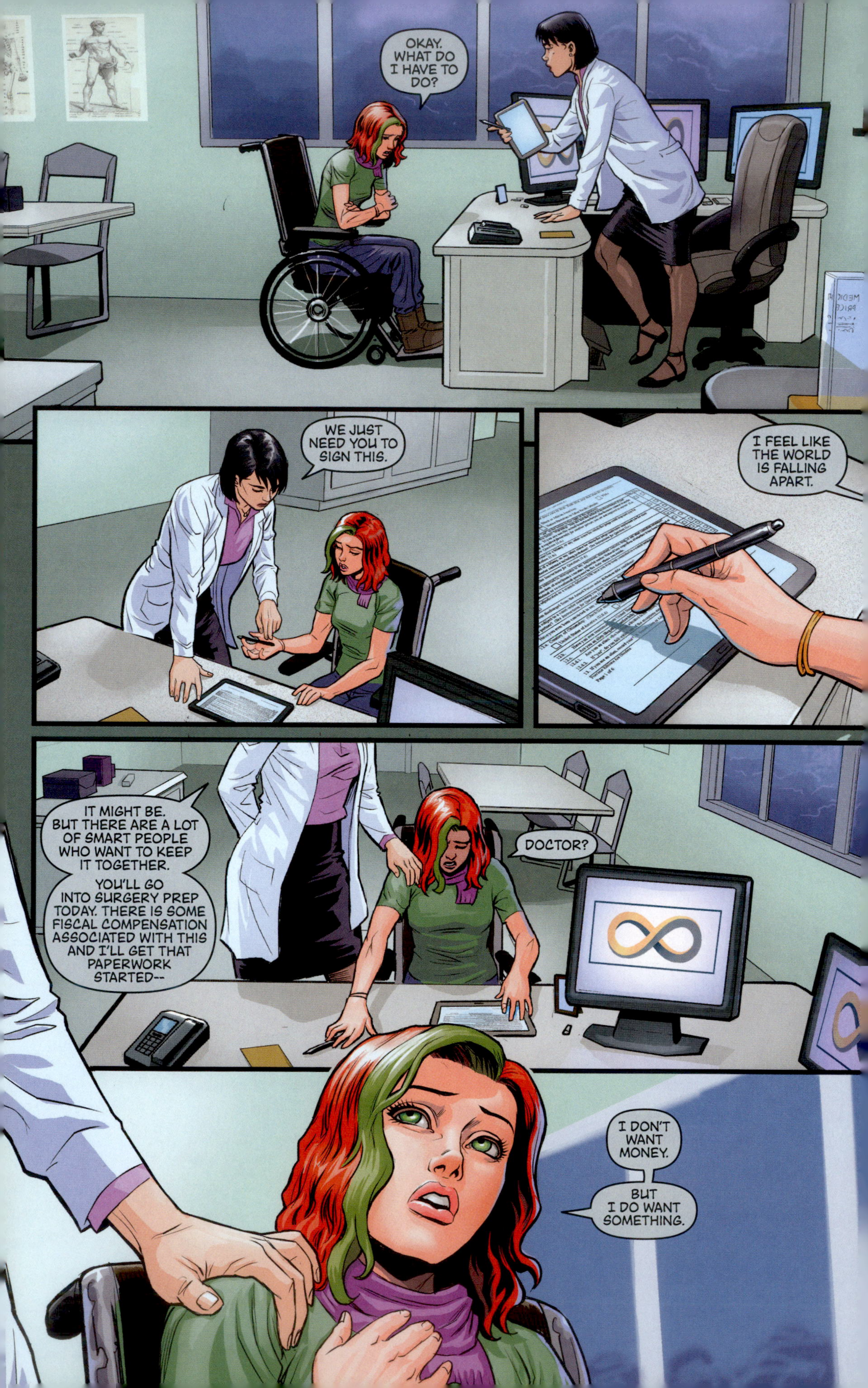
OKAY. WHAT DO I HAVE TO DO?
WE JUST NEED YOU TO SIGN THIS.
I FEEL LIKE THE WORLD IS FALLING APART.
IT MIGHT BE. BUT THERE ARE A LOT OF SMART PEOPLE WHO WANT TO KEEP IT TOGETHER.
YOU'LL GO INTO SURGERY PREP TODAY. THERE IS SOME FISCAL COMPENSATION ASSOCIATED WITH THIS AND I'LL GET THAT PAPERWORK STARTED--
DOCTOR?
I DON'T WANT MONEY.
BUT I DO WANT SOMETHING.

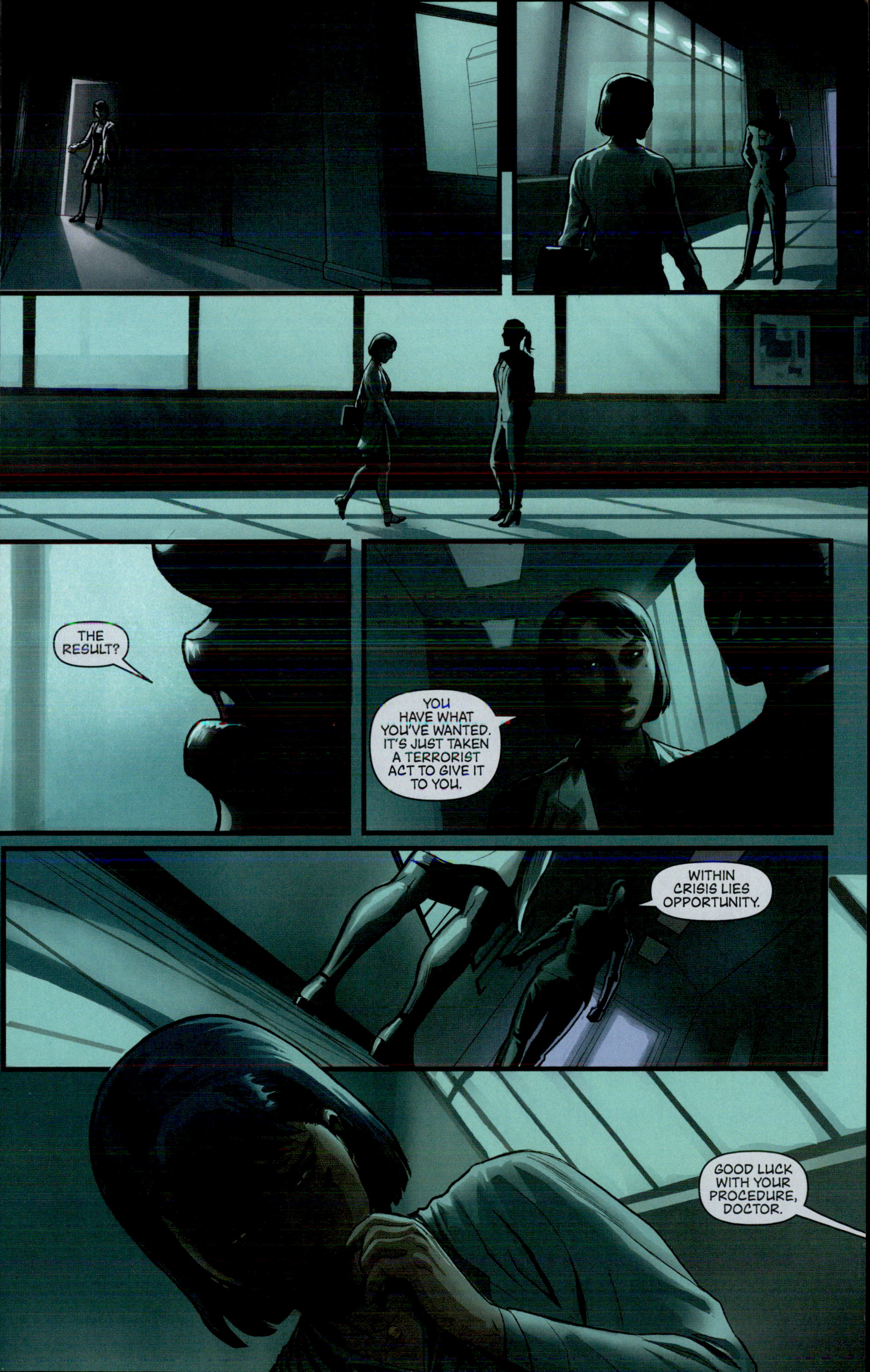
THE RESULT?
YOU HAVE WHAT YOU'VE WANTED. IT'S JUST TAKEN A TERRORIST ACT TO GIVE IT TO YOU.
WITHIN CRISIS LIES OPPORTUNITY.
GOOD LUCK WITH YOUR PROCEDURE, DOCTOR.

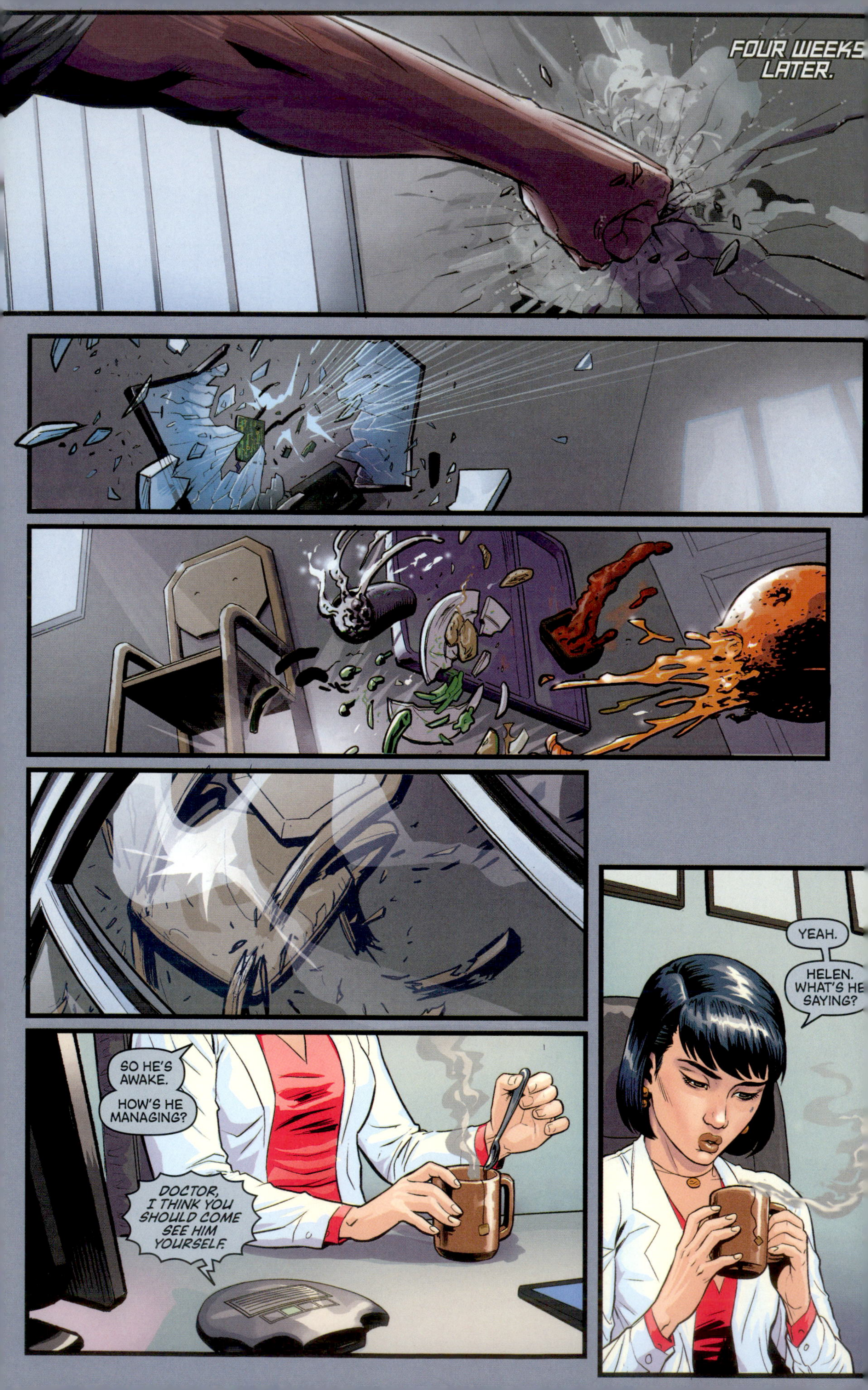
FOUR WEEKS LATER.
SO HE'S AWAKE.
HOW'S HE MANAGING?
DOCTOR, I THINK YOU SHOULD COME SEE HIM YOURSELF.
YEAH.
HELEN. WHAT'S HE SAYING?

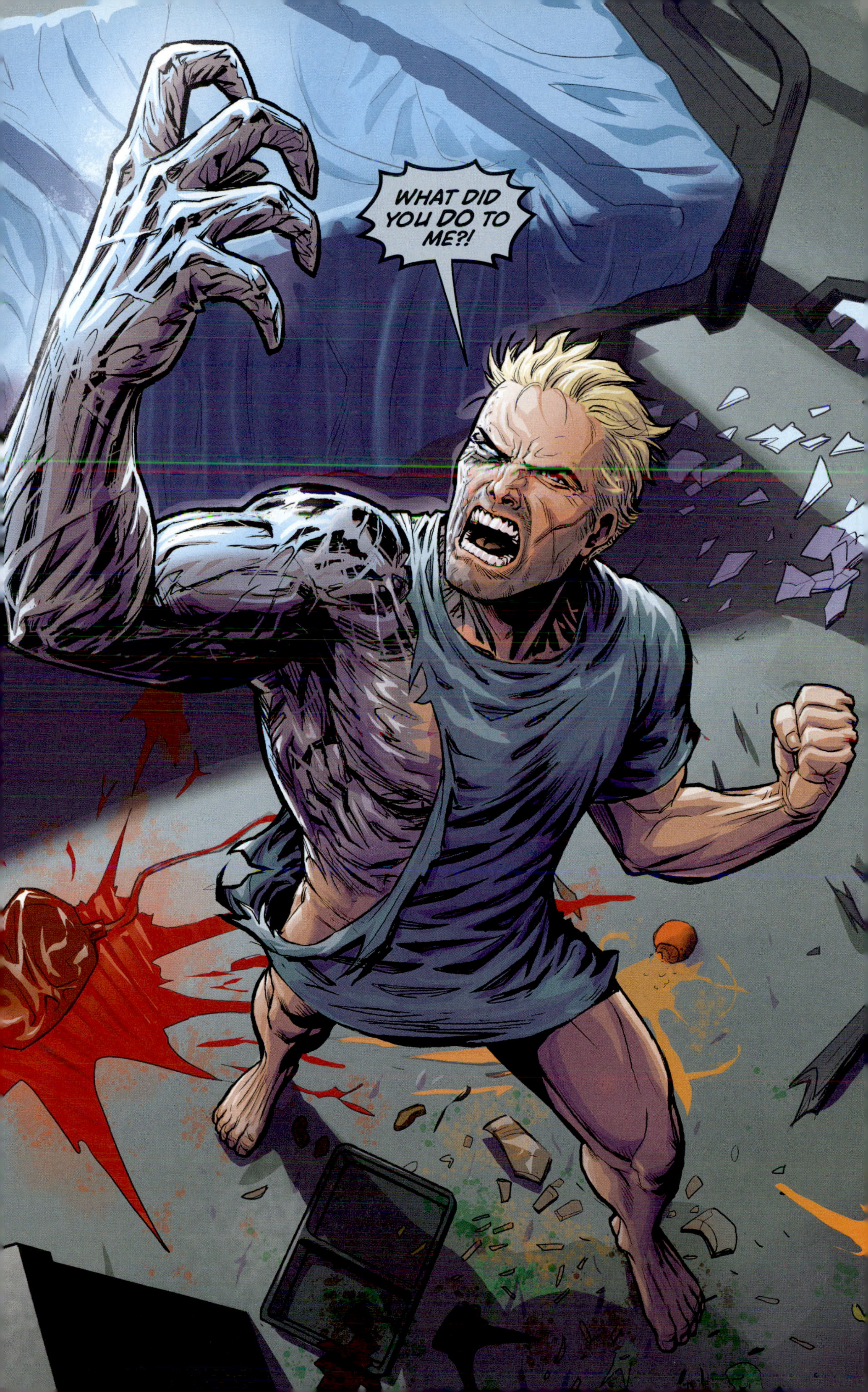
WHAT DID YOU DO TO ME?!

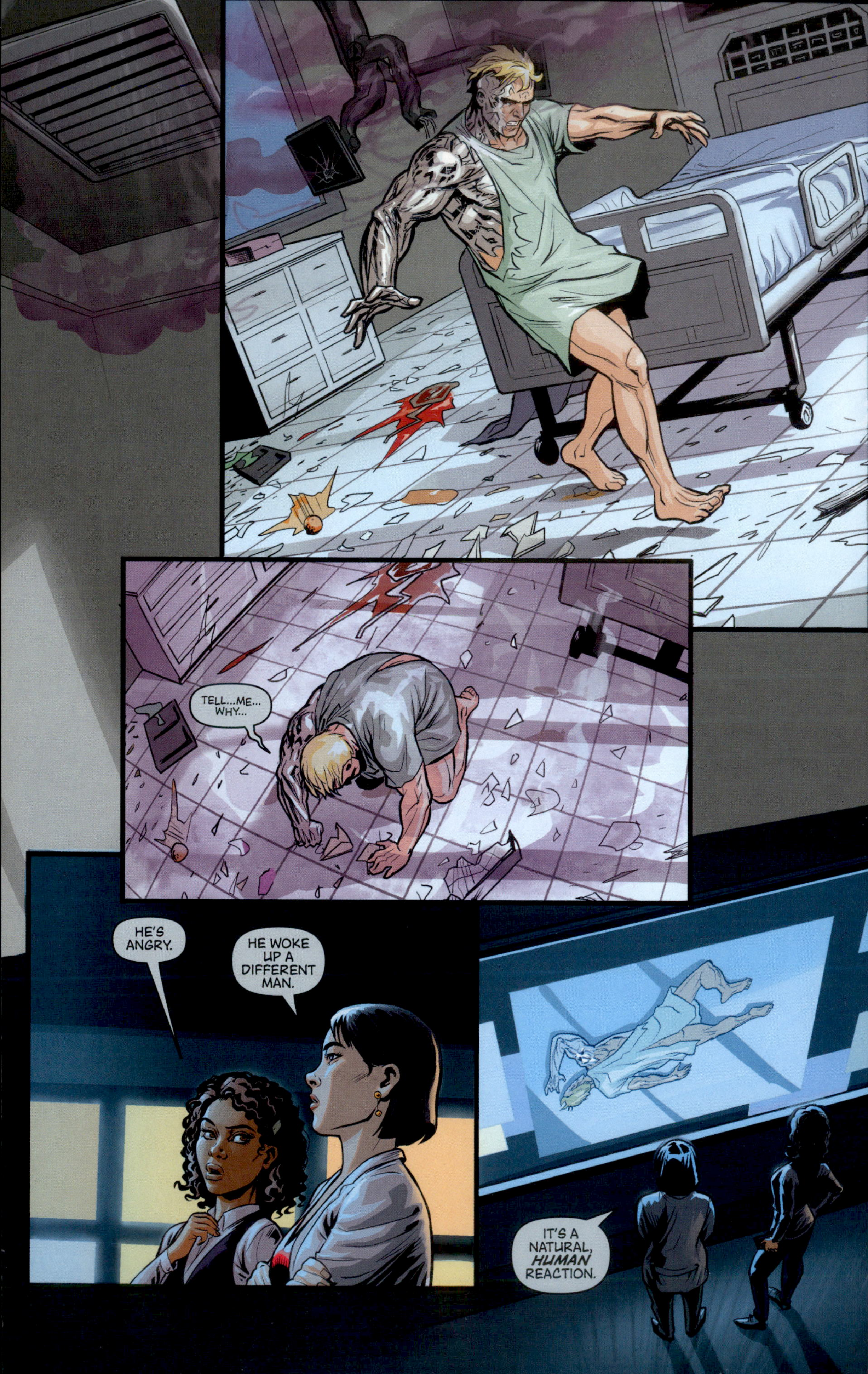
TELL...ME... WHY...
HE'S ANGRY.
HE WOKE UP A DIFFERENT MAN.
IT'S A NATURAL, *HUMAN* REACTION.

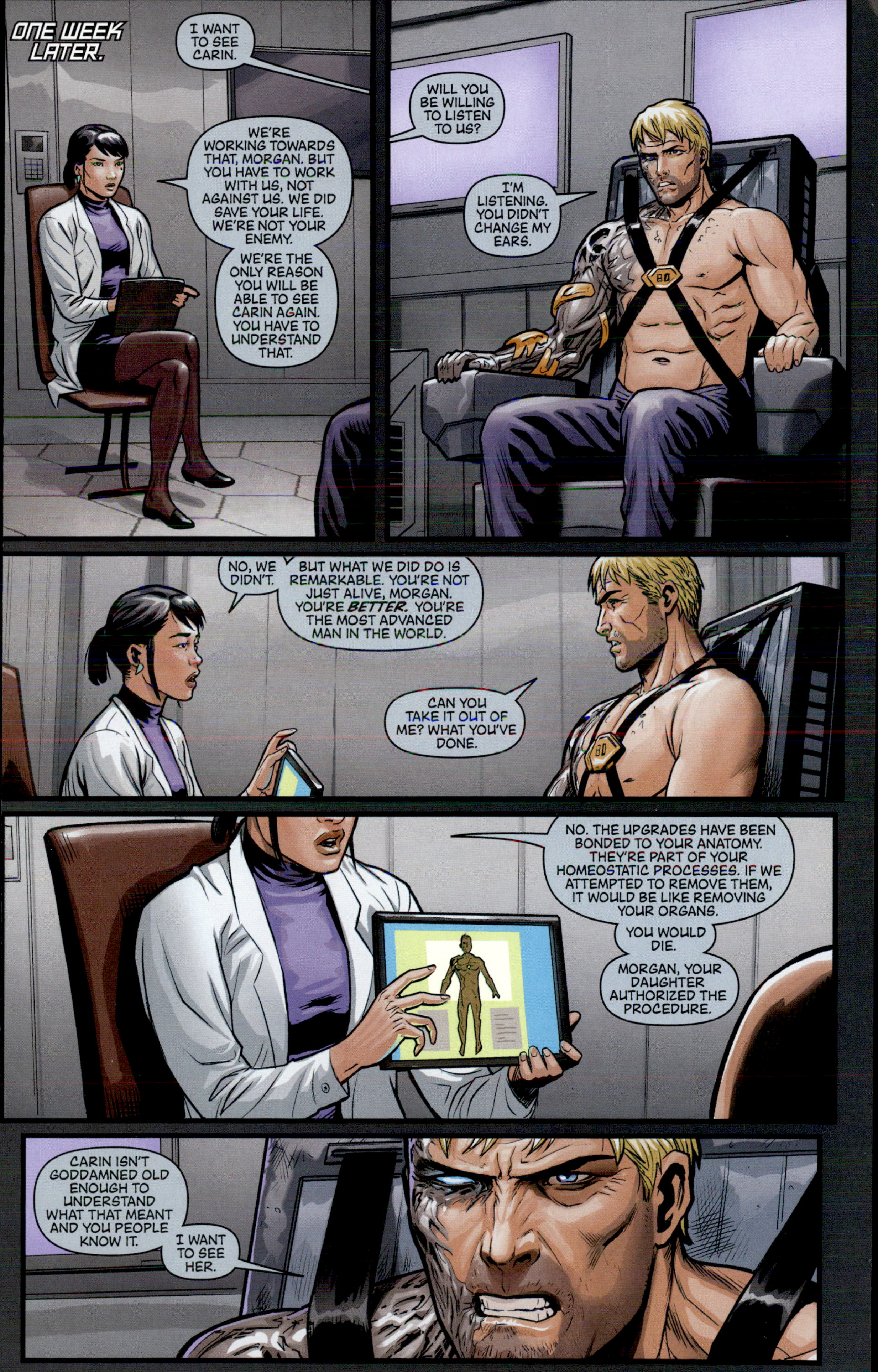
ONE WEEK LATER.
I WANT TO SEE CARIN.
WE'RE WORKING TOWARDS THAT, MORGAN. BUT YOU HAVE TO WORK WITH US, NOT AGAINST US. WE DID SAVE YOUR LIFE. WE'RE NOT YOUR ENEMY.
WE'RE THE ONLY REASON YOU WILL BE ABLE TO SEE CARIN AGAIN. YOU HAVE TO UNDERSTAND THAT.
WILL YOU BE WILLING TO LISTEN TO US?
I'M LISTENING. YOU DIDN'T CHANGE MY EARS.
NO, WE DIDN'T.
BUT WHAT WE DID DO IS REMARKABLE. YOU'RE NOT JUST ALIVE, MORGAN. YOU'RE *BETTER.* YOU'RE THE MOST ADVANCED MAN IN THE WORLD.
CAN YOU TAKE IT OUT OF ME? WHAT YOU'VE DONE.
NO. THE UPGRADES HAVE BEEN BONDED TO YOUR ANATOMY. THEY'RE PART OF YOUR HOMEOSTATIC PROCESSES. IF WE ATTEMPTED TO REMOVE THEM, IT WOULD BE LIKE REMOVING YOUR ORGANS.
YOU WOULD DIE.
MORGAN, YOUR DAUGHTER AUTHORIZED THE PROCEDURE.
CARIN ISN'T GODDAMNED OLD ENOUGH TO UNDERSTAND WHAT THAT MEANT AND YOU PEOPLE KNOW IT.
I WANT TO SEE HER.

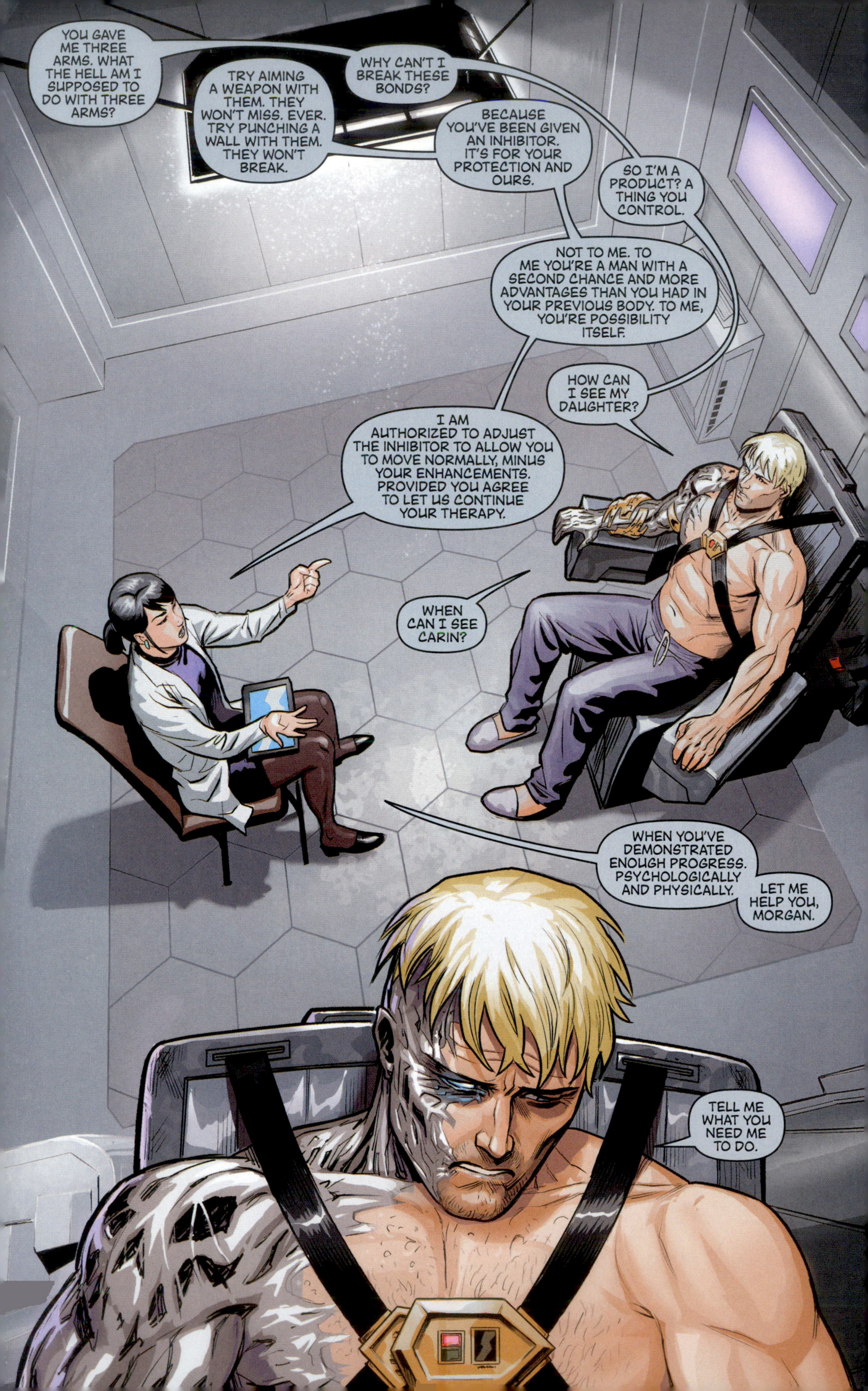
YOU GAVE ME THREE ARMS. WHAT THE HELL AM I SUPPOSED TO DO WITH THREE ARMS?
TRY AIMING A WEAPON WITH THEM. THEY WON'T MISS. EVER. TRY PUNCHING A WALL WITH THEM. THEY WON'T BREAK.
WHY CAN'T I BREAK THESE BONDS?
BECAUSE YOU'VE BEEN GIVEN AN INHIBITOR. IT'S FOR YOUR PROTECTION AND OURS.
SO I'M A PRODUCT? A THING YOU CONTROL.
NOT TO ME. TO ME YOU'RE A MAN WITH A SECOND CHANCE AND MORE ADVANTAGES THAN YOU HAD IN YOUR PREVIOUS BODY. TO ME, YOU'RE POSSIBILITY ITSELF.
HOW CAN I SEE MY DAUGHTER?
I AM AUTHORIZED TO ADJUST THE INHIBITOR TO ALLOW YOU TO MOVE NORMALLY, MINUS YOUR ENHANCEMENTS. PROVIDED YOU AGREE TO LET US CONTINUE YOUR THERAPY.
WHEN CAN I SEE CARIN?
WHEN YOU'VE DEMONSTRATED ENOUGH PROGRESS. PSYCHOLOGICALLY AND PHYSICALLY.
LET ME HELP YOU, MORGAN.
TELL ME WHAT YOU NEED ME TO DO.

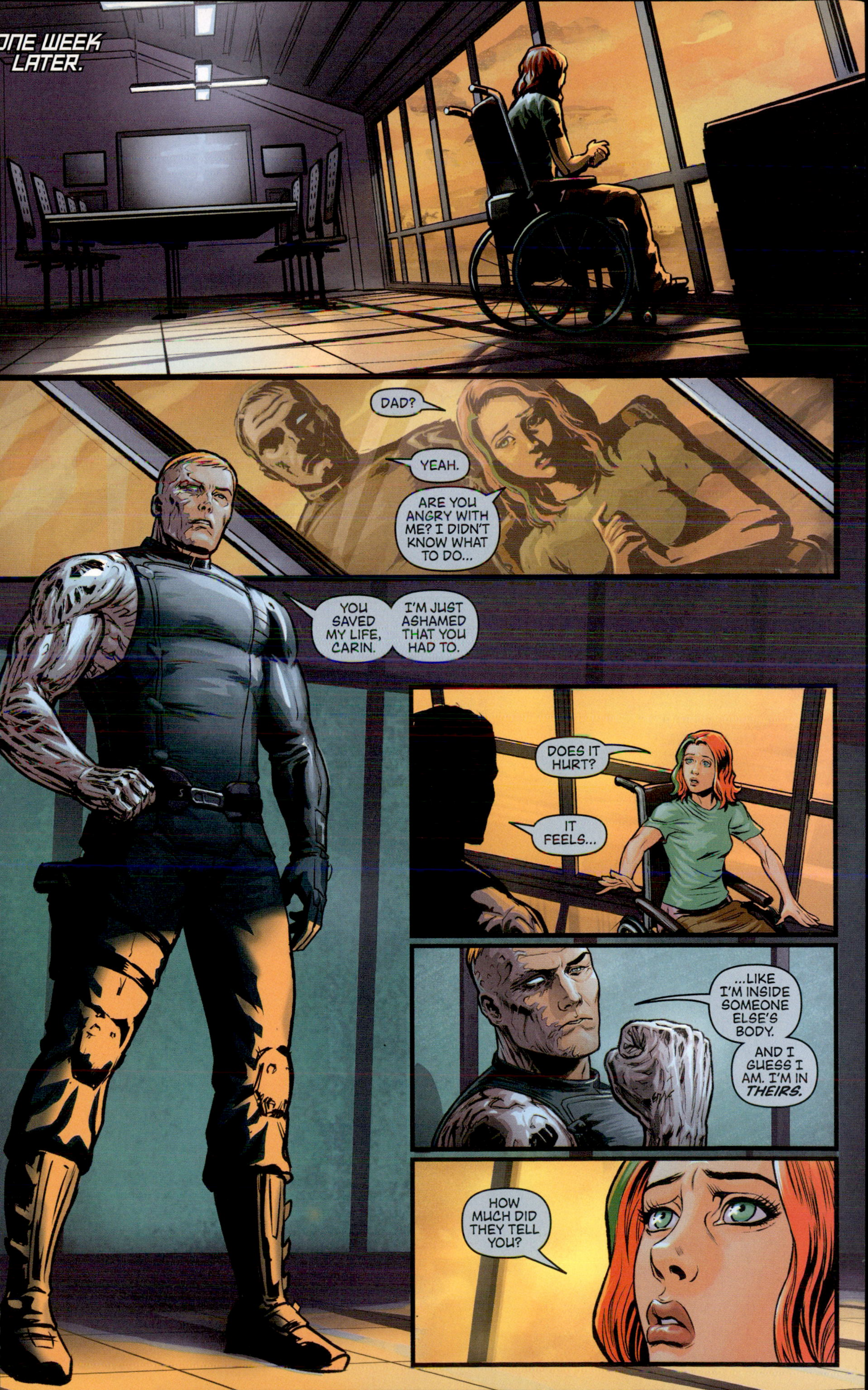
ONE WEEK LATER.
DAD?
YEAH.
ARE YOU ANGRY WITH ME? I DIDN'T KNOW WHAT TO DO...
YOU SAVED MY LIFE, CARIN.
I'M JUST ASHAMED THAT YOU HAD TO.
DOES IT HURT?
IT FEELS...
...LIKE I'M INSIDE SOMEONE ELSE'S BODY.
AND I GUESS I AM. I'M IN *THEIRS.*
HOW MUCH DID THEY TELL YOU?

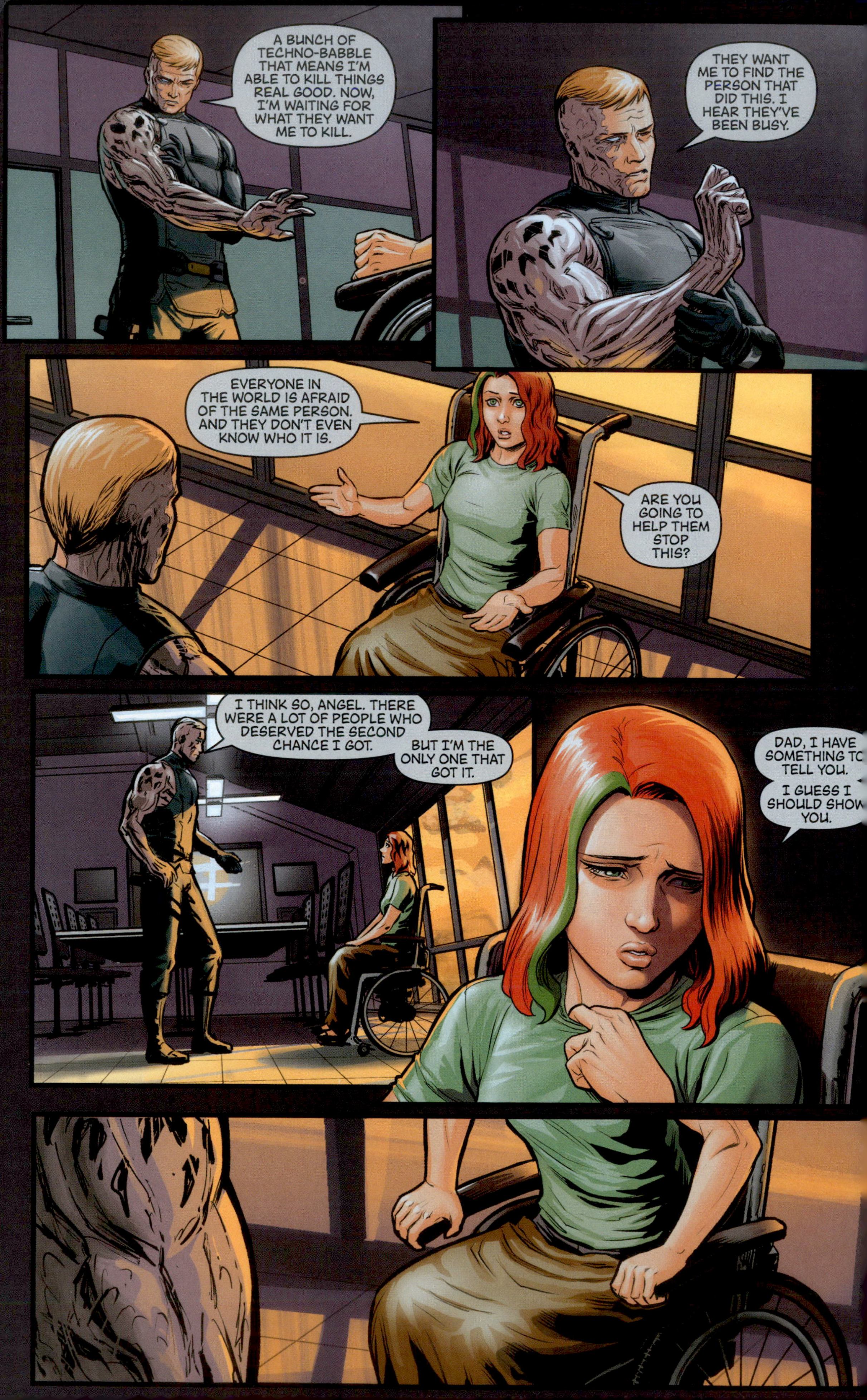
A BUNCH OF TECHNO-BABBLE THAT MEANS I'M ABLE TO KILL THINGS REAL GOOD. NOW, I'M WAITING FOR WHAT THEY WANT ME TO KILL.
THEY WANT ME TO FIND THE PERSON THAT DID THIS. I HEAR THEY'VE BEEN BUSY.
EVERYONE IN THE WORLD IS AFRAID OF THE SAME PERSON. AND THEY DON'T EVEN KNOW WHO IT IS.
ARE YOU GOING TO HELP THEM STOP THIS?
I THINK SO, ANGEL. THERE WERE A LOT OF PEOPLE WHO DESERVED THE SECOND CHANCE I GOT.
BUT I'M THE ONLY ONE THAT GOT IT.
DAD, I HAVE SOMETHING TO TELL YOU.
I GUESS I SHOULD SHOW YOU.

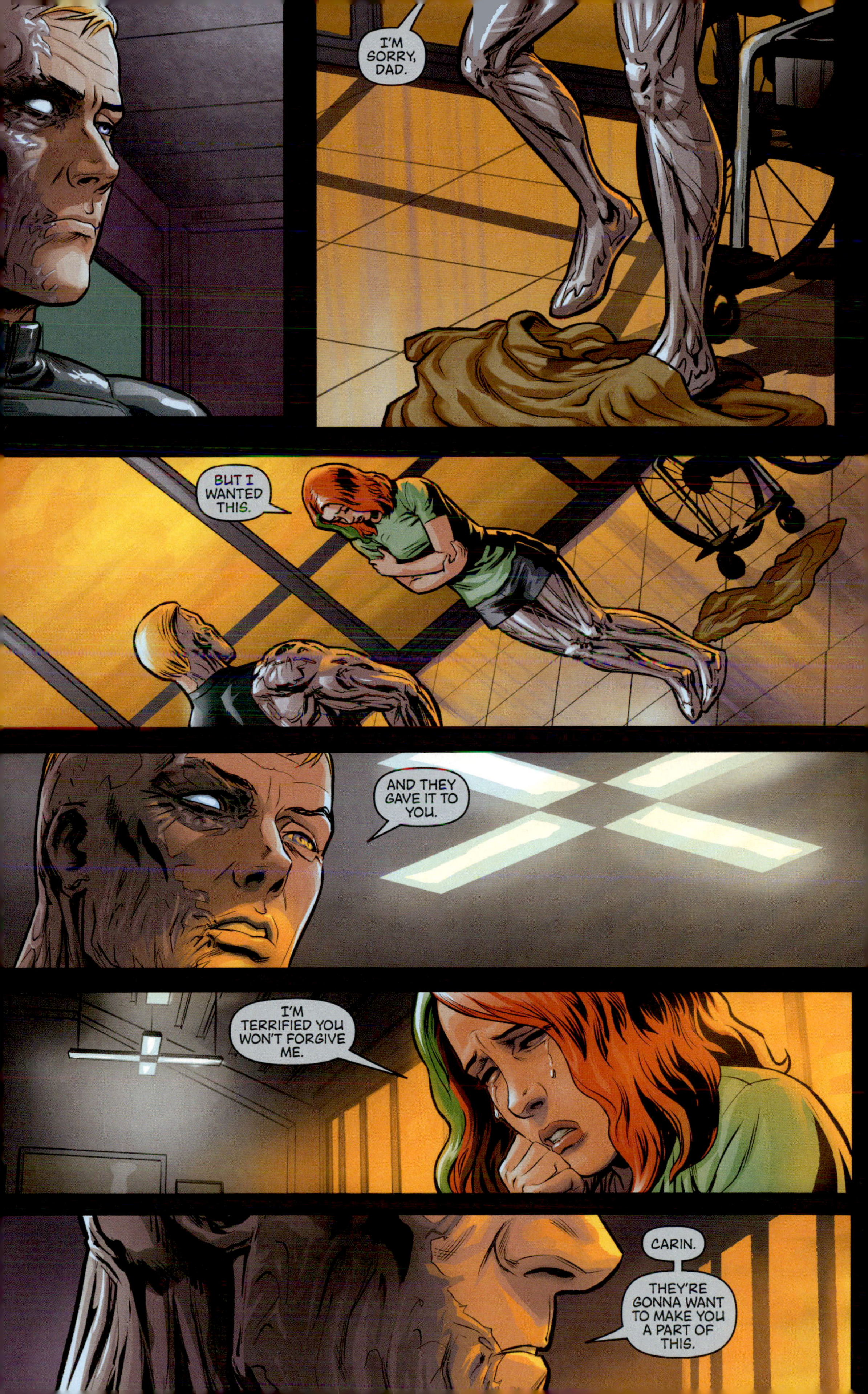
I'M SORRY, DAD.
BUT I WANTED THIS.
AND THEY GAVE IT TO YOU.
I'M TERRIFIED YOU WON'T FORGIVE ME.
CARIN.
THEY'RE GONNA WANT TO MAKE YOU A PART OF THIS.

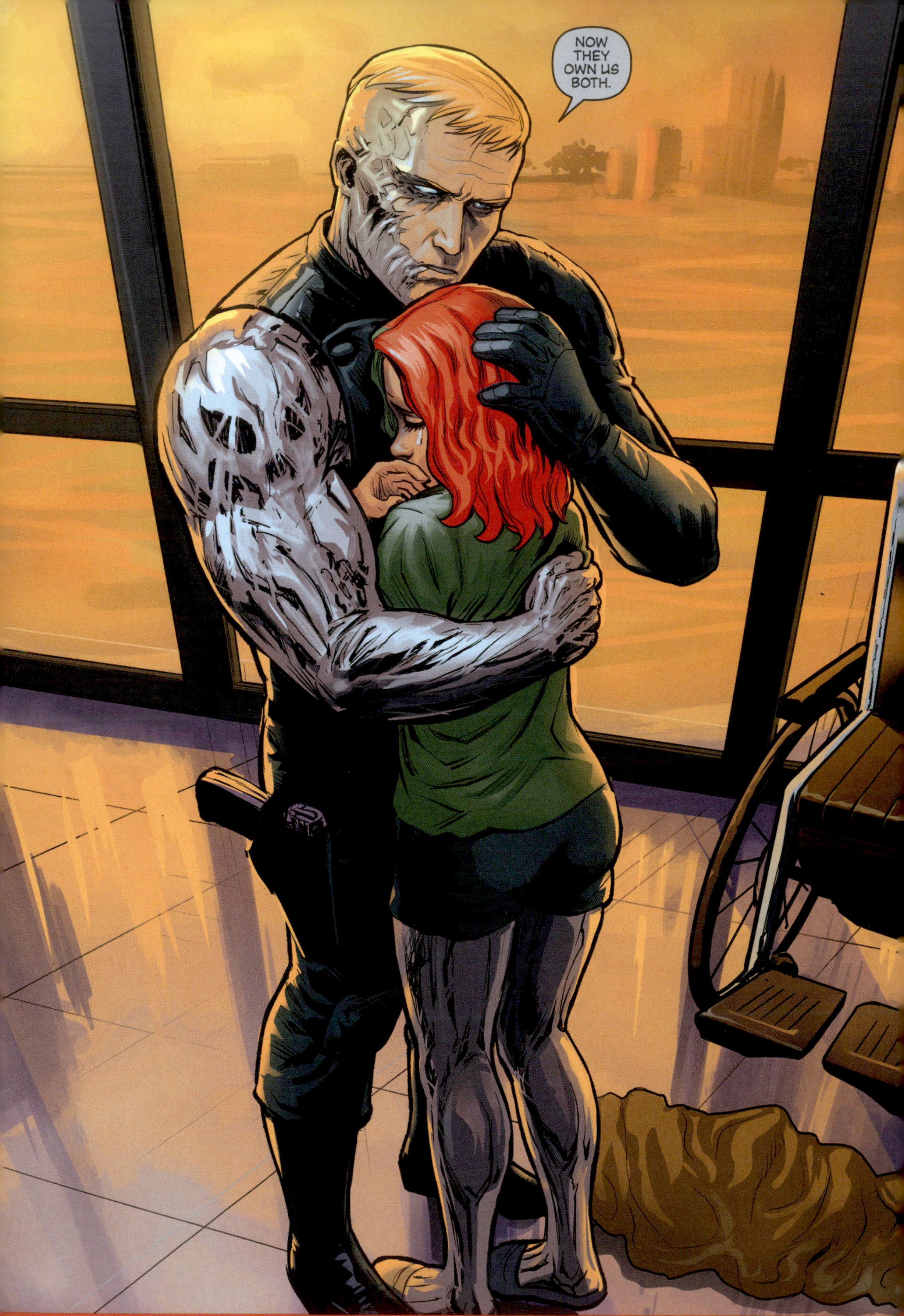
NOW THEY OWN US BOTH.

CONTINUED IN CYBER FORCE AWAKENINGS VOLUME 1
AVAILABLE NOW

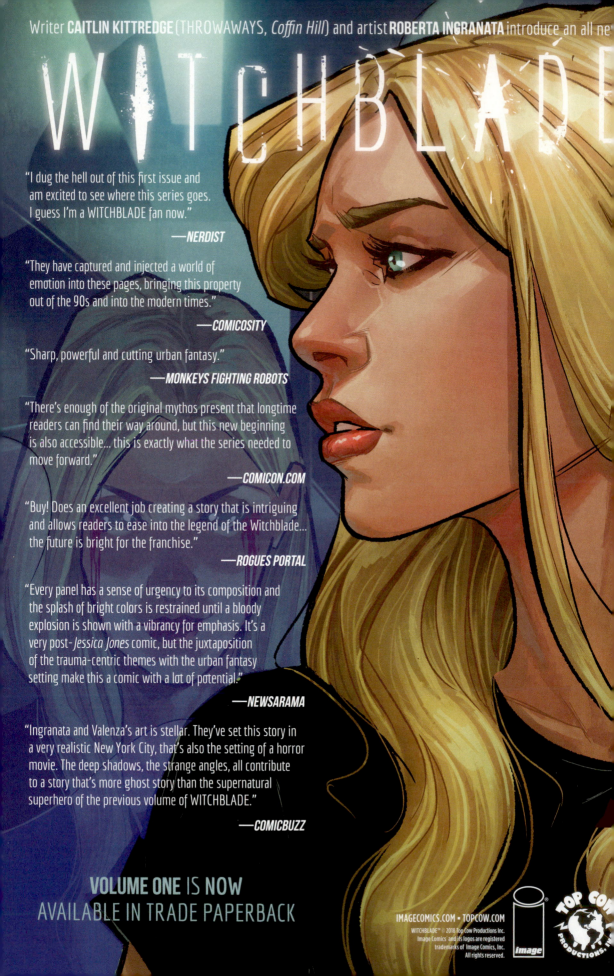

Writer **CAITLIN KITTREDGE** (THROWAWAYS, *Coffin Hill*) and artist **ROBERTA INGRANATA** introduce an all ne

WITCHBLADE

"I dug the hell out of this first issue and am excited to see where this series goes. I guess I'm a WITCHBLADE fan now."

—*NERDIST*

"They have captured and injected a world of emotion into these pages, bringing this property out of the 90s and into the modern times."

—*COMICOSITY*

"Sharp, powerful and cutting urban fantasy."

—*MONKEYS FIGHTING ROBOTS*

"There's enough of the original mythos present that longtime readers can find their way around, but this new beginning is also accessible... this is exactly what the series needed to move forward."

—*COMICON.COM*

"Buy! Does an excellent job creating a story that is intriguing and allows readers to ease into the legend of the Witchblade... the future is bright for the franchise."

—*ROGUES PORTAL*

"Every panel has a sense of urgency to its composition and the splash of bright colors is restrained until a bloody explosion is shown with a vibrancy for emphasis. It's a very post-*Jessica Jones* comic, but the juxtaposition of the trauma-centric themes with the urban fantasy setting make this a comic with a lot of potential."

—*NEWSARAMA*

"Ingranata and Valenza's art is stellar. They've set this story in a very realistic New York City, that's also the setting of a horror movie. The deep shadows, the strange angles, all contribute to a story that's more ghost story than the supernatural superhero of the previous volume of WITCHBLADE."

—*COMICBUZZ*

VOLUME ONE IS NOW
AVAILABLE IN TRADE PAPERBACK

IMAGECOMICS.COM • TOPCOW.COM

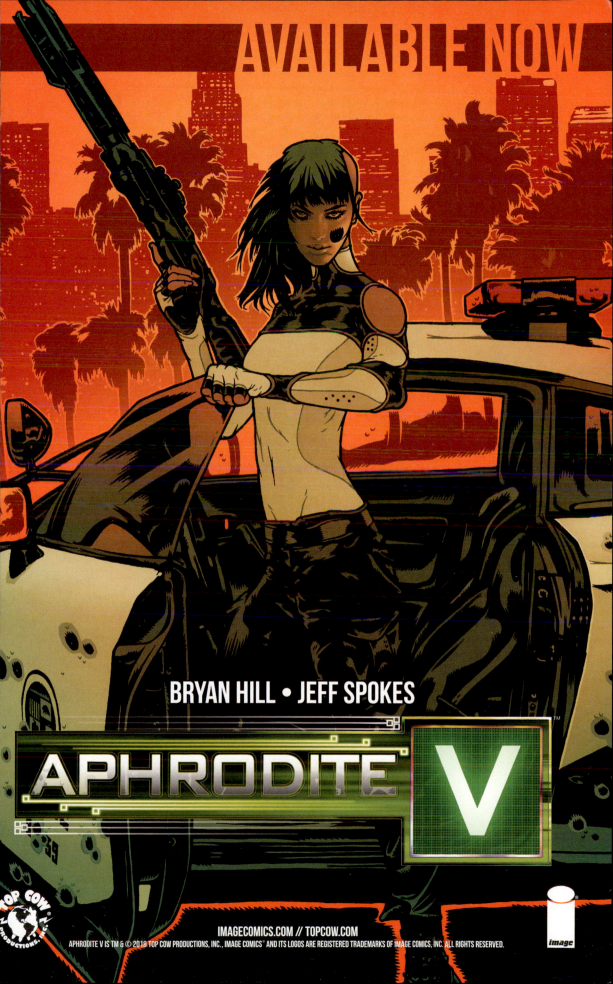

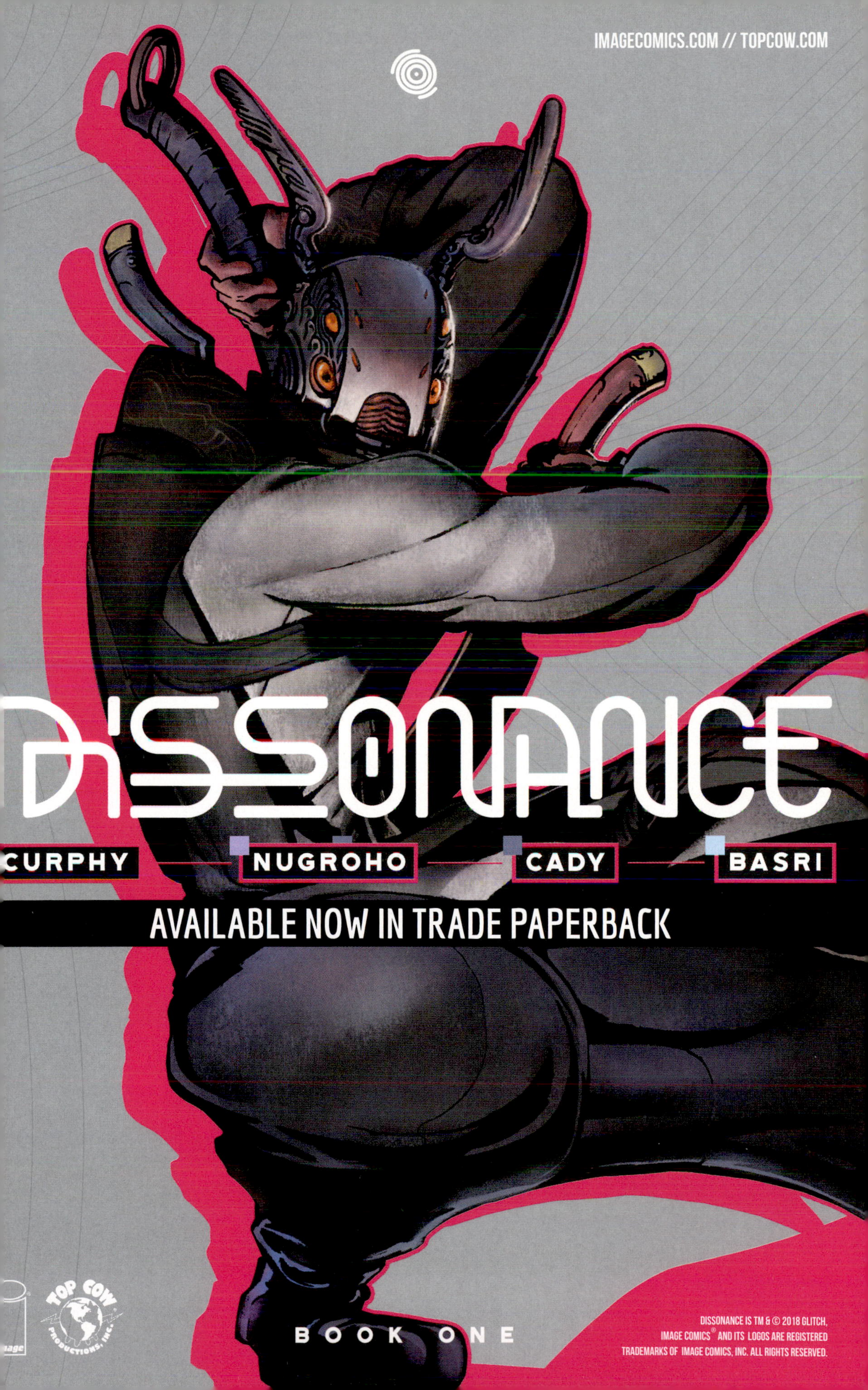
IMAGECOMICS.COM // TOPCOW.COM
DISSONANCE
CURPHY
NUGROHO
CADY
BASRI
AVAILABLE NOW IN TRADE PAPERBACK
BOOK ONE
DISSONANCE IS TM & © 2018 GLITCH, IMAGE COMICS® AND ITS LOGOS ARE REGISTERED TRADEMARKS OF IMAGE COMICS, INC. ALL RIGHTS RESERVED.

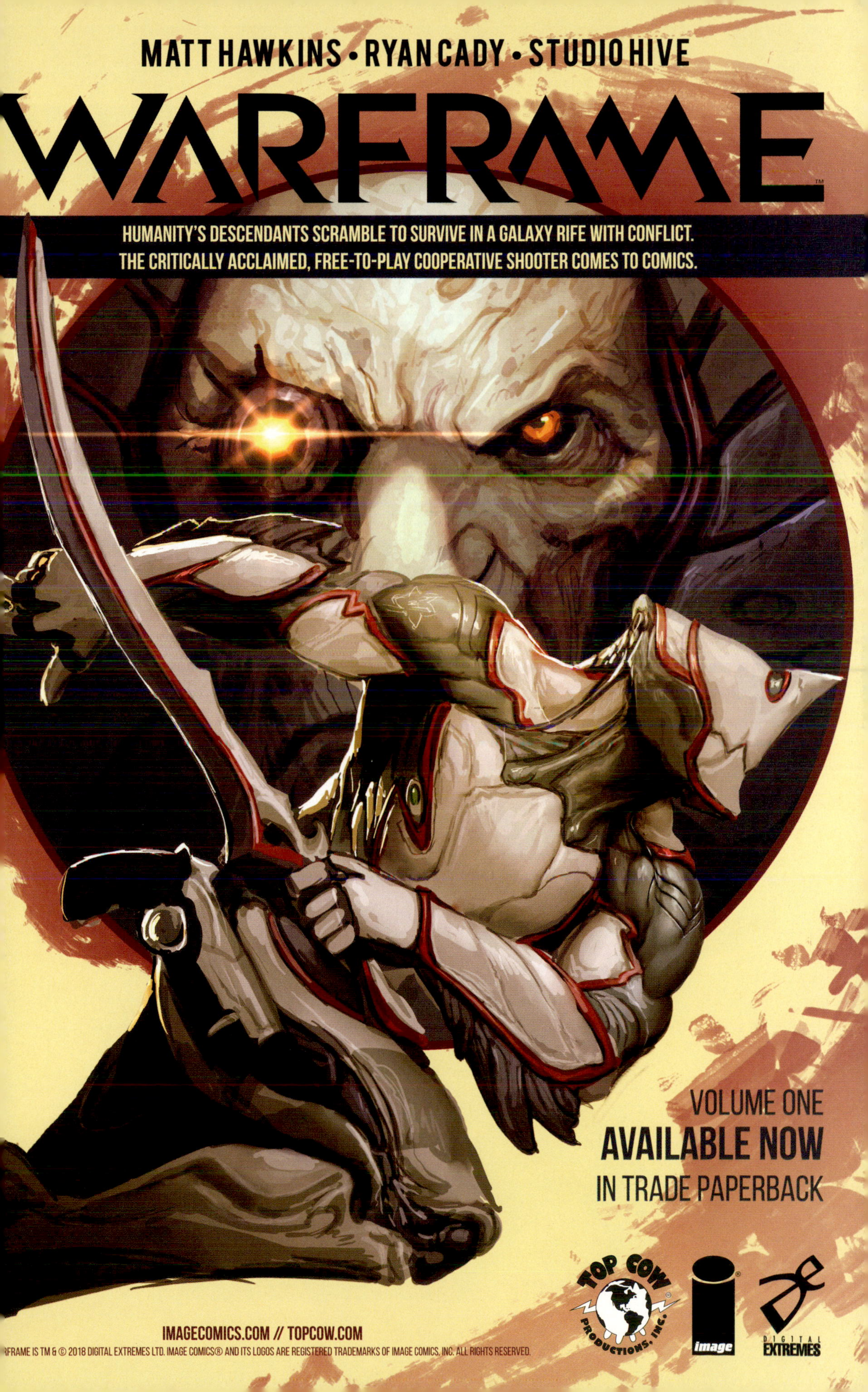
MATT HAWKINS • RYAN CADY • STUDIO HIVE
WARFRAME™
HUMANITY'S DESCENDANTS SCRAMBLE TO SURVIVE IN A GALAXY RIFE WITH CONFLICT.
THE CRITICALLY ACCLAIMED, FREE-TO-PLAY COOPERATIVE SHOOTER COMES TO COMICS.
VOLUME ONE
AVAILABLE NOW
IN TRADE PAPERBACK
TOP COW PRODUCTIONS, INC.
image
DIGITAL EXTREMES
IMAGECOMICS.COM // TOPCOW.COM
RFRAME IS TM & © 2018 DIGITAL EXTREMES LTD. IMAGE COMICS® AND ITS LOGOS ARE REGISTERED TRADEMARKS OF IMAGE COMICS, INC. ALL RIGHTS RESERVED.

GOD CVMPLEX

DOGMA

AVAILABLE NOW
IN TRADE PAPERBACK

"BOTH FRESH AND
BRILLIANTLY EXECUTED."
—ComicsVerse

JENKINS —— LIE —— PRASETY

BOOK · ONE

RYAN **CADY** ANDREA **MUTTI** K MICHAEL **RUSSELL**

INFINITE DARK

THE INFINITE DARK
HIDES AN INFINITE HORROR...

AVAILABLE
OCTOBER
2018

IMAGECOMICS.COM • TOPCOW.COM

The Top Cow essentials checklist:

For more ISBN and ordering information on our latest collections go to:
www.topcow.com
Ask your retailer about our catalogue of collected editions,
digests, and hard covers or check the listings at:
Barnes and Noble, Amazon.com,
and other fine retailers.

To find your nearest comic shop go to:
www.comicshoplocator.com